By

J. Jerome

ISBN 978-1-7364438-0-4 (Paperback) ISBN 978-1-7364438-1-1 (Digital)

Prologue

The feeling permeated inside all of them and ate away at their very souls! That feeling was as strong as the acts of aggression that were going on just a few feet outside of the place that they all remained huddled in. It was not supposed to be like this; how could this happen? Even though this is something that they had all feared could, and would happen right along with every other American, no matter their ethnicity. The feeling that a gift, a savior, a messenger, or messiah had been taken away in the blink of an eye, on this day in 1968 was unbearable. But still, they all tried to remain calm and be rational.

Not Don, "We should be out there!"

"For what?" replied Frank. "So, we can be ignorant right with them and risk our lives too, and the lives of our families? Anyway, what you gonna do if you go outside fool?"

Frank was always the cooler head in all situations, a 39-year-old black man, well educated. A bachelor's degree in social science, married, one child on the way, and the head of the Civil Rights office in this small rural town a few miles south of Baltimore. Frank was always the one who tried to stop the fights, got people together. So, following in the massive footsteps of someone such as Dr. King was only natural for him. Frank always felt that he wanted to stand up for injustice and speak out against indifference but never did until being inspired by Dr. King. For Frank, trying to talk some sense into Don was natural, even though he was being torn apart inside just like the rest of the group.

As Frank reflected on his life and purpose, Don hastily replied, "Get some damn justice, that's what!"

Frank just gazed at Don for a few seconds and then began to have a look around the room slowly to judge the expressions of everyone else in the room to see if he could tell if they felt the same way.

First was June. A smart, 24-year-old college student who faithfully worked at the office day in and day out, spending tireless hours organizing all the church visits, sit-ins, and demonstrations that took place in, and around town. Frank glanced next at Mary, the grandparent in the office. Mary's face was still as stone for she had already lived through some of the worst of times, so this night only added to the pain that filled her heart. Mary only worked with the sole purpose of hope. Hope that someone or something could give everyone a fair shake at life and a chance to be able to live a good life. The blank stare on Mary's face made it hard for Frank to continue to look at her or say anything without breaking down crying. The tear wells and marks on Mary's face almost told the story of not only her life but the struggles of the entire African American race. As Frank turned to look at Reggie, all he saw was the frightened unsure young man that would probably go along with anything that the majority would do.

"You damned fool! Don't you get it? That's what they want us to do!" Yelled Frank. As he continued to look back and forth at everyone. "What y'all think? We should do that. We should go and open these doors and let them fools come tear this place apart just like they tearing up the rest of the town?"

"But we should do something for justice! At least, for respect for all of us!" Shrieked Reggie who was sitting next to Don listening and buying into Don's murmur of obscenities as Frank addressed the group.

Frank quickly replied, "If we can open these doors tomorrow and help rebuild this town, that would well honor everyone!"

As Frank continued to try and calm the group, the riots went on outside. The entire town burning and in peril, no one dared to throw an object at the window of the office or try to enter. Maybe it was because the group was huddled in the back with all the lights off and only the faint sound of the transistor radio replaying the same sad news over and over. Maybe it was the poster boards taped to the windows that graced Dr. King's face and excerpts from his speeches. Anyhow, the group was safe as long as they stayed in the office until the riots died down. Soon, all the discussion turned loud and was on the cusp of being an argument, with everyone crying and angry but knowing deep down, rioting wasn't what Dr. King would want. Emotions ran over until the room was filled with shouting, and just as Don got up and started to move towards the front room of the office, the entire group was abruptly startled by the ringing of the phone in the front.

"Aw man, my heart almost jumped up out my chest," said Don.

Everyone startled by the sudden phone ringing, and ringing, and ringing, and ringing while no one moved.

Still startled at how Don almost jumped out of his skin, Frank said to June. "Well, ain't you gonna get that?"

June hopped up and quickly walked to the front room of the office and answered the phone. As she answered the phone and began to listen to the person on the other end, it was hard for her to try and pay attention.

This was because Don was standing right there bugging her. "Who is it? Is it about what happened? Who is it?"

"Everyone be Quiet!" June yelled out to the group.

Don could somewhat hear the voice on the other end of the line, and it was a woman, with an anxious sound, sort of loud, almost a yell.

Then June yelled out, "Oh my God! Frank! Frank! Get the phone! Hurry up!"

"What's wrong?" Said Don as Frank rushed into the room to get to the phone.

As Frank listened to the person on the other end of the phone, his face became distressed and he started to look panicked and pale. He hung up the receiver and turned to walk back to the back room.

"You good Frank?" asked Don, and he repeated the question about 3 times before Frank said anything.

Frank had just got the news that his wife Anne had gone into labor, but he was not in a happy mood because the person on the other end of the phone was his wife's sister Tricia. Tricia's news was as devastating as the entire night itself! Tricia had just relayed to Frank that Anne was not doing well and there was a risk of losing the baby during labor. As Frank's mind swirled, everyone around him was trying to get his attention. But it was too much for him. For this day to begin with the loss of such a great man! Now the possible loss of his firstborn was entirely overbearing. It is crazy that they always say that your life flashes in front of your eyes in the moment of death. Yet Frank; was experiencing something similar. As everyone was patting him on his shoulders, grabbing him, trying to get his attention; Frank mentally left the room and his body:

With a beautiful grin and brightness of her light brown eyes, Anne gazed into Frank's face as they twirled on the dancefloor clutching each other's hands, moving to the soft song playing in the background.

"Don't you just love this song baby?" Anne said softly to Frank as she rhythmically moved to the beat of the music and Frank's lead on the dancefloor.

"Sweetie; I could dance with you all night long!" Frank readily replied to Anne's gesture as they moved in closer to embrace during the slow dance. Just as Frank began to feel Anne's breast press up against his chest...

Don snapped him out of his gaze trying to get his attention, "Hey! Hey! Hey Frank!"

Frank suddenly jolted back into reality and was back in the office in the room with everyone else. He began to speak slowly. "It's Anne, It's Anne and the baby! Don, let me use your car!"

"Is she okay?" said Mary.

No reply from Frank, just the repeat of; "Don, let me use your car, I got to get to the hospital."

Don grabbed his keys and said, "Come on!"

7

But Frank said, "No, you need to stay here! We need all the men we can, to stay here and protect this place. I can make it, I'll be fine."

Don, of course in disagreement, replied quickly to Frank. "I'm coming man! You are in no mental state to drive brother!"

Frank snapped back at Don again; "I said I need you here man!"

Mary tried to intervene. "Frank, listen to Don. We will be okay here. We have Reggie too."

Frank looked at Mary and replied as respectfully as he could. "Mary; no disrespect, but I need Don here! He is better served here with you all tonight! I said I'll be fine!"

After a bit more back and forth within the group, everyone eventually gave into Frank's will, as they usually do. Frank was their leader, so they would always listen to him in the end. One by one, everyone wished him a safe trip to the hospital as they gave in.

"Please call us as soon as you get to the hospital," June said softly as Frank slid one arm into his leather jacket.

"Yes, let us know what's going on up there Frank!" Mary said, as Frank completed dressing his jacket to his frame and grabbing Don's car keys in one final motion before heading to the front door of the office.

Frank went to the front door and opened it slowly and slipped out the door trying not to fully open the door and draw attention to himself, for he didn't want to put anyone inside at risk. As he walked cautiously to Don's car, he passed people in the neighborhood who he talked with daily and they did not even notice him. These people were so full of rage that he did not look familiar to them. He saw police in the middle of the street hosing down people who were looting and rioting. He saw some police guarding some of the white-owned businesses while the black barbershops and hole in the walls were being ravaged. *"My lord help us!"* Frank said to himself as he approached Don's car checking it out before trying to open the door. Everything looked clear so he got in and started to drive. Suddenly as he began to drive the caution left his mind and he thought about Anne and the baby and he became anxious again. He took off and began to speed down the avenue right past a group of police, but their hands were full already, so they paid him no mind. Frank soon came to a point in the center of town and he had to abruptly stop in the middle of the main street. He almost ran into a group of young men who were in a hurry and it looked like all of these boys had arms full of stolen merchandise and could barely run trying not to drop any of it. Disgusted, Frank threw the car into park, swung the door open and stuck one foot out to stand, and began to scream at the boys.

"Why not show some respect! That's not helping the cause!"

One of the young men just turned to look at him but none of them stopped running. Frank slowly got back into the car and pulled off again and began to speed along. As Frank sped down the winding road; he kept veering in and out of his lane. He was mentally distracted by the situation. He was also trying to tune the radio with one hand and steer with the other. Fumbling with the radio dial, hoping to hear the magnitude of the night and the effect on his hometown. From one station to the next, all the broadcasts were focused on the assassination, the protests, and the rioting. One was still playing earlier broadcasts of the news that had broken earlier in the day. Just as Frank gave his full attention to guiding the vehicle; he noticed the gas hand on the car (was just barely touching the "E". Troubling was this because the hospital was clear across town; at least 12 more miles away. Frank knew he needed gas, but the town was a horror show. It would be next to impossible to get gas in this situation without running into some trouble, or police with bad intentions. As he weighed his options of trying to push it with hopes of not running out of gas; or thinking about where he could safely stop; Frank remembered the old gas station on Rooney street. Rooney was a long road with all houses, but a makeshift gas station built on a garage. Anthony's garage. Yep, in the hood, Anthony had started out being the neighborhood mechanic, then kept adding things to his house and his garage, until he had a full-blown business established right in the center of the neighborhood, with nothing but houses surrounding his business. How convenient. How Anthony got away with this in Baltimore? In the '60 s with no trouble from the police? No one knew. Whispers were that Anthony was moving heavy drugs out of that establishment for the Italian mob across town. Therefore, he had undisclosed police protection. Either way, Frank started to head over there to see if Anthony was open in the madness. Frank figured that everyone had left their neighborhood to go downtown to tear shit up. As Frank approached the dark residential block – low and behold, he saw the porch and garage light on at Anthony's house. Boom! Once again Frank had the correct hunch.

He pulled up to the garage door and began to feverishly peck at the car horn with hopes Anthony would pop out as he usually does. Just as Frank turned his head to look back and forth from the front to the back of Anthony's house; Frank heard sudden stuttering and banging. It was the engine struggling to continue to run due to the gas dissipating fast. Now Frank was getting extremely nervous. As he sat there, he contemplated turning off the car until he could confirm if Anthony was home. Yet he was also afraid to turn off the car, for fear of it not starting again. Frank started to survey the yard for gas cans to see if he could get lucky and get a few leftover drops in a can left behind from a car repair situation. Looking front to back; left to right at the yard, Frank was suddenly startled by a loud bang.

"Boom!" The loudest bang you could ever hear, and it was Anthony using both hands to pound on the trunk of the car that Frank was sitting in.

As he scurried to the driver-side window of the car where Frank sat, "Aye brother! What's up with you?" Anthony yelled out to Frank to get his attention and pop Frank out of his trance of surveying the yard. "Franky!!" Anthony called out with a comical tone. "What is up with you my brother? You alright in this crazy shit out here tonight man? Ain't nobody fucking with you? Are they?"

Question, after question from Anthony, hurled at Frank; before Frank could even get a chance to reply. Maybe it was just the heightened intensity of the night that had Anthony in such a series of moods. Defensive, inquisitive, and protective.

Finally, Frank was able to get a word in edgewise. "Hey brother." I need a bump of gas partner. Trying to hurry up and get over to the hospital!"

"Whoa, whoa! Hospital?" Anthony replied with much surprise. "Somebody hit you?" Anthony said as he leaned into the car window with an inspectors-like look as if he would be able to examine Frank for any injuries. "You good?" Anthony continued with another question as he looked Frank up and down in his seat in the car.

"Nah man; I'm okay. Just about to run out of gas and won't be able to make it over to the hospital."

"Yeah man; who's at the hospital?" Anthony replied with a question.

"It's Anne man." Frank came back with the answer with a half-angry/half concerned tone. "I gotta get over there now man. She's in labor, and the Docs say it ain't looking good."

Anthony stepped back from the window in a little disbelief; "Ah shit my man! Let me take you over there, shit! Hop in my truck."

Frank declined politely; "I got it. Appreciate it, but just need a bump of gas, if you can spare it? I left my wallet at the office rushing out to get to the hospital."

"Aww shit my brother. You know I got you. I'm gonna top your tank off right now and get you on down the road. Give me a quick minute."

After a few minutes, Anthony had filled the gas tank up as Frank anxiously waited for him to finish. Anthony gave the back of the trunk a quick two taps to give Frank the indication that he was good to go. As Anthony moved from behind the car, Frank threw the car in reverse to back out of Anthony's driveway and began to back up.

As he reversed past Anthony standing there; they both nodded at each other with a speechless acknowledgment that Frank had to go, and he was good. Anthony had helped his buddy out and knew Frank needed to get to his wife. With no hesitation, after backing out of the driveway; Frank scorched off onto the road to head back towards the hospital in a raging hurry.

Soon, Frank was driving down a dark road that ran up in between the town forest preserve. As he rounded a curve, he began to see lights in his rearview mirror and hear sirens, of course, it was the police. Frank pulled over to the side of the road and tried to remain calm. His gut for some reason was telling him not to stop because he was so worried about the baby and Anne. As anxious as he was, he stayed cool and waited for the officer to approach the car. As Frank looked in his rearview mirrors, he could see that two officers were coming, one on the right side of the car and the other coming up on the left. The officer on the driver's side tapped on the window and Frank slowly grabbed the handle to wind the window down, as not to show any sudden moves to startle the cops. It took a while because Don's car was not one of the best; hell, it barely ran at times. Frank finally got the window down to hear the officer begin to question him.

"Are you in a hurry?"

"Yes Sir." Replied Frank.

The officer looked up at the other officer on the left side of the car and said, "Oh we got us a smart one here!"

"No sir, I just need to get to…" Before Frank could finish explaining why he was in a hurry the officer came with a snapping reply.

"Did I tell you to speak boy?"

Frank tried to explain, "I just need to…"

But he was interrupted again, this time by the other police officer, "He's gonna be some trouble."

"Get the hell out of the car boy!" Yelled the officer standing right next to Frank's window, and as Frank reached for the door handle there was suddenly a loud bang and Frank slumped over onto the steering wheel.

In shock was the officer standing next to Frank's window; now with his uniform covered in blood from the bottom of his chest to his mid abdominal area; he hopped back and hollered, "Hey! What the hell did you do? What the fuck man! Are you fucking crazy?! What did you do?"

The second officer ran over to the driver's side of the car and grabbed the other officer by his shoulders and began to talk slowly to him with his face pressed close up against his ear. "Listen! It looked to me like that nigger was reaching for a weapon, that's what I saw, you understand?"

The first officer was shaking and trembling in disbelief. You see this young man was somewhat new to the force and he only had intentions of searching the car because of what was going on that night, not killing an unarmed man. The first officer tried to get a grip on himself and started to speak.

"But there's no gun! There is no gun!" He kneeled and eventually sat on the ground, leaned up against Don's car, right under the back-passenger door behind the seat where Frank's dead body laid slain.

The second officer replied, "Calm the fuck down! Now you just wait a minute! Think about it! We can push this car over there in that ditch, go get you cleaned up, and go back to our regular beat until the shift is over. By the time they find this dead motherfucker, so much would have happened in this town after tonight, it'll look like a mystery. Hell, they might even call us to the scene when he's found."

The first officer, still extremely nervous and afraid, barely calmed a little and said. "Are.... Are you sure? That we won't catch no heat for this?"

"Trust me!" Replied the second officer. "The way those niggers out here acting tonight, anything goes. Trust me! Now help me push this car in the ditch."

The two officers proceeded to push the car into the ditch and hurried up and jumped in the squad car and raced off. The sad thing is that there was a strong to definite possibility that they could and would get away with such a heinous crime.

To Lose and to Gain

As Frank's dead body lay inside Don's car in that ditch; back at the office, the phone began to ring again. June went to answer the phone to find that it was Tricia again wondering about the whereabouts of Frank. "Hello, has Frank left yet?"

June replied to Tricia, "Yea, he been gone for more than an hour and a half now. He ain't made it there yet?"

Tricia answered anxiously, "No, that's why I was calling back, to see if he left and let him know that it's not looking good and please hurry."

June then replied to Tricia, "He should probably be there soon because he ran out in quite a hurry. You know how bad it is out there, it's probably a tough drive."

"Yea you right! Hopefully, it will be soon." Said Tricia.

As Tricia hung up the phone, she hung her head because she was so distraught with Anne not doing well with labor, she felt that Anne needed Frank to be there. Tricia knew that just Frank's presence would add value to the troubled situation Anne was in because Frank was Anne's rock. As she headed back to the room with Anne, Tricia was stopped by one of the doctors and he asked her to follow him to the waiting room.

The doctor began to address Tricia and started to ask about Frank. "Ma'am, are you immediate family for Anne Tibbs? Can her husband make it?"

Tricia answered the doctor, "I am her sister, Patricia Wilson. Well, I called him, and he should be on his way."

Then the doctor continued, "Are there any other relatives present?"

Tricia replied, "No! Just me. What is it? Is it going to be okay?" Tricia began to tremble, and her eye wells began to fill with tears.

The doctor took a step back and looked long and hard at Tricia because he knew that he was bearing more bad news. "Well, the baby is at risk as you know, but there may also be a possibility that if she has this baby, her life may be in danger. Now, I've talked with your sister..."

As the doctor continued to try and explain, Tricia waivered and almost fell into his arms, but somehow kept her composure. The doctor noticed Tricia's imbalance and put his arms out as if to try and catch Tricia, but she remained standing and attentive to his reply. The doctor knew he would be able to continue but knew that what came next would devastate Tricia. "Your sister made it clear that she wants this baby to be born no matter what."

Tricia got a little dizzy again as she took in all of this and sighed as she mumbled, *"Oh My God,"* to herself. "Do you mean?" Tricia looked the doctor right in his eyes looking for confirmation about what he claimed Anne had confirmed.

The doctor looked back at Tricia seriously and replied to the best of his strength. "What I'm telling you is that your sister feels..."

Tricia immediately ran off from the doctor knowing what he was going to say. She just couldn't believe that not only Anne would declare this, but that it was even an option and it was just too much to bear. The doctor tried to stop Tricia and continue to explain the decision; he couldn't stop her. She headed back to the room where Anne was, to talk to Anne about what was going on. Tricia entered the room slowly as not to wake Anne if she was sleeping. Anne was in a deep gaze, almost a trance, with a life-or-death decision now hers to make, she chose to let whatever was to happen, happen and leave it in God's hands. Of course, Anne was growing restless herself wondering where Frank was.

With barely any strength to even talk, her first question to Tricia as soon as she snapped out of her deep thought and noticed that her sister was again sitting in the chair next to the bed. "Oh, girl how long have you been sitting there? I didn't even see you there." Now heavily medicated with whatever the doctors could give her that would help her cope with pain, but not harm the baby. "Did you hear about where Frank is?" The questions came spewing out back-to-back, almost like a pressure release from the deep thought that she was just locked in.

Tricia slowly replied, "I called the office, they said he been left! And maybe it's bad traffic because of what happened tonight."

Anne replied in her pain, "Yea, you are probably right. Ohhhh!" With a painful yell from the instance of jolting pain that belched out of Anne's little face. "It hurts so bad! Frank! Get here soon!"

Tricia, trying to be the calm encouraging older sister looked at Anne and gave her a certain stare and said, "He will!"

Anne just looked at her sister with a ghostly expression. With no more words exchanged between them for a few minutes, it was like they were communicating through telekinesis. For they both began to cry as Anne clutched Tricia's hands extremely tight. Tricia, wanting to ask Anne about her decision to have the baby delivered no matter what, but she was hesitant with a huge ball of anxiety in her belly; she could not talk. At the same time, Anne was giving her a look that Tricia was all too familiar with. This was the same look that Tricia got five years ago from their Aunt Justine as she died in their house in front of Tricia while she was staying as a house guest.

As a little more time passed and Anne's fever began to climb to dangerous levels, the doctors tried to maintain it, but it was fast approaching the midnight hour and still no word or sight of Frank. The doctors were growing more and more anxious to induce Anne's labor for fear of losing either Anne or the baby. Even though the danger was there, the doctors hoped to be able to save the baby with Anne being okay also. As Anne lay there groaning in discomfort and pain, Tricia had since gone back in the waiting room to make calls to try and locate Frank. She even called the police and gave them a description of Don's car in hopes that they would find him. With no apparent luck, Tricia walked down to the hospital cafeteria to get some snacks and coffee, to try and calm her nerves. As Tricia entered the cafeteria, she looked toward the vending machine and saw an older woman bent over with her right arm lodged in the bottom dispense area of the snack vending machine.

"My Goodness." The older lady said with disappointment.

"Excuse me. Can I help you?" Tricia said as she approached the lady that seemed to be either stuck or busy trying to retrieve her snack from the clutch of the vending machine.

"Oh, thank you sweetie." The little old lady replied. But "I'm just trying to get my peanut bar. It's stuck behind the door."

Tricia jumped into action to help. "Let me give it a try."

As the lady lifted up from bending over, they looked into each other's eyes. Both women had pain in their eyes. Pain from what this night had brought. Bringing them both to this place, this hospital, to be in a position of hopelessness and helplessness. Then to add to the turmoil, a vending machine that was not working right to dispense. What else could go wrong? Then suddenly, success! Tricia was able to retrieve the peanut bar for the lady and hand it to her.

"Thank you so much sweetie. Can I buy you a snack?" The lady said in appreciation to Tricia.

"Oh, no thank you ma'am." Tricia answered promptly. "I got it. But I appreciate it."

The lady in turn replied to Tricia in the same manner; "I appreciate you. Thank you."

It was as if they both heaped so much appreciation and respect upon each other just to try and cope with what was going on with them in the hospital. As the lady sat down in the cafeteria, Tricia put a few coins into that same snack machine hoping that the sour candy she chose would not get stuck just like the lady's peanut bar.

"Well! No sticking for this piece of candy." Tricia grabbed it as it dispensed from the machine and turned to go and sit at the table across from where the lady had setup.

"Oh. Come on over here and have a seat with me sweetie. I owe you some conversation or something. If it'll help you tonight?" The lady offered up to Tricia in gratitude for Tricia just helping her out with her vending machine snack.

Tricia quickly glanced at the lady with a slight grin and said, "Thank you." As she walked to the same table the lady was sitting at to grab a seat across the table directly in front of the lady. "So, my name is Patricia."

The lady nodded her head with wisdom and replied, "I am Ethel." Ethel went on to talk, "What has you in this hospital tonight sweetie?"

Tricia's face turned to stone when thinking about how to answer Ethel's question. Tricia didn't know what was to come, after the doctor's news about Anne and the baby. She wanted to be jovial and reply about the fantastic news of her baby niece being born, but she knew that no one knew how the night would turn out. Especially with the still long-awaited arrival of Frank in the balance.

"I came in with my sister who's pregnant. Tricia started to explain as Ethel immediately wanted to congratulate.

"Oh, is that so…." Ethel said.

As Ethel began to form a congratulatory reply to Tricia; Tricia stopped her short to interrupt. "Well, it's not going well. There have been some major complications and now the doctor just told me that my sister could be in big trouble. And her husband is taking forever to get here."

In an empathetic mood from receiving Tricia's response; Ethel replied to Tricia, "Oh my, sweetie. I am so sorry to hear that. Let's pray baby. God will help."

Again, Tricia cut in on Ethel's speech, "I just don't understand tonight. What happened today? Now this! My sister!"

As the tears started to drop and bounce on the table in front of Tricia; Ethel got up from her seat and came over to Tricia's side to comfort Tricia. "I'm so sorry baby. God will make a way. I promise you. Let's pray." Ethel said once again. Then she grabbed Tricia's hands and began to speak a Prayer:

"My Lord and Savior Jesus Christ. Wrap your hands around this young lady and her family and bring peace and healing to allow this family to get through any trouble tonight and make it home safely to love and be there for each other. Protect them Father. Give Patricia the strength to deal with whatever your will is on this night of sin. God, guide this young lady to become stronger than she has ever been in her life. All praise to you Lord. Amen."

Tricia recited Amen along with Ethel as Ethel finished the Prayer. While wiping the tears from her eyes, cheeks, and upper lip; Tricia looked up at Ethel and with so much gratitude, repeatedly began to say thank you to Ethel. Over and over and over again. Ethel embraced Tricia from the side as Tricia sat at the table while she leaned in.

"Sweetie. God has got you. Whatever this night brings you – you are made for it. God has made sure of it!"

With that, Tricia dried her eyes again and grasped Ethel's hand tightly as Ethel began to round the table back to her seat and sit down slowly. Next, with a murmur of speech, Tricia finally got some more words out. "I am so sorry Ethel." It's not all about me and my family. What brought you here tonight?"

Ethel then replied to Tricia. "Oh, baby; my husband is having knee surgery. He should be okay. He's just got so much going on with blood pressure and everything, the doctor said it'll be a rough operation for him. He just went back, but God will get him through it. I know it!"

"My God Ethel." Tricia replied in disbelief. "You are an amazing woman!"

"Well, what do you mean sweetie?" Ethel took a bite from her peanut bar.

Tricia replied. "I mean, just the positive attitude you can have with everything that happened today and your husband."

Ethel replied to her. "Sweetie, I've been through a lot. But there are so many that's been through far more than me, struggling. I'll be fine. My husband will be fine. I think about those babies that lost their great daddy today. Now, that's where God needs to reach out and raise his hands for protection."

Tricia nodded her head in agreement with Ethel and sat quietly eating her sour candy; but couldn't help but think about Anne. For a few more minutes, Ethel continued to talk to Tricia to try and cheer her up. At this point, Tricia was listening to Ethel; but only heard sounds, no words. Not as if Tricia were purposely being rude to Ethel to ignore; Tricia's mind was just all over the place. And though she had effectively discontinued actively listening to Ethel, Tricia did continue to nod her head and smile as Ethel continued to preach and try to console Tricia.

After about 20 minutes of Ethel talking to Tricia, and Tricia acting to listen, Ethel raised from the table and said a final; "Baby bless you and your family. I am going to go down to the waiting room with my family to check on them. Do you need me to stay with you?"

Tricia looked up at Ethel and replied, "Oh no. You've done so much for me in just a few minutes. Thank you so much Ethel. I appreciate you."

Ethel began to grab her purse and jacket from the chair at the cafeteria table. Ethel had a feeling of satisfaction that she had given some good advice and gospel to Tricia and that Tricia had taken it in well. Even though, Ethel had recognized that Tricia had tuned her speech out, but probably not on purpose.

As Ethel left out of the cafeteria, she looked back at Tricia with one more comment and waived, "God be with you Tricia!"

Finishing her candy, Tricia went to the coffee vending machine as she prepared to go back to Anne's room. Upon her return to the floor in which Anne was roomed, Tricia encountered a huge scurry of nurses and doctors whisking past her onto the elevator as she was getting off. She feared the worst, dropped her coffee, and ran toward the room that Anne was in. As she rushed into the room to find it empty, she turned back to the main nurse station to ask what happened. While in the whole melee the nurse was trying to get her attention.

"Miss, they took her to emergency labor. I was trying to tell you as you ran past."

Hysterically replying, Tricia said. "Emergency labor? Oh no! Where? Tell me where?"

The nurse replied, "Floor 2, room 342B, they won't let you in, but they'll tell you were to wait."

Tricia gave the nurse a muffled, "Thank you." Then, she hurried back to the elevators. She headed to the area where the room was and found the waiting room for emergency labor. She impatiently sat and waited; periodically getting up and making a full lap around the entire waiting room. The room was cold and had only a few more people waiting there. As she passed each window in the waiting room, she would stop to look out as if she thought she would see Frank coming. Maybe she just felt that something was wrong and looking out the window would make him get there soon. Either way, it sort of kept her mind busy and off of horrible thoughts of losing her soon-to-be niece or even her sister. As a little more than three hours went by, a doctor soon entered the waiting room. As he entered, all the attention of everyone in the waiting room turned to him. By now, the count of people had grown over the hours. Cousins, aunts, uncles, co-workers of Anne's and Tricia's had since arrived at the hospital. The onlookers also included strangers awaiting news about their loved ones in operating situations that night. They all turned to the doctor in hopes that he would be letting them know what was going on about their loved ones.

The doctor took a few steps in the direction of the middle of the room and looked around until he made eye contact with Tricia, he called out her name and said, "Patricia. Patricia Wilson?"

She answered, "Yes!?" He told her to come with him. They went out to the hall for a little privacy and as he began to talk, Tricia interrupted him by asking, "Is the baby okay?" By now, she had thought and prayed so hard that she somehow felt that Anne would automatically be ok. For Anne was strong, she knew Anne. Anne could pull through anything.

The doctor looked at her and said, "Yes, the baby is okay, seems to be a healthy baby girl." Then he bowed his head in disappointment with an ill look upon his face.

Tricia's heart dropped because she knew by the expression on the doctor's face what he was about to say. "Don't tell me!" She said as tears began to fill up the wells of her eyes.

The doctor said, "I'm sorry Miss Wilson, she didn't make it through."

As Tricia let out a loud shrill like that of a cat being bitten by a dog, she fell into the arms of the doctor and passed out from the news. She could not take it. After hours of trying to save the baby and Anne, Anne's blood pressure got to dangerous levels and she went into cardiac arrest just as the baby breached, they could not resuscitate her. In the wake of brand-new life, this new mother could now only watch over her daughter from the heavens. The doctor had some nurses take Tricia to a room with a bed as they tried to get her to come to. After a few minutes she did, only to see that she was in a room full of nurses and doctors. As she moved her eyes about the room through a blur, she saw the doctor who had given her the bad news and noticed he was inquiring about the father. She thought to herself, *Still no Frank? Please Lord let him be alright.*

The doctors noticed that she had come to and began to speak to her. "Please Miss, try and stay calm, and don't move. We want to talk to you, ask you about the deceased and the newborn."

Tricia cried out, "Deceased!?" And temporarily blacked out again.

After they woke her again, the doctor went on, "We still have not heard from the father of this child. Are there any grandparents who can come and sign papers and whatnot?"

She replied somberly, realizing the reality of the situation. "No. It's just me and Anne." Through the well of tears and anguish that overcame her again; Tricia managed to speak as she struggled with the pain of the reality of the situation. "I can sign any papers."

"That shouldn't be necessary," the doctor said, and then asked, as he led with an inquiry. "Well, with the assumption that the father will be here to take the baby. Do you know what the couple had planned to name the baby if it were a girl? We can start the paperwork and the father can sign when he arrives."

As Tricia laid her head back again, the tears flooded her eyes and the deep throbbing pain in her soul continued to tear to shreds any resemblance of hope for anything. Tricia envisioned all the good times spent with Anne. Tricia got a vision of them growing up together. Suddenly she was sitting on the floor of their back porch:

Wearing a pink and yellow dress. Anne was sitting across from her in a red outfit with a big blue bow in her hair holding her favorite baby doll.

As Anne looked up at Tricia, Anne slowly rocked the baby doll back and forth. She looked at Tricia and said, "When I grow up, I'm going to have a baby girl just like this and I'm going to name her…"

In what seemed to be an hour of daydreaming to Tricia, and oh so real, but was just a few seconds; she looked up at the doctors and nurses slowly as she dried her eyes from the monsoon of tears and with the faintest voice that she could get out, Tricia replied.

"Priscilla!" They wanted a girl named Priscilla!"

New Beginnings

A Light rain drizzle covered the grass, mist from that rain filled the air as the tears ran down Tricia's face. "Let us not grieve what the Lord has taken from us. Let us rejoice in the lesson of what the Lord has given us in times of grief. Let us acknowledge that there will be times our loved ones will be called upon by the Lord." Those were the words that Pastor Shaw recited as he went on with his sermon at the burial. Tricia stood there, lost in a daze remembering her beloved sister. Heavily grieving; thinking back to their youth, and all the things they use to do:

"You can't catch me.... Hahahaha.... Anne laughed as she ran around the tree trying to escape the grasp of Tricia.

"Stop playing Anne, I tagged you; your it!"

Still running away from Tricia; Anne replied. "No... Nope, you didn't; you're still it!" Both girls laughing hysterically as they gave chase to one another.

Just as Tricia was zoned out reminiscing about her childhood with Anne, she was startled by a touch on her shoulder. The funeral director gently touched her to get her attention, as he could tell Tricia was not present.

"Are you ready?" A whisper into her left ear to snap Tricia back into reality and the present.

Shaken a bit, Tricia started to recognize where she was. "Oh... Oh, yes. I think I am ready."

She slowly walked up to the podium in the cemetery to give the eulogy. Tricia realized two caskets lay before her. Her precious sister to the right and her closely loved brother-in-law Frank to the left. So tragic; a double funeral and Tricia was standing there acting as if she had all the strength in the world to stand before all these friends and family members to speak about the lives of these two people that she cared for so dearly. Tricia strongly grasped the podium to keep her balance, but she was determined to speak the light of the life of her departed sister and brother-in-law. Determined to let everyone know just how much they both meant to her and the entire family.

"Anne was... Anne and Frank were..." Pausing as everyone sat looking at her with encouragement.

Now the tears filled up her eyes as she tried to gather herself, choking on her words as she tried to begin to speak again. A man got up from his seat in the front row to the right of the caskets; from the family row and walked up to the podium and wrapped his arm around the shoulder of Tricia and whispered something in her ear that the guests of the funeral could not hear. Then he moved his hands to his side and with his right hand, he placed it on top of Tricia's left hand that rest upon the podium and clinched the back of that hand to support her. It was almost as if his grasp sent power into Tricia because as the family in the front row began to smile at this act of love and encouragement; Tricia began to speak again – this time clearly and concisely, with the tears drying up a bit as she delivered the powerful Eulogy. "My sister Anne and her husband Frank were the base of this family, the base of this community!" Tricia went on and on for about 22 minutes before she would break down again. All with Uncle Bill standing by her side. It almost seemed that she had zoned out again and wasn't giving the eulogy of a lifetime as she spoke so eloquently about the two lives that were so impactful to the family. As she went on and on, with the occasional; *"Umm Hmmm" and "Preach"* from the crowd, the burial service slowly turned into an outdoor church service to honor Frank and Anne. Tricia continued to praise their lives to the family and friends gathered before her. Feeling relieved and now somewhat able to deal with the grief. This day will be burned into Tricia's memory for the rest of her life. As her new life began; without Anne, without Frank, with a new niece that she desperately wanted to ensure grew up properly.

***

Sitting looking through family photographs, reminiscing about all the good times and bad and what could have been, Tricia placed herself in a time machine and she felt like she was talking to Anne about what they were going to be when they grew up:

Sitting on the edge of the bed as Anne was at the top by the headboard. Anne went on about how she wanted to have 5 or 6 kids, marry a rich man and live uptown in a nice house.

As the two of them laughed and joked, Tricia was awakened out of her daydream to the sound of a bell and the voice of a girl calling out her name.

"Aunt Tricia! Aunt Tricia! There's a man at the door." Tricia snapped out of it and gathered herself as she closed the photograph book, wiping her watery eyes from the intense reminiscing at the sound of her name being sung. It was her niece, Priscilla, wearing her favorite sweater with green and white stripes and the buttons at the bottom missing. A young brown skin girl with beautiful puffy, curly hair, and a very pronounced face. A pretty little face, with astonishing features that were sure to develop into a beautiful woman. Priscilla was singing Tricia's name, as she did quite often. Priscilla had a great singing voice for a young girl. She often sang around the house but didn't take it seriously or indicate she wanted to pursue singing, at least at this young age. Tricia went to see who was at the door.

As she approached the front hall to go to see who was at the door, Priscilla came running up to her saying, "I ain't never saw him before, he looks like the police or something."

Tricia smiled at her and kept walking towards the door as she said, "Go on back to your room and stop being so nosey girl."

Tricia always had to tell Priscilla to stop being nosey, at 13 years old now, attending school and very smart, Priscilla was quite the inquisitive one. Raised to this point in her life alone by Tricia, Priscilla was in every bit just like her mother Anne. After that horrible night of losing her sister and brother-in-law, Tricia took custody of Priscilla because there was no one else that would or could. Tricia's mother and father had long died before the night of Anne's death and Tricia was the closest relative remaining to raise the baby. So here they were, in the house that Anne and Tricia grew up in, which was left to the two of them when their parents both died in a bad automobile accident. It was Priscilla and her aunt Tricia just making it through life, together. The doorbell rang once more as the man outside seemed to grow impatient, Tricia opened the door.

"Good afternoon," said the man. "I'm Mr. Thomas from the State Attorney's office and I would like to have a few words with you, Miss Wilson, right?"

"Yes, that is me. Please come in, right this way, please have a seat at the table, I will get you something to drink."

"Oh, I would appreciate that, it's really hot today." said Mr. Thomas as Tricia went into the kitchen to prepare some lemonade for the man and herself, she could not help but feel a little antsy and somewhat afraid about what the man could be here for. She entered back into the dining room where the man was sitting, looking at some papers that he had pulled out of his briefcase.

"Well, I'm here to talk about the death of Frank Tibbs; that was your brother-in-law, I believe?"

"Yes, that was him," replied Tricia.

"I understand that you are the lone relative that was able to take in his daughter?"

"Yes, that is me." Replied Tricia.

He continued. "Well, I know that back when things happened, your family got the word that he somehow lost control of his vehicle and ended up in a ditch and that's how he passed?"

"Yes, that is correct, it was devastating because that's the same way both my parents went," said Tricia.

33

"Well as a man of the law, it brings me great heartache to tell you that, it's not what happened at all."

Tricia replied to him; "What do you mean?"

He replied. "You see, even though those were the results given, this still was considered an open case because there were many deaths that night that were similar. So, it is our job to continually investigate open cases, just so happened that the people working in the attorney's office before I got here were in on what happened and covered it up."

"What Happened!? What do you mean!?" Tricia asked the man.

He paused and then answered, "In my team's re-investigation and examining the evidence and records, I found that there was a bullet hole found in the head of Mr. Tibbs. That part of the paperwork had been discarded, but I dug up the originals from the vault.

"Oh my God!" Tricia said.

"Miss Wilson, basically what I'm trying to get at is Mr. Tibbs was murdered that night, there was no accident."

"But I don't understand," said Tricia, as she went on. "He was the sweetest, kindest man, who would want to hurt him?"

Mr. Thomas replied, "Well, unfortunately, amid the ruckus that night two of our very own went on a little killing spree of Negr... I mean people taking part in the rioting that night, I guess figuring they could get away with it."

As Tricia's eyes began to fill with tears from thinking that this is what happened and reliving that night in her head, the man was about to go on. Tricia cut him off. "Frank wasn't doing any rioting. That's not Frank."

Mr. Thomas intervened on her comment, "I think you should be able to feel a little comfort in knowing that those two men could be brought to justice." He said, hoping to calm her. "That brings me to what else I'm here for. Seeing that these cases were covered up by our own and no one followed up to investigate for so long, each family is entitled to file suit for the incompetence and negligence of the police force and you could stand to get some amount of money that could help you with raising the child; and make them serve the justice they should. You know, for the pain you all have suffered."

Tricia replied, "Well, what's right is right, but I don't want to have to put Priscilla through any unnecessary things, you know. What would we have to do? Would Priscilla have to be involved? How much time would it take?" The questions spewed out of Tricia back-to-back as she immediately thought about the long-term effects on Priscilla.

He answered. "I know what you mean Miss Wilson, but there should be some justice for your family." "Unfortunately, in this case; you will need to be ready to fight. Long and hard. And the courts would want to meet his daughter to ensure that you have been taking the great care that you have, to build the case of what she is missing out on without her father in her life."

Sitting there thinking about what Mr. Thomas just told her, Tricia was thinking about everything she had been through, everything she had been trying to protect Priscilla from.

She replied with her final answer, "As long as we have closure and each other, we will make it." Tricia said with hesitation, "I just don't want to be digging up old sad memories, she's doing fine in school and we don't have many bills, we will make it."

As the man stood up, he opened his briefcase and grabbed a folder out of it. "Please, at least take this."

Tricia, now standing up as well asked, "What is this?"

Looking at her with a serious face, "This folder holds everything you need to fight this case. It has the officer's statements about the incident; the forms that look like a cover-up, and also some information on what I consider the courts would grant you monetarily if you fought and won. I just did some preliminary numbers. But, of course, nothing is guaranteed. I also wrote my number on the top of the inside of the folder, so you can reach me anytime." As he paused, before getting ready to leave, he made another comment, "Understand, this case remains dead without you or a family member taking action. These two officers probably have and will continue to do this to other families. I just feel you needed to know your options and get justice."

He closed the briefcase and started to walk towards the front door as he kept a steady look into Tricia's eyes as he said, "Okay, just don't hesitate to call me if you feel you've had a change of reasoning."

Tricia looked back at him and told him, "Yes, yes I will do that if I need you."

The man opened the front door and headed down the front stairs to get into his car. He sat out in front of the house looking at it for a few minutes, maybe trying to understand Tricia's mindset, and he thought to himself that maybe it is not all about revenge or money to everyone. For him to see a young black woman, single, trying to raise a child after practically losing everyone close to her and not want to try and get some financial gain to at least ease her worries, he could do nothing but admire her as he put his car in drive and slowly pulled off. As S.A. Thomas pulled off, Tricia stood at the window next to the door wondering when she should talk with Priscilla about what happened to her father. She had already given her the explanation of what happened to her mother, telling her that God called her home and wanted her in heaven to help. Saying that God told her mother her work here was done because she had brought such a special girl into the world. As she turned away from the window to get ready and go and check on Priscilla, she noticed Priscilla sitting at the table in the spot where the man was sitting just staring off into space. Tricia called out to get her attention as she walked towards Priscilla.

"What are you doing sweetie? You're being nosey again?"

"No, I'm hungry. Why did the man come Aunt Trish?" said Priscilla, calling her Trish for short like she sometimes would do.

Tricia hesitated a little trying to come up with something that wouldn't provoke more questions from the inquisitive Priscilla. "Don't worry baby, everything is fine, he was trying to sell something."

As she hid the folder behind her back, trying to think of a place to hide it. What Tricia did not know is that the whole time the man was there, Priscilla was hiding and listening on the stairs. Priscilla heard every word, and even though she now kind of understood what really happened to her daddy, she still did not understand fully. She still would need an adult to sit her down and explain every detail for her adolescent brain to process and comprehend. So, she decided to pretend she wasn't listening to their conversation and never brought it up to her aunt again. Besides, all Priscilla ever had were pictures of her parents and the long stories that Tricia would tell her about them as memories. It was difficult for the girl to feel hurt, for Tricia had taken such good care of her and virtually given her everything she needed. Tricia grabbed both of Priscilla's cheeks on her little chubby face and kneeled to look Priscilla right in the eyes.

"Baby listen. No matter what. I'm going to always take care of you. I'm going to always be there for you. And make sure you are alright! You hear me?!"

Priscilla shook her head yes to agree with her loving Aunt. The two of them were tight. Inseparable.

"What I will tell you is that your daddy was a great man. He was so, so nice to everyone. But for some reason, he always had to deal with enemies."

"Enemies?" Priscilla asked.

"Yes, people who tried to go against him, even though he was kind to everyone."

"But why?" Priscilla asked. "What did he do to the enemies?"

"Just know that your daddy had a way to remove them. He would never hurt a fly, but he always knew how to deal with people the right way to remove them and protect your momma and me."

Tricia had just explained to Priscilla how Frank would diplomatically deal with people that got in his way, or at least she was trying to do that. Not knowing that Priscilla took the explanation and understood it in a way that her daddy would eliminate opposition no matter what. From this point on, in the back of Priscilla's mind; she knew her dad didn't play around. At least, according to her aunt Tricia, he just had a way.

A little part of Tricia felt guilty for not telling Priscilla the full truth, but for some reason, she felt that the girl did indeed know. It was like an unspoken thing that they both kept to themselves, both felt that each other knew that the other did know. Tricia grabbed Priscilla's hand and said, "Come on, let's go see what we can fix to eat. You want your favorite?" Priscilla loved to eat a piece of toast with a little butter and sprinkled it with sugar no matter what time of the day it was, and she would always wash it down with some milk. Other than breakfast and dinner, Tricia would let her eat that snack any time. There was not always much to eat in the house anyway. With Tricia working at a little restaurant as a waitress at the end of the block, she did not make much money, just barely enough for them to make it. Lucky or blessed, it may be, Tricia did not have a mortgage on the house because her father worked hard and worked multiple jobs and had just paid it off before the tragic accident.

As Tricia sat Priscilla down to the table with her snack, she reminded Priscilla that in a few, they were leaving to go to Choir rehearsal down at the church, "Don't take all day eating, you know we got to go to the church."

"Yes ma'am" Priscilla replied.

Priscilla loved Choir rehearsal, it allowed her to let that powerful voice of hers out, but still not be provoked to fully reveal it. She could blend in with the Choir and fulfill her desire to sing. While Priscilla ate her toast, Tricia went into the living room of the house and sat at a desk that was set up in the corner next to the front window. There she sat thinking about Frank. Thinking about Anne. Thinking about what Mr. Thomas just told her. She took out the paper that Mr. Thomas used to write his office number and began to write notes. As she wrote, she documented what Mr. Thomas just relayed to her about Frank's real reason for dying. As tears filled her eyes, she began to get emotional.

Priscilla yelled from the kitchen, "Can I have some more milk?" Gathering herself and quickly folding the paper up she just wrote on; Tricia put the paper in a box under the china cabinet where she kept all the important papers; wiped the tears and went into the kitchen with a smile.

"Of course, sweetie. Then you go on and get ready to go. Hurry up girl."

It was about ten minutes to six o'clock and Tricia and Priscilla were headed on their way to the church. As they walked down the block, they got the normal hello's from all the people in the neighborhood.

"On y'all way to the church ladies?" Said old Mr. Simpson who stayed at the end of the block. Priscilla, nodding her head yes as Tricia said hello to the man.

"Oh, such a pretty dress for a pretty girl," said Mrs. Handy, the nice lady in the neighborhood who would look out for anybody and always willing to lend a hand.

Priscilla could only blush at the compliment as they continued to walk along.

"Hey Tricia, don't forget that we giving Tracy a birthday party this coming weekend, I'm sure Priscilla wouldn't want to miss it!" Gina, the lady that lived down on the next block from them said as they passed by.

It was a friendly and family-oriented atmosphere in the neighborhood, and it seemed like everyone took a special interest in Tricia and Priscilla because they all knew about their story. The two of them soon approached the church where a few groups were standing outside congregating. Some groups were children and some adults. Tricia let Priscilla go off to be with the children as she talked with some of the adult members while keeping a peripheral view of her.

"Girl, I don't know how you do it," said May, a member of the same age as Tricia whom she had known for most of her life, for they had both attended grammar and high school together.

"Do what May?" Tricia asked.

"Girl you a good soul, you spend all your time raising that girl and you miss all the parties." Said May.

Tricia then answered, "Yea I know, but it's worth it, I gotta make sure she's okay."

"Oh, I know girl, I'm not knocking you, your blessings are coming!" May said just as they began to follow the groups into the church, behind Pastor Shaw, as the kids ran ahead trying to make sure they got their favorite seats during the rehearsal.

As the two women followed the children into the church, Tricia could not help but notice Roy; one of the young deacons of the church staring at her with his usual goofy smile as he waved from the front of the church. Tricia knew that Roy had a thing for her, he even tried to kiss her once back in high school, but he never seriously pursued Tricia because he was too shy to say what he felt. So, for years there was always this flirtation going back and forth between them. Trying not to lock eyes with Roy, a sudden voice began to grab Tricia's attention.

"Hey there sweetheart." It was Priscilla's Dad's old friend Don. Don would stop by the church from time to time. He was still deeply involved in the civil rights movement, becoming more and more of a figurehead in the region. "I hear you doing good with your niece."

Tricia nodded to agree as she began to talk and take a lean in to hug Don. "Thank you. It's been a while since we've seen you Don. So good to see you."

Don quickly replied, "Yes, very good to see you too. I just saw your little bundle of joy has grown up quite fast." They both had a chuckle about just how big Priscilla was by now.

Tricia replied, "Yep, she is a whole handful too. But I wouldn't change a thing."

Then Don replied, "Yes ma'am! I tell you; you know there is nothing I wouldn't do for you and that girl. Frank was like a brother to me. And that means y'all are my family. Forever!" Don went on, "I mean it. Don't ever hesitate to come to me."

Tricia looked at him with much admiration and replied. "Thank you so much Don. It means a lot to us."

Don replied, "You got it sweetheart." As he slowly turned to begin to go into the church to visit everyone else before the choir began. "Girl, that ain't Wendy over there, is it? Let me go on over there and speak. You know she gonna take it personally if I don't."

They both laughed as Tricia agreed with his assessment of Wendy's disposition. Tricia went into the church to find Priscilla had gone with the other children; and then to get to her seat for rehearsal, she couldn't help but keep searching the building to locate where Roy was sitting. She couldn't help herself. May walked up beside Tricia again to go and sit next to her, like they always do at rehearsal.

Tricia made sure to downplay any liking of Roy in public, although she liked him just as much or even more than he liked her. She often dreamed of going out with him someday and sometimes replaced her last name with his. At times when alone, standing in the bathroom mirror with the door closed and locked saying, *"Patricia Wetherspoon."* Trying to get a feel for it. But in church they always acted cordial, not speaking directly to each other, just saying hi and speaking through other members. They would often stand in group conversations not inputting one word, just occasionally glancing at each other trying not to draw attention to themselves. One thing was for sure, they liked and lusted after each other, but they restrained it in church. Though Tricia was everything that Roy wanted in a woman; strong, beautiful, now in her mid-30's, a chocolate complexion slim frame woman with the most telling deep brown eyes and long thick full hair, he also played it cool not to let on his feelings. As Tricia and May walked side by side down the aisle, May nudged Tricia on the elbow and whispered while trying not to move her lips talking through her smile.

"Y'all need to stop fooling around and get together girl."

Tricia began to blush while saying, "What are you talking about? I just only said hello."

May laughed and said, "I know, that's the problem. It won't hurt you to go over there for once and have a decent conversation with the man, y'all not kids anymore."

As the two sat down on a bench right behind the children, Tricia started to think to herself just as the organist began to warm up. Tricia had spent over the last decade in recluse, mourning the loss of her sister and brother-in-law and trying to raise Priscilla. Like May said, she did indeed miss all the parties because once she was done mourning, she was so busy trying to provide for Priscilla. The members of the church proceeded with the rehearsals; adults first, and then kids after, allowing Priscilla to get that beautiful voice out. Suddenly there was no more music and May was standing over Tricia while Priscilla was at her side grabbing her hand.

She rose from her deep thought to hear Priscilla saying, "Aunt Trish, I gotta pee, I'll be right back."

"Okay." Tricia replied as she realized she had missed the whole rehearsal thinking about how she was going to start living her life, thinking, *"Just because I got Priscilla doesn't mean I can't live."*

May touched her shoulder and said, "Girl you ok?" You weren't hitting those high notes like you usually do."

Tricia answered, "Oh, yea I'm good, I just got a little headache."

Still trying to conceal her intentions about Roy. The next thirty or forty minutes were consumed with the usual seemingly endless chatter of the adults while the kids sat anxiously ready to leave. Tricia found herself in that group of people again standing at an angle across from Roy.

Again, trying to catch a glance at him secretly, and then for some reason she built up her nerve and belted out, "Deacon Wetherspoon. Can I talk to you for a second?"

Surprised and looking at Tricia now, "Of course!" He eagerly replied as they walked off away from the group.

Roy led Tricia into the front vestibule of the church, and they began to talk. This was it! They finally took a step toward uncovering the feelings that have been pinned up inside both of them for years. This initiation? Maybe it was Tricia's built-up courage? Maybe it was Roy's slick way of cautiously flirting just enough with Tricia to get her to ask him to talk? Either way, here they were! Finally, about to hash it out.

"How are things?" Roy asked.

Tricia gave a sheepish look and replied, "They've been alright."

For some reason, Roy knew what was going on here, so he decided to cut to the chase and finally spill his guts about how he felt about her.

"You know Tricia, I never lost that crush I had on you back in school. Matter of fact, it probably has grown a little." Roy said to her with his newfound confidence. Maybe all these years he just simply needed some type of confirmation from Tricia before he could open up? Either way, it was finally happening.

"Is that so?" Tricia said in response to his gesture as she continued to slowly give in to him. "Well, I guess you alright with me too!"

Roy smiled back at her, "Just alright huh?" Roy said with a grin. "If I'm just alright then why I always catch you staring at me?"

Tricia rolled her eyes and laughed as she responded, "No, that's you, you're the one who stares at me all the time." As Roy began to laugh with a tone of denial, Tricia gathered herself and got a little more serious. "You know, on Sunday I'm making a nice big dinner and you are welcome to come to share it with us, I always seem to cook a little too much. Like I'm expecting someone."

With no hesitation, "Oh yea, I'll come by, just give me the time and I wouldn't miss it for the world." Roy said with a smile that seemed to stretch from behind his left ear around the other side of the back of his head. Just as the date was set, Priscilla walked up and noticed the two talking and grabbed Tricia's hand, but she did not say a word.

As Tricia began to walk off, she looked back at Roy and jokingly said, "Don't stand me up, I'll come to find you." Roy just stood there and watched her walk away until he could not see her anymore as the church doors closed behind her.

Birds of Promise

On the walk home, Priscilla began one of her nosey spells again because she had been watching from across the church as Tricia and Roy talked the whole time. As Priscilla started to ask questions Tricia kept this smirk on her face with each reply to Priscilla. She had this feeling inside, a feeling she had not felt since she last saw her sister or her parents. A feeling of content or fullness, like she knew that this was meant to be.

"What did he want Aunt Trish?"

Tricia replied, "Baby, he's just a nice guy that I grew up with wanting to talk to me, that's all." Tricia answered awaiting the next question from Priscilla.

"The other girls at church say he likes you, Aunt Tricia."

Laughing cautiously at Priscilla's comment; Tricia replied the best she could. "Oh, baby we just friends, but who knows. But he will be coming to have Sunday dinner with us this week."

Priscilla looked up at her aunt with malcontent and said, "Uh, he can't come to our house, I don't like him!"

Tricia looked back at the girl and said, "Don't start with me, he's alright. Trust me, it will be ok."

Priscilla did not answer her. From that point, all the way back to the house Priscilla got quiet, and everything

47

Tricia said was met with no reply. As the two entered the house and began to take off their shoes, Tricia grabbed Priscilla's shoulders and crouched down to Priscilla's eye level and looked at her with the most serious face imaginable.

"Listen to me baby, you don't have to worry about anything, it's always been just you and me and, in the end, it will always be you and me. I just think he's a good person, and I need some new friends, I promise you I will always be there for you and nothing is going to change between me and you, I promise. Do you understand?" Tricia said as she touched both cheeks on Priscilla's face and kissed her forehead.

Priscilla looked at her aunt with watery eyes and hugged her as she replied, "Do you promise?"

Tricia replied as they both hugged each other as tight as possible and shared a heartfelt cry. "I do, I do!"

Sunday came fast. Here it was just after 3 in the afternoon; Tricia and Priscilla had just arrived back home from church service that morning.

"Go ahead and take your church clothes off and put on that new short set I bought you last week Priscilla." Tricia yelled to the girl as Priscilla dropped her bible and bag to jet up the stairs in a scurry as she usually did after a long morning of what she considered "boring" church service. Honestly – Priscilla only looked forward to church to be able to sing and play with her friends in the basement when they would sneak down there to act as if they had to use the bathroom one-by-one to get a break from the preaching and singing. Of course, the children would linger in the basement and the bathroom as long as they could during service. That is until an adult would come and kick them out of the bathroom from doing whatever shenanigans they were up to. But as Priscilla yelled back down the stairs to her aunt to obey the order, "Yes Ma'am!" she turned down the hall of the upstairs and went to the spot she always went right after church; and sometimes on Saturday afternoon. She perched herself on the back window stoop to look at the birds that enveloped the tree in the neighbor's yard. This wasn't just a couple of birds. For some reason, this tree would house hundreds of birds. At times, a couple hundred. And those birds would sing and sing and sing. Priscilla found it soothing. So aware was this young girl. So unconventional for her age. But every Sunday afternoon; there she sat, on the upstairs back window stoop admiring nature. It put her soul at peace, calming her.

Every time she would try and get her Aunt Tricia to come to look at the birds; they would start to fly away. By the time Tricia did come to the window, the few times she stopped what she was doing to appease Priscilla, half or more than half of the birds would be gone. Just flew away. Tricia's message to Priscilla about why the birds would seemingly only allow her to see them was that the birds were gathering at the direction of her Mom and Dad. To visit and spend some time with their baby that they never met. Such a touchy way to describe this situation to Priscilla, such a young child, but it was something that Tricia took a chance to do a few years back. Partly to stop the child from running up and down the stairs on Saturdays and Sundays to try and hurry up and get her to "Come look!" but it worked. By now, Priscilla would only come back after visiting the birds and calmly explain what most of them were doing in the tree that day. Also explaining that her Mom and Dad were right there with the birds singing to their baby. Such a questionable, but a sweet gesture that was formed from the fib of an adult to a child to appease them. But sweet indeed. Tricia was just finishing up putting the plate settings on the dining room table as Priscilla came fumbling down the stairs.

"Aunt Tricia, the birds were singing my favorite song. They were extra special today."

"That is wonderful sweetie." Tricia replied with a huge smile as she turned to acknowledge Priscilla's Sunday afternoon ritual. "Go into the kitchen and get me the forks, spoons, cups, and napkins. I'll get the knives when I bring in the food." The two of them worked for the next few minutes to set the table family-style for the dinner with Roy. Surprisingly, Priscilla was not acting out and upset about the dinner. Maybe out of respect for Tricia, she was just going to be accepting of this dinner with Roy. In Priscilla's mind, she was thinking more in the line of *"Get this over with this one time and I won't have to worry about Roy anymore."* Just as Tricia was opening some windows to get a good breeze flowing through the house, and to cool off the house from the heat of the oven that had just raised the temp in the home quite a bit from the cornbread, baked macaroni and cheese, roast, and peas that Tricia had prepared, there was a subtle knock at the door and then the bell. Like a giddy schoolgirl, Tricia got excited about her date; even though this was dinner for three.

"Priscilla, go make sure I turned off everything in the kitchen on the stove while I get the door." Tricia wanted to make sure she could properly greet Roy at the door without Priscilla hovering behind her. As Priscilla headed for the kitchen, Tricia turned to the mirror by the door to check her outfit, hair, and makeup. She wanted to make sure she looked her best for Roy!

There the three of them sat. All enjoying the fantastic dinner that Tricia had prepared, but an awkward silence was in the dining room as they partook in the meal. Then, the youngest person in the room broke the silence.

"Why do you like my Auntie?"

"Priscilla!" Tricia replied to the girl's question in shock with emphasis.

"No, no, it's okay," Roy said with a grin on his face. Then he leaned toward Priscilla with warmth and said, "I just like her, I like her a lot. I always liked her even in school when we were little."

"Uh um! You didn't know Aunt Tricia in school." Priscilla replied to Roy with a snarky tone. Tricia couldn't help but bust out laughing at Priscilla's comeback to Roy. Tricia gathered herself to come to Roy's defense in the conversation.

"But Priscilla, we did go to school together when we were little. About your age. You know the little boy Johnny in your class that you said threw tissue at you, but then your friends said he only did it because he likes you? But you don't like him? Roy used to be my Johnny." As they all started to laugh, and Priscilla laughed with a weirded-out look upon her face; Roy jumped in on the comment to straighten it out.

"But I didn't throw no tissue at your aunt, and she did like me."

51

"Really!?" Tricia replied to Roy. "You that certain that I liked your big-head self!?" They all laughed heartedly again. Then Priscilla got quiet as the two adults got into the closing exchange.

"I'm just saying, way back then, sitting in the classroom, I knew that one day Patricia Wilson was going to..." as he steaked his fork into his cornbread slice,

"Fix me some delicious cornbread." Then he stuck his fork into his roast.

"Bake me the most succulent beef roast in the world." Moving the fork onto the baked macaroni and cheese.

"And blow my mind away with the cheesiest mac and cheese I ever tasted."

As they all began to giggle, Tricia joked back at Roy, "But my peas ain't good enough huh?" The two of them burst into louder laughter while Priscilla was uncontrollably grinning and giggling at the child's play-act of the two grown folks. As the night went on, Tricia and Roy continued to talk about growing up and the stories from the neighborhood and those stories fascinated Priscilla. Eventually, Priscilla finished her food, and politely took all of the plates to the kitchen sink for her aunt and followed directions to go get ready for bed. Tricia and Roy continued to talk over a glass of wine for about another hour until he prepared to leave the house for the night. Tricia walked Roy to the door and Roy thanked Tricia for such hospitality and a great dinner, as they held hands in the doorway. Looking at each other deep in their eyes. Roy didn't take advantage of the moment and kiss Tricia, but she got up on her toes and gave Roy a peck on his cheek; then he backed away from the entrance of the front door and backed carefully down the front stairs onto the sidewalk and left waving as he walked away from the house slowly.

***

Roy and Tricia moved extremely fast after that Sunday dinner that they shared, as awkward as it may have been at the dinner with Priscilla being snarky and cracking jokes at every turn toward Roy. Roy tried to keep the small talk at the table. Priscilla kept quiet and reserved around Roy; other than the few jokes, something in Priscilla, as unknowing and naive as she was, made her not feel she could trust Roy. Maybe it was the feeling of jealousy that she had towards him because she was afraid of losing the only person she ever had in her life. Amidst all these feelings Priscilla had, she was cordial as a young girl could be to a person they did not like. A couple of months passed by with Tricia and Roy going out on numerous dates, trips, and church gatherings. Tricia made sure that Priscilla was always along for everything, sort of trying to keep her promise to Priscilla, of never leaving her alone. Although Roy's feelings toward Tricia continued to grow, he was uneasy about not being able to spend much time alone with Tricia. Roy wanted to take things a step further so he planned an elaborate night where he would cook dinner and then they could later go out to dance, but he knew that getting Tricia to let someone keep Priscilla would be the hang-up, besides, Tricia never allowed anyone to watch over Priscilla for her; even when she did pick up some hours at the local diner; Tricia would only work during the late school hours. It was always the two of them, since Tricia only worked the hours at the restaurant that Priscilla was at school, she would always walk Priscilla back and forth to school each day, so this would be tough for Roy to pull off, but he had a plan.

Turns out Roy's mom was the woman in the neighborhood that everyone trusted to babysit for them, she even babysat Tricia a few times when she was young, so Roy decided to ask his mom to do him a big favor before he finalized the plans for the evening. Roy was driving as he was thinking out everything and soon arrived at his moms' home. He hopped out of the car and ran up the front stairs as he would always do since he was a little boy; skipping every other step as he went up the stairs. Just as he was about to dig out the key to the door from his pocket his mother opened the door startling him,

"Hey Roy, you didn't tell me you were coming today, I could have called you so you could stop and pick me up some onions boy."

"I'm sorry momma, I was kind of just driving through so I stopped," Roy said with a smile. As his mother walked out to the porch to water her plants, he gave her a peck on the face. She continued to conversate with her son,

"Seems to me that you coming to visit me less and less boy."

"Aw mamma, I'm just a little busy, you know with work and the church and all." He said keeping his slick smile upon his face.

"Yea and all. I know your time is going to that girl now, but anyway how is she doing?" His mother said as she turned back around to face him.

"She's doing good momma. Speaking of Tricia, I kind of need a favor from you momma." Roy said as he walked up to his mother and put his arm around her and walked next to her back into the house. "I wanna do something special for her momma. See I got this nice dinner planned out and then we can go out dancing on Saturday, but she never has a babysitter." Roy said as he gave his mother that sly smile that he would give everyone when he was asking for a favor.

His mother kept walking into the kitchen as she gave him his answer, "I guess it wouldn't hurt, I'm keeping the Jones's and Williams girls that night since they going out of town with the church, so I guess I could make it a camp out for the girls. Priscilla is surely invited." As if she knew that Tricia would be apprehensive to have anyone watch over Priscilla. Roy's mom knew that inviting Priscilla to a sleepover chaperoned by her would do the trick. A little part of her wanted to see Roy be settled down with a woman and possibly marry finally, so she was all for helping her son if that was what it meant.

"Ooh thank you, momma, I owe you big time," Roy said as he grabbed some of her homemade chocolate chip cookies from the cookie jar.

"That must go with the whole list of other things you owe me for, big time, huh boy?" She replied as she chuckled to herself. Roy gave his mother a peck on the cheek again as he headed toward the front door saying goodbye to her. Roy hopped back in his car as happy as he could be, now on his way to meet Tricia and give her the good news about their night out he had planned.

Later that evening while Tricia was helping Priscilla finish up some homework, there was a knock at the door, of course, as Tricia approached the front door to see who it was, Roy was standing there with a dozen flowers and a huge smile upon his face.

"Hey baby, these are for you."

"Oh, how sweet," said Tricia as she took the flowers while giving him a big kiss and hug. Roy came in and took off his coat and hat and had a seat on the couch in the living room as Tricia returned to the kitchen where Priscilla was putting away her schoolbooks.

"What are you doing?" said Tricia. "I know you're not done with the math yet."

Priscilla looked up at her and replied, "I finished the last two by myself." Tricia looked at her leery, but she did not bother to check behind the girl, she took her word for it. As Priscilla continued to gather her school supplies, Tricia was putting her flowers in a vase as she said,

"Those math answers better be right! But anyways don't you like my flowers?" With this big grin awaiting Priscilla's response, but once she finished putting water into the vase and turned around Priscilla was gone from the kitchen. Tricia thought to herself, *"Crazy little child, just like her mamma!"* She headed back into the living room where Roy was sitting reading the newspaper, he had in his bag all day and said,

"Give me a minute baby, I'll be right back."

"Okay", he replied as she went to the stairs and began to yell.

"Priscilla, you alright up there?"

With a muffled, "YES!" Priscilla answered.

Tricia continued to yell upstairs, "Well draw your bath and get ready for bed and I'll be up there to tuck you in, Okay."

"Yes ma'am." said Priscilla.

Tricia went on into the living room and had a seat next to Roy as he continued to read an article in the paper. She began to rub on the back of his head as she would always do until he gave her his full attention. Soon they were locked into a deep passionate kiss that seemed to last for days, though only a few seconds.

"What brings you here tonight mister? With gifts?" Tricia asked with a giggle.

"No reason, just something special for my girl that's all," Roy said as he put away the paper and sat back to relax.

"Alright, don't be expecting me to go all out and buy you nice gifts mister!" Tricia said with a sassy tone.

"Naw baby, I just been thinking about you all day, so I decided to stop by before I go home and turn in for the night. But I do got some plans for you."

"Oh, is that right?" As Tricia turned and straddled Roy and began to repeatedly peck on his bottom lip.

Roy, distracted and aroused now, continued to try to explain with just faint whispers, getting out a word after each kiss planted by Tricia.

"Yea, I wanna make a special dinner for you and then take you out to a surprise spot."

Tricia stopped and stared at Roy for a few seconds. "That's so sweet baby, but you know I can't leave Priscilla alone, so that night won't be so romantic, now would it?" Roy looked at her and began to laugh as a way to cover his nervousness about the plan for his mother to watch over Priscilla, seeing that he knew how Tricia was about Priscilla, so he was extremely apprehensive about telling her that part.

"Well baby, that's what else I was gonna tell you, my mother said that night she was throwing a sleepover for some kids from the neighborhood and she invited Priscilla to come over, too. So, what do you think? What a coincidence, huh?"

Tricia, with a surprised look got up and stood in front of him.

Roy then said quickly to try and defuse any problem that could come from Tricia discovering his plan. "Hey, now it's not what you're thinking baby. I just want to be able to spend a little quality time alone with you that's all." He had a feeling that Tricia would get the impression that he was just trying to dump Priscilla off on anyone, so he was about to go on the defensive.

"It's cool with me!" Tricia said much to the surprise of Roy. "I just have to see if it's Okay with Priscilla, that's all."

As Roy jumped up off the couch and grabbed his coat and hat, he could not hide his excitement.

"I'm telling you baby; you will not regret it. We going to have a good ole time." Roy said as he gave her one more kiss and headed to the door. Tricia followed him to lock up the house. Grinning hard as she was both flattered and impressed by Roy's surprise and planning.

She stood in the doorway and took a short glance over the neighborhood before she closed the door. It was about 7:45 PM and dark outside by now, but as Roy's car pulled away from in front of the house, Tricia imagined the two of them together forever and him not leaving after just a short visit. She continued to look back and forth at neighbors walking up and down the block, the older kids being called into the house because the streetlights had come on. Then her imagination made her feel like it was the middle of the afternoon and the sun was still shining bright, even picturing herself in a wedding dress being carried over the very threshold she was standing at by Roy. That's the way Roy made her feel. By the time she snapped out of it, Priscilla was tugging on her hand.

"What are you looking at Aunt Trish?"

Tricia snapped out of her trance and began to close the door and she answered Priscilla. "Nothing sweetheart, just looking. Are you okay? You ran up those stairs mighty fast once Roy got here."

"I'm okay aunt Trish, just a little sleepy."

"That's good to know, let's go to bed."

Tricia knew that Priscilla wasn't telling her the truth about why she rushed upstairs, but she didn't feel like there was anything to worry about either, so she decided to let Priscilla go on to sleep and tell her about Roy's plans tomorrow. Tricia tucked Priscilla in and went to bed herself, back in Priscilla's room she lay there in the dark thinking about all the fun times she and Aunt Trish shared. Just the two of them, going on trips, visiting friends and family, she even treasured the grocery errands. Tricia was all she had, and she couldn't imagine being without her, but she felt like Roy was coming between them and it made her sad. As she turned on her side and clutched her pillow tight around her head, she began to pray. Priscilla would always say the same prayer every night. She would ask God to protect her mommy and daddy up in heaven, protect her aunt Tricia, the people in the neighborhood, and she would always end with asking that she and Tricia never be apart. With an Amen, she would dose off to sleep. This time it took a little longer for her to dose off because she felt the part about her and Tricia never parting was in danger. With tears in her eyes, she slowly fell asleep while thinking about Tricia and Roy together. She just couldn't accept Roy, even though she never disrespected him or said anything to let on about her feelings about him. There was a bit of jealousy that she could not let go of. She wouldn't dare object Roy directly to her aunt Trish because she saw that Tricia was happy, so she decided to keep it inside.

A Night Out

As the light from the window glowed through Priscilla's eyelids, she began to awake to the smell of breakfast. Tricia was downstairs in the kitchen making Priscilla's favorite. Blueberry pancakes with bacon and scrambled eggs. Priscilla lay there thinking about Tricia and how much she loved her aunt. For some reason, she felt that she was being selfish about Roy and should put on a happy face for the sake of her aunt. "It's pancakes sweetie," the voice of Tricia pierced Priscilla's ears as she rolled over in the bed. She could hear Tricia creeping up to her door, so she lay there pretending to still be asleep. The door eased open with that old noisy sound that would always startle Priscilla.

"Are you woke, sweetie?" Tricia said as she touched the back of Priscilla's head and gently pushed her.

Priscilla answered slowly, "Yes Ma'am."

Tricia with the reply; "Are you hungry? I made your favorite."

Priscilla rolled to face her aunt and let out a jovial, "Ummmm. Sounds delicious."

Knowing that she needed to talk to her, she put her hand on Priscilla's forehead and began to stroke her hair.

"How would you feel about spending the night with Mrs. Wetherspoon?"

Priscilla looked at Tricia with surprise. "What do you mean Aunt Trish?"

"Well, Roy told me that she is having this special sleepover for some of the kids in the neighborhood and she asked if you would come too."

Priscilla surprisingly got excited and jumped up out of the bed and started pacing back and forth. "Oooh, that would be fun Aunt Trish. Who else is coming? What should I wear? What should I pack? What is she cooking?" Question after question, Priscilla asked much to Tricia's surprise. Tricia didn't know how to react to Priscilla's enthusiasm. She was expecting her to be upset or sad, neglected. But here she was, happy and jovial about going to play with the other kids. Maybe it was a rush of emotion that went through her, from holding in all the feelings about her aunt and Roy. Maybe without even knowing it, Priscilla had a surge of relief with the thought of her and Tricia getting a break. Here it had been every single minute, of every single day, of every single year of her life, spent with her aunt. So, without any persuasion, Priscilla was going over to Roy's moms for a night and Tricia and Roy would finally get their much-needed time alone.

***

The night had arrived. Tricia was anxious, Priscilla was excited, Roy was happy. All their thoughts and feelings were somewhat intertwined but separate as this night would set a precedent for a new beginning for the three of them. As Tricia checked through Priscilla's bag to make sure she had everything; toothbrush, underwear, socks, pajamas, extra clothes, she caught herself. Almost like a parent getting ready to send their first child off to college. For most of Priscilla's life, Tricia and Priscilla ate, slept, talked, walked, and did everything together since Priscilla arrived on this earth. All they had was each other by fate and choice. So, to spend a night apart was going to be something to endure. At the very same time, Priscilla was upstairs going through her preferred choice of toys to bring along to the sleepover. She paused and got a little scared. She didn't know how to be without Tricia by her side. She didn't know what to say without asking Tricia's opinion. Then Priscilla almost jumped up into the bed from the floor in one leap as she heard the stern voice of her aunt Tricia. "Priscilla, are you about ready?" As she snapped out of her current trance, Priscilla began to get excited again about all the fun she was going to have that night. She grabbed her toys, her jacket and began to head down the stairs as she had thoughts of the pizza, the games, the ice cream, and the stories all the girls would tell. Priscilla just about slipped and missed a stair as she daydreamed on the way down the stairs but kept her balance as she approached the landing and her aunt standing there, with a curious smile on her face.

Priscilla fumbled near the door with all her packed bags – she had packed as if she was going on a sabbatical to another country, Tricia turned to open the front door. Just outside the door at the curb was a 72 Bonneville, sky blue and all these little heads were poking out of the back window with excited eyes. Just as Priscilla noticed the car outside, and Tricia raised her hand to wave assurance to the driver of the car; Mr. Wetherspoon popped out from the driver's side of the car and walked around the front to get to the stairs of Tricia's home. Mr. Wetherspoon walked away from the car toward the house and he slightly turned to the car and said, "Girls, y'all be cool while I pick up Priscilla." Ole Edward was Mr. Wetherspoon's name, Roy's father, though they stayed at odds a lot and no one knew why. Everyone in the neighborhood loved and respected Edward. He was the elder statesmen of the neighborhood. He was known for fixing things and just looking out for everyone. Tonight, his duty was to go around and pick up all the girls for the sleepover at the direction of Mrs. Wetherspoon. In the back of the car were some girls from the church and school that Priscilla knew. Jackie, a girl that was in Priscilla's classroom. Jackie and Priscilla were cool with each other, but not super close friends. Then there was Susie; Susie was a girl from the church. Susie lived a little far; just about a town over, but her parents continued to attend the local neighborhood church. Then Carla and Charity; these two were sisters and members of the church as well. They lived just around the corner from Priscilla. Last was Denise, Denise was Roy's adopted sister; for Mr. and Mrs. Wetherspoon had decided to adopt a young girl at their older age, because they wanted to help a kid that had been affected by drugs in the neighborhood. Denise only knew the Wetherspoons' because her parents gave her up as soon as she was born.

The five teen girls jostled back and forth sticking their tiny heads out of the back window of the Bonneville to see what was going on at the porch of Tricia's house, while anxiously awaiting Priscilla to come to get in the car to join them and begin the "Girls night out," or at least that's what these teen girls had the nerve to call this sleepover. So funny. Nevertheless, they were overjoyed to be able to have this night.

"Hey there!" Edward said to Tricia as he approached the top step. "Got some bags for me?"

Tricia replied, "She's got a hold of the bags, but thank you, Edward."

"Looks like they are ready for some fun times tonight." Edward said, just as Priscilla hopped out from inside the vestibule of the house and onto the porch to grab Tricia's arm and perch up on her toes for a kiss on Tricia's cheek, to begin the goodbyes for the night.

"Well, hello there little lady!" Edward said to Priscilla as she was half-way paying attention to him, and half-way looking down at the car full of girls trying to read their facial expressions and sign language that was telling her to hurry up and come get into the car.

"Hi, Mr. Wetherspoon! Thank you so much for inviting me to the sleepover and for picking me up!" Priscilla said with the sweetest tone of respect.

"Aww; you're welcome little lady. But I'm just the chauffeur tonight. Thank my wife when you get to the house."

Tricia then intervened and told Priscilla, "Go on, go get in the car; I know it's killing you."

"Love you, Aunt Tricia!" Priscilla said as she grabbed her bundle of bags of clothes and toys and ran down the stairs to go jump into the car with the other girls, Finally!

Priscilla got in the car and began the "Girls night out" officially. The girls got loud and boisterous and started laughing and talking with all the excitement that was built up within them anticipating this night. Back on the porch were Tricia and Edward.

"Well, I see my knucklehead boy done finally found him a real good friend!?" Edward said to Tricia with a sarcastic tone. As Tricia began to reply, Edward cut in again, "I'm just saying that boy gave me so many headaches and is always getting on someone's nerves. I'm just happy to see him with someone as nice as you Tricia."

Tricia replied. "Aww, well thank you, Edward, I appreciate that."

"I guess between church involvement and you; I can finally stop worrying about his knucklehead ass." Edward said as he began to get ready to turn and walk back down the steps to go to the car.

Tricia replied in Roy's defense as she didn't know the depth of Roy and Ed's issues with each other, "Well, I promise you, he is a very respectful man; y'all have done a great job raising him. He treats me and Priscilla well."

"That's good, that's good!" Edward replied again and then went on. "Your girl is in the best hands tonight. My wife is going to make sure these girls have so much fun, that they'll pass out and won't want to get up for church tomorrow." They both laugh as Edward walked toward the curve and got ready to get back into the car.

"So that is the plan? I am picking her up at church, right?" Tricia said to Edward as he grabbed the car door handle.

"Yes Ma'am! See you at service in the morning!" Edward got into the car, and the girls calmed down a bit from their raging energy of laughter and jokes. Edward started the car to drive off and waved at Tricia goodbye, and so did all the girls in the backseat.

Edward's car pulled away from the curve – just then; Roy's car rounded the corner to approach the house. Tricia saw this in her peripheral, so she decided to stay on the porch. Grinning from ear-to-ear as Roy pulled up in front of the house and began to park; Tricia couldn't contain her excitement. Here it is, the two of them finally get to go out on a date; just them. No Priscilla tagging along. Not that Priscilla was any trouble. They just wanted and needed to grow their relationship at this point. Only Lord knows how bad Roy wanted this. Roy threw the car in park and jumped out to jog around to the passenger side. Before opening the door, he ran up the porch stairs to deliver a single rose to Tricia. He reached up to her with the rose and then kissed her right on the lips. They hold the kiss for about 12 seconds, and they stood there on the front porch embracing each other.

"I'm going to go ahead and lock down the house and I'll be ready," Tricia said as she gently pulled away from Roy's embrace around her hips. Nodding his head in silence with a grin; he turns and goes back to his car to open the passenger door and wait for his date to come out of the house. Tricia reemerged from inside the house and locked the door. Purse, keys, and the single rose in tow; she skipped down each stair like a scene from *"The Wizard of Oz"*, as Dorothy skipped the yellow brick road. Just as jovial as she could be, Tricia lifted her dress off the ground as she turned to sit down in the car as Roy held the door open for her. "You are so beautiful Tricia!" Roy said as he held the door handle for her. Once Tricia was inside the car securely; Roy shut the door and rushed over to the driver's side to officially begin the long-awaited date night. Back in the car, Roy leaned over to give Tricia another long passionate kiss. They could not contain the feeling they had been curtailing when they couldn't be alone. Roy started the car, then began to fiddle with the radio.

"I got that Isley Brothers record. Want to hear it, babe?" Roy asked Tricia as he fumbled with the radio.

"Sure! Whatever you like is fine with me. I'm sure we like the same songs." Tricia replied with a grin still on her face that could not be wiped away. As Roy began to pull off from in front of Tricia's house, the sounds of *"Groove with You"* by the Isley's blasted from the windows of his car, setting the stage for the perfect date night.

At Mrs. Wetherspoon's house, the girls had not too long unloaded from Edward's car and went into the house to start their "Girls night out." Upon entering the house with Edward, Katherine (Mrs. Wetherspoon) Had a table set up with popcorn, candy, and soda. Then another table set up with pizza, cookies, and cake. This was all in the dining room. Just off to the right of the dining room was the living room; in there were plush floor pallets laid out in front of the couch facing the TV and board games galore, stacked on the floor next to the pallets. Oh, boy, were these girls in for a fun night. "Welcome young ladies. First thing I want everyone to do is to go upstairs, wash your hands, change into your pajamas, set out your church outfit that your parents sent; then come on back down to eat." The girls all marched upstairs to the order of Katherine while giggling and laughing and continuing with the horseplay.

"Hey darling, I'm going to be out in the backyard with Donald having a couple of beers if you don't mind?" Edward said to Katherine as he leaned in to kiss her on the cheek.

Katherine replied. "No problem dear! Do you want me to put you a few slices of pizza up?"

"Just one will do for later sweetie." Edward replied as he walked into the kitchen to grab a pack of beer and continue to head towards the back door of the house.

Roy and Tricia had arrived at his apartment and gotten comfortable. Tricia parked on his couch in his living room. Roy in the kitchen putting the finishing touches on his self-proclaimed award-winning pork chops. As Tricia sat there looking around observing a man-pad. The pictures of famous singers on one wall, Ali's picture on another, and a raggedy bookshelf packed to the brim next to the TV.

"So, you like to read I see?" Tricia said with a slightly lifted voice to reach into the kitchen right next to the living room in the quaint apartment.

"Oh yes!" Roy replied. "I got a decent collection. So, would you like a soda, a beer, or some wine; cause you so fine!" Roy said in a singing tone jokingly.

Laughing at Roy's joke and his singing; Tricia replied, "I'll take a beer if you don't mind."

Roy replied while laughing, "Oh my! Look at you! Drinking with the big fish in the sea." Roy jabbed at Tricia's want for a beer above soda or wine. As he entered back into the living room to deliver the drink order, he slid onto the couch right up next to his date and threw his right arm over her shoulder while handing her the cold beer with the left hand. Then he leaned in for another kiss.

As she began to kiss him back, she slowly tapped the bottom of the beer can on the end table next to the couch to make sure not to drop it since her attention was not on the table. After about a good 3-minute session of making out; a loud beep started to repeat, and the slight smell of smoke permeated the apartment. "Oh shit!" Roy yelled as he pulled his lips apart from Tricia's and jumped from the couch. "My pork chops!" As Roy got into the kitchen to fling the oven door open, he satisfyingly found that the smoke was only a result of the juices from the pan that the pork chops were in, dripping onto the bottom of the oven. He had caught a break. As he quickly reacted to grab the pan out of the oven, he bumped his wrist on the hot oven rack while clumsily reaching for something to wipe the bottom of the oven; foolishly not waiting for the oven to cool down. "Ahhh Shit!" He yelled out in a brief pain. All the while, Tricia had left the couch too, and was standing in the entrance of the kitchen doorway laughing at Roy.

"Hahaha!" She couldn't contain it.

"Oh, you think that's funny, don't you?" Roy turned saying as she continued to laugh. "I'm good though. No big deal." Then he started to laugh also.

"Put some butter on that burn to stop the throbbing," Tricia advised. Then she went over to the icebox and grabbed the butter and sat Roy down at the kitchen table to nurse her man from his burn wound.

Stuffed full of food and candy; the girls were all sprawled all over the living room floor with every board game in the room open and playing them one by one as re-runs of Soul Train played on the TV in the background. Katherine had long gone into the kitchen to clean up, while Edward was still out back chatting it up with his buddy Donald. The whole house was quiet now, except for the girls laid out talking about this, that, and everything. Katherine; as sweet as she was to all the kids; ran a tight ship. So, she gave the marching orders to the girls about not getting too loud in the night but did not put any time limit on when they need to go to sleep. She just told them not to be loud.

"I hate all those boys in our class," said Jackie, Priscilla's classmate.

"I know! They are so stupid and stinky!" Priscilla said, giving her input on the subject.

"They are, but I got a boyfriend," said Susie, as all the other girls looked at her surprised and in unison said,

"OOOOO…" then began to laugh wholeheartedly. "He lives next door to me. I let him call himself my boyfriend so he can bring me candy from his daddy's candy store." Susie continued trying to justify liking a stinky boy to the group of girls. Then Charity said, "That's it! Make them give you some good stuff right away." All the girls started laughing hysterically again and continued the girl-talk throughout the night with the fun.

With the delicious dinner that Roy took his precious time to prepare for Tricia now over. They sat back on the couch appreciating each other. Not many words; a lot of kissing and touching. With short breaks for sips of liquor that they each had on the end tables at either end of the couch. While they continued to feel each other up and down and explore bodies, Roy stopped for a breath and mentioned the dancing they had planned. While looking at his watch; all while Tricia was unbuttoning his buttons one-by-one on his blue button-up shirt; Roy got out a question between kisses. "Shouldn't we go ahead and head out to the dance hall now?" No answer from Tricia. Just more and more kisses on his neck and chest as he tried to coerce the topic again. "You ready to head out yet?" Barely able to say those words as Tricia mounted his lap, still kissing him everywhere, now on his lips included. Finally, Tricia leaned back from him and stopped kissing all over him, but only to begin undoing her blouse; she replied with the most devious and sexy smirk as she looked Roy deep into his brown eyes so seductively, "As far as I'm concerned, we already have started dancing for the night. So, let's dance a little more, and a little dirty!" Roy, taken aback a bit was shocked that this was coming from the responsible, respectable, and shy Tricia. Nevertheless, Roy wasn't a fool! He reached back for the lamp behind the couch to turn the lights out and then started to attack Tricia with the same intense passion or even more than she was giving. Needless to say, their night ended how they both had planned it. Sans, the actual dancing in a dance hall.

As all the girls were dosing off, Carla and Priscilla remained the lone two awake. These two girls were kind of close. As close as Priscilla had gotten with anyone in her life other than Tricia. They always sat together at church and would be the first two to fake a bathroom run at church to get a break from the service.

"This might be the most fun in my life." Priscilla said to Carla.

"Yep!" Carla agreed nodding her head, now beginning to dose here and there as well. "I always wanted to ask you a question, Priscilla." Carla turned over on her side to deliver the question to her friend as she was trying to stay woke in the night.

"What's that Carla?" Priscilla replied.

"I just always wondered what it is like to have just a momma?" Carla said. "I mean, I'm not trying to say that you should feel bad for not having a dad, but since me and my sister have always had both our parents, I wonder what you feel like?"

"No, I don't feel bad." Priscilla said.

Then Carla replied to try and explain her position more. "I know, it's just me and my sister; I think we are spoiled."

"No, you're not spoiled," said Priscilla. "It's just not the same for everyone." Not taking any offense to what Carla was saying, Priscilla simply answered in the best way she could. "My aunt always told me that God took my parents to watch over me from heaven to make sure I was guided right." Priscilla went on, "I know that is not the truth, but I accept it. I accept that something bad probably happened to my parents, but I am happy that I have Tricia. I know that if I ever find out something bad did happen to my Mom or Dad; I'm going to do something about it. Aunt Tricia being good to me or not." Carla, while slowly dosing off; kind of woke up to the empty threat that Priscilla put into the atmosphere, with a look at her like she just couldn't believe what she had heard. Though she was still dosing off, it was almost like she was dreaming Priscilla was getting irritated at the thought that her parents suffered or were wronged in their deaths.

Tension

As the days, weeks and months passed on; Roy was hanging around the house more and more. By default, or on purpose due to his affection for Tricia; he was taking on more of a Man's role in Tricia's household. Roy still had his apartment a few minutes away. But now, he and Tricia were close. Priscilla was still indifferent to Roy being around so much. On a bright sunny Saturday morning, you could find Priscilla perched in her familiar spot in the upstairs back window looking for the birds to sing to her. Tricia was preparing to go out for some shopping with Priscilla. Roy had come over that morning to do some yardwork for Tricia. Very convenient it was for Tricia now. To have Roy ready and willing to cut the grass and fix stuff around the house. Tricia was able to discontinue having the neighborhood yard guy coming to do the grass for the house since Roy was around so much.

"Priscilla! Come on down and let's get ready to go to the store!" Tricia yelled up the stairs to Priscilla.

"Yes Ma'am!" Priscilla answered after about a one-minute pause of still being entranced at her bird-watching habit. Just outside in the front yard was Roy; in an old oily, dirty set of overalls crouched down tiddling away at an old lawnmower, trying to prime the engine and get it to start. Going back and forth with priming, then pulling the ignition string, priming, pulling the ignition string, and again. Only to pause to take a deeper look at the engine components to make sure he didn't miss anything while trying to get the lawnmower ready to start. Standing in the doorway was Tricia, now watching Roy as he was in a ritual of crouching and standing and pulling; trying to cut the grass as he promised. Tricia was just standing there admiring her man, taking on the yard duties for her, "free of charge."

Tricia watched Roy until he finally got the lawnmower to start. With the loud motor finally churning; and Roy getting going; here came Priscilla barreling down the stairs to come to get ready for the store as she promised Tricia. Bending down to grab her shoes, with her puffy, curly hair and wearing her favorite sweater with green and white stripes and the buttons at the bottom missing. She sat next to the front door right behind Tricia standing in the doorway with the screen door partially propped open; Priscilla got her shoes on for the trip. Roy began his up and down motion of the front lawn from the curbside to the edge of the house, and then Tricia approached him with a yell to let him know that they were leaving, trying to speak loud enough to have a volume over the mower because they both knew it wouldn't be a good idea to turn that mower off now that he'd finally got it going. With the elevated screech of her voice, "We are about to go to a couple of stores," Tricia yelled, as Roy acknowledged with a head nod. "I left the back door unlocked, and the shed unlocked for you." Tricia continuing to yell over the lawnmower as Roy nodded again. Then Priscilla ran down the stairs to the curb to join her aunt, and they began to walk west, away from the house toward the midtown market for shopping. Perhaps they would grab a few groceries, perhaps some clothing and shoes. These types of Saturdays were what Tricia would call spontaneous weekend days with Priscilla. She just wanted to get Priscilla out of the house and give the girl some type of adventure. They headed off as Roy continued to mow the grass looking at them as they walked away.

With a toy in one hand and candy in the other, Priscilla stood just behind Tricia as Tricia held a blouse up to the nape of her neck while standing in a mirror in the clothing department of Max Mart, the main clothing store in midtown. Tricia would decide on each article of clothing carefully, then put it in a cart; then she would grab the next item to examine. Priscilla standing next to her aunt, not bothered by the shopping because she had already been pacified in the previous two stores with the toy and candy. Piece of clothing after piece of clothing, Tricia would investigate as she shopped. Therapy it was! This is what she had left beside Priscilla and now Roy. Shopping used to be her favorite activity with her sister Anne when they were coming up. Oh, how she missed shopping with her sister. But Priscilla played the role of shopping companion very well. Just minus all the talking and advice on which blouse to get.

As Tricia finalized the items in her cart, she let Priscilla know it was time to go. "You see anything you wanted in here?"

"No Ma'am. Those shoes are nice, but I don't need new ones." Priscilla was a bit frugal to be young.
Be it genuine, or acknowledgment that she didn't want to be a burden and try to spend all of her aunt's money,

Priscilla didn't ask for much. With that confirmation, Tricia began to push the cart to the front of the store to check-out, where Tony was the cashier as always on the weekends. Boy did Tony think Tricia was a hot piece.

"Hey hey there, Priscilla! Who is this beautiful Miss America that you have with you, young lady!?" Tony joked to Priscilla, as Priscilla and Tricia laughed.

"Boy, stop playing with me!" Tricia said to Tony. "You know my man wouldn't like that." Tricia swiftly followed up with her jab at Tony.

Then Tony replied sarcastically, knowing that Tricia and Roy were an item. "Oh, oh oh – it's like that now!?"

Tricia rolled her eyes with a grin and reply, "Yes sir! Tell him Priscilla." Priscilla stood there looking at both of them with a weird look, and in an awkward position since she didn't particularly like Roy.

"I guess she got a boyfriend." With a turned-up lip toward them.

"Girl you know you are something else. Gone on out the store. Here I come after I pay." Tricia continued to finish paying for her items as Tony continued to flirt, while Priscilla sat on the stoop of the outside of the store waiting on her aunt.

After an eventful day of shopping for clothes, food, and just getting out to spend some time together, Tricia and Priscilla finally got back home. Roy, now sitting on the front porch in the shaded part of the porch on this nice, hot weekend day, with a cold beer in hand. Roy was observing the crispy cut grass that he had just finished a few minutes before the ladies arrived back to the house. Tricia slowly walked up the stairs looking Roy in the face with this satisfied expression on her face; satisfied from having a man in the house? Satisfied with having someone to help with the house chores? Or just simply satisfied with the thought of knowing she now had two people in the world that genuinely cared for her. Priscilla and Roy! As Tricia approached Roy to begin to do a quick show and tell of what she had gathered while out with her niece; Priscilla ran straight into the house while Roy was about to take the opportunity to have some small talk with Priscilla.

"So, what did you bu…." Before Roy could finish his question to Priscilla, the front screen door slammed shut.

"Sorry about that baby." Tricia tried to apologize for the girl's actions.

"Oh no, I get it!" Roy replied. "She's still got to warm up to me being around so much." Roy followed his comment to Tricia with the glow of understanding that he was the extra person in this three-way relationship. That gave Tricia a bit of calm in the situation as she sat beside Roy to begin to pull out blouses and household items that she had purchased on the trip to the mid-town market. As the two of them sat there on the porch, they continued to talk, and then Roy mentioned he was going to have a card party at his place, but it was a long list of people. "Yeah, so it's the card party I told you we usually do a couple of times a year. All of my buddies, some of their lady friends, and if they must bring them, then kids are always invited. As Tricia listened to the guest list, food menu, and narrative of the card party extravaganza, she began to feel left out and then spurted out the unexpected.

"Have the party here!" Roy stops in mid-sentence to look at Tricia with quite a surprise on his face.

"Huh?" Roy asked in disbelief. "Did you just say have my party here?" Roy asked again as Tricia began to form her mouth to answer with a definitive,

"Yes!" once again.

Hesitant to accept, Roy said, "Okay…. If you are sure?" with a very puzzled look on his face.

She continued, "Yeah, then we can invite both our friends to mix and mingle." So, there it was, Tricia was going to be hosting a neighborhood card party cook-out at her place with Roy. Maybe Tricia's ambitious suggestion to have the party there was due to a bit of jealousy of the women that would be at Roy's house? Or maybe it was just to be around him even more. Who knows? But here it was. A party was going to be planned. Now the task of telling Priscilla and hoping Priscilla would not feel like Roy was taking over hers and her aunts' life. After continuing the small talk on the porch, Roy and Tricia entered the house to put away the bags from shopping. Priscilla was parked in front of the TV; trying to watch what was left of the Saturday cartoons, since she had missed most of them while out with her aunt. "Hey sweetie!" Tricia said to Priscilla as she walked past the living room where the girl sat laughing at the cartoons on the screen. "Take my clothes bags up to my room and put them on the bed for me."

Priscilla replied quickly, "Yes Ma'am!" Priscilla popped up from the floor to jog to her aunt and grab the bags from her. Roy and Tricia continued into the kitchen to put away the groceries that they had bought while out.

"I think I may cook up this ground beef and make some burgers tonight," Tricia said as she reached to open the refrigerator door.

"I think whatever you make is a great idea." Roy said as he turned to Tricia with a jar of pickles in his hand to help her put everything away. Just as the two of them finished putting the groceries away, Priscilla made her way back down the stairs and into the kitchen.

"Do you want a nice juicy hamburger for dinner?" Tricia said to Priscilla as she came into the kitchen.

"Yep! That sounds delicious aunt Tricia. Can I help cook?" Priscilla said to her aunt as she began to grin at the thought of having her favorite Saturday meal.

"In that case, my work here is done for now." Roy said with slight sarcasm to both. "I am going to make myself more useful and go back out and water the lawn until dinner is ready."

As Roy started to leave to go back outside, Tricia said to him, "Whatever!" as she swung a loaf of bread at Roy in a fun playful way. Then Tricia and Priscilla began to take out the pans they would use to prepare the Saturday meal.

The clinging sounds of metal rang from the dining room as Tricia stood at the front door of the house looking out to the sidewalk. Forks and spoons followed by plates banging as Priscilla set the table for her aunt as instructed. Tricia stepped out onto the porch briefly to inform Roy that the meal was ready to consume, "Food just about done Roy!" Then turned to go back into the house to finish helping Priscilla set the table. Roy was standing out on the sidewalk talking to Tricia's down-the-street neighbor James Simpson. James had lived in the house down the block since Tricia's parents owned this house. A very stoic man. Sort of the block watchman. James always kept tabs on everyone and everything that happened on the block. So, now talking to Roy was no different. James was slowly getting to know Roy, as Roy was being around more and more. James noticed Roy was taking care of the house for Tricia. James used to offer to do all of the outside caretaking for Tricia ever since she and Anne were living there without their parents.

"Well, I'll talk to you later," James said to Roy as Roy began to head back towards the front porch to go into the house and clean up for dinner.

"Same to you Mr. Simpson! See you!" Roy said as he went up the stairs and into the house. Roy entered into the house to head towards the bathroom to wipe himself down before sitting for dinner with the two ladies, he slightly turned to look into the dining room to glance and caught eyes with Priscilla as she was just finishing putting the plate of hamburger toppings on the dining room table for the meal. Priscilla looked at Roy and rolled her eyes at the man. *"How rude"*, Roy thought; but made no reaction and continued up the stairs to go ahead and wash up for the meal. The three of them sat at the dining room table putting together their hamburger sandwiches, with little to no conversation. So, Tricia decided she'd take the mantle to break the silence of the trio.

"So, Roy, you sure you want to have the card party here?" Tricia decided to bring up a question to Roy as if it was his idea in front of Priscilla.

"Oh…. Oh…" Roy stumbled with his answer, as he was caught off guard at Tricia's question since she was the one that suggested having the party at her house.

"There's going to be a party here?" Priscilla inquired, butting into the adult's conversation.

Tricia replied to her. "Yes, sweetie. Roy is planning a nice get-together, and I think we should do it here." Tricia now taking ownership of the party planning. Continuing to try and make this event palatable for Priscilla. "Then some of the grown folks will be your friends' parents, and your friends can come too." Tricia backing up her planning reveal.

"Yep!" Roy supporting Tricia's proclamation as if they needed to explain to Priscilla. They were the adults. Right? Looking at both of them, Priscilla neither confirmed nor denied that she would be fine with the party happening at their house.

Roy tried to add on to justify the party. "I mean, you and the other girls can probably play jump rope in the yard while we play cards."

Then the unexpected happened.

"Nobody asked you! You shouldn't even be here right now!" Priscilla said with such a disrespectful tone.

Then immediately, Tricia said with authority in her voice. "Priscilla! Apologize right now!"

Roy immediately intervened, "No need to apologize, I understand."

Tricia said immediately. "No! You better apologize Right Now!"

With a nonchalant look in her eyes, Priscilla let out the faint non-impactful words, "I'm sorry." While rolling her eyes.

"I'll deal with you later." Tricia said with an angry tone. From that point on during the dinner, Priscilla said not another word. Just body language that was obvious toward Roy with negativity. As Tricia and Roy continue to talk about the plans for the party, the food, the drinks; Priscilla kept on with the negative body language toward everything Roy would say. This made the night very tenuous as the three of them finished eating dinner.

Later that evening, after finishing up dinner, Roy had grabbed his jacket and began to head toward the door, with Tricia in tow, while Priscilla was still sitting at the dining room table drawing and coloring in her notepad.

"I'm sorry Roy!" Tricia said while rubbing on his back as he exited the house. "I'm sorry, she just has to get used to you... Us...." Tricia trying to piece her words together carefully.

Roy replied. "You don't have to apologize Tricia. I get it. She just doesn't like me."

Tricia quickly replied. "No, no! She just takes a long time to warm up to people." Tricia added on to her defense and apology. Tricia grabbed Roy's hands and pulled them towards her waist. "Believe me, you are someone I want in my life. For you, I'll make whatever sacrifice I have to make."

"But!" Roy replied immediately. "Of course, there will always be a but!" Tricia looked at him, trying to soften the blow of the exception.

"Yes, Priscilla and I have only ever had each other. So, sometimes it's tough to let anyone in."

Roy, in an attempt to defend his loyalty, "I know, I know Tricia. But I've been around a long time now, do a lot of good for both of you." Roy defended his position in their little three-way family.

Tricia agreeing to his defense, "Just trust me Roy. Priscilla will come around, and before you know it, the two of you will be better friends than me and her. I bet!"

Roy, looking at Tricia in the eyes as he pulled his hands away to begin to walk down the stairs. "I hope you're right baby, I hope you're right." Roy kissed Tricia on the cheek and turned and walked down the stairs to go to his car. As he put the car in gear to drive away, they both waved goodbye for the night.

***

As a mix of R & B and disco hits emerged from the standing speakers that Tricia had moved from the living room to the back porch; Tricia continued to prepare side dishes with the help of Priscilla. Priscilla, not all the way bought into the idea of a party at her home, hosted by Roy. Yet, she was giving in slowly since she'd learned that some of her church and schoolgirl friends would be in attendance since their parents would be coming to the party. She had a little grin on her face as she shucked the corn to help her aunt prepare the food. Just outside on the patio was Roy, manning the barbeque grill. Attending to burgers, hot dogs, polishes, and pork chops. Roy had a thing for pork chops indeed.

"Priscilla, hand me the can opener so I can get the peaches open to make the peach cobbler." Tricia instructing Priscilla.

"Yes Ma'am!" She readily replied. As the two of them continued to cook, the back-porch screen door flung open as Roy burst into the kitchen dancing a two-step to the music playing. All while opening the refrigerator with one hand, swinging around to grab a beer, and taking Tricia's hand to try and get her involved in the dance steps in the kitchen. Priscilla looking on with a smirk on her face at what Roy called himself doing. "Boy, what are you doing?" Tricia said as she laughed and gave in to Roy's dancing fever. "My hands are all sticky from peach juice and butter Roy!" As she continued to laugh hysterically. Priscilla began to laugh as Tricia and Roy danced around the kitchen. Would seem to be a breakthrough for the makeshift family of three, or soon to be makeshift family. Priscilla was enjoying herself in the company of Roy. What a breakthrough it was!

As the night went on; "You better not cut me out, partner!" May screamed across the kitchen table to her spades partner Dennis. Sitting counter at the table was Tricia and Dan, trying their best to win the best of three fight or flight tournament of the card game spades that Roy had planned out. Tricia's best friend from church brought these two young men as plus one and two to the party to have some fun. Dennis, the drummer from the church, and Dan, the church's handyman. All of them were having a lot of fun at this point. In the front room was the remainder of the adult invitees; talking, laughing, and drinking, some dancing to the music that played. At least a group of 7 to 8 adults. A few small children sitting on the living room floor playing the board games that Tricia borrowed from the Wetherspoons for the party. In the back yard, were Roy and three other guys standing around smoking cigarettes and having a couple of drinks, talking about current events. In the distance were Priscilla, Jackie, Susie, Carla, and Charity; all the girls from the sleepover at the Wetherspoons except for Roy's sister Denise. Denise didn't make it to the party today because she was back at home sick with the summer flu.

The 5 girls were jumping rope in the dirt, off next to the patio where Roy and the guys were standing. Laughing, and jumping rope, and making jokes were the girls.

"Woo, I'm getting thirsty," Carla said as she jumped out of her turn in the jump rope circle.

"Me too!" Jackie said as she took a break from jumping. Priscilla and Charity wined down the swing of the rope while Susie finished her round of jumping. The girls began to head towards the back stairs to go into the house and raid the cooler for juice, water, or pop. Whatever would be allowed since they haven't eaten anything at the party yet. While the girls file up the stairs, Roy kept his eyes on Priscilla in a weird way as she bounced up the stairs. Mike, one of the guys in the backyard with Roy tapped him on his shoulder to get his attention because he noticed Roy's ongoing stare at the girl.

"Hey man, you alright?" Mike said. Roy jumped as he replied,

"Uh, yeah... Yeah; I'm good! You know, those kids, always up to no good man."

Apprehensively agreeing with Roy, as the other two guys had a separate sidebar, "Yeah.... you Right." Mike agreeing but feeling weird about what just happened.

As the girls barged into the kitchen, in the front room, Dan hopped up from the table while slamming his hand of cards on the table. The remaining Ace, King, and Queen of spades.

Dennis yelling out, "What the Fuck! Man, how did you get all that!? Who dealt this shit!" Everyone at the table falling laughing.

"Let's take a break before we go to the next round y'all." Tricia said as she rose from the table still laughing.

"Yes! We need a break!" Dennis said as he walked toward the front of the house and Tricia and the others followed. Now, the girls were in the kitchen looking down into the cooler filled with beverages. Jackie, with her hand down deep into the cooler, half of her shirt sleeve-soaked from trying to move beers around to grab pop and water, whatever the request from the group of girls.

"Uhhh! This nasty beer they drink." Jackie said as all the girls giggled.

"I know!" Priscilla agreed.

"I like my pop in a glass." Carla said as Charity laughed and commented,

"So, fancy! My sister has to be so sophisticated."

"Shut up!" Carla said with a snappy reply.

Priscilla took the lead, "I'll get you a glass miss fancy."

Since this was her house. Then, Roy entered back into the kitchen, stumbling a bit from all the drinks he'd had so far. Getting way past his alcohol limits. As he came into the kitchen, the girls quickly got quiet and stopped their stories as if they were trying to keep all their girl secrets hidden. Priscilla now perched on her toes reaching up to the cabinet just above the sink to get Carla a glass for her pop; fully extended to the furthest of her reach with one finger on a glass trying to twist the glass out toward the edge of the cabinet to grab it as it fell. Roy goes up right behind Priscilla and reached over her to grab the glass. Disgustingly pressing himself up against Priscilla's butt while grabbing the glass. Then slamming the glass on the sink counter right next to Priscilla. Priscilla felt the engorgement of Roy pressing up against her and immediately felt uncomfortable and got a sick feeling in her stomach; dropped down to her feet flat, then turned and ran to the stairs passed everyone in the party and up to her bedroom. Roy, drunkenly stumbling, turned, and looked at all the girls as they stood there in disbelief of what they just witnessed. "What!? Next time use a fucking chair!" Roy said with no remorse for what he just did as he went to the front of the house and began mingling with the other adults already dancing and talking in the front. As the girls stood in the kitchen with sick and afraid looks on their faces, they all one-by-one put down their beverages, and slowly followed each other upstairs to Priscilla's bedroom.

"So, what's up with the card table?" Roy said as he enters the front room where part of the adults were huddled, the other part outside on the front porch. As Dan turned to reply to Roy, Roy observed the girls making their way upstairs. With a suspicious look in his eyes, he pretends to not see them. "Boom, boom, boom." Carla banged on Priscilla's bedroom door. "Open the door, Priscilla!" Charity said as Carla continued to knock. Bang, bang, bang; Carla knocked on Priscilla's door as the girls all take turns speaking through the closed door, trying to get Priscilla to open the door.

"Come on Priscilla, let us in!" Said Jackie.

Then, followed by Susie. "We need to talk about what just happened!"

Then Charity chimed in, "Priscilla, come on, let's go down and tell your aunt, we need to tell!" The lock on the door made a clank and the door became ajar. As the girls entered the room, they could see that Priscilla was curled up on her bed balling with tears on every pillow and the sheets.

"We can't tell on him!" Priscilla said as she wiped tears from her eyes and snot from her nose.

Carla replied with a justified attitude. "Yes, we can, and we will!"

"I can't do this to Tricia," Priscilla said to the other girls as their faces formed undeniable disbelief. "Auntie Tricia is happy for the first time in her life, and I go and mess it up!"

Priscilla continued to blame herself as the girls were all on the bed to embrace Priscilla and try to talk some sense into her.

"You can't not do anything!" Jackie said.

"You don't need him around here Priscilla." Charity followed the sentiment of Jackie. All the girls were crying and trying to persuade Priscilla to build up the courage to tell on Roy.

"I just can't do anything to hurt Tricia! I can't…" Priscilla said as Jackie embraced her, and they began to rock back and forth.

With one last effort, Carla offered, "We will go with you and tell what we saw Priscilla."

Then, looking up at the ceiling of the room, Priscilla proclaimed. "One day I'm gonna get him!" The girls continued to cry as the party downstairs went on into the night.

Secrets and Fear

A beautiful blend of birds, sunbathing and singing as Priscilla sat in the window seal observing her little winged friends as she would always do. Residue still hung over the house from everything the prior night. Residue from the barbeque, the cigarette smoke, the loud music, the laughter, and worse still; the unforgivable act that Roy performed in the kitchen that not only violated Priscilla but most likely scarred the group of girls from this point on. Yet, here she sat, in somewhat of a daze. Staring off at the tree trying to find some peace of mind. As she keeps having flashbacks to last night, and the point of Roy's grotesque body pressing up against hers as she reached for the glass in the upper cabinet in the kitchen. Flashbacks of the look on each girl's face as she turned to look at them and their reaction while running upstairs to her bedroom. Flashbacks of the immense pain, embarrassment, and guilt she felt as she did run away from the incident. Yet, she was still trying to determine if her friends were right about going to Tricia, to out Roy. Or if she is right about not wanting to ruin something that Tricia seems to hold dearly? Her aunt's relationship with Roy. Priscilla took in the view of the birds and then began to softly sing to herself to try and calm her thoughts and nerves. Letting her beautiful voice soothe herself from the anxiety of the happenings and what was to come. Down in the kitchen, Tricia was just finishing preparing breakfast, then Roy popped in from the backyard, back early to take care of some more housework for Tricia as promised.

"Good morning to the most beautiful woman I know walking God's green earth." Roy, with the early morning charm to appease Tricia as he walked up behind her and grabbed her waist.

"Boy, stop it! You are crazy!" As she laughed and then turned to kiss Roy. They embraced and continued to laugh and hug as Tricia pulled away to continue to finish prepping breakfast. Then Tricia walked to the stairs to get Priscilla down for breakfast. "Priscilla! Breakfast is ready! Brush your teeth and come down." Priscilla jumped down from the window seal and then went into the bathroom to begin freshening up for breakfast. She knew that Roy was back this morning and felt uncomfortable about him being there and was trying to think of a way to not upset Tricia in any way about what happened last night, but didn't want to go downstairs, but did it anyway.

"Good morning Auntie." Priscilla came into the kitchen to hug her aunt as she would often do in the morning.

Then Tricia said to her as she placed Priscilla's plate on the table with a glass of orange juice. "I made one of your favorites!"

Then, trying to act normal, Roy spoke to Priscilla as he started to exit back out to the yard. "Good morning!" No reply from Priscilla as she ignores him bluntly.

"Do we have any whip cream?" Priscilla asks her aunt. "For the waffles?" One of Priscilla's favorite breakfasts was waffles, and she would always ask for whip cream. Tricia did notice that Priscilla did not say anything to Roy. She thought about questioning her niece but chalked it up to perhaps Priscilla being distracted by the waffles and wanting whip cream.

"I have to run down the street to pick up some vegetables from Miss Williams garden. You'll be fine while I run down there?" Tricia asked Priscilla.

Priscilla looked at her aunt while she began to consume the breakfast spread and thinking about the fact that Roy was in the backyard working. She felt uneasy about it, but this wasn't anything out of the norm. Tricia would often run next door, or down the street and leave Priscilla in the house for a few minutes. Never an issue. Still not an issue for Tricia, as she had no idea about what had happened between Roy and Priscilla last night. Begrudgingly, in her mind, as it may have been, Priscilla played it off and nodded in agreement of her aunt running down the street for a few minutes, as not to tip off the friction between her and Roy. At this point, it is just so unnerving that Priscilla would go out of her way to protect her Aunt; but she did. She did because she loves her so much and just wants Tricia to stay happy.

After grabbing a couple of grocery bags for the haul of veggies that Miss Williams would give out, Tricia jumped into her shoes and got ready to head out down the street. Miss Williams was the lady on the block that grew all her food. Surprisingly, a vegan in the 80's. Miss Williams was a health nut, but she encouraged everyone on the block to eat healthy, just like her, so she would give away some of every harvest. Miss Williams would always give Tricia and Priscilla way more than anyone else. As she had a special place in her heart for the girl and her aunt as she used to be very close friends with Tricia's parents. With the backdoor screen propped open; Tricia yelled out to the yard, over the banging coming from the yard of Roy trying to fix on the garage door that had been in disrepair for months. "I'll be back!" Roy nodded his head in acknowledgment as he continued to work on the garage door that was broken. Then Tricia ran her hand through Priscilla's hair as she walked past the girl, still eating breakfast. "Be right back sweetie." Then Tricia darted out of the front door to head down the street. Now alone in the house, Priscilla felt very afraid but hoped that Roy would continue to work and not come into the house while her aunt was gone. Taking this chance was not wise. She knew in her soul that she should have told on Roy by now. Or at least, went down the street to Miss Williams' with her aunt. But so stubborn was Priscilla; to take on the weight of being the one to take care of Tricia's feelings. How dare she! But this was Priscilla; strong and stubborn, just like her late mother, father, and her aunt.

As Priscilla started to get up from the kitchen table to put away her plate, she noticed that all of a sudden, the noise that Roy was making outside in the backyard had stopped. Her heart started to pick up the pace of beating, as she feared he was on his way into the house. Priscilla

95

rushed to try and get her breakfast setting cleaned up and get out of the kitchen to try and avoid Roy. She fumbled with the plate as she held it over the garbage can to scrape off the remaining crumbs. Roy inquired as he entered, already knowing the answer. "Your aunt went down the street to get the vegetables huh?" He was trying to present a front that everything was normal between him and Priscilla. Trying to play it as if he didn't do anything to her. Priscilla ignored him and continued to scrape the plate clean. "She loves to go get those veggies, it's nice what Miss Williams does, giving away food." Still arrogantly talking to the girl as if they were cool. Roy's ignorant stance on the temperature between the two of them was appalling, even to a young girl such as Priscilla. Yet, she continued to ignore him. Not a glance, not a word. Then Priscilla; dead set on making her way quietly out of the kitchen before having to reply to Roy, dropped the plate into the sink and went over to the table to grab her glass that had contained the orange juice she was drinking. "So, you just going to ignore me!?" Roy said, this time with some anger in his voice. Priscilla still ignoring him. "You need to respect your elders!" Roy, now raising his voice a decibel higher. Priscilla was determined to ignore Roy and not say anything to him. Roy rushed over to Priscilla at the table and grabbed the back of her head, with a full hand of her hair and pushed her head onto the table and held her there. "Listen to me you little muthafucka!" Priscilla shaking so uncontrollably with so much fear, thinking if she should try and do something, not knowing what he would do to her next. "You better learn to respect me!" Priscilla, pinned to the table with tears coming from her eyes now, still not making a sound. Roy continued with serious threats. "I'm your aunts' man, and I ain't going nowhere! And that little stunt you pulled last night, going upstairs, and slamming your door. That is disrespectful. You better get used to me being around you little bitch!" Tricia was walking up the front stairs returning from her visit down the street to Miss Williams.

In the distance, they could hear Tricia speaking, "Okay girl…. I know, I know… Yep, she got plenty more where this came from, go down there and get you some…" Roy quickly released Priscilla's head from being pinned to the table and allowed her to stand back up, as he watched her anxiously try to walk away from him shaking so from fear of what just transpired. Priscilla rushed past the sink and threw the orange juice glass in the sink and made her way to the stairs. He began to turn and prepare to walk back out to the yard to avoid having to explain anything, even though he knew now that the girl was petrified of him and wasn't going to say anything. Priscilla quickly walked away from the kitchen to try and hurry upstairs to avoid Tricia seeing what just happened.

Tricia entered the house as Roy was leaving out of the back door, and Tricia saw Priscilla's little feet just reaching the top stair and turning down the hall towards the bedrooms. Feeling an uneasiness; Tricia had a gut feeling something wasn't right.

"Priscilla, I'm back! Everything okay?" Tricia feeling like something just was amiss. Priscilla was standing right at the top of the stairs behind the wall by the stairs, not saying a word to her aunt. Constantly wiping her tears from her face, heaving, and breathing uncontrollably trying not to cry out loud. She was just a footstep reach from revealing herself to her aunt at the top of the stairs, face wet with tears, and shivering. But she remained hidden right there and silent.

After about three minutes of silence and Tricia heading into the kitchen to put down the bag of vegetables, Priscilla finally replied yelling down the stairs, partially broken voice, "I'm okay!" Hearing Priscilla's reply, Tricia was standing in the back doorway watching Roy work on the garage door. Tricia knew something wasn't right but couldn't put her finger on it; especially with Roy still in the same place he was when she left, and Priscilla's dishes in the sink, and Priscilla upstairs as usual. She left the feeling she had alone.

Priscilla, now alone in her room, with the door locked. She tried to make sense of the whole situation. So unfair was this situation, for a girl, so young to have to be in; and have to be the one to have to decide how to handle it alone. As she sat there, on her bed, legs crossed, shedding more and more tears; all she could do is think about the horrible way Roy was treating her. For some reason, she was blaming herself. Ignorantly thinking that, if she wasn't there, in the way. Tricia and Roy would be happy together. She convinced herself that maybe Roy was only acting this way toward her because she was in the way. So silly of Priscilla to feel and think this way, yet she did. Then she began to go through some stages of dealing with the issue. As she had just got it in her mind that it was her fault; she then started to think with anger. She began thinking of ways she could try and get rid of Roy. Now an about 15-year-old girl could in no way kill a grown, over 6-foot man physically. But, could she get her hands on a gun? Should she try and stab him some way? All these violent thoughts were going through her head as she went through the motions. Next, she began to think of the best ways to tell Tricia. That's if she could muster up the courage to do so. Maybe she could do it while she and Tricia were out on one of their shopping trips? Perhaps she could write a letter for her aunt telling her about the two incidents and leave it in her room on her pillow, allowing Tricia to read it and then come confront her to talk about it? As she went through all of her options, the only thing that resulted was to try and make sure her aunt would remain happy. So, telling was not the first choice in her mind. Lastly, Priscilla began to think of how she could just leave. Yes, leave! But, of course, she had nowhere to go. So, this notion was by far the most farfetched and dangerous one to choose. As she began to think about leaving her aunt alone with Roy, all she could do is continue to cry harder. She could not vision herself without Tricia. Steadily weighing options, Priscilla cried herself to sleep into a nap.

A few weeks had passed since the party night and the last incident. Roy was just about living there by now. Priscilla hated it, but she remained steadfast for the sake of her aunt. Somehow, Priscilla had managed to avoid much interaction with Roy, and there hadn't been any more incidents. Perhaps Roy also knew that he had crossed the line way too much, and any day, Priscilla could reveal the secret of how he treated her. But he knew that the girl was scared to death of him; so, he had that in his pocket. There was a real tension between Priscilla and Roy, and Tricia was slowly starting to notice the tension as she tried to stay ahead of it. At this point, Priscilla had shut down a lot, and Tricia noticed it. This is what made Tricia aware of the tension between her man and her niece. Over the past couple of weeks, Tricia had tried to drop little hints to allow Priscilla to reveal what was bothering her, but Priscilla continued to deny anything is wrong. She just told her aunt that she had a headache or was tired, to avoid talking about what was bothering her. Through all of these feelings, Priscilla had even thought to seek counsel from an outside source. After multiple times of trying to bring herself to build up the courage to tell Tricia; she ultimately never brought herself to do it. Last week she even cornered Pastor Shaw before church to try and get advice on how to handle it; but turned around and changed her story of why she wanted to talk to him, she just couldn't do it.

Today, Don arrived back in town, and he made his way over to Tricia's house to check in on them like he always did. The doorbell rang and Tricia answered to see Don standing on the porch with his back partially turned away from the door as he looked around the neighborhood and observed what was going on up and down the block.

"Hey there Don." Tricia said as she opened the door fully to welcome him into her home. With a huge hug, they embraced and then began to start walking toward the living room to sit on the couch and catch up. "You know D....." Just as Tricia sat down to begin the dialogue; Priscilla came bursting down the stairs frantically running towards Don to give him the biggest hug ever.

"I miss you, Uncle Don! I was about to go outside, and I heard the door and knew it had to be you, Uncle Don."

As she continued to head towards him and as Don stood back up to catch the oncoming hug from Priscilla, he was laughing aloud at the pure joy he shared with this girl and her aunt, as Priscilla squeezed him. It was like Don was her uncle. She always thought that Don was a family member, even though he wasn't. But he might as well have been, as close as he was with the entire family and how he continued to keep up with Tricia and Priscilla. He felt it was his duty to Frank, as he had always expressed to Tricia. Just as Priscilla and Don embraced, down the stairs came Roy. In the corner of his eye, Don noticed Roy coming downstairs and immediately thought to himself, *"What the hell!"* As Don turned his head toward Tricia, Priscilla let go of him from their hug, his face said it all with no words.

While Priscilla headed out to the front porch, and Roy continued into the living room, Tricia started to explain, "Don, you know Roy. He's been staying a lot lately to help out around the house and be our protector." While Tricia formed a muscle pose with her right arm to emphasize the protector part. Don was looking suspicious at the whole ordeal, glanced at Tricia while she gave the excuse, and then turned to extend his hand out to Roy. As he shook Roy's hand, Don had a weird feeling about it all but did not comment, as it wasn't his place. The three of them could feel the disapproval in Don's demeanor though. They all sat down and began to catch up.

After about a good hour of casual conversation, Tricia got up, "Let me make us some snacks and tea."

As Tricia went into the kitchen, Roy said, "I'll be right back, I'm going to run down to the corner store and get a pack of cigarettes. Anyone want anything?"

Both Tricia and Don replied, "Nah."

Don was starting to go into the kitchen with Tricia. While Roy was just getting into his car, Priscilla pulled up on her bike and dropped it in the grass as she hopped off in one motion and ran up the stairs, bursting into the front door.

"You're still here Uncle Don?" She proclaimed as she ran into the living room with a heavy grin on her face; Don saw her, so he sat back down to talk with the girl. "I just went on an adventure with my friend's Uncle Don! On our bikes! Let me tell you the story." Priscilla went on and on telling Don, as Tricia listened from the kitchen as she prepared some sandwiches and tea for the four of them. Tricia grinning and laughing to herself as she could never believe how patient Don was with Priscilla and her stories. Tricia had the quick thought of maybe one day, Roy and Priscilla could get that close and comfortable, trying to envision Priscilla and Roy sitting in the living room on the couch talking just the way Don and Priscilla were. But knowing that it was probably unlikely. She continued to prep lunch.

"So, Priscilla!" Don said to cut off Priscilla's ongoing storytelling. "How are things here with Roy being around the house?" Don was no fool. Don so loved both Tricia and Priscilla very much, and the fact that he felt something was not quite right, made him inquisitive. And what better way to become inquisitive than with a child, who would be more honest than an adult. Don had planned to confront Tricia about what he perceived as awkward energy in the house with Roy once he went into the kitchen to help with lunch. But since Priscilla was going on and on; he felt it was a good opportunity to try and get some answers right now. To the question about Roy being around the house; Priscilla's whole mood and expression immediately changed, and Don saw it.

"Well, I go outside a lot, and play in my room, or go to the store with Aunt Tricia," Priscilla answered. Don noticed that the girl did not include Roy in her answer. Oddly enough because the question was about Roy. He knew something was up and was starting to get agitated.

"So, do you and Roy ever go to the park? Play games when he's around?" Don continued to dig for answers.

"I like to have company over when Tricia lets me. Then I'll try and watch the birds from the window a lot."

Again, Priscilla ignored answering directly about Roy, Don couldn't take it. He placed his hand on Priscilla's shoulder as he rose from his seat on the couch.

"Sweetie, that is so nice," looking her right in the eyes as to acknowledge that she was uncomfortable about Roy, talking about him or anything. "I'll be in the kitchen with your aunt. You should go and freshen up for lunch." As he headed into the kitchen. Priscilla looked at Don with some confirmation of the fact that they were both on the same page, she started to go towards the stairs to follow his direction.

"Yes sir, Uncle Don." She replied as she went up the stairs.

In the kitchen, Don was on a mission. He was going to get to the bottom of what was going on here.

"Mmmm! Ham and cheese! My favorite!" Don said as he entered the kitchen. "You know, I've been meaning to ask you about Roy, Tricia!" Just as Don was about to start questioning Tricia about the situation, the front screen door opens, and Roy returns.

"Heeey y'all! I got some potato chips too! To go with lunch!" As Roy came into the kitchen with his bag, Don decided to leave it alone.

"What were you about to say, Don?" Tricia asked as Roy got in the kitchen and placed the bag onto the kitchen table.

Don, replying to Tricia and acknowledging Roy all at once said as he looked into the bag that Roy just put on the table. "Oh, nothing sweetheart. Good move my man. And they are the barbecue flavor. A man with similar taste."

"Aww yeah! You know it, man. I'm about to go have this smoke in the backyard." Roy said as Don was done inspecting the bag from the store.

"Okay, lunch will be ready soon." Tricia said as Don began to follow behind Roy to the backyard.

"I'll join you, Roy." As the two men made their way outside into the yard, Don couldn't help himself. He had already pretty much figured out the whole situation in his head about the tension in the house. One thing he knew was this. There was no tension in the house before Roy started coming around a lot. So, Don being Don, he decided it was a good time to confront Roy to ask about Priscilla.

"Hey man! Is it me? Or does Priscilla seem to act a little different lately?" Don started up to see what he could get Roy to voluntarily give up about the situation.

"What do you mean?" Roy answered as he lit his cigarette.

"Just saying, I was sitting and talking to her, and every time I brought you up, she seemed to change her disposition, just saying." Don replied to attempt to poke a bit, but still allow Roy to back himself into a corner.

"Bring me up!? What the fuck does that even mean, man!?" Now being defensive, it's like Don got what he wanted immediately.

"Whoa, whoa whoa!" Don replied. "Hey man, why the anger brother?"

Roy interjected, "I'm just saying, you come around here now and again and you think you can come and question me!"

Don was about to get into his ready-to-fight mode and decided to himself in his mind, *"Fuck it!"* Don began to further accuse Roy of making her act funny. "I'm just saying brother, it seems like it's you! You seem like the reason for Priscilla acting weird. I just need to know that everything is okay, and ain't no funny business going on in this house."

Roy, now extremely defensive and angry, "What the Fuck! Funny business!? Man, who the fuck do you think you are, you ain't they family motherfucker!"

They grabbed each other up, Don threatened to kill him. "If I hear anything about Tricia or Priscilla being hurt in any way! I swear, I will come back here and take yo bitch ass out muthafucka!" Just as Roy was thinking about taking a swing on Don, Tricia popped out of the screen door.

"Lunch is served, fellas." She saw them tangled up and said, "Is everything alright?" The two let each other go and made up an excuse.

Roy first. "These damn hornets back here babe. I was trying to avoid one, and almost tripped. Don caught my fall."

Tricia replied hesitantly, "Oh… Oh okay," partially believing the story.

As they all went into the living room where Tricia had set the table for lunch, Roy said, "I'm going to hit this bathroom right quick before we eat." As Roy went upstairs to the bathroom, Priscilla came in from the front porch where she had been ever since she freshened up as Don had told her. She was out in the front waiting for Tricia to get done preparing lunch.

"Listen here, sweetie." Don looked at Tricia as she finished setting the table and Priscilla took a seat. "I just remembered; I have to head down to the church by a certain time to meet with Pastor Shaw about some business."

"Aww, not so soon!" Tricia said as both she and Priscilla were disappointed that he was stating he had to leave.

"Maybe we can all get together for dinner before I leave town this time?" Don offered up as a consolation of him having to depart.

"Well, take your sandwich with you, I'll wrap it up." Tricia went into the kitchen with the sandwich as Don and Priscilla headed onto the front porch.

"Listen here, sweetie! I know something ain't quite right here. You find me if you need help. Understand?" Standing in front of Don with a helpless look in her eyes, Priscilla agreed with Don, as Tricia came back onto the porch to hand him the now wrapped sandwich. He kissed them both on their cheek one at a time, then walked off the porch to get into his car and pulled away.

Roy came out onto the porch, trying to act surprised, "Hey, where is he going? He has to leave so soon?"

Tricia replied to Roy as she waved at Don's car pulling off, "Yeah, he forgot he had a meeting with Pastor Shaw." As the three of them, all stand on the porch staring at Don's car leaving; Priscilla was locked in on what Don just told her. Does she use Don's offer of help to expose Roy? Or does she find another way? Roy standing there thinking to himself, that he must find a way to put Don in his place and out of their business there at Tricia's house. With arrogant nerve, feeling as if Don was the one in the wrong for having a feeling something was amiss in the house as it was. Tricia, standing there thinking to herself that something was not quite right with how Don left. He had to be making some excuse. She was feeling deeply that she should drill Roy to find out what happened in the backyard because what she saw as she was coming out to the backyard was far from Don trying to help Roy avoid a hornet. As they all went into the house one-by-one, Priscilla went into the kitchen with her lunch plate, while Tricia and Roy sat at the prepared dining room table for lunch with the two of them small talking while they enjoyed the lunch. All three felt a void in their relationships.

The Unthinkable

As the birds chirped outside the house as loud as they could, in the usual fashion, it was early, and Tricia was in the kitchen preparing breakfast as she normally did. This Saturday morning had so much in store, as Tricia and Priscilla were going to be heading back to midtown for some girl's day out shopping as they would do. While Tricia was flipping pancakes, Roy came into the kitchen to grab her around the waist and kiss her on the neck.

"Stop it fool! You're going to make me burn the pancakes!" As she slapped his hands away from her waist.

Roy laughed as he heads out of the kitchen sarcastically saying, "You know it's all your fault! Being so sexy!" Then he headed out to the front yard to get ready to do the lawn care that he so graciously had been doing for the duration of the summer. Roy being around was now a staple. Somehow, Priscilla had been able to maintain her will to allow Tricia to be happy with this guy. Even though he long had deserved to pay for being a creep to her and who knows how many other girls in the neighborhood. Not that there had been any talk about Roy, but if he had the nerve to get inappropriate with Priscilla, his lady's niece, who knows how bold and disgusting he could be. As Tricia completed the breakfast spread and removed everything from the stove, she noticed she hadn't heard a peep from Priscilla this morning. Of course, Priscilla has to be upstairs in that doggone window watching those birds as she normally did on the weekend. This is the first thing that comes to Tricia's mind when she questions why she hadn't seen the girl yet.

Tricia finished up in the kitchen and began to head upstairs, planning to sneak up on Priscilla while she watched the birds. As she turned at the top of the stairs and began to head toward the back window, she didn't see Priscilla sitting on the window stoop as she usually would. With a mild panic, Tricia immediately turned to go to Priscilla's bedroom, knowing she would find her still in the bed that morning, which would be out of the norm. As Tricia approached the bedroom door that was partially ajar, she pushed the door to get a glimpse of the head of the bed in Priscilla's room to find that she didn't see her lying in the bed. As Tricia's heart started to race, she flung the bedroom door open to fully survey the room; still didn't see Priscilla in the room as she entered and panned in a circle. Tricia went into full-on panic mode and her heart was literally about to pound a hole into her chest. She fumbled over her own feet as she tried to turn around to check the remaining rooms upstairs, knowing that she just walked past the bathroom that was not fully closed and she didn't hear any noise in there. "Priscilla!" She screamed out as she ran down the hall back to each room, pushing each door to check into the rooms as she scoured the hall. Though she yelled at the top of her voice in fear for anyone to hear her; Roy, outside, did not hear her over the now in-use lawnmower.

As her brow was now sweating and she went back to Priscilla's room again to double-check, she yelled out again, "Priscilla!" As she surveyed Priscilla's room again to come up empty of the girl's presence in the room; all of a sudden Tricia jumped almost to the top of the door as she heard the smallest voice, partially hoarse faintly speaking her name, "Aunt Tricia." Priscilla said as she had just come out of the bathroom that Tricia had not fully entered in her panic of trying to find the girl. Tricia, now with eyes full of tears and all the panic that could be in her chest, turned to see Priscilla standing in the hall, yellow and pale and looking fully depleted of hydration. Tricia ran to her and fell to her knees to hug Priscilla.

With the embrace, she was crying and asked, "Where were you!?"

Priscilla replied, "In the bathroom. I don't feel well."

Tricia not remembering that she didn't fully go into the bathroom, "But I didn't see you in there."

As Priscilla looked up at her aunt, removed from all of her energy, she replied sheepishly, "I was on the toilet, My stomach is hurting bad."

Tricia now starting to calm down took her right hand and placed it on Priscilla's forehead. "Girl you are burning up! You must have caught a bug. Let's get you back in the bed." As the two of them head back to Priscilla's room to lay her down, Priscilla looked at her aunt with admiration to see just how panicked she was and just how much her aunt was worried about her. She knew that she was loved so much by this woman. Tricia tucked Priscilla back into the sheets and removed the blanket, then turned on the fan in the room; Priscilla could barely move to use any energy to thank her aunt. "Oh my God! You need to stay in this bed! And we were going to go to your favorite shops in midtown today; that can't happen now!" Priscilla laying there helpless, not able to reply; she just looked at her aunt to nod and agree with Tricia's statement. Tricia went on and on now that she had gone into take-care mode for Priscilla, "I do have that dentist appointment today in mid-town though. I can't miss it! Or it'll be months before I can reschedule the appointment." Priscilla started to fall asleep from lack of energy and the comfort from her aunt; plus, the used-up energy she just expended in the bathroom, looked up at her aunt perplexed about the statement of not being able to miss her dental appointment.

"Roy is outside doing the grass and I should be able to get back before he is done."

Priscilla jumped up into an upright position on the bed suddenly. "I'll be okay to go to midtown and with you to the dentist Aunt Tricia." Priscilla knowing that it was not a good idea for her to be in the house with just Roy hanging around; outside mowing the grass or not.

"Girl lay down. What are you doing?"

Then Priscilla with a helpless look in her eyes as she looked up at Tricia from her laying position since she laid back down still nervous as ever said, "I... I just don't want to be in the house all by myself Aunt Tricia."

Tricia replied. "By yourself?! Roy will be outside doing the yardwork as I said. So, you won't be by yourself, Priscilla." Tricia tried to convince her that it'd be okay for about an hour or so.

Then Priscilla tried to rebuttal with an excuse for her aunt to stay, "Yes Ma'am; but you know since it's the weekend, those bike boys always be trying to do some crazy stuff around the block too." Referring to a group of teenage boys in the neighborhood who broke into yards and stole some things, and even painted on some houses a couple of weeks ago. As Priscilla grasped for straws for reasons to keep her aunt at home with her or let her go with her to the dentist; sick or not, Priscilla could not help but get close to telling her aunt about Roy. With a serious look in her eyes, Priscilla propped herself back up on the bed and began to wipe tears from her eyes as she began to speak.

"Aunt Tricia!" With a very stoic tone this time. "Can I tell you something very serious?"

Tricia swung her full attention to Priscilla to try to convince the girl that she'd be okay replied genuinely. "Yes baby, what is it?"

Priscilla replied, "It's about Roy."

Now Tricia was very intrigued and concerned as she leaned into Priscilla and grabs her hand.

"What about Roy baby?" With much concern on her face as her eyebrows scrunched up while she looked straight at Priscilla for the continuum of her statement.

"Well, I need to tell you seriously about Roy. It's just that…" Priscilla paused again as she wiped some tears from the well of her eyes.

"Go on girl. What is it?" Tricia replied.

Priscilla tried to go on, "I… I just don't like him. But I know you do. And you love him." Tricia began to try and intervene on the statement as Priscilla grabbed her aunt's arm to indicate that she wasn't done speaking. "I just want to be able to spend as much time with you before you marry Roy or something, and I'll be left out and won't be able to be with you, Aunt Tricia." Breaking down now into a full-blown cry, Priscilla fell into Tricia's lap, as Tricia tried to calm her down and explain that Roy didn't interfere with their relationship. "Awww, baby. I've told you time and time again. What Roy and I have, has nothing to do with what you and I have." Priscilla, sobbing so, knowing she just blew her chance to tell on Roy. But she just couldn't bring herself to do it. She was crying so mightily hard out of disappointment in herself for not going through with telling about Roy. Fitting, because now Tricia just thought she was comforting Priscilla about feeling alone in the threesome of her relationship with Roy and herself.

Tricia looked stern at her and said, as she grasped Priscilla's hands, "Look! I will never leave you. I will never ask you to leave me. Roy or no Roy. Understand baby?" Now, with the missed opportunity, Priscilla felt hopeless, drained even. She fell back onto her pillow and gave in. She gave in to being left alone with this creep right outside her window while her protector, her mother, her aunt left her alone in this huge house for over an hour. But, the sheer disappointment in herself for not growing the moxie to tell on that jerk was all too draining of an event. Especially coming so close to doing it. Now she lay helpless agreeing to be left alone to allow her aunt to step out to take care of her business on this afternoon weekend day. Knowing and hoping that the obvious would not happen. Knowing and hoping that she could just fall asleep from the fever medicine Tricia was administering to her, sleep off this bug, and wake up to her precious aunt back at home, preparing lunch, and everything back to normal. As Tricia closed the top on the fever medicine, she grabbed the cold towel she had just prepared while Priscilla was dosing in and out of her thoughts in the bed, drained from the previous event. "As I said, You'll be fine. I'll be right back as soon as this dentist appointment is done. I was going to pick up some groceries, but I'll come right back. This tooth is killing me. Okay, baby?" Priscilla, now half-drugged and wore out from crying and anguish, nodded, and dozed off in the bed. Tricia pulled the sheet up on Priscilla's shoulder and kissed her on the forehead. She could already feel the fever starting to break, so she slowly crept out of the bedroom and slightly pulled the door up ajar. Tricia quietly headed to her bedroom to grab her purse and keys to head to her appointment; she crept to be sure not to wake Priscilla. In Tricia's mind was the fear and anxiety in Priscilla's little sick face as she lay in the bed. Tricia still trying to decipher the true reasons why Priscilla is always so uptight about Roy; about seeming to not want to share her aunt with anyone; specifically, this man. As Tricia found herself exiting the back door of the house, she cleared her head and chalked it up to just knowing that Priscilla had been through so much. Much like herself. *"That has to be why she is so uptight and defensive!"* Tricia finalized her thoughts as she approached Roy in the yard.

"Hey sweetie!" Tricia said to Roy as he turned off the lawnmower to hear her. "Well, I am about to head on to the stores and my appointment and Priscilla is not feeling all that well. She's up in her room sleep since I gave her some medication. So, she should be fine, and sleep right on until I get back."

Roy looking and nodding at Tricia while she informed him of Priscilla's condition.

"Alright baby, I'll be out here making sure the house is watched while I work. As long as she needs nothing from me, we should be good! You know I'm no babysitter!" Roy said to Tricia with a firm look on his face.

Tricia replied to him with a snark, "What you say?"

Roy quickly came back in rebuttal to his stupid comment, "You know I'm joking baby. I'll do whatever y'all need of me."

Tricia looked at Roy with rolling eyes, "You better!" as she prepared to get ready to leave. Just as she started to leave, she explained to Roy that she shouldn't need him to do anything. If much; just go and check on Priscilla's fever if he had the time to, but it's not necessary. Then she grabbed his dirty hand and kissed him on his cheek and started to walk on down the gangway of the house to the front sidewalk from the backyard. Just as she got about half-way to the front, Tricia thought about something she wanted to tell Roy and stopped short to go back up to him. As he was about to restart the lawnmower, he saw Tricia coming back in his direction, so he paused on restarting the machine.

"Besides, maybe if she can see you trying to help her through this bug, she'll lighten up about you and me and not be so awkward around you?" Roy agreed with a weird look on his face; that of a lying criminal because he knew the truth about him and Priscilla but let Tricia go on to the dentist and continued to mow the grass.

As Priscilla lay in the bed, wrapped in her covers sleeping like a log; her body trying to fight off what seemed to be a temporary bug. Possibly from food, or germs outside, she was recovering. Uninvited, Roy was standing just outside her bedroom door, peaking in at Priscilla. Checking on her, as he promised Tricia, Roy stood at the door looking in at Priscilla. Priscilla slightly woke up to turn over in her bed, and there Roy stood. Still half-sleep and extremely drowsy from the medication, Priscilla was startled and scared, but too weak to yell or jump.

"Wha... Wha... What do you want?" In such a whimpering voice. She was still waking up and gaining her consciousness back as he stood there.

"I'm just checking on you as your aunt asked me. You need to relax."

"Bu.... But..." Priscilla tried to muster up a defensive statement to Roy's proclamation.

He continued, "I'm just checking as I promised, I'm going to take your temperature, and I'm back outside, relax!"

Priscilla began to tremble as she continued to gain full awareness as she tugged on her covers tight to clutch them closer to her body. Roy sat on the side of the bed, Priscilla inched over to the middle of her bed, now feeling extremely uncomfortable with Roy sitting right next to her on the bed. He grabbed the wet towel and placed it on one side of her forehead while using his free hand to reach up and place the back of his hand on the other side of her head. Priscilla, now shaking tremendously.

Roy said, "Okay, so you're not as hot as your aunt said you were when she was leaving. So that is a good thing." As Priscilla lie there shaking and silent, she would not take her eyes off Roy's hands. She could not bring herself to look at his face. All she could remember was the kitchen incidents, and it was making her feel sicker as he rambled on speaking in a manner of being someone that genuinely cares for her. All the while Roy was speaking to her, kind of diagnosing her, somewhat even speaking words of comfort to a sick person; but Priscilla heard absolutely nothing. Her thoughts and eyes trained on his hands, hoping that maybe, just maybe he does not try anything close to repeating what happened in the kitchen. She is so scared, she is about to pee herself in the bed, but holds all her muscles tight; still not hearing him, as he talked in her mental background, "Blah, blah blah…." Roy took his hand that was previously on her forehead for the temperature check and grabbed a piece of her covers, wet towel still in his other hand, he maneuvers the towel down to Priscillas chest, "I just want to make sure that you are fully relieved of your fever Priscilla." With the most disgusting, demonizing trick he could find, he tries to justify touching her with the towel on her chest. She felt like she was about to throw up all over her bed. "I told you to relax girl! I'm trying to help you!" The nasty, unrelenting trash that Roy was. He was intent on trying to pursue this God-forsaken attempt on the young girl.

Finally getting some strength from recovery and fear, Priscilla let out a shrill, "STOOOOP!" Her defense word drawing out in anguish just like the situation she was trapped in. In the same instance, she pulled the covers back up to her neck and slid over to the other edge of the bed. Still unable to muster the strength to jump out of the bed, as she was still feeling the wooziness from the sick pit of the stomach pain of realizing what Roy was trying to do. Now a struggle began to ensue, as Roy pulled back on the covers to yank them down from her chin, going back in towards Priscilla's chest again.

In an instance of rebuttal and restrained energy, Priscilla yelled out one more time, "I said Stop!" At the same time, finally jumping up from the covers and reaching past Roy to the nightstand and grabbing the pencil that was laying on her notepad all in one motion, she stabbed Roy on the back of his hand that was tugging on the covers. She jumped up from the bed and stumbled to the floor right at her bedroom door as she was trying to run away. Roy was shocked and stunned by her action. He was not ready for Priscilla to fight back. "Ahhhhhh.... You little wench!" As he fell to his knees next to the bed grabbing his stabbed hand with the other, looking at the pencil perched out of it like a flagpole, blood starting to gush out of his hand. Priscilla stuck him good. "Come back here!" Roy said as he was trying to both build up the courage to pull the deeply wedged pencil out from the back of his hand and stand up to give chase to her. Priscilla managed to get a bit more energy and stand herself up on the frame of the bedroom door. As she glanced back at him; she noticed the rage in his face and could not help but think that this man was about to try and kill her. Adrenaline hit her and she took off down the stairs, grabbed her shoes and tucked them under her arm like a football, and made a b-line for the backyard. Dashed out to the yard and into the alley and just kept running for what seemed to be her life to her. Roy finally gathered himself after pulling the pencil out of his hand and tossed it across the room. He stumbled down the stairs and headed to the front door cursing up a storm. As he noticed the locked front door, he quickly pivoted to the kitchen and jetted to the back of the house, pushed open the screen door with fury, and burst out into the yard and out to the alley. By this time, Priscilla was nowhere in sight. He stood in the alley, turning back and forth, looking to the west end of the alley. Then looking to the east end of the alley, no sight of the swift-footed Priscilla. Just as he was about to yell out her name, he stopped himself. He began to think like a piece of trash again and shifted to cover his tracks. He knew that Priscilla wouldn't come right back because she was so scared. He headed back up to the house to try and not draw any more attention to himself or the house and began to plot a plan to cover up what just transpired. He also planned how to refute anything Priscilla would say when she did come back. It's unreal what the sick-criminalistic mind will do.

Disappearance

As Roy entered the back of the house; he ripped the screen door half-off its hinges and goes into the kitchen to the sink and began to clean his stab wound on his hand from the pencil to get rid of the blood. As he stood at the kitchen sink; he was being careful to use bleach to clean up his trace. As he finally got the hand to stop bleeding with the cold faucet water, he grabbed a bundle of napkins, applied pressure to his hand, and went back upstairs. Roy headed right back into Priscilla's room and pulled the cover off the bed and threw it to the foot of the bed on the floor. Then he looked around the room for the pencil he tossed earlier. He found it with no problem, and put it in his pocket, then left the room. Now he was nervous, but still steadfast in covering up his actions. With ill nerve, Roy went back out to the back of the house and grabbed the lawnmower and pushed it to the front of the house. His hand wrapped with a cloth. Roy started the lawnmower; then began to mow the front-yard as if nothing had even happened. After about forty more minutes, Tricia arrived back home as she saw Roy finishing up the front yard. Roy was careful to take extra time to do the front now. He purposely tried to waste time to set up Tricia to find the house wrecked in the back door, and Priscilla missing. As Tricia approached the house, Roy tried to pretend that he didn't hear her over the noise of the hedge trimmer. Now done with the grass in the front and back of the house, Roy was trimming the bushes in the front of the house to complete the day of outside chores in his usual manner.

"Hey baby, I'm back." Tricia said at the top of her voice to him as he cut the bushes. Roy didn't acknowledge her. She walked next to him but not too close, and he acted as if he was startled by her presence.

"Oh; hey sweetie." As he powered down the hedge trimmer. "Didn't see you there! Just about finished with everything."

She wanted to see if he checked on Priscilla. "How is she? Did she get up at all?"

Trying to pretend like he forgot to check on Priscilla, Roy looked at Tricia with a fake confused expression on his face for a few seconds, then gazed up at the sky preparing to reply to her. "Oh… Oh…. I didn't get a chance to check on her. Was so busy trying to finish up. But she never came outside, or anything; she must still be sleeping!" Lying right to Tricia's face like the evil man he was, Roy put down the trimmer and said to her, "Let me finish up, then I'll come in and get cleaned up and help you out with Priscilla.

Tricia replied. "Oh baby, don't worry about it. I gave her a nice dose of medicine; so, she probably would sleep through everything for these last couple of hours. Just come on in whenever you are done with everything."

As she prepared to go into the house, Roy smacked her on her ass, to make sure he stayed in the character of a man not being aware that Priscilla was missing, or that he was the reason for her being gone. Tricia went up the stairs and entered the house.

After a few minutes, Roy was getting nervous. For he would have thought that Tricia would have come running out of the house by now; after seeing the back door tore off the hinge; Priscilla's room empty, and the girl missing. Wanting to be ready to act as if he was surprised, Roy started to put away all the yard tools and try his best to remain patient for the fall-out from Tricia. About another 2 minutes passed as he remained outside waiting. Something seemed too weird to him. Now he began to think he had left something that would get him caught. He started to re-envision the moments between him and Priscilla as the girl struggled to get away from his terrible grasp, thinking to himself, Did I leave something? Another half a minute, still no sign of Tricia! Roy couldn't take anymore, so he began to walk toward the side of the house and was planning to run into the backdoor to act as if he found the house broken into. Just as he was about to approach the side walkway of the house; an unbelievable loud shriek emerged from the walls of the home. Tricia screaming at the top of her lungs. "Oh my God! Roy! Oh my God! Roy! Oh my God! Roy!" She kept repeating as she ran toward the exit of the front of the house. "My baby!" Now was the time for Roy to put on his award-winning acting hat. As Tricia stumbled down the front stairs, Roy ran towards her to grab her as he was yelling now as well.

"What is it, sweetie? What is it!?" Acting surprised as he grasped her while Tricia fell to the ground crying out to the sky.

"Where is my baby!?" She cried out.

"What are you talking about Tricia!" Roy said with force as he cradled her on the grass in the front of the house, trying to pretend to be caught off guard.

"She's gone! She's gone!"

Again, trying to act surprised Roy said, "Who's gone, Tricia? Calm down! Talk to me!"

As Tricia sat there on the ground trying to speak through the flood of tears to Roy; she was now drawing the attention of the neighbors who were stopping to try and help the situation. With the crowd starting to swell, she finally proclaimed with clarity what was going on. What Roy already knew but pretended not to know.

"I... I... went into the house to use the bathroom." Tricia shaking uncontrollably as she tried to explain what happened. "The back d... Back... Back door was broken into!" As the neighbors continued to crowd around; Roy got up and tried to lift Tricia from her knees to look her in the eyes and wipe her face.

"Wait!" Roy said. "Broken into!? What do you mean the house was broken into? I have been out here the whole time!" With pure fakeness, Roy tried to continue to act like he had no clue that something happened while he was doing yard work. "No-way! That can't be true Tricia! Can't be true!" By now, the neighbors had taken the liberty to call the police as they heard about a break-in. All the while, Roy had walked Tricia to the front step and sat her down on the bottom step. "I'll be right back!" Roy said while grabbing a rake to enter the house through the front door. Now trying to act as a detective trying to go and inspect the house, and supposedly secure it. Shortly behind him was John; the neighbor from across the street, who was responsible for calling the police in the melee. As the two men entered the front door of the house, a few women neighbors surrounded Tricia on the porch as she continued to sob.

"What the fuck!" Roy shouted out as he entered the kitchen and glanced at the back door tore off the hinge. Displaying clear frustration and surprise in front of John to play the role. With a look of disbelief on his face, John just stood there bewildered as he stood behind Roy observing the damage to the kitchen and the house. "She has to be here hiding somewhere!" Roy said to John as he turns to head up-stairs. Acting like he had a hunch that Priscilla was still in the house. As the two men look all over the house for Priscilla, the police finally arrive outside. With a good size crowd now in front of Tricia's house, the police try to park and get close to the curb. Tricia continues to sob as the police began to exit their vehicles and walk toward the house. Back in the house; John and Roy finish checking every possible place for Priscilla. Roy is frustrated with the fact that John had taken the liberty to help him. Knowing in his mind why the girl is not there anymore. But he continues to play dumb to look for Priscilla.

Then John began with questions, "Man; I saw you were mowing the lawn all morning. You didn't hear or see nothing man?" John now drilling Roy honestly due to concern for the girl.

Naturally, Roy is offended, and just barely catches himself from exposing who he is to John. "What! What you trying to say, man?" John jumping back in surprise to Roy's response to a simple question is when Roy realizes that he needs to be cool.

"I'm sorry; just trying to figure out how someone could just walk right in here and take her!" John replied to Roy's defensive response to his question.

"Nah man, Nah man!" with a whimper in his voice now. Trying to act hurt in front of John as to not give any clues. "I didn't see anything. But I should have!"

Now kicking the baseboard that was near the both of them to act out aggression and frustration of the situation. John quickly grabs Roy's shoulder and consoles him.

"Nope brother! It's not your fault. Don't blame yourself, man. It's just crazy that a sicko would even do this! Is all I'm saying." As John consoles him, Roy nods his head in agreement and acceptance of John's apology or deferment.

"Let's go outside and see what the cops can do; I think they are out there now." Then John turns to go outside, and Roy looked him up and down from the back with a devious and sneaky look because he knows he duped John into believing he is a victim of this situation too. John and Roy get back onto the front porch, they see the police questioning Tricia trying to figure out the scene. Three more officers begin to enter the house to tape off everything and investigate.

"We checked and she's not here, and no-one is in the house," Roy said as the police breeze passed them on the porch.

"Thank you!" One police officer said in passing. Roy and John get closer to being in on the conversation, and quickly realize the cop is brow-beating Tricia for a run-away case.

"Just saying ma'am; was she happy? A lot of the kids in this neighborhood run away all the time. Nothing new here." Roy hears it and acts as if he is taking offense; very convincingly because he knows that she is not a runaway.

"Excuse me, officer. What did you just say to her?" The officer, with a burly build and rough-looking white face, looked up at Roy standing at the top of the porch in response as if he were about to charge Roy when his partner grabs his elbow.

"Is there a reason you are here Mr.?" The cop said to Roy after he is half restrained.

Roy replies to the cop, "I'm her man! I'm always here!"

The cop looking at him with disgust, "Well can you or anyone give me the details of the perpetrator who supposedly took the girl?"

Roy replies in defense, "What does supposedly mean?" Tricia jumps up from her seated position on the stair to question the officer, with one of the neighbors grabbing her. In the confusion and tension, the second officer tries to pacify the situation. "Excuse me ma'am; can I talk to you and your boyfriend over here." As the detective stares at Roy while he heads up the stairs to enter the house and aid in the investigation of the premises.

Roy said, "All I know is that I was mowing the lawn, and as I was finishing up, Tricia came home, went in the house, and then came out screaming. I didn't hear or see anything while I was working." Then he turned to Tricia as the officer wrote down his statement; "I'm so sorry sweetie. It's my fault. I should have checked on her."

Tricia grabbed Roy's hand and excusing his self-blame, "No it's not your fault babe; you thought she was sleep."

The cop tries to begin digging into the details. "So, your niece was sleeping the whole time?"

Tricia gives a reply, "Yes, you see she was ill this morning, so I gave her some meds and went to the store, knowing Roy was outside I knew she would be okay in the house. I…. I just didn't…" Roy grabs her to embrace Tricia and hug her as she continues to explain to the cop.

The cop immediately said. "Interesting, so she was alone in the house!"

Tricia defends herself. "But Roy was here!"

The cop responds, "Okay, I think I have enough."

The other police officers start to exit the house and huddle up to discuss everything. As they walk away from Tricia and Roy, one officer said to the other, "Clear breaking and entering in the back. We have to hope she's alive." Tricia overhears and faints into Roy's arms. One officer notices and quickly radios for an ambulance. Tricia was overwhelmed by it all and it took her out. Roy, as he propped Tricia's head upon his chest to keep her from collapsing to the ground could not help but glare at the male cop again as if he wanted to drop Tricia and launch at him to kick his ass. The cop did not spare his evil look either; throwing them right back at Roy as he continued to walk towards his car. As the medics arrive to tend to Tricia, the police wrap up their investigation for now, and Roy convinced them that he was a bystander to the situation as they leave.

"Ma'am... Ma'am. We are going to be leaving now." The lady officer spoke to Tricia as she is zoned out. The medic snaps Tricia out of her daze by nudging her shoulder.

Then Tricia sat perched on the back of the ambulance. "Oh, oh, I'm sorry; what was that you said?"

The officer replies again, "Take my card, we'll be in touch as soon as we get any leads. I promise you; we are going to tear this town apart looking for your girl."

As all the police presence leaves and the neighbors disburse back to their homes, John offers help, "I'm right across the street if y'all need me, Tricia." Roy nods to John as Tricia said with a whimpered, "Thanks, John."

Roy and Tricia remain on the porch, just talking about all the events of the day, trying to re-in act how someone could have possibly got into the house with him in the front, and take Priscilla without him knowing. Tricia trying to think through what could have happened, praying that Priscilla is alive and well, and they plan to canvas the neighborhood all night. Tricia is doing all the mind-bending work of planning to find Priscilla, and trace what happened; while Roy is pretending to also try and figure out how something so random could have happened right under his nose. But Roy couldn't care. With his sick ways, he is hoping the girl doesn't turn up. But he pretends and is getting ready to walk the blocks tonight with Tricia to find Priscilla. As they plan, a few other neighbors come back and offer to help look as well that night.

Tricia noticed Roy's hand is cut, and she grabs the bandage, "What happened to your hand?"

"Oh, no big deal; it happened when I was trying to fix the mower when it got clogged one time today."

Tricia stares at him, then back at his wound, then back at him, and back at the wound again. Roy is getting a little worried she sees something to disprove his story, he is cringing to think up a lie to spill to her. But Tricia is just lost right now, not knowing what to believe, doesn't question his reason for the cut further, and he escapes having to go into more detail.

Later, as the sunset, and dawn appeared, Tricia and Roy locked the house down and went out to the street to join the group of neighborhood friends who had banded together today to canvas the area for Priscilla. They had a plan to walk block-by-block and alley-by alley to check in every corner and every park for her. They gathered at the corner of Tricia's block and they plan the search. John is there again as promised, and it seems to bother the hell out of Roy. As if he can feel that John will be the one to uncover the truth.

John then suggested. "I think we split up into three groups; one man by three women."

One of the neighbors agreed with John, "Yes, I think that is a good idea."

John confirmed and further suggested. "Okay, then let's do that, and maybe meet back here in about 3-4 hours?" Looking at John, Roy couldn't help but feel like this guy was going to be his downfall.

But Roy played along, "Man, great thinking! I don't know what we would do without you tonight my man."

Roy grabs Tricia's hand as they begin to pair into groups, only to make sure that he stays by her side and no one else can put any doubt into her head about what happened at the house earlier. They part ways and begin the night search. The first of many searches they would do until Priscilla is home safe.

Running

The gym teacher barked orders to the summer school gym class to get them in line for the daily calisthenics. "Everyone in a single file line so we can start the class! Stop goofing around Ben! Angie! Stand up straight!" Mr. Coleman yelled at all the kids still goofing around, but slowly getting in order as they would always do, holding out to the very last second to be mindful of Mr. Coleman's directions in gym class. As the class went on, a blurred vision of everything was coming into focus as Priscilla woke from her slumber behind the gym room bleachers and saw the class forming through the thin gap in the bleacher seats. Here she was, in the neighborhood high school hiding out after running from Roy and his vicious rape attempt. At least that is what she thought was going to happen. She also can't help but think that he could have possibly been about to murder her so he could have Tricia all to himself. Either way, she was lucky to escape. And here she was, in the high school hiding behind the gym room bleachers wrapped in a rug she grabbed in her escape into the school on the way in. She had been in the school for a few days now. Hiding. How? While running away that day, she ran as fast and as hard as she could but kept running into cars and groups of adults who for sure would have tried to help her, but she didn't want any help.

While running, she ignored everyone that kept trying to stop her or grab her or help her. She just ran. Until she saw that the dock door on the back of the school was wide open with a garbage truck backing up to it for the weekend garbage pickup. She took her chance and ran up to the door while the truck was backing in, running on the passenger side of the truck she hopped up onto the dock and skirted into the building, and ran down the hall until she found an empty classroom. She stayed in the classroom for only a few minutes because of the chance of being exposed; she then ran again down the halls of the school until she saw the gym room door, looked in, and ran in there and quickly under the bleachers to hide, shaking so. Since that day, the only opportunity she's had was to go into the gym teacher's office and steal the rug that was under his meeting table in the office to use as a blanket under the bleachers. That is where she had been for two days. Hiding, hungry, and scared. Trying to think about her next move. While under those bleachers, at night, alone, in that gym, Priscilla used her singing voice to soothe herself. Afraid and alone, just as she had come into the world as an infant, she sang songs to herself to get through the night. Thinking, should she go back to Tricia's house and tell. If she should go to the police. She just didn't know what to do. Still in the mind that she doesn't want to ruin Tricia's life, and change the way Tricia feels about Roy, even though he was evil.

She had to make a move now. After the gym class disperses and the teacher shuts it down for the days' summer session, she waits for him to exit the office and the gym to make her move. He finally leaves, she appears from behind the bleachers to make the move. Goes into his office creeping in, and then trying to search through his desk drawers for some sort of snack or anything. Just as she is rummaging through his desk drawer, she hears a noise. He's coming back!! Now she is locked in his office and is sure to be caught! She looks up toward the ceiling, too high for her reach. She sees the furnace return gate on the wall ajar. That's the ticket! But when she goes to pull on it to try and hide in the return chamber, she notices that it is only ajar because one of the screws is missing, and the other three screws are secure. What now!! Mr. Coleman is right at the office door! She looks around the room, quickly determining that she had run out of options for hiding. Her mind switched to the realization that she will be marched right back to Tricia and Roy. And will have to decide to tell on Roy or be quiet and risk being abused. Her heart is pounding! He grabs the door handle. She began to cry. He twists the knob! She is sweating from the brow and now balled up in the corner of the office by the wall. He enters the office. Priscilla shaking uncontrollably... The door opens and Mr. Coleman walks into the office. "What did I do with those car keys!?" As he looked around the office. Priscilla, in her last-minute hiding spot under the meeting table in his office, now sitting balled up clinching her knees with her back to the mid-post that supported the table, trying to be as quiet as she possibly can, while Mr. Coleman was looking for his keys. Suddenly, Priscilla inadvertently bumps her leg on the chair that she pulled up close to her under the table. Looking over his shoulder from hearing the bump, Mr. Coleman suddenly began to try and figure out where the thump came from. Canvasing the office, he looks at each corner, and then walks over to the window and parts the mini blinds to look out into the gym; quickly determining that the noise had to come from outside of the office since he didn't see anything in the office with him. As Priscilla continued to stay hidden under the table, he turns back to his desk and sees that his keys have fallen on the floor next to his chair. "Shit! I dropped them on the floor!" Mr. Coleman let out a giggle to himself. *"Shoot!"* As he began to crouch down onto the floor, bracing his knees as he grabbed the edge of the desk. He reaches the floor and slips a bit and almost falls but catches himself as he reaches for the car keys. Priscilla is under the table across from his desk and is looking him right in his eyes as he grabs the keys. In her fright, she feels that he sees her. She was almost compelled to jump up and run out of the office to escape because she knew she had been caught. But she remained seated under the table as Mr. Coleman grapples to raise back up to his feet. Even though it seemed like they locked eyes; the scared person always feels they've been caught was the case. Suddenly, the office light is turned off and Mr. Coleman leaves the office, and the lock engages as Priscilla exhales.

As the entire neighborhood is on alert looking for her, Priscilla finds some clothes in the gym and a hooded sweatshirt and sneaks to the lunchroom tiptoeing around the school past the cleaning crew and other summer staff. In the lunchroom, she finds the stack of bagged prepared lunches for the summer program. She grabs two of the bags; carefully verifying that the two she grabbed contained peanut butter and jelly sandwiches. Thinking ahead as she knew that she didn't know what was to come in the days ahead. Stuffing the bags into the hooded sweatshirt pockets and scurrying back out of the lunchroom, she knew she had to decide on her next move. Making her way down the hall, looking for another room to hide in, and sleep overnight before she tried to continue her new journey of being alone; being independent, by circumstance. She found the science lab, looked into the door, and noticed that there was a supply closet in that lab. It Seemed like the right place to hide out and eat a sandwich and relax. Looking around before grabbing the science lab door, she quickly went into the lab. As she walked past the Bunsen burners and science equipment, she is intrigued by everything as she made her way to the supply closet. Priscilla entered the supply closet and looked around to make sure there is a spot for her to get low and hide and rest. She saw that there was a spot in-between the last two shelving units in the back of the closet. Boom! That's where she'll be for the night. Priscilla crouched down onto the floor to try and get comfortable in her new temporary habitat. Then she heard some laughter and a door slam! Oh No!!! The lab had visitors. Now what?

"So, as I said earlier; I would like to have the display set up right here in the front of the room." The voice led with instructions as two burly men walked into the lab. The directions came from a woman's voice; must have been the science teacher. "Perfect! Perfect! We will be set up nicely for getting ready for our summer fair!" The woman's voice continued to talk as loud thumps progressed as the two men carried in tables and pieces of furniture and set them up in the front of the lab. "Thank you, thank you!" The science teacher continued as the men worked. "Back there in the lab storage; that's where you'll find any tools you might need for the setup. I'll be right back. I need to go get some of my bags from my car!"

With a short reply as he sat down a large end of a display case; one of the burly men said, "No problem ma'am! We'll check in there to see what we can find!"

Once again, Priscilla seemed to be cooked! The men were coming toward the door, and she was in the back of the supply room, but how could they not see her? She had to try and figure out yet another escape! As the first burly man opens the door to the supply room, he is fumbling with the wall, trying to locate the light switch. Priscilla is still in a mid-hide, trying to find a coverage spot to not be seen. The first switch that the man flipped turned on a fan in the supply room; subsequently buying Priscilla a few seconds. By now, she was thinking that she'd just make a run for it once the two men entered the supply room since the lights were off. Just as the man finally found the light switch and began to gaze around the room, his eyes fixed immediately onto the back of the supply room where Priscilla was sitting in between the last two shelving units. But she wasn't there! He made his way down the aisle and quickly found a hammer and turned to make his way back out to the lab as the other man had continued to set up the displays.

"I found some tools buddy."

The other man replied, "Alright. Let's hurry up and get this done. I'm ready to go to a bar."

Both men belted out laughter as they continued to work. As they did, Priscilla started to climb down from the top of the shelving unit that she had crept up so slowly in the dark as the man fumbled with the light switch. Like a spider, Priscilla had climbed up the unit and lay flat on her stomach quietly while he looked around for tools. Trapped again! Priscilla decides that maybe the school is not the place to hide out anymore. Since the man left the supply room door open as he walked away, and the science lab room door was propped open by the teacher while she went back to her car, Priscilla saw an opportunity to run again. Just as the two men began trying to set up a display cabinet and securing it to the wall, she jetted towards the lab main door. The wind from her scamper made a few papers lift off of one of the tables and it caught the attention of the men, but they were busy trying to maintain their balance of the display case and couldn't fully turn around to see what had made the papers fly. She entered the hallway and ran to the right down the hall. Just as the science teacher was turning right into the hall that the science lab door was, she just barely missed the dash of Priscilla running away from the class. The teacher dropped a bag of items she grabbed from the car trunk. Priscilla had managed to get away again. But in the back of her mind, she could not help but think that perhaps she should not be running from these people. Maybe she should be letting these people help her. Because they hadn't done anything to her. Never-the-less; she ran again. Not knowing where she was headed this time; she still ran as fast as she could to get away from the school. As the science teacher entered the science lab, she noticed a wrapped muffin laying at the entrance of the room floor. As she kneeled to pick it up, she looked at it and knew that it was from one of the school summer lunch bags; but knew that she hadn't seen it before leaving out of the lab just a few minutes before.

"Did any students happen to come in here?" She inquired to the two men working on the other side of the room. Both men looked at her bewildered as they continued to work on the display case, and she looked around the room, went towards the supply closet as well, didn't see anything else unusual, and carried on with her planning.

Priscilla managed to get out of the school unscathed and into the alleys again. She walked hurriedly and wondered all around the town; she just didn't know what to do! Didn't know what her next move would be. While walking and ducking in and out of alleys and people's yards and business docks she migrates to the bus station in town because she knows it is always open. She remembers this because she was reminded of the times when her aunt would talk about the late-night bus rides her mom and Tricia would have to take out of town for funerals or weddings when they were growing up. At this point, she figures she can hide there, scavenge some food, use the bathroom, and not feel out of place like the school, because there are always people at the bus station. She knew that people may not question her being there. Just take her as a girl who is there with her parents waiting on their bus to depart. On the precipice of her 16th birthday, she knew that she was just about at the age where some people may question her being in a bus station alone, and some people wouldn't question it at all. After scoping out the station, where all the drivers and managers were; she headed into the cafe area to see what she could find. By now, the two lunch bags she had stolen from the high school lunchroom were all mushed-up from the activity of her trying to get away from the school. As she entered the café area of the station; she sat at a bench and pulled out the bag that managed to remain in the hooded jacket pocket. Mangled from the run; all that remained was a smashed peanut butter and jelly sandwich, barely recognizable. She instantly saw that someone had left a tray with an apple and a juice box on the table across from her in the row. She swiftly got up from the table and grabbed both the apple and the juice and kept walking toward the bathrooms of the bus station and dived into a stall, locked the stall and put the seat cover down on the stool to sit and reluctantly eat the apple and drink the juice in the stall. As she sat in the stall uncomfortably, hour by hour, different women come in and out of the bathroom to do their business. Sometimes leaving behind smells that she only thought were possible from men! The cleaning lady would tug at the door, not knowing she was in the stall and it startled her; but she didn't leave the stall. As she sat and sat, she began to doze off and put her legs up on the seat to use her knees as a pillow while she slept. The next morning, she wanted to get out and walk around the station to stretch her legs. Just as she was about to get up and unlock the stall door to come out, she heard a commotion of a mother and daughter arguing with each other.

"Hurry up! So, I can let the driver know that you're going to be coming to the bus before it leaves!"

Another voice replied, "Whatever!" Priscilla heard the back and forth of this mother and her daughter.

"My stomach is hurting!" the girl replied to her mother as Priscilla stayed standing in the stall and not emerging just yet. As not to interrupt their spat.

Then the mother yells again, "You know I have to be at work in an hour! Hurry up!"

The girl's voice replied with disrespect again to her mother. "You can just leave like you always do! I know how to get on the bus! Like I always do when you send me off to Dad so you can be with all your boyfriends!"

Angrily replying, the mother yelled at the girl, "Listen to me Dammit! You are just like your no-good father! I'm going out to let the bus driver know you'll be out shortly! You better not miss that bus! I'm leaving for work after that! Have fun with your father!"

With another disrespectful reply, the girl came back with, "I'll make it on the bus! Just like I always do! Don't I?!"

As the mother began to exit the bathroom angrily, she gave one last reply to her disrespectful daughter, "You ungrateful little twirp! Who bought your bus ticket? I'm leaving your bag here on the counter right here in front of the stall you're in. Everything you need is in the bag! Enjoy the rest of the summer!"

The mother stomped away from the stall and exited the bathroom. At the same time, the girl flushed the toilet to drown out her mother's last rebuttal. Priscilla quietly unlocks her stall door and eases out of the stall and walks over to the sink in front of the stall that the girl that was arguing with her mother was occupied. Priscilla turned on the water and began to wash her hands. As she does so, she is scoping the bag left behind by the mother. Seems that even though the girl was disrespectful to her mother; her stomach must have been upset, as she was in the stall groaning from obvious stomach pain as she did her business. Priscilla continued to scope the bag to the left of her on the counter and noticed some cash and a ticket sticking out of the front pocket of the bag. Thinking to herself that she needed some cash to figure out her next moves; it was too tempting. She turned on the water faucet to the highest level to make more noise, and then gently pulled on the envelope sticking out of the front pocket of the bag. As she pulled slowly, she peeked over her right shoulder to make sure the girl was still using the bathroom. She noticed the envelope had two twenty-dollar bills and a bus ticket. The bus ticket; as she continued to pull on it and finally deciding to take the envelope and make her escape out of the bathroom, read:

Chicago/10:20AM/#321

Journey

Now that Priscilla had stolen the bus ticket and the money; she knew she needed to get away from the bathroom as fast as possible, to make sure the girl didn't come out and find that the bag had been tampered with and the ticket was gone. Priscilla entered the Great Hall of the bus station and was trying to get away with the money. Thinking that she'll have to find a new place to hide out since the bus station would soon become a place where everyone was looking for some stolen money. She looked up at the huge clock on the wall of the bus station in the Great Hall and noticed something! The huge clock, fancy and made from brass read 10:09 am. Suddenly, an idea came into Priscilla's head that had not even crossed her mind in the day and a half that she had spent hiding out at this bus station thinking of where in town she would go and hide next. Why did her next hiding spot have to be in town? She instantly turns and heads toward the bus terminal; now walking at a pace that was almost running; knowing she had a small chance to pull this newfangled plan off. As she scurried through the great hall and into the bus terminal, she slightly looked at the envelope in her left hooded jacket pocket at the bus ticket again, making sure not to catch any attention or stop moving while doing so. She noticed a name on the ticket,

Angela Anderson while reading the top of the ticket again and then looking up to verify as she continued towards all of the buses in the terminal. While looking for the bus number, she was also getting nervous about the name on the ticket, knowing she would have to prove she was Angela. The number, 321, She kept repeating in her head. 321! Then, in the corner of her eye, she sees it! Bus #321. Quickly, Priscilla hops in the line of people slowly inching along to board the bus. As each person gets to the front of the line; they all, in what seems to be one motion, hand the driver the ticket to verify with one hand, hand the porter their suitcase or bag with the other, places one foot on the first step of the bus, waits for the okay, then enters the bus, step-by-step and vanishes onto the bus. She wanted to take note and do the same as to not seem nervous or suspicious. As she finally gets up to the front of the line, she fakes like she is the other girl who was arguing with her mother in the bathroom a few minutes earlier. The bus driver looks her up and down with some doubt on his face. Now she knows she's exposed! How would she pull this off? What should she say to fool him? Just as she was about to formulate some off-the-wall lie to get on the bus, the driver began to speak to her. "You must be the girl whose momma just came and told me you were in the bathroom and not to leave you behind, Angela?" Priscilla, eyes wide open, in shock now, as she was scared to death, just shook her head up and down in agreeance with the driver. "Lucky you got here on time!" the bus driver continued. "I would have hated for your ticket to be wasted, young lady!" Again, in disbelief that something was going her way, Priscilla nodded again with the driver and placed her foot on the first step of the bus. The driver punched the ticket and went to hand it back to her. "I get it! You're scared to ride by yourself. You'll be fine. There are some other kids on here too. Gone on ahead." Onto the greyhound to Chicago, she was headed. In disbelief that the driver didn't fully verify she was Angela, him just trusting that he was told a girl was coming soon.

As she walked down the bus aisle looking for a spot to sit, she passed some weird-looking people, some old people, and some folks that plain looked at her like she was a criminal for her black skin! Then, just as she was about to head to the very last seat next to the toilet at the back of the bus; she heard a voice. "You don't want to sit next to the shit hole! You'll regret it!" A young girl, about her age, possibly a little older, very light complexion, beautiful thick long wavy dark hair, and full lips and eyebrows, got up from her seat and stepped in front of her into the aisle and held her hand out as to offer up the window seat next to her. Priscilla again, with shock in her face, not believing that she was about to pull this off, quietly said, "Thanks!" and slid into the seat next to the window. As she sat down, she noticed a commotion outside of the bus. It was the girl from the stall arguing with the security and the manager. Priscilla's heart dropped again! This is it! She knew she'd soon be getting escorted off of the bus! As the girl was outside the bus explaining to the manager that she should be on the bus and that someone on the bus must have stolen her ticket; the driver glanced at everyone in the rearview mirror and seemed to look directly into Priscilla's eyes only. Knowing he was about to tell her to get up and come to the front of the bus; Priscilla started to lift just as the driver began to speak. "Everyone please ignore the craziness outside the bus, settle in, and get comfortable as possible. We have a long road to Chicago. I'll try to make it as enjoyable as possible!" Then the bus began to move slowly in reverse just as the girl next to Priscilla grabbed her wrist as Priscilla was raising since she thought she was caught. "You okay?" The girl said to her. As the bus continued to maneuver to position to leave the bus station, and the girl outside the bus got more and more rambunctious with security and the manager, Priscilla realized she had pulled it off! She looked at the girl in the next seat as she began to lower her butt back down into the seat and just shook her head yes. In disbelief of everything that just happened to her. Everything that just happened to her not only today! But the last week or so. Did Priscilla just manage to leave all of her troubles behind? Without breaking up Tricia and Roy? It seemed so! It seemed so!

"I'm sorry for grabbing you! Just didn't want you to fall as the bus started to move." The girl next to Priscilla said as the bus finally departed the terminal and it looked like Priscilla was driven away from her fears.

Priscilla replied to the girl as she continued to adjust how she sat in the window seat. "No, no. It's my fault! I was just looking at what was happening outside the bus."

Looking at Priscilla with a suspicious look, the girl just nodded and replied, "Oh... Okay." About fifteen minutes passed as the bus got out of town and onto the highway. All the while, the girl sitting next to Priscilla kept looking at her, then looking away and observing the entire bus. As if she was waiting for Priscilla to strike up a conversation. The girl didn't want to probe, given the first encounter with Priscilla was awkward, to say the least. But she knew that she'll be spending the next 12-15 hours next to this strange girl and knew she would eventually need to talk to her, or at least she thought so. While the girl tried to figure out how to make an introduction and strike up some sort of conversation with her; Priscilla was leaning her head on the window and gazing out into the view of the bus passing fields, trees, and towns. As she sat there on the bus surrounded by all these strangers, Priscilla zoned out and placed herself back on the back window stoop at Tricia's house. While the bus zipped past all of the scenery Priscilla was able to mentally take snapshots of each tree that they drove by. Oddly, she was locked in on those trees, and just like back at home, she was able to look at the birds that enveloped every tree along the highway. Seemed impossible to do; but at this point, after everything she had been through this week, it seemed as if the same birds were following her from the neighbor's tree and were keeping her path safe. Again, just like back at home, or at least in Priscilla's mind, this wasn't just a couple of birds. Each tree she framed housed hundreds of birds, just like the neighbor's tree. Though Priscilla could not hear outside of the bus; the birds were singing, to her. Just like being back home sitting on the window stoop; in her mind, she heard those birds singing as they zipped by on the highway in this bus. Perhaps this was therapy for her to absorb the previous adventure and encounters and still stay sane and calm surrounded by all of these strangers. Priscilla used the mental sight of seeing the birds in the trees and the imaginative implementation of the sound of those birds singing as soothing, just like home. At least what used to be home. Home now was unknown to Priscilla. Ahead was the path, and she didn't know where it would end. Only that right now, the path was headed to Chicago. Priscilla began to dose in and out; yet as she did, she thought deeply to herself and vowed to never run again. Make everyone pay! Thinking about Tricia telling her how her dad removed obstacles. Of course, Priscilla had initially interpreted what Tricia was saying back then wrong. But with what Roy tried to do, and Tricia not acknowledging the type of person Roy was; Priscilla decided from this point on; she would make sure she would never be used and will remove any obstacles in her way.

Back in Baltimore, the search had not stopped! Everyone that knew her was trying to find her. "Lord! If there is any way you can give me a sign. A sign to let me know that my baby is okay. Bring her back to me, please God! Please!" Tricia shedding tears as she sat on the front porch crying and praying for the return of Priscilla. For days, the entire neighborhood had been looking for Priscilla. The police kept getting what seemed to be promising leads, but nothing ever fully materialized. Such as the deli owner in town telling the police that he was sure he saw her running in the alley when he emptied his garbage. Or some landscapers telling Tricia that they think they saw her near the high school a few days ago. Every time Tricia got some news, or the police gave an update to her; Tricia would go to those locations and look for Priscilla, just like she was a detective. With Roy in tow every time. They exhausted almost every measure looking for Priscilla. What was there left to do? But let the police do their job. That seemed to be lacking in reliability at this point. Placing his hands on her shoulders as she cried, Roy sat next to her on the porch and tried to console her, as he did every day now.

"Baby, we are going to find her. We're not going to give up." Roy said, trying to give Tricia some type of encouragement.

Tricia began to blame herself as she had been doing daily. "It's my fault! It's all my fault!"

Roy cut Tricia off in her self-blame. "No! Stop that!"

Roy was there for her, but in his mind, he knew why Priscilla was gone. He knew what happened that day she disappeared. But still pretended to act like he was trying hard to find Priscilla just like everyone else. Tricia suddenly perked up from her slouched crying session and turned to Roy with a look in her eyes that resembled evil. Out of nowhere, she went off.

"You're right! You are fucking right!" Now ripping Roy's hands off of her shoulders. "How in the fuck did you not see the guy?" At this point, she began to stand up. "How in the fuck can you stand your stupid ass in the front yard and let a big ass teen girl just fucking get taken right under your idiot ass nose? You asshole!" By now, Tricia was standing up, two steps below Roy, screaming and yelling, and wildly throwing open-handed punches at his chest as she cursed him out, blaming him for not catching the person that took Priscilla. Neighbors and walkers-by started to stop and rush toward the two of them to try and get control of Tricia. John and a few other women neighbors tried to hold Tricia down as Roy moved out of the way of the flurry of anger that Tricia expelled.

As they slowly got control of Tricia, the whole episode was a huge outlet of raw emotion from the buildup of Priscilla becoming missing, them all searching for Priscilla, and Tricia trying to keep a steady head as each day added up with Priscilla missing. Seemed very normal for a mother to breakdown and act up in fury for their missing child and blame the last person that was close to that child. Everyone that was there and trying to calm her, knew in their minds that this was a perfectly normal response to the stress of the days prior. But the sad reality that no one but Roy knew was that he was guilty of the whole thing and hiding it. So, Tricia was more than justified in flailing and lashing out at him with blame; but for now, he would continue to get away with being able to push this incident off as Tricia just being overwhelmed with emotions. Roy yelled out, "Baby!" "Baby!" Roy was able to get into the group and embrace Tricia on the ground after the neighbors detached her from swinging on him. "I understand baby! You're hurting! We're all hurting!" Tricia snapped out of her rage and looked at Roy in his eyes, and just slumped over whining in his lap. Emptied of all of her energy, nothing left, she just laid there in his lap as John and the other two women neighbors rubbed her back to pacify her with Roy holding her head on his lap. They all just sat there on the sidewalk in front of the steps for minutes. Roy, staring off afar as he rubbed her head, thinking to himself that he was close to being found out, and not knowing how he could keep hiding this secret.

On the bus, Priscilla's view came into focus as she looked down at the tray in front of her attached to the seat ahead. A Thermus cup of hot coffee was sitting there. The aroma is what caught her attention from her slumber that she had dozed off into while observing the birds in the trees that the bus passed early in the trip. Now, deep into the highway and country, Priscilla finally awoke to this thermal cup of coffee and looked over to her seat partner to see her looking at her and smiling. The girl next to her spoke, "Fabiola!" Priscilla looked at her confused, then looked at the cup of coffee, back at the girl, then out of the window of the bus, and back at the girl. "Everyone calls me Fabi!" Priscilla nodding her head in agreement to the girl's sudden introduction, but not speaking. Fabi, a girl of Mexican descent, about Priscilla's age or just a bit older was sitting there trying to make a new friend. Taking it to the next level to introduce herself to Priscilla to further the extension of making her comfortable on this long bus ride. While trying to gather herself from the nap, Priscilla reaches down to the thermal cup and cradles it to lift it to her nose and take a big sniff. She gets a whiff of the strong black coffee smell infused with milk and sugar to awaken her senses. She then takes a sip and sits back into the seat more comfortably. Fabi then reaches in her bag, which seems to be packed with all the essentials for the trip and takes out some butter cookies wrapped in a napkin, removes two from the napkin, and extends her hand to Priscilla to offer them up as a companion to the coffee she just gave Priscilla. Priscilla took the cookies from Fabi's hand as the two girls made contact in the exchange, further confirming the comfort level between the two. Fabi began to engage in a conversation.

"I get it. You're all by yourself. First bus ride. Normal to stay to yourself." Fabi went on to allow Priscilla's actions. As she crunched on the corner of a cookie after placing one down on the tray in front of her, then sipping a bit more coffee, she cleared her mouth.

"I'm Priscilla." Finally coming to the certain reality that this girl, this new stranger was going out of her way to make her comfortable and welcome. "Thank... Thank you, Fabi." As Priscilla continued to nibble on the cookies and sip the coffee and try to prepare herself to talk to the girl.

Fabi started first as she allowed Priscilla to finish eating. "I'm from Chicago. I was just here to help one of my aunts take care of her husband for part of the summer. He is sick. So, my Abuela sent me here on the bus after school let out for summer to help. He's not doing better, but I have to go back now."

Finally finishing the impromptu breakfast; Priscilla wiped her mouth with her sleeve and began to respond to Fabi. "I'm sorry, I have just been through quite a bit lately, and I'm here just trying to go and visit my uncle in Chicago." Priscilla, thinking quickly and deciding not to be honest with Fabi just yet; thought swiftly on her feet to lie about going to visit an uncle. Priscilla remembers Tricia talking about spending some time in Chicago with her uncle, so she thought she would use this story to let Fabi feel ensured that she was on this bus with a purpose and not just freelancing as a passenger who stole a ticket and pirated a seat. Priscilla still didn't know who to trust, so lying right now was the only option, even though Fabi seemed to be cool.

Fabi replied, "Oh, okay; I see. Well, here we are, both in the middle of trips to visit an uncle, for different reasons. Your uncle isn't sick? Is he?"

Priscilla replied. "No, just visiting him."

Fabi went on after her reply. "I see." As the talker, she was making it a bit easy for Priscilla to engage since she had to do minimal talking. "I wish I could stay in Baltimore longer. But my Abuela wants me back because my cousin is not reliable. He's always out all night and all day, so my Abuela needs me back. You know, Chicago is rough, with a lot going on. I know my cousin is a part of that. Do you know what I mean? The 'lot' going on in the city?" Priscilla kept nodding in agreement, even though she didn't get what Fabi was saying. "I'm sorry; I'm talking too much." Fabi said after going on a few minutes rant about back home in Chicago.

Priscilla said in response to Fabi's apology for talking too much. "No, no; it's fine to talk about home, you can tell me more. There is so much I can tell you about back home in Baltimore too." Priscilla gives up as an offering to Fabi to allow a level playing field in this new – unlikely friendship. As the bus drove on, the hours flew by and they made a couple of stops, and the two girls exchanged more and more information about each other. With Priscilla finally opening up and telling Fabi more about herself, about Tricia, about their neighborhood. But stopping short to mention anything about Roy and what happened in the previous days that led up to this bus ride. Fabi; the talkative one; let Priscilla know more and more about her and Chicago and everything. As they sat on a bench at one of the bus stops while people went to the bathroom and the bus fueled back up; Fabi even went into talking and telling more about her cousin, many people suspected he was a big-time drug dealer with a crew. Fabi mentioned that her cousin; Christopher was a pretty powerful individual in the streets up north. "Yeah, my cousin is a boss!" Fabi kind of bragged. "Everyone in the city knows not to mess with him!" Priscilla was very intrigued by all of this drug talk that Fabi was revealing. She had heard about the drugs and how they affected the neighborhoods in Baltimore but was never exposed. Fabi went on as they noticed that the passengers were beginning to re-board the bus for the last leg of the trip. Fabi said, "Can I tell you a secret?" Priscilla opened her eyes wide as the two girls waited in line to get back on the bus, but then nodded in agreement. As the two of them sat back down and the bus began to close up and pull off. Fabi went on. "So, my cousin is trying to find out who killed his brother Angel." Priscilla, now looking intrigued and surprised by the amount of sharing by Fabi. Fabi goes on, "He's so obsessed that matter of fact, the apartment that his brother was killed in, my cousin won't allow it to be rented until his brother's killer is found and he's avenged!" At this point, Fabi realizes that she may have said too much. She finally stops for a few minutes to allow Priscilla to talk. "I'm sorry; did I say too much?" Fabi asks Priscilla.

Priscilla said in response to let Fabi know that she would keep the secrets and that she was not thrown off so much by the talk. "No, No, No; it's okay!"

Relieved and convinced, Fabi said with a bit of a chuckle, "Okay! I just don't want to chase you away my new friend!"

Priscilla responds as she places her hand on the back of Fabi's hand, "Trust me Fabi. I have seen a lot lately. I'm not afraid of what's to come."

Both the girls chuckle in their reality of acknowledging that they both have been grown up far too fast! Yet they go on talking as the bus drives on. Fabi goes on to tell Priscilla more about her cousin; telling her about how he goes to the apartment his brother was killed in a lot to morn. "Weird," Fabi said as she told the stories. She said, "They heard my cousin put up a fight, but got choked out. The police of course haven't found the murderer." Fabi goes on, "They don't care! One less drug dealer, I suppose." She continued to feed Priscilla information about it, "They think it's the other crew up north, maybe over jealousy of money. But the police claim that they have a tip that it could have been a southside group of money movers, but that crew doesn't have a motive." The depth of information that Fabi knew was astounding! That she was sharing it with Priscilla was even more impressive and unbelievable. "Besides, the south side crew; they do business with my cousin all the time." Fabi, not realizing how much she was sharing with Priscilla, just repeating hearsay from her cousin and rumors. She was telling Priscilla that her cousin is the south side crew's connection to drugs, so they wouldn't be stupid enough to mess up their money. But her cousin will without question kill whoever he finds out did it. Priscilla is blown away by this talk. But she plays along as if it is no big deal to her as Fabi told it all on the remainder of the trip. The rival north side crew blames the crew from out south's leader – believed to be a pimp who is an awkward dresser, they call him Ricky. He wears a huge earring lined with diamonds. But her cousin just doesn't believe it's that crew that is responsible for his brother Angel's death. When Priscilla can finally get some words in edgewise; she asks Fabi about the location of Madison in Chicago; trying to figure out where her uncle lives in the city.

"Fabi, do you know where Madison is in Chicago?"

Fabi looks at Priscilla and responds, "You mean the street, right? I think I can tell you how to get to that street."

Priscilla responds to Fabi, "No, no; it's a town, my aunt always talked about a town called Madison where my uncle lives, it's by or in Chicago."

Fabi answers. "To be honest, I'm not sure. There is a Madison in Wisconsin as a town, but I never heard of a town called that in Chicago. Just a street." Fabi finishes trying to help Priscilla figure it out and offers up; "We can ask my cousin if you want when we get there."

Big City Dreaming

The bus pulled into the downtown Chicago station, the girls prepare to part ways in this new friendship. They depart the bus and promise to stay connected. Fabi handed a torn piece of paper over to Priscilla as they exit the bus together. "Here is the number and address to my Abuela's house." As they arrive at the front of the bus station, Fabi is anxiously looking for her ride while Priscilla is aimlessly looking around. Fabi probes at Priscilla.

"Your uncle on the way?"

Priscilla lies to not make the situation uncomfortable. "Huh!? Oh! Ummm... Yeah... He Shou..."

As Priscilla tries to finish conjuring up the lie about her uncle arriving soon, Fabi sees her ride, "Primo!" As a brown and tan van pulled up to the curb, Fabi got excited. The driver door opened and a young, handsome man, looking to be in his early twenties, with a beard and a firm face appeared from the van. "Prima! You're back!" Christopher said as he got to the curb and placed one hand on Fabi's bag and used the other to embrace her and half-way lift her up off the curb onto her toes as they hugged, and she kissed him on the cheek.

"Ay Dios Mio! What a long ride!" Fabi proclaimed to her cousin as he put her bag in the back of the van and closed the doors. Priscilla still standing there looking at them interact, was a bit put off by the closeness of these two cousins. For Priscilla hadn't experienced being close to anyone but Tricia. So, to see family act this way was new to her. She just stood there taking it all in. Atop of the experience of witnessing closeness between family, Priscilla was also admiring the handsomeness of Christopher. She was taken aback by his smooth beard and easy eyes and nice build, also his soft tone as he spoke to Fabi to catch up on what she had been doing in Baltimore.

"Who's your friend?" Christopher asked Fabi. Looking Priscilla up and down, quickly sizing up that she was younger than him, much about the age of his cousin.

Fabi explained. "Oh, this is Priscilla, we met on the ride here. Sweet girl." As she grabbed Priscilla's elbow to tell her cousin how nice Priscilla was.

"That's good." Chris said. "Do you need a ride anywhere?" He extended to Priscilla.

"Huh!?" Priscilla standing there gazing at Chris, a bit lost. "Huh; Oh! No, No, my ride should be here real soon."

Fabi, looking around noticing that most cars had already left from picking up the passengers on the bus, and no other cars were starting to approach the station, was a little concerned for her friend.

"You sure girl? We can take you over to your uncle's house if you want."

Priscilla, trying to combat the situation and allow them to go ahead and leave to save herself face, "No, I'm fine. But I thank you for everything."

As she moved in and gave Fabi the biggest hug she could. They embraced for about a minute as Chris began to get back into the van.

"I'll be fine." Priscilla said to Fabi as they embraced on the curb. Thinking in her mind that she survived in her small town for about a week, and how bad could it be here in Chicago?

"Okay. You got the number and the address. Call. Or shit, just come to the house. You see how we are. My Abuela would love you." Smiling and giggling, trying to hold back a tear that was pursing the left eye, Priscilla agreed, shaking her head as they let each other go. Knowing that she hadn't experienced love like what she just saw Fabi and Chris express. In public! Fabi got into the van, and Priscilla began to walk in the opposite direction down the street. While Fabi was getting in the van and closing the door, Chris was turning up the music and at the same time telling Fabi, "You know we have to go and get some of those crazy good donuts down here before we leave downtown. I think it's just a few blocks down there." Pointing down the street in a direction to the right of the van as he put the van in drive and pulled away from the curb.

Here she was. Priscilla, in a strange city. Walking in the downtown area, alone. This is not where she thought she'd be last week. As she walked block by block, looking up at the ridiculousness of the large skyscrapers in this city, much different than the small town in Baltimore she lived. Or at least the neighborhood she stayed in. Sheltered by Tricia in between the 8-block radius of the school, store, home, and church all of her life. This was way different! But alone! That was pressing, as each stranger walked by her and looked her up and down! She didn't know where she was going as she walked. Just aimlessly walking. She remembered she had the forty dollars that she had stolen with the bus ticket and was trying to think of how to best use it and stretch it out while she kept walking and thinking about her next moves. The pit of her stomach was hurting her so bad. So bad with anxiety. She didn't know what she was about to do. She knew she didn't have places she was familiar with to go and duck into like back home. She only saw the strange faces. Some of those faces as they passed her on the street seemed to be looking at her with mischief. Especially some of the older men. After walking about five or six blocks, and maybe some of those in circles, she decided to sit at a bus stop to gather her thoughts instead of walking aimlessly. Should she go back to the bus station? Use the forty to buy another ticket back to Baltimore? Go back home to Tricia and avoid this strange new predicament she was in? Thinking and thinking she did, as she sat there at the bus stop. As she sat and thought, a few more minutes passed and then suddenly the sun disappeared, and the clouds started to roll in just due east of her. Looked like rain was coming soon! But off in the distance, there was a tree. An empty tree as she first glanced at it and looked away, still trying to plot her next move. Then she turned back toward the direction of the tree she saw, and it seemed as if the same birds were following her from the neighbor's tree to the bus, and now here in Chicago. There they were. Again! Keeping her path safe, just like back at home, or at least in Priscilla's mind, this wasn't just a couple of birds. The tree, now in the distance, here in Chicago just in sight downtown; housed hundreds of birds, just like the neighbor's tree. Again, she stayed glued looking at the tree and got into a daze as if she were using the tree full of birds to guide her next move. As she sat there zoned out staring at the tree, suddenly she could feel a drop or two sparingly begin to hit her face from an angle. The rain from those clouds she saw earlier was slowly approaching the area she sat. As she began to snap out of her daze, she began to look away from the tree and then suddenly focused to see a van parked in front of her, and someone yelling at her as her vision un-blurred from her daydream of the birds in the tree.

"Priscilla!" "Priscilla!" "Priscilla!" After saying it a few times, Fabi jumped out of the van and rushed over to her and grabbed her wrist, and said, "Come on with us! Get in the van." Pushing Priscilla into the side door of the back of the van and getting in behind her and pulling the door closed.

Fabi went on with the questions as Chris drove off. "Why didn't you be honest and say you had nowhere to go!?"

Priscilla, finally fully aware of her surroundings again, looked at Fabi, then looked at Chris as he drove in the rain drizzle, and began to try and lie again. "I was waiting for my uncle, but he never came. I tried calling his number, but no answer. So, I decided to wait for him."

As Chris drove on, he looked at Fabi through the rearview mirror and gave her a look like he knew this girl was lying to them.

Fabi chimed in. "Look Priscilla, you don't have to lie to us. We got you. You can come with us."

Chris intervened. "Hey, we have to ask Abuela first. And I don't know if she'll be down for it. She's nice and all, but lately, it's been tough. So, we'll have to wait before we spring this on Abuela."

Fabi interjected, "So, what do you suggest we do Chris?"

Then Priscilla added to the conversation. "No, no need to take me with you or ask. You can just drop me at another bus station, and I'll find my uncle somehow."

Both Fabi and Chris looked at each other again in the rearview mirror, and both thought about the same plan simultaneously.

"You thinking what I'm thinking?" Fabi said, followed by a response immediately from Chris.

"You thinking what I'm thinking?"

Priscilla parted the conversation as they plotted. "Ummm... I don't know what y'all are thinking, but I'll be fine if you just drop me at the next bus station. I have a little money." Priscilla said with defiance as the two of them planned the next move to take in their new friend from harm in the streets.

"Don't be foolish Priscilla." Fabi went on as Chris drove. "We been driving around downtown for about thirty minutes looking for a donut shop that we just realized has closed. As we were about to turn around and head home, there you were! Still down there, sitting on a bus stop staring off into the sky. No, No. You are not fine, and okay. At least let us help you until you locate your uncle. If you have an uncle here?"

Taking offense to the long rant that Fabi just went on; Priscilla tried to defend herself. "Wait a minute! You don't owe me shit! And I don't owe y'all shit! I know how to look out for myself, and I can find my...."

As Priscilla was trying to defend her independence to both of them, Chris cut her off. "Look! I don't know you at all." With his voice raised and a bit of thunder in it with frustration and some anger by now. "We could have ignored you when we just saw you sitting there. Fabi could have ignored you on that long bus ride. This city is not forgiving. Trust me. You fucking need us. At least until you figure something out. It's clear you're lost dammit!" Fabi and Chris looked at each other again in the rearview mirror, and this time Priscilla even caught his eyes in the mirror as he finished his speech. After that stern talking from Chris, all three of them were silent for the next couple of miles. After the defense that Priscilla was trying to play just before the silence. She finally gave in and stopped all of the lies and just sat back and took in the ride. Chris stopped talking the rest of the way and turned up the music as he drove. Fabi just sat back, next to Priscilla, holding her hand and occasionally looking over at her to get a reaction from Chris chewing her out. Nothing. Priscilla remained quiet and just let it happen. Seems that after weeks of fighting and running, she finally decided to just let it happen. Let something conceivably good happen to her for a change. At least she knew that Fabi was sincere, from the last day she just spent with her, she felt she was sincere. Besides, at this point, Priscilla began to plot in her head that at the very least, Fabi told her all that dirt about her cousin Chris. That he's this big-time drug dealer; she could escape and go to the police and rat Chris out if they tried to do any harm to her. In her mind, though she had surrendered to what could turn out to be a good situation in the interim; she was planning an escape route.

As he passed the light on the corner, Chris pulled to a curb and put the van in park. "I have to go to the store and get Abuela that cornmeal she asked me to get. Do y'all want anything out of the store?" Looking back at both Fabi and Priscilla as he began to exit the van.

They both said in unison as he left the van. "No, nothing!"

Just as he was about to close his door, Chris looked back into the van at Priscilla and said, "We promise we are going to look out for you; okay?!"

Fabi replied as she waved her left hand to shoo him out of the van. "Just go into the store Chris!

You okay now?" Fabi asked Priscilla as they sat.

Priscilla tried to reply to her, "I just, I just…" As tears began to run down her face.

Fabi, now rubbing Priscilla's back, "It's okay. You can let it out."

Priscilla murmurs more, "I just have been through so much. In these… In these…" As Priscilla was trying to hold in her tears and snot, she was losing it emotionally. Just her sitting here thinking that these two strangers were talking of looking out for her! Taking her in! Making sure she was good! It was all too much to accept and realize without getting emotional. Because she kept thinking back to Roy, and how he treated her from day one of meeting her. The situation was just too much to understand and take in. The two girls sat there while Chris was in the store and talked it out until

Priscilla calmed down. After a few minutes, Priscilla did calm a bit and the girls began to giggle and laugh a little. Fabi was good like that. She could get anyone to laugh and turn a bad situation into a reason to be happy.

As they were laughing, Chris jumped back into the van. "I got it!"

Fabi looked at him and quickly replied, "Got what!?"

He replied. "We can set her up in the garage, and let her find her uncle, then she can leave before Abuela even finds out she is there."

Fabi responded, "Okay, but what if Abuela finds her while gardening?

Chris replied. "She won't. Until she finds her uncle, you and I can go and pull the garden in the morning for Abuela and turn on the water. Okay?" Chris's plan seemed to be foolproof. Nodding her head, Fabi agreed, and Chris threw the van into drive and pulled away from the curb.

New Family

Driving and cultivating the plan to hide Priscilla; Chris parks the van in the driveway and Fabi told her to stay in the van until they come back for her. At the same time that they are pulling into park, their grandmother is eager to see Fabi and is hurrying out of the house as fast as she can to come and see her sweet granddaughter. "La Nieta! Fabiolita!" Their grandmother approaches the van as Fabi quickly exits the van to ensure that her Abuela doesn't see Priscilla sitting in the back. Christopher also hops out of the van and comes around the other side of the van as Fabi and her grandmother embrace in the tightest hug imaginable. Christopher wraps his hands around them to join the hug, and also tries to steer them away from the van and toward the house. As they all begin to walk to the house, Priscilla climbs over to the driver's side back row of the van and delicately parts the curtain on the back-van window. Seeing Fabi's and Chris's grandmother gave Priscilla a feeling of wholeness. For some reason, just seeing this lady and her interaction with Fabi, and how she is openly expressing how much she misses Fabi gave Priscilla such a fullness of love in her chest. Not that Tricia did not show Priscilla all the love in the world and take care of her to the fullest extent. Priscilla realized just how much of a burden she may have been on her aunt as she was growing up, smart mouth, sometimes being defiant. She also realized that Aunt Tricia was always so busy with the business of taking care of her. As the three of them: Fabi, Chris and Grandma disappeared into the house, Priscilla sat back on the back row of the van and began to sulk. She was missing Tricia, missing home, missing her friends. Thinking about home. Thinking about being in Church goofing around with her friends. Thinking about the sleepover, the fun part. Trying not to think about when Roy messed everything up. So many things going through her mind. As she sat and cried in the van, she reached into her pocket to find the stamped bus ticket and the forty dollars. Holding the ticket and staring at it; she focused on the top label and the word Baltimore. Just reminiscing and missing her neighborhood. She continued to stare at the ticket and then began to look at the two twenty-dollar bills. Turning them in her hands, she was thinking about running away from Fabi and Chris and going back to the bus station to buy a ticket home. What was stopping her was the fact that she had no idea where she was. Just finding a way back downtown would be half the battle in this plan. As she sat there weighing to run or not, she remembered her vow to herself to never run again. Make everyone pay! She again slipped into thinking about Tricia telling her how her Dad removed obstacles. She lifted her head and decided to not let sadness and longing ruin her. As she sat for what seemed an eternity while Chris and Fabi bought time; she began to think of the incidents that happened with Roy and became infuriated. She began to think about the day when the States Attorney visited Tricia and she stayed in the background eavesdropping. The day when she started to figure out that her father wasn't in a regular accident the night he died. All of these thoughts took over her mind and got her angry. Her mentality turned her ruthless. This young girl was sitting in a stranger's van, plotting, wanting revenge on everyone! Maybe this was just a reaction to the sadness? A reaction to the situation of being lost. She had a new mindset and was not going to cry anymore.

After about an hour, Christopher emerges from the house, hurrying back to the van and the passenger side. As he slid the door open; he found Priscilla sitting, just staring off into space. "Come on. Let's go; we've got to get you into the garage before she notices." Priscilla gets up and grabs his hand to exit the van and follow him up the side of the house away from the van and onto the garage side door. As they scurry, Priscilla couldn't help but notice the rich spread of greens and vegetables that Chris's and Fabi's grandmother had cultivated in the backyard. They enter the garage and Priscilla surveys the building to see what her next couple of days would be. She saw boxes stacked in the back-right corner. There were shelving units in the left-back corner that held plant vases and yard and garden supplies. Right in the middle was a vintage car, a Ford, or a Dodge, partially covered, with the passenger side revealing the front window partly. The entire garage was a bit dusty, but overall, pretty clean for a garage.

"So, this is where I'm supposed to stay?" Priscilla said with a flip-mouth tone.

Chris replied to her comment. "What? You're not serious? Are you?"

Priscilla, getting defiant replied, "I'm just saying. I could just go and find my uncle and have a bed. Have a sink and a toilet."

Chris shot back at her unappreciative comments. "Fuck it! Then go. We're trying to help you!" As he turned away from her to open the side door and extend his arm as if to tell her to go ahead and leave now.

Coming to reality and knowing that she needed to play the long game; she came to her senses. "I apologize. I'm just so tired and have been through so much. I shouldn't have said all of that."

Turning back toward her; Chris looked her up and down and accepts her apology. "Okay, look. We just want to help you find your uncle and get you to where you need to be. Okay."

As Fabi emerged into the garage door, toting a pillow and throw. "You guys alright?"

Chris turns to look at Fabi with a partially upset face and replies; "We're good."

Fabi looked at both of them and said, "Oh, okay, I thought I heard yelling."

Priscilla now replied; "Nah, we good."

Fabi goes on to explain the plan to both of them; "So look, You can sleep on the back seat of the car. Just open the back door and slide in. For the bathroom, the basement door is always open, and there is a bathroom down there, and Abuela never goes in the basement since Poppa died. Sneak in there when you need to but be careful."

Chris started to enter his input on the plan; "I'll bring you food every time we eat. Abuela won't pay attention to me, since she knows I like to eat outside sometimes." They had the plan, now they just needed to tread lightly around grandma until Priscilla figured out her next move.

Fabi asked. "So, how do you plan to locate your uncle? Chris, she says he lives in a town in Chicago called Madison?"

Chris, looking perplexed because he hadn't heard of that either. "Isn't that in Wisconsin?" They all stood there looking at each other trying to figure it out.

Priscilla broke the awkwardness; "Don't worry about it. I'll sneak out and try to search the bus lines to find it. I just appreciate what you are doing for me. I promise I won't stay in your hair for long."

Chris stopped her and offered. "Stay as long as you need."

After a couple of days and nights of hiding out, slipping in and out of the basement to use the bathroom; today was a particularly hot morning and Priscilla was stretched out in the back seat of the car knocked out. Probably getting some of the best rest she ever had. Chris was up from hanging out all night with his crew, and Fabi was still sleeping. For the last couple of days, Chris and Fabi had been doing the morning gardening duties to keep grandma away from the garage. But today, they were slipping. Abuela; humming and singing to herself was out in her straw hat; pulling weeds from the garden and plucking any veggies that were ripe to pull. Now she was looking for some fertilizer to lay in the garden and entered the garage. Walking directly over to the shelving to find what she needed, she didn't even look toward the car. As she reaches up to pull a bag of fertilizer from the middle shelf; a small metal hand shovel fell and hit the garage floor. As the tool banged the floor; it caught Priscilla's attention and woke her from her slumber, Priscilla's foot banged up against the driver's side door from being startled by the tool falling. Grandma got a bit startled as well and placed the bag of fertilizer on the garage floor and turned around to try and figure out where the bang came from. All Priscilla could do was cover her head and her body up and pray that she wasn't found. Abuela walked around the car and looked behind the garage door that she left ajar, thinking that maybe a critter got in. Seeing nothing, she moved over to the side of the garage where the boxes were stacked and looked in between the boxes to find nothing. At this point, she was standing there with her hands on her hips and wondering, and about to just go ahead and move on with her day. Priscilla's right foot slipped off of the leather seat and slightly hit the floor of the car. Not making a huge noise, but another small sound that was enough to allow grandma to hear it. Now Abuela went toward the car, the front, and lifted the car cover on the front driver side to look in. She saw nothing out of the normal. Then grandma went around the entire car and went to the side where the car cover was always partially lifted. The side where Priscilla was entering in and out of the car each day. As Abuela moved the cover a bit to look into the back seat of the car; Priscilla was sweating and shaking in fear; Abuela was shaken by a loud voice.

"Abuelaaaa…" Fabi called out to get her attention. Just as she thought she saw a sheet with a lump in it on the back seat and was about to investigate further, Fabi entered the garage yelling looking for her and she let the sheet go.

"La Nieta! You scared me!" Fabi sees that her grandmother was sneaking around the car, and quickly ran over to her and grabbed her hand.

"Yes, I'm sorry Abuela. I woke up to help you with the garden."

Abuela replied as the both of them turned and Fabi grabbed the fertilizer bag and they exited the garage and Fabi closed the door behind them. "Oh, okay sweetheart." Priscilla breathed a deep sigh of relief and removed the cover from over her head and sat up in the car to look around the garage to see no one. Priscilla knew she needed to do a better job of getting up and out of that garage and finding out her next move. She just didn't know where to start, but she knew this wasn't going to work long-term.

Later that night as they sat to eat dinner; Fabi and Chris were acting extremely nervous due to the incident earlier when Fabi had narrowly got grandma out of the garage before finding Priscilla.

"This dinner is so delicious Abuela." Fabi said as they all enjoyed the dinner grandma prepared, using mostly the vegetables from their garden.

"Yes! Very delicious as usual Abuela." Chris said as he walked past his grandma after grabbing lemonade from the fridge and kissing her on her forehead before placing the lemonade jug on the table and sitting back down.

Grandma, now probing at the dinner table, averting from their normal dinner time chat that usually includes talking about old family stories. "You children have been very quiet ever since you got back from the bus station a couple of days ago."

Fabi then reacts to the questioning from her grandmother. "Huh Abuela?"

Chris tries to jump in and defend their recent demeanors. "I think that Fabi is just tired Abuela. And you know I've been working nights lately, so that's it. We are probably just tired Abuela."

Their grandma looks at both of them and nods in agreement, seeming to bury the immediate controversy of the conversation. Both Fabi and Chris look at each other and notice that they may have diverted the questions from grandma and then they began to laugh and talk about old times, as usual, to finish the family dinner for the night. As they finish up dinner and conversation, the time passed quickly. All the while, Priscilla is in the garage getting hungry and having to pee from being unable to sneak in the basement because grandma was highly active, in and out of the house all day up until dinner. She contemplated sneaking in the basement while they were eating dinner but didn't want to make any noise and alert grandma as they ate. But she was getting desperate while sitting in the back of the car. Fabi and Grandma are now beginning to put away food and cleaning the dinner dishes as they prepare to wrap it up for the night. Chris, sitting at the table, about to get up and help. Fabi is running water in the sink, rinsing dirty dishes. All of a sudden, grandma walks over to Chris where he sits at the table and reaches over his shoulder with a plate of food. The plate is lightly wrapped in a napkin and she places it on the table right in front of him. Chris, with his eyes bulging huge now, looking at the plate grandma just dropped in front of him. Fabi stops in mid-fill of the sink with water and let go of the faucet to turn around and see what the thump on the table was. Chris looks down at the plate, looks up at Abuela, looks back at Fabi. Grandma removes her apron and folds it to place it on the edge of the table and then turns to begin to exit the kitchen. "When both of you finish cleaning the dishes, I've already fixed your friend in the garage a plate of dinner. You can take it out to her, or why not invite her in and let her sleep on the couch. Aye Aye. the back seat of Poppa's old car cannot be as comfortable as the couch. And I would like to meet her tomorrow! Buenas Noches Nietas." Chris and Fabi stayed frozen in disbelief. Fabi was sure that she got grandma out of the garage before seeing Priscilla. And how could she possibly have figured out it was a girl under the cover? Even if she saw the cover. Perplexed they were, to say the least!

As Fabi and Chris finished cleaning the dishes and the kitchen, they stayed so silent and didn't speak a word. Still couldn't believe that Abuela saw her. Now they feel like Abuela knew the whole time, ever since they arrived back from the bus station, and let them carry on with the charade. They finish, Chris grabs the garbage, and they head out to the garage.

"About time! My goodness, I think I'm about to die from hunger today." Priscilla goes on and on as she sat perched on the hood of the car as the two of them enter the garage empty-handed. "Where's dinner? It smelled so good."

Chris began to speak. About that. Grandma knows. She found you." Priscilla jumps down from the hood of the car as if she were about to flee, Chris grabbed her and said, "Calm down, calm down. She told us to let you

173

come into the house to sleep." Chris and Fabi stood there looking relieved as Priscilla was looking shocked.

"Yep." Fabi added in, "Somehow, she knew you were here the whole time, we think."

Priscilla responded as they all stood there. "Wow! Wow!"

Chris waved his hand as he turns to go back to the house and exit the garage. "So, come on."

All three of them in disbelief; they go into the house. Priscilla entered the house and instantly began to look around and observe everything. She looked at pictures on the wall, the décor, she notices a strong-faced man in most of the pictures with Abuela. The beauty of this woman in the pictures that she caught a small glimpse of from hiding inside of the van through the van curtains just days earlier. Priscilla now, saw that this was a gorgeous woman in her prime and once had a handsome husband on her side. There were other pictures; of Fabi as a tiny girl with Chris and another boy. That must be Angel; Chris's brother that Fabi spoke of on the bus ride. He was also as handsome as Chris, looked just like him, but older. Priscilla was just taken aback by the homely safe feeling of their house. Much like how Tricia kept the house back in Baltimore, similar vibe, but more love and softness due to more people being there. She didn't speak any more that night. Matter of fact, none of the three did. Probably due to the shock of being outsmarted by their grandma they were trying to outsmart. It was irony. They prepared the couch for Priscilla for the night and they all retire to go to sleep. The next morning, as Fabi, Chris and Priscilla slept late, there was the smell of breakfast in the air as Abuela prepared a good morning meal. As she set the table, putting the different breakfast dishes on the center of the table, Chris could hear the dishes clanging together and began to wake up. He headed into the kitchen to see his grandmother sitting at the table reading the paper and drinking some coffee. As Chris went to grab a plate to prepare, as usual, next entered Fabi into the kitchen; she peeked in to see her cousin and grandmother in the kitchen and then stopped short to reverse into the living room to go and wake up Priscilla. Walking up to the couch, Fabi saw that Priscilla was already awake and just lying there on the couch.

"Good morning sleepy head!" Fabi said to Priscilla even though she knew Priscilla was already woke.

Stretching and yawning, Priscilla looked up at Fabi and returned the greeting, "Good morning!"

Fabi smiled and said, "I'm sure you can smell the delicious aromas coming from the kitchen. I left you some towels and an extra toothbrush on the bathroom sink. I also picked out some clothes for you out of my closet that you can wear. Looks like we are about the same size. But feel free to grab what you want if you don't like what I picked."

"Thank you!" Priscilla replied as she jumped up from the couch and began to fold her blanket neatly and place it on top of her pillow on the left-hand edge of the couch. As Fabi was leaving to go back into the kitchen, Priscilla stopped her, "Ummm... Which way is the bathroom?" Fabi pointed in the direction of the bathroom down the hall to the left as they both chuckled realizing that Priscilla had only been within these walls for less than 12 hours.

Now sitting at the kitchen table taking in breakfast; Abuela, Fabi, and Chris were all enjoying the food that was prepared as Priscilla finally made her way into the kitchen after freshening up. So shy was she; Priscilla peaked into the kitchen from the hall first before placing one foot into the kitchen and coming in. With her back sitting to the hall in her seat at the kitchen table, and still glancing at the daily newspaper to the left of her breakfast plate, Abuela knew Priscilla was hesitant, "Come on in my dear. I don't bite!" Fabi and Chris looking at Priscilla with the eyes of welcoming and also laughing at their Grandma's sweet comment. "You are very welcome in my home." Abuela went on, "As a friend of my Nietas." Priscilla finally entered fully into the kitchen and reached for the remaining vacant kitchen seat and pulled it slowly from the table and sat at a plate that had already been prepared for her while she was in the bathroom.

"Good morning Ma'am!" Priscilla said immediately upon sitting and looking at Abuela face to face, close up for the first time. Observing grandma's pearl-colored hair with a touch of brown color still there to see. Observing the beauty of her smooth skin and firm cheekbones. Looking so much like the pictures on the wall that Priscilla looked at last night as she entered the home. Priscilla was in awe of the beauty of their grandmother. The small, sweet lady's demeanor made it even easier for Priscilla to get more comfortable in the situation.

"They call me Abuela, but my name is Marisol. I'll accept whichever is more comfortable for you my dear." Abuela said; formally introducing herself to this young stranger in her home.

"Thank you so much for letting me stay the night. I promise, I will be moving on soon, and getting out of your way." Priscilla offered as not to be a burden on Marisol.

"Nonsense. You can stay as long as you like dear. What brings you to Chicago?" Marisol went on to ask as Fabi and Chris just looked on, already knowing Priscilla's story; or believing they knew, yet staying quiet, allowing Abuela to find out for herself, being respectful children in the presence of their beloved Grandma. Priscilla, not ready to reveal to anyone that she is a runaway, stuck to her story that she had told Fabi and Chris.

"I came to visit my uncle, but I am having difficulty locating where he stays. But I'll find him soon! I'm sure." Marisol, looking at Priscilla with apprehension, not fully believing the story, but with wisdom, feeling that this girl had experienced some things, didn't pry. Marisol just nodded her head to the story as acknowledgment and commented here and there as Priscilla talked and gave reason for being in a big city such as Chicago alone at her age.

"Well, until you find him, you have a home." Marisol commented to bring the conversation to a close. "These two. They will help you with anything you need. One condition. She needs to have chores and school. She continued, Christopher. You will take her to the school to see how she can register when summer is over. If for any reason you don't find your uncle." Marisol, knowing the story was a lie that Priscilla presented; instantly went into her mode of the belief that in America, any kid considered a minority needed an education. Especially, the ones under her roof.

"Yes Abuela." Chris replied and nodded. "I'll take her first thing tomorrow morning to see what needs to be done at the school."

Marisol nodded in agreement; "Good, good!" Then, With a smile on her face and reaching out and placing her palm on Priscillas chin; "And you can help these two clean up and garden around here dear."

For Hire?

The next morning, after breakfast and Marisol getting to know Priscilla a bit more; with Priscilla telling as much as she could without revealing the full truth. Chris was looking at his watch telling the time of 15 after 10 am and is ready to go.

"Are you ready?" Chris said to Priscilla. At the same time, Fabi was grabbing her bag to leave as well.

"You can drop me off at the library, right!?" Fabi said to Chris as she grabs the last piece of breakfast meat from the table right as Chris was about to do the same.

"Whatever!" Chris responds in a snippy tone to Fabi.

"You all be careful!" Marisol said to the group as they prepare to exit the house. "And watch out for my new little friend!"

The three of them load up into Chris's van and head down the street. After riding and talking along the way, Chris finally pulls up in front of the library upon his first stop to drop off Fabi. She mocks Chris as she gets out of the van.

"Be back by 1 stupid."

Chris replies snippy as Priscilla laughs at the sibling rivalry the two cousins display. "Whatever!"

As he pulls off and began to drive again, Chris felt it was time to see if he could get some more information out of Priscilla. Especially since she's been so guarded, and he knows that she is not telling everything.

"So, What about your uncle?" Chris leads in his investigative tone.

Priscilla replies, "Huh?" And continues. "What about my uncle?"

Chris responds. "I'm just saying; you've been hanging out with us for a little while now, and you haven't been beating down the streets to find where he lives." In a moment of exposure, Priscilla was left to try and fumble a reply to him.

"I… I just need to try and figure out where this Madison town or suburb, as you all call it is." Chris looking at her in the rearview mirror with suspicion as he drove along.

"You know what I think? I think you need to cut the shit and be real about why you are here in Chicago." Shocked at his forwardness, and honestly getting a little afraid as she realizes that she is alone, in a van, with this guy she's only known for a few days. She tries to keep her cool and not let her nervousness get the best of her.

"What do you mean cut the shit? I told you everything you need to know about me!" Priscilla snaps back with fierce aggression as she attempts to defend her lies. Figuring it'll make Chris back down. "I just need to figure it all out."

Chris, still not believing her story decides not to push any further as he drove, because he had a little more in store for her anyway. In his mind, what comes next would expose the truth or reveal more of the lie. While pulling into a forest preserve park, Chris looks back at Priscilla in the back of the van and began to park in a spot away from anyone. Priscilla asks as Chris finishes parking. "Why are we in the park?" With her clinching the buckle of the seatbelt, the only thing within reach, thinking she would have to try and use it as a weapon somehow. As he parked, her mind could not help but glance back to the day when Roy attacked her and caused her to run and be in this situation. As he parked the van, Chris replies to her and notices how anxious and nervous she is.

"Don't be afraid of me. I have a proposition. An offer. Let's say, a take it or leave it deal."

Clinching the seat belt buckle tighter in her fist, Priscilla replies, "Take it or leave it? I don't know what you are getting at, but I will get out of this van and run and holler and either never come back or get someone's attention." Trying to insist to Chris that she was not about to just sit and take whatever the hell he was about to try and do, Priscilla even balled up her face in an angry expression to try to intimidate him.

"Settle down. Settle down. Listen!" Chris began his offer to Priscilla. "I know that Fabi told you some stuff about me. About my brother, that was killed?" Looking at her for a response of confirmation. Priscilla nodding as she remained ready to do something. "I run a business here. A business that.... Let's just say, a lot of people don't know what I do. Don't know what is involved. I think you can help me with my business."

Looking at him with confusion on her face, Priscilla was a little afraid to respond to him. Just sitting silent, looking at Chris for about a minute, and Chris looking at her for some sort of response, she finally said something back. "A business no one knows about?" with more confusion on her face. "I'm not sure I get what you mean?" Chris looking at her knowing he had her full attention now, goes in with his plan.

"Look, I know that you have no one here, and you don't want to go back to where you came from." He goes on. "I can tell that you ran from something. Something that scared the shit out of you. You are way too young to be here by yourself. And not in a rush to try and locate your family, your uncle. It looks to me that you need to be able to establish yourself here in this city. I can help you do that." Priscilla, looking the most confused and bewildered; yet intrigued by the beginning of his proposition, sits up in her seat to listen, and subconsciously lets the grip of the seatbelt buckle loosen. Still trying to maintain the nonchalant demeanor to his proposal; Priscilla tries her best to downplay the fact that she now wants to hear what he has to say.

"You don't know what you are talking about. I'm not even old enough to live by myself yet." She replied, trying to be smart assed toward him. Chris knew he had her right where he wanted her now.

"Exactly! You are not old enough to live by yourself yet! So, you're going to help me in my business, keep your fucking mouth shut! Make some money to put away while living the good fucking life under my Abuela's roof! Or else!" Saying this to her as he hit the locks button to lock the van doors on her. Fear crept back into her body at the response of his authoritative voice; She tried to stay cool.

"Kee... Keep my fucking mouth shut? Let me out!" Then she yelled! Let me out now!" Chris, now ready to do whatever he needed to do, took off his seatbelt and got up on his seat to face her. He grabbed the back of his seat to act like he would climb over to her and do something.

"Listen Dammit! As I said, you're going to work for me and make some money until you can go on your own, or you can get the fuck out of this van now. Start walking, and get lost, and never contact me, Fabi, or come to my Abuela's house ever again! Your fucking choice! And if you tell anyone about what I'm saying, I'm going to make sure you fucking regret it! You understand me?"

Now shrunk into a ball in her seat as she looked at Chris, who displayed much rage; she just nodded her head and whined as she couldn't keep a teardrop from her eye. Chris backed up from gripping the seat and tried to calm down. As he could see she was so visibly on the verge of a breakdown. Besides, he just saw an opportunity to use her to make some money. And in a sick way, felt he could help her in the interim. "Look, I'm sorry I had to yell at you. I didn't mean to scare you. I just want to help you get your own, that's all. If you're going to stay here in this city, you'll need to be able to have some money and take care of yourself. You can't stay with my Abuela forever. Hell, I don't even plan to do that." Saying all of that, with a lowered tone now, hoping he'd get Priscilla to calm down and listen. He took a chance and sat back down in the driver's seat and hit the unlock button to the van doors. Priscilla, now looking at the back of his head, thinking should she try to do something, or just run, she was just shell shocked and didn't know what to do. "There! You can go. I'm sorry."

Chris said in a very calm tone as he sat there, not looking at her. "The door's unlocked. You can go and live free in the city, or find your way back home, do whatever you want. I won't stop you." Sitting there, still thinking about what she should do, Priscilla was now frozen with an indecisive disposition. She could tell Chris never intended to hurt her in this escapade. She knew his threats were a bluff to scare her into doing what he wanted her to do. But still, she could tell the difference in what Chris just displayed in comparison to how Roy acted the day he attacked her. Priscilla knew there was a difference. Something in her could feel that, ultimately, Chris would never lay a hand on her. But he wanted to get a point across to convince her to work for him. She just didn't know what that work would entail. But did she want to find out? She knew she didn't want to run anymore. And had no intention of trying to find her way back to Baltimore soon. Her uncle, she didn't even know where to start on that. Besides, even though there was an actual uncle that lived in one of the Chicago suburbs, it was an all too convenient story to spew whenever she was pressed to explain why a 16-year-old girl was in Chicago alone. After about fifteen minutes of silence, and the opportunity for her to run away from Chris, with Chris just sitting there patient, she finally gave a response to his offer.

"Okay. I'll do it. But I'm not anyone's prostitute! If that's what you're thinking, you got another…"

Chris cuts her off. "Prostitute!?" Laughing while he replies. "I'm sorry Priscilla, You have to excuse my language, but I make way more money with what I do than selling pussy does! Hahahahaha…" He started to laugh hysterically. "Hahahaha..." Priscilla looking embarrassed for suggesting it now; Chris laid it on even more, "Plus, you don't have much to offer a pimp right now little one!" Priscilla, now turning red with embarrassment, for thinking that Chris wanted to pimp her out, and feeling a little ashamed that he called out that perhaps she was not even equipped to sell herself on the streets; she just looked at him and rolled her eyes and replied,

"What do I have to do then!?"

Chris started the van up and put it in reverse to back out of the parking spot. "Come on, I'll take you to get a sandwich at my favorite spot. Then we'll go and get Fabi. You just be ready to go to work bright and early in the morning, and we can never talk about this conversation we just had. Understood? But, to work for me, you'll have to pretend that you're in school, so Abuela and Fabi don't know. We'll tell them that the school Fabi is in wouldn't accept you, so we had to register you in the next district. This way I'll have to drive you to school all the time, and you can come with me to work for me. Of course, we'll do some weekend jobs too." Priscilla nodded in agreement, half-way looking out of the window out into the forest preserve trees through the cracked van curtain as Chris exited the park. On the ride, she stayed quiet. Chris didn't say anything either. He just proceeded to drive and slightly cranked up the volume on the van radio to play the station hits. As he drove down the street, Chris suddenly stops at a random building and turns the radio down. Priscilla questioned Chris stopping at a different location than what he prior mentioned.

"Why did you stop here? I thought we were going to the sandwich shop?"

Chris just stared at this building. Looking at the second floor. "This is where it happened! This is where they found my brother. Damn!"

As Chris began to get choked up. Here it was, what Fabi had told Priscilla on the bus. Chris couldn't let go. Couldn't let go of what happened to his brother, and where it happened. He sat for another 3 minutes before pulling off. Priscilla was taken aback by this but understood that he was grieving and chose not to question further. While Chris drove on down the road and kept quiet and kept the awkwardness going along the ride, Priscilla started to zone out and pulled the curtain open even more and slid over closer to the window. The birds that use to envelope the tree in the neighbor's yard appeared. This time, flying in unison at what seemed to be right along with the path of the van. She just sat and watched the birds fly as they drove. Steady with the watch of the flight of the flock. Suddenly, the van arrived at the library and parked to await Fabi to emerge from the building. Priscilla still zoned out, though the birds were gone. Chris tried to get her attention.

"Hey! Wake up. Are you going to be okay? Trust me. You have nothing to worry about tomorrow morning! You sure you're going to be able to keep quiet about our discussion?" Chris continues to probe as they wait for Fabi to come out of the library. Priscilla snaps out of her daze and looks up to acknowledge Chris talking to her.

"I'm okay. We'll see what you are talking about tomorrow."

Fabi runs out of the building and up to the van. "Open the door stupid." Fabi said to Chris as she pulled on the door handle trying to get into the van. He unlocks the door; she climbed in and he put the van in drive and began to pull off as she put on her seatbelt.

As they drive, Fabi turns around to Priscilla, "So, did you like the school?"

Priscilla, looking at her, not having the same level of excitement that Fabi carried into the van. "Yeah, it was okay." With absolutely no enthusiasm in her response.

Fabi looked at Chris, then back at Priscilla, and went on with the questioning. "So, are you in? Can you start school when I go back?"

Priscilla, still with no real emotion in her voice. "Yeah, I think I'll be okay."

By now, Fabi is confused and getting a little irritated by the short responses from Priscilla. Looking at Chris again, trying to see if his face would give some clues to what was going on, and what happened between them in the last few hours, but yielding nothing; Fabi just turned back into her seat in the van and reached for the radio dial as she let out her last opinion on the ride back home. "Well, excuse me you two party poopers. Chris stayed quiet and just looked at Fabi with a serious expression, then at Priscilla through the rearview mirror to try and gain confidence that she would keep their secret, and he continued to drive home. Dinner came fast, and the night went by quickly as morning appeared as fast as what seemed to be a blink of an eye. The previous night, Priscilla and Marisol got even closer over dinner as they talked and mainly Marisol told Priscilla old stories about the old days when she grew up and came over to America with her family. Priscilla ended up going to sleep on the couch listening to Marisol tell those stories until Marisol decided to go to bed. But this was morning. Chris was ready to go. Bright and early, outside, at the van after pulling weeds out the garden, waiting for Priscilla to get up and come on. Marisol, up as usual in the early hours; knew that Chris worked hard. Didn't know what he did at work. Figured he did construction. At least that's what Chris sold to his grandmother for as long as he'd been contributing money to the household. Either Marisol didn't know what Chris did for work, or she knew and didn't reveal that she was aware of it. For reasons only she knew.

"Are you taking my friend with you?" Marisol said to her grandson.

Chris replied, "Yes Ma'am! She wants to make some money, so the guys on the sight can use her to help with the clean-up. A good way to make a few dollars and the guys need the help."

Marisol, feeling suspicion, but not allowing her face to show it, simply replied with a confirmation. "I see. Sounds good my boy."

Chris goes back to the van to get in and get ready, as Priscilla heads to the door, and as she walks past Marisol, Marisol hands her a grocery bag with a sandwich and an apple in the bag. So sweet, their grandma was taking a shine to Priscilla and was beginning to look out for her as one of her own. Chris pulled off and they were off on their secret journey. For now, a secret to Priscilla as well.

Orientation

Chris exited the highway, far away from the neighborhood that Abuela's house sat. Long was the drive, about an hour and a half. Priscilla thought she was lost when she first got to Chicago! The drive to this "Job" Chris was about to have her do was so long, she felt like he was about to take her back to Baltimore. After exiting the highway, Chris pulls into a residential neighborhood, then follows the road up to a street that led to a bunch of huge old buildings that looked like factories. All the while, Priscilla is paying attention. Thinking that she needed to remember where they went after the highway exit – 34B. As if she knew where she was. No chance! But she did it anyway. Upon driving closer to those old-looking factory buildings, Chris pulled into the gates to enter the yard of one of the buildings, and then drove to the back and proceeded to park next to a dumpster right by a dock door of one of the buildings. He parked and Priscilla sees a guy standing outside of the building door that was next to the dock door. He was standing there smoking a cigarette and just staring at the van as it was parking. While putting the van in park and turning off the ignition, Chris looked over to Priscilla. "Look, be cool. These guys are not going to do anything to hurt you. Once we show you the job, they'll make sure you're protected

189

and can work. Okay?" Priscilla looking weary of the whole situation just nodded and agreed to what he was saying. Hoping that she would indeed be okay with what was to come. They get out of the van and approach the door. The guy standing there had just finished his cigarette and extinguished the butt. He gave a head nod to Chris and began to look Priscilla up and down. "She's cool. She's with me." Chris said to obtain passage for Priscilla. "This is Vic. He looks out for us, makes sure no one comes around, and tries any funny business." Vic looks at Priscilla again as he turns his head from Chris's explanation of his role. He gives her a nod to indicate her being welcomed into the building. Now they both enter. Upon entering the factory, Priscilla is immediately taken aback. To the left were crates stack as high as she could see. To the right, there were stacks of black duffle bags piled high. Straight away, she saw a few more guys sitting around a table counting money. Off in the distance in the immediate corner to the right were multiple pickup trucks lined in front of the overhead door, looking ready to pull out. There was a set of stairs in the back of the factory that led to an office with blinded windows and a single door. This whole setup was making her feel extremely uncomfortable yet intrigued. As they approach the table, one of the men got up from his seat to greet Chris; walked around the table and embraced him with a huge hug.

"Christopher. Been a while since I've seen you." The man, much older than everyone in the room was short, bald with a greyish beard.

"This is Carlos. He is like a father to me. Grew up with my father and taught us all." Chris explained the role of the older man. Carlos began to talk and ask about

Priscilla as he turned and looked Priscilla right in the eyes. Measuring her up to see if he could detect anything out of the ordinary in the girl.

"And who is this young lady that I get the pleasure to meet?" Chris answered, "This is Priscilla." Then continued. "She is a friend of Fabi. In town, alone, and in need of some cash. So, I figured we could use her to help out on our runs."

Now with his hands in his pockets and walking in a circle around Chris, Priscilla, and the entire table, still looking her up and down, "I see." Carlos said as he began to interject questions to probe at Priscilla. "Sweetie, why are you in this mean city alone? A bit young for that, right?"

Priscilla, looking and trying to prepare an appropriate answer for the elder man. "I am here to find my uncle and help him out when I do find him. But Chris told me that he could get me some work to allow me to make a little money in the meantime."

Carlos, looking at her, having a hard time believing her story replies, "Find your uncle huh? Okay, I hope you do find him. But now let's get down to the business of things and introduce you to the crew. Your new job!"

Carlos walks back to his seat at the table and as he sat down, he began to go round the table. "This is David; he's my best driver." David was about the same build and height as Chris, just a lighter skin tone, looked as if he was more of Filipino descent. Carlos turns his head to the right and points to Andre, "This here is Andre; he is the money man." Andre, a heavy-set black guy with a raggedy mustache and beard was standing there looking at Priscilla with a stupid grin on his face as he's introduced. Carlos, now turning back to the left and looking over at George; a tall skinny fellow, Mexican with a skull cap on in the summer for some reason. "George is the eyes and the product man. He makes sure we always have enough product available for distribution. I assume you met Vic outside. He's the enforcer for us. Extra protection you could say." Now standing there getting the full run of the crew, Priscilla was, even more, intrigued, but also growing nervous about the word "Product" that Carlos just mentioned. She was eager to find out what this product was, and what her role in this new job would be. It was killing her at this point. Carlos, now done with the introductions stands back up and addresses them all, "Let's get the day started! Chris, come to the office with me. Young lady, why don't you go with David and Andre to do a run to see what your new job will be." Chris looking at Carlos weary, but not questioning his instructions, gives Priscilla the look of it being okay, as he also looks at Carlos to get confirmation that she'll be safe with the guys. Carlos nods at Chris and they turn to head up to the office to talk as David and Andre begin to fill and throw a duffle bag onto the back of one of the pickup trucks as Priscilla stood there watching. While the two guys loaded the truck, George began to count the money on the table. Everything that just happened was so much for a young girl to take in. She knew that this job and operation wasn't on the straight up and up. But she still didn't know what she was getting into, or her role yet. She just knew that she trusted Chris by now and that even Carlos, mysterious as he was, did not seem harmful. Nor did the rest of the guys. Praying to herself in her mind; she was hoping that none of this would be illegal. Though the huge stacks of money on the table said otherwise. However, she was determined to find out what this operation was. As if she had a choice in the matter either way. After loading the truck, David gets in and told Priscilla to get in the back. She looks around and glances up toward the office that Chris and Carlos disappeared into and then turns to go ahead into the backseat of the pickup. Hoping that this all turns out fine. But having the gut feeling that she wasn't being told everything. With George still counting money, the overhead door opens. Andre also climbed into the pickup truck and they head out. Priscilla, still incredibly nervous about it all, just sitting gripping one hand in the other, and hoping she'll come out of this fine. As the truck heads out and the overhead door closes behind them, and Vic is standing outside of the factory watching them leave and observing their path out of the factory yard, David cranks up the radio loud, so loud that Priscilla is caught off guard and is startled by the levels. David and Andre both start nodding their heads and singing along to the song on the radio as they coast down the road; "Welcome to Hotel California…." As they ride, Priscilla is paying great attention to every street sign and road and landmark. Even though she didn't know where she was, for this ride, she decided she would try her best to bookmark her surroundings just in case she had to make a quick getaway from these two guys. Yet, she also felt that she knew Chris would not allow her to leave with these guys if there was a real danger. Very strange that Priscilla had developed such a level of trust in Chris in such a short time. Perhaps it was because of the bond she and Fabi made since the bus ride? Or maybe it was the growing relationship that she and Marisol were nurturing each day, and her learning in these last days that Chris would never do anything to disappoint his Abuela; and that now included herself.

Music still bumping as they drove, David had now been driving for about 20 minutes, and they were approaching a neighborhood with many blocks of row-houses. Kind of looked like duplexes. Reminded Priscilla of the project homes her cousins lived in when Aunt Tricia use to take her to visit family back home. David carefully pulls to a curb away from all of the row-houses and then puts the truck in to park and places his arm on the headrest of his seat and turns to Priscilla.

"Okay little lady, here we go. I want you to go with Andre and just watch what he does, don't say a word! Don't look weird. Don't ask any questions." Priscilla looked at David and confirmed that she understood his directions, while she notices that Andre grabs a gun out of the glove box and cradles it in his hand and is checking that it's loaded. She keeps her cool and pretends not to see the gun. But now she is getting scared. David finishes giving his instructions as Andre puts the gun into his waistband.

Trying to show some calm and readiness, Priscilla responds with a bit of a shaky voice, "I hear you, I'm ready." Wanting to ask what the gun was for, but not wanting to provoke either of them to do or say anything that would harm her, she just followed directions. Andre hopped out of the truck and went to the bed in the back and uncovered the bed to grab the duffle bag. Priscilla carefully climbed out of the truck also and went to stand near Andre getting prepared to follow his lead. Andre gives the okay, and they start to walk toward the second set of row-houses.

"Okay. We gonna take this bag up to this door and go in and give it to someone inside. Once we give up the bag, we'll get a key to a mailbox in the mailroom. We go in the mailroom and hit the box and then get the fuck out of here as fast as we can, got it?" Andre looking at her with bulging eyes expecting agreeance.

Priscilla looks at him and replies in agreement, "Yep, I got it!"

Then Andre added one last thing as they moved into the apartment, "Number one rule, never, under any circumstances, go in the apartment! No matter what! Understand?" She looked at him with big eyes in response and just agreed, as she could see he was very serious about that part. They approach the third door on the second row of the row-houses. "Stand to the right of the door the whole time." Andre instructs Priscilla. Then Andre knocks very lightly just two times, then steps back out of the door view to the left. Suddenly, the curtain on the window next to the door moves a bit, but Priscilla failed to see if someone was in the curtains, Andre still looking straight at the door. The door opens slightly ajar, with no visibility into the house as all of the lights are off. Andre drops the duffle bag onto the ground right in the crevice of the door opening. The bag gets snatched from the ground and a small baggie is tossed outside of the door. Andre looks down at the baggie, and then at Priscilla and kneels to pick up the baggie. Priscilla could see that there was a single key in the baggie. Andre turns and starts to walk swiftly as the door slams behind them as they leave from the row-house. Now Andre is headed for a building that is located directly in the center of the row-house complex. It's the mailroom he mentioned when he was telling Priscilla what they would do in this exercise. They approach the door to the mailroom, and Andre takes the key out of the baggie and puts the key in the keyhole on the knob of the door to turn the knob and he opens the mailroom door. They both enter, and Andre looks at the back of the key as he walks. Priscilla is observing what he's doing closely and notices that he keeps looking up at the mailboxes after he glances at the key. He's trying to match the number on the key to one of the boxes as he walks swiftly. As she watches him, she can tell he's done this so many times, because he's not even watching his step as he walks down the long aisle of mailboxes looking for the right number. Then boom, "23!" Andre calls out as he takes the key and sticks it into the mailbox, turns it, and opens the door. In the box, there is a stack of neatly wrapped brown paper rectangles. Andre starts to grab them, about five in all, and takes out a bigger paper bag from his pocket that was folded into a square. As he popped the bag open with one hand, he began to drop each brown box into the big paper bag. Closes the bag by rolling the top down to secure it, slams the mailbox shut, locks it, then hurries to exit the mailroom. Priscilla in tow, they both exit the mailroom building and Andre heads toward the truck parked with David sitting in it. As they make their way back to the truck, on the way Andre walks by an actual mailbox and opens the lid, and oddly enough drops the key into the mailbox. Priscilla, witnesses this and is extremely confused by it as she continues to follow Andre. Everything, though it all looked illegal, made sense until he dropped that key into a mailbox. Her mind was suddenly thrown into a loop as they approached the truck to get back in with David. That key in the mailbox move was messing with her head! She needed to know what that was about but didn't think this was the time to ask. She figured she'd find out in time, but she was perplexed, to say the least.

With the both of them back in the truck and the brown bag secured, David rips the pavement as he presses the gas pedal on the truck as they pull away from the row-house complex. Priscilla, in the back seat of the truck, being tossed around like a ragdoll because she didn't get to fasten her seatbelt before David pulled off, is still thinking about that key drop into the mailbox. As David and Andre talk about the drop while David drives, they both begin to bounce their heads to the music again. Priscilla, now fastened in as they hit the highway this time; is now replaying the whole occurrence in her head, each step, trying to think if she did indeed see someone at the curtain. If she saw anything else in particular in or around the mailroom. Also, thinking to herself that, This can't be it? This is not what Chris brought me here to do? She sat back and just observed and listened to the two guys bragging about the drop and the ease of it and stayed silent. As David exited the highway and approached a stoplight, he turned down the radio and began to talk to Priscilla.

"So, did you pay attention to everything?"

With Andre chiming in as well, "Yeah, did you see what I did back there?"

Priscilla, eager to connect all the dots of the minutes before doing the drop; especially the key in the mailbox readily agreed. "Yep, I saw everything! I saw every step, how everything was done! Is that going to be my job now?"

Both David and Andre began to laugh loudly as they shook their heads at her. "Hold on short-bread!" Andre said to her as they finish laughing. "The time will come. We just want to make sure you didn't miss anything."

David, agreeing with what Andre just said to Priscilla, "Yeah, you didn't miss anything? Did you?" Looking at both of them with a sure stare, she replied with some air of confidence, knowing in her mind that she was just as confused as she was when Chris first drove up to the factory a few hours ago. But she wanted to make sure they understood she was ready for whatever, and also reported back to Chris that she was cool on the trip.

"Nope! I didn't miss a thing!"

The two guys, still chuckling a bit, but impressed with Priscilla's composure turned the music back up and began to groove again. Priscilla was dying to know about that darn key in the mailbox but decided to wait for the right time to ask. They continued to drive until they arrived at a burger joint and pulled into the driveway.

David, pulling up to the order window; looked over his shoulder at Priscilla, and asked, "You eat burgers, right? You have to be hungry by now?" Priscilla replied with a yes over the music, and David proceeded to roll down the window and order. "Let me get ten cheeseburgers, five fries. That's all." It was clear that either David was ordering for a group of people, or he was an extremely greedy dude. The food order gave Priscilla some peace of mind, and a feeling of safety as well. With all of this being new and weird, and scary wrapped into one; she knew that some of what he ordered included food for Chris. So, she felt good about knowing they were taking her back to Chris after that crazy run they just pulled off. They pull up to the factory and Vic gives them the okay to enter as the overhead door opens to allow David to drive the truck in. The overhead door closes behind the truck and David parks. When the truck is parked, and Andre opens his door and gets out holding the big paper bag from the run, Chris and Carlos walk up to the truck as Priscilla opens her door. Chris looks at her to get confirmation that she is okay. She gives him a look of security, but also a face with an expression full of questions. As David gets out and heads over to the table where George is still sitting, counting money, Priscilla goes over and stands next to Chris. Carlos grabbed the paper bag from Andre and began to inspect it to make sure everything was there. While Carlos inspects, Andre stands there and Chris bumps Priscilla with his elbow on her arm.

"You good? Seems like everything went okay, Huh?" Priscilla was caught off guard by the overture of Chris because she thought they would all be quiet as Carlos inspected the goods.

But she turned to Chris, and replied nevertheless, "Yes, it was smooth."

Chris looking back at her after looking over at Carlos and Andre, "Good, you should be ready now!" Carlos hands the bag back to Andre and both of them begin to head toward the table where David and George are now sitting. Chris and Priscilla in tow as Carlos stands next to the table.

Then Carlos starts talking to Andre as he stands over them. "The young lady did well? No panic?"

Andre replies as he sits back in his chair and places his hands behind his head. "Man, she wasn't scared at all! Went along with the program like a champ."

Looking around at everyone, Carlos knew what he had to do next, "Chris, David come with me." Carlos began to head toward the set of stairs to the office. Then as he walked with the two guys following, he glanced over his shoulder at Priscilla and said, "You too young lady, come on with us. Time to talk business." The four of them headed up the staircase to the office. George and Andre remained seated at the table goofing around and laughing at a joke George just made, while Andre began to open the paper bag that he obtained during the run. It was time to break down the prize from the run. While Carlos moved forward with the next steps for Priscilla.

They enter the office; Carlos sits on a couch on the left wall at the end and grabbed a cigar to light and reached for a bottle of whiskey that was sitting on the end table next to the couch. Carlos cradled the cigar in his palm while also trying to pour the whiskey into a glass that looks previously used. Chris goes and sits at a desk in the office, facing them. Andre grabbed the chair on the other side of the desk and turns it toward Carlos, while Priscilla sat on the other end of the couch that Carlos sat. Finally getting his liquor poured and taking an initial sip, Carlos lights the cigar, puffing to get it lit right, and looks over to Priscilla, "You don't mind?" As if he needed her confirmation to smoke his cigar. At this point, Priscilla acknowledged that Carlos was the man in charge of all of this. A stark difference from the stories that Fabi told her on the bus ride. It didn't take away any of the respect that she'd built up for Chris, but she still knew that Chris wasn't as in charge of whatever this was, as Fabi made it seem.

She replied to Carlos as she surveyed the lay of power, "No, it's fine."

Carlos, taking a few tugs on the cigar as he began to speak, "Andre tells me you were cool and calm on the run. I like that! You seem that you will do well out there." Priscilla, looking at Carlos as he smoked and talked to her while Chris and Andre paid close attention.

"I... I think I did okay. It was weird." Being as honest as she could. Thrust into this situation, an unsavory profession, she replied to a question about her witnessing and being a part of a shady, stealthy business exchange. Carlos chuckled at her response and went on.

"So, since Chris brings you to us, and you seem to need help with getting some income, I want you to take Andre's place on the type of run you just witnessed. Lately, Andre has gotten too noticeable in the streets. We need to keep him covered for a while, and you would be the perfect unknown on these runs." Carlos, scooting to the front of the couch and turning more toward Priscilla as he leaned in her direction. "You think you could handle that? Being the new Andre for us?" Priscilla looked at Chris first before giving a response. As if she needed to confirm with him that she should take this offer from Carlos. Chris stayed quiet, giving all respect to Carlos to broker the deal. Yet, he did give an acknowledgment with his eyes to her that it was okay to take this deal. She looked at Carlos and gave her a confirming response.

"Yes, I can do it. I'll be ready, and I'll do a good job! I remember everything that happened and everything that Andre did on the run." Sitting back again on the couch as he reached for his glass of whiskey; Carlos looked content.

"Good then! Very good. The only thing left to do is plan the next couple of runs, and of course, young lady, let you ask any questions. I know you have questions? But before you're questioning you must always remember. Never. Ever. Go into an apartment or spot alone. Never!" Carlos put her on the spot to finalize this business arrangement to make sure she understood all that was involved, and at risk for her. Priscilla looked at Carlos, then at Chris, and next David, then sat up erect to begin to respond to Carlos.

"I do have two questions, if you can answer them?" Again, making her eyes stroll around the office before continuing. "What is in those brown packs? And what was the key in the mailbox about?" Two essential questions for a business setup such as this. Two questions that she hoped would get answered but wasn't expecting to be disappointed if the answers did not materialize.

Carlos put his glass down, giggled a bit, looked at Chris, and said to him, "My man Chris! You brought us a buzzsaw, a tough one. I like it." Taking a tug at his cigar again, Carlos looks at Priscilla and said, "Okay, you want to know, I'll tell you."

Searching

Priscilla sat in a factory office, with strangers that she just met, and Chris; whom she's only known for about two weeks. 700 miles or so away in Baltimore; the hunt to find her continued. Tricia getting weaker, more stressed, and breaking down by the day, as they continue to look and fail to find her. Today, Tricia was out shopping for groceries since she hadn't been able to do it because of the day-after-day searching for Priscilla. Tricia had been neglecting the house, church, everything, including Roy. But anyone should understand the hurt and pain of a mother who's lost their child and the police made no progress or had no leads in a couple of weeks. Each day that passed, tore at her soul. Tricia decided to go to the store, to try and get some type of normal back in her life as if that was possible without Priscilla. Normal for her these days would include at least eating food for a change. Which she hadn't been doing on a regular anymore. Here she was, in the grocery store, with her cart and a few items in it. Hoping to do this shopping, and maybe go home and cook something to ease her mind, perhaps allow the police to work, the neighborhood volunteers to search, and pray that while she cooked, someone would bring some good news. News that her precious Priscilla had been returned to her. Tricia rolled the cart over to the produce section and began to pick through the grapefruits, squeezing each one as she placed them in the produce bag that she had just grabbed and popped open. As she placed one grapefruit into the bag and moved her eyes back to the rack to grab another, in the peripheral of her left eye, she saw a glimpse of a girl standing by the apple cart, about in her teen years, puffy, curly hair like Priscilla, and wearing the sweater that Priscilla would often wear when they shopped together. The sweater with the green and white stripes and the two buttons on the bottom missing. As Tricia turned her head fully in the direction of the young girl, with excitement that she has just seen Priscilla; she shoves the cart away from her in preparation to run over to the girl she's seen. As she runs over to the girl. She hears a shrill and then notices that the young girl in the green and white striped sweater is no longer standing by the apple cart. At the same time, the produce manager is standing by the greens and kneeled with one hand on Tricia's half-full cart, and his other hand on his right knee. Tricia stood there, tears filling up in the wells of her eyes realizing that she didn't see Priscilla. Her heart now feeling more pain than she'd felt all week due to the disappointment of the missed opportunity of having her baby back. Did she see Priscilla? Did Priscilla not see her and leave the store before she got the chance to go over to her? Tricia was lost.

After wincing in pain for a bit from the cart ramming his knee, the produce manager goes over to Tricia to deliver the cart back to her and try to see if she was okay because he witnessed the whole ordeal; Tricia flinging the cart and starting to run over to the girl she thought she saw, thinking the girl was Priscilla.

"Excuse me miss. Are you okay?" As he pushed the cart back in front of her. "You tossed the cart and it hit me in my knee. I'll be okay, but just want to make sure you're alright miss. You seem very troubled." The produce manager, still favoring his knee as he checked on Tricia's wellbeing. "Do you need me to call anyone?" Tricia, snapping out of her daze of thinking she saw Priscilla, and realizing that she just had an episode, looks at the produce manager and replies with embarrassment on her face.

"I am so sorry! I am okay. I just, I just..." Not knowing how to explain to the produce manager what just transpired; she just continued to say that she was okay, as she grabbed the cart from him. The produce manager looks at her as she grabbed the cart, and he began to walk away, saying to her once more that he could help if she needed it.

"I'm right over here if you need me miss." Layered with embarrassment, now thinking that everyone in the produce section and even the entire store saw her episode; Tricia hurries to the front register to check out with her groceries and try to get out of the store. Hoping that no one else approached her about what just happened. She exited the store and entered the parking lot to go to Roy's car to load the groceries. She was bent over into the trunk, moving some of Roy's junk around to make room for the bags of groceries, when in her ear, she heard a laugh across the parking lot. That was the laugh of Priscilla! Tricia dropped everything she had in her hands that she was moving around in the trunk and turned her head left and right and around to locate the sound of the young girl's laughter. When she finally located the sound; she again saw the puffy, curly hair like Priscilla's, and a girl wearing a sweater with green and white stripes and the two buttons on the bottom missing. Tricia sprang into action this time, with a purpose! She was not going to let Priscilla get away again. This time the girl in the green and white striped sweater was just about to get into the back of a red Lincoln town car that had a man sitting in the driver seat looking like he was about to pull off as soon as the girl got into the car. Tricia dashed across the parking lot, leaving the cart full of groceries, and Roy's trunk wide open and quickly approached the red Lincoln. As she got closer and closer to the car, and the girl was in the motion of getting in the car; Tricia was not mistaken this time. It was clear! This girl was Priscilla! As Tricia ran toward the car, she could see that the mannerisms and movement of the girl matched perfectly to Priscilla. The girl's hand that grasped the side of the door as she held it for support to lift her leg into the car looked just like Priscilla's hand! Tricia reaches the car, yells out, "Priscilla!" Grabbed the girl and turned her around to embrace her, and the girl is scared out of her mind and began to scream from the surprise of Tricia grabbing her. The man jumps out of the driver's seat and pushes Tricia down upon the ground.

"Get your fucking hands off of my daughter you crazy bitch!" Furious, the man, goes on more of a tangent, cursing Tricia out as she lay on the ground, everything bruised, including her mental.

A woman appears from the passenger side of the car and bends down to help Tricia up, "Andy! Stop! This must be a mistake!" the woman, understanding that Tricia had mistaken her daughter for someone else, but the man still angry and cursing, as the girl sobbed in her daddy's arms. The man, disgusted with the situation, takes his daughter over to the passenger side and sits her down to calm her. The lady stays with Tricia and walks her back to Roy's car, as Tricia, highly embarrassed tries to explain to the lady that Priscilla is missing for weeks and she thought the lady's daughter looked like Priscilla. The lady having sympathy, said she understood and helped Tricia load her groceries, and assured Tricia that she was okay to leave, and she would go calm her husband and daughter down. Tricia gets in the car, shuts the door, and just collapsed upon the steering wheel crying harder than she had cried in years. She sat there crying for many minutes that felt like hours. Sitting there, praying to the Lord, over and over for peace of mind. Tricia eventually finds her center and brings herself to start the car and pull off. As she exits the grocery store parking lot, she drives past the red Lincoln town car and sees the lady explaining to her husband and the man is still angry, while the girl was sitting, wiping her eyes. The girl looked nothing like Priscilla.

After driving around the neighborhood, trying to gather herself, Tricia arrives back home and gets all the groceries in. Roy comes down from upstairs, basically living with Tricia now that Priscilla has been gone, under the cloak of helping Tricia through all of this. He came into the kitchen and began to help her put away the food while checking on her as they talk. Tricia asks Roy can they sit down and talk as they have lunch. She planned to make some sandwiches for them so that they could talk about everything that has happened with Priscilla. Roy, feeling like Tricia was up to something, agreed and said he was going to go out into the backyard for a smoke while she prepared the lunch. Tricia agreed and proceeded to fix the sandwiches. After she sets the table, Roy appears back into the kitchen from the backyard and his smoking session and they prepare to sit down to eat. As they sat, and Roy began to chomp on his sandwich, Tricia was fiddling with a potato chip on her plate, but not eating just yet. "Roy, we need to talk. I need to tell you about something that happened to me today, what's been happening to me lately while we look for Priscilla." Roy, chewing a mouth full of the sandwich as he listened, looked at Tricia and gave her confirmation that he was paying attention. Tricia continues to tell the events, "I… I keep seeing her. But it's… it's not her." Roy puts down his sandwich and just stares at her, while he tries to understand what she is trying to tell him.

"You mean to tell me, you've seen Priscilla?" Roy asks with seriousness because his mind always goes back to not wanting to be found out about being the reason for Priscilla's disappearance.

"That's just it. I haven't seen her. I just keep mistaking other girls for her. And it's driving me crazy." Tricia said as she began to sob. "I think I need help. I need to go see someone, talk to someone. Until I… I get my baby back." Roy, trying to comfort Tricia, gets up from his chair and goes over to her side of the table to embrace her from behind.

"We are going to find her. I promise! You don't need to talk to anyone. You've got me, baby." Tricia, getting more frustrated, takes Roy's hands off of her shoulders and raises them from the table.

"I knew you wouldn't understand. I made an appointment with a psychiatrist, just to get me through this until she's back. Plus, I've been very sick every single morning. Not like you have noticed." Now the tone began to change as Tricia got more frustrated and began to express unhappiness with Roy.

"Wait! Are you blaming me?" Roy said as he stepped back and let Tricia get up from the table.

"No, that's not what I'm saying. I just think that you could be more supportive through this. It seems that you are not trying as hard as everyone else to find her!" Tricia replies with a shot to Roy's pride.

He replies now with an angrier tone, "What the fuck does that even mean? Be more supportive? I've been with you every fucking day since she's been missing!" Tricia, now full-on crying replies as she takes her plate and stomps into the kitchen and slams the plate against the garbage can to dump the sandwich that she barely even touched.

"You just don't get it, Roy! You are only in it if it benefits you. I noticed how you haven't even shown any hurt for my baby being gone. And don't give me that man-grieving bullshit."

Roy, now extremely mad, slams his hand on the wall to cause a loud bang right next to Tricia's head by the garbage can. "I'm not going to take this shit. You must be fucking crazy. I've been here for you and that fucking girl for everything! Cleaning, fixing, doing everything."

Tricia cuts him off in the middle of his rant. "That fucking girl? That fucking girl? You know what! I was right! It is your fault! You don't care! I'm going to my psychiatrist appointment, and there ain't shit you can do about it! Matter of fact, you can fucking leave since you don't care!"

Roy, standing there in amazement, hurt and mad, but also knowing in his mind, it is his fault. Just looks at Tricia and turns to go upstairs with no words. Tricia, now with a face fully wet from tears and almost dizzy with the pain of hurt continues to grab the plates and starts to wash the dishes as she curses to herself. After about ten minutes, Roy comes back down the stairs with a bag in tow and walks to the doorway of the kitchen, with the bag in view, but does not speak. Just stands there and looks at the backside of Tricia's head as she is wiping the sink with a dishtowel. Tricia sees Roy in her peripheral but does not acknowledge him or say anything. He looks at her for another minute and then turns and walks out the front door, slamming it mightily behind him. Tricia drops the dishrag and runs to the front door. Looking out of the glass on the door and watching Roy drive off, Tricia falls to her knees at the door crying out and stays there all-night sobbing. Now having lost her baby girl and her man. She felt she was losing a grip on everything in life. She didn't know what to do.

The next morning Tricia is sitting at the dining room table with a cup of coffee, peering out of the window to see when Roy's car was going to pull up. Knowing him well, she knew he would turn back up this morning to apologize and they would make up and make things right to continue to look for Priscilla together. She stayed up all night preparing her apology for blaming Roy for everything. Eventually, her coffee turned cold as she tried to continue to sip it, about two hours passed and it was time for her to go to her appointment. Tricia, feeling the weight of losing Priscilla and now what seems to be Roy, gets up and finds the strength to get out of the house and head down to the psychiatrist. As she walks down the street to get to the bus at the corner that would take her, she hears a voice calling her name from behind. She turns to see it is her neighbor John.

"Tricia, you okay? I saw Roy leave yesterday in a rush it seems. Is everything okay?"

Tricia, not wanting to reveal the truth, lied as she replied to John. "Yes John, everything is good. Roy... Roy just had something he needed to get to quickly when he left. An appointment. Speaking of an appointment, I'm on my way to one now."

John cuts in with an inquisitive look on his face, "Oh okay. Just, making sure you're good. And I wanted to let you know that this weekend on Saturday we are leading another search party through the neighborhood for Priscilla, wanted to let you know it starts at six so you could join. You can ride with me to the meet-up spot. We refuse to give up while these lazy cops half-ass the job looking for your girl."

Tricia, standing there looking at John, realizing that there were so many people that did care, got mad again in her mind at Roy. Thinking that this should be Roy leading a search party looking for Priscilla. "Thank you so, so much John." She reached out and grabbed his hands and cradled them in hers. "You just don't know how much it means that you would do this for me."

John nodding and looking at Tricia in her eyes, "Anything for my folks in the neighborhood Tricia. Priscilla is the daughter of this block. This neighborhood. We look out for our own." Looking at John, Tricia held back tears and let him know she needed to go to make her appointment. John asks. "You sure you don't want a ride to the appointment?"

Tricia declines, "No, you've done so much already. I'll see you at six on Saturday. Thank you so much John."

She lets his hands go and turns to walk away from him to get the bus on the corner. As Tricia disappears onto the bus and it pulls away, John remains standing right where they just talked watching her leave. Then he turns and walks back over to his house. At the opposite corner sat Roy in his car, he just watched the whole scene with Tricia and John. Roy, of course not knowing anything that was said, assumed the worst, especially since he saw them embrace hands as they talked. Roy pulls off and turns to the left in the opposite direction of John's house screeching his tires with anger.

Acclimation

While Tricia was going through the emotions of losing Priscilla and then Roy, and going crazy back home; in Chicago, Priscilla had just experienced one of the wildest stunts she'd ever witnessed. That ride with Andre and Dave was something else! She still couldn't believe what she had just taken part in. Chris and Priscilla were preparing to leave the factory after all of the events of the run. Carlos explains what the key was about to Priscilla, but not what was in the packs. "So, young lady. The key in the mailbox!" As he chuckled to himself. "That is our neutral spot with our suppliers. We took an empty mailbox and set it up on the opposite side of the complex from the real one, so the postal service doesn't bother it, or us. We have an agreement that if we successfully obtain the supply, we return the key to the box for the next run. If the supply is not there, we keep the key. If we ever have to keep the key. Let's just say, that is not good for the supplier." Priscilla looked confused by what Carlos just said but continued to pay attention. Carlos continued as Chris, Dave, Andre, and George paid attention as well; all looking at her to see if she could handle what she was being told. "That brings me to you, young lady. You are now the new Andre for us, okay?"

Looking at her with a serious face. As if she had a choice in the matter.

Priscilla looks at Chris first, then back at Carlos, then at the other men in the room. Then she agrees by nodding her head. "Yes, yeah. I'll do it! I want to make some money." With assurance in her voice, as if she were all of a sudden, this Boss. This grown woman out of nowhere. Looking at her, then at the guys, Carlos gets up from his seat, and places his hands on his hips as he surveyed the room.

"Good then. We are all set." He proceeded to tell her she will begin doing runs next week. One a week to start, then increasing. Chris then shakes Carlos's hand, grabs a small blue bag, and gives Priscilla the look as if it were time to leave. She turns to follow Chris as she kept looking back at all of the men. They exit the factory door to head to Chris's van as Vic is standing outside of the door, now grabbing it, and holding it for Priscilla after Chris opens it and exits. As Chris drives home, at first it is noticeably quiet between the two of them. Priscilla, still trying to accept that she had just become an accomplice of an operation that is for sure illegal, in Chicago! Wow! What a difference a couple of weeks make. She is just taking it all in as she reflects on what she'll have to do, remembering what Andre did, step-by-step while they were at that housing complex. Trying to accept that that was her new job, and she couldn't mess it up, for fear of what Carlos might do. As Chris makes a right turn onto the expressway, he looks at Priscilla.

"You got nothing to say? No questions? Come on now. I know you do."

Glancing at Chris, then back out of the window, then back at him again, Priscilla finally began to speak. "You didn't tell me you were a drug dealer."

Chris began to laugh. "Drug dealer. No one said we deal drugs." Turning fully toward Chris now in her seat on the passenger side, she stares him in the side of his face as he continues to drive down the expressway.

"I'm young, but I'm not stupid Chris. What else could be in those brown packs?"

Chris looks over at her as he continued to drive, "Look. You don't need to be concerned with what's in them anyway. Just try and focus on not messing up the run, and everything will be fine! Can you do that? And make some good money until you decide to go out on your own? Here, or wherever you are from."

Priscilla replies with a snap in her voice, "I'm from Baltimore. It's cool. I can handle so much more than you will ever get to find out about me Chris."

Chris, noticing the attitude in Priscilla that just appeared, laughs a bit before replying to her. "Okay, okay. Just don't mess up the good thing I got going with Carlos, and we'll be straight." As they continued to drive and talk about the runs, Chris explains a little more to Priscilla, without giving up the whole story. In between his explanations, Priscilla continues to snap with attitude tones, to try and act like she is ready, or at least convince Chris that she is indeed ready, and won't mess anything up. They come to a total understanding as they go back and forth on the ride. Chris realizing that Priscilla was a buzzsaw, not a pushover. He learned on this ride home that he may have to pay attention and keep an eye on

Priscilla because he may be dealing with a Boss who is not aware that she is one.

Back at the house as Chris pulls in the driveway, Abuela and Fabi are walking from the backyard out to the front of the house and greets the van. "Well. You two look like you had a long day of work." Marisol said as she held a basket of vegetables in her arms. Chris turns the van off, jumps out, and grabs the basket from his grandmother. Fabi goes over to the passenger side of the van where Priscilla is getting out.

"Damn girl. I feel like I haven't seen you in a week." Laughing as she said it to Priscilla. Priscilla gets out and is laughing too.

"Girl, you didn't tell me your brother works with some dudes that have a very junky operation and need a damn maid." Priscilla cleverly concealing the facts about what they'd been doing all day.

Not knowing if Fabi even knew about the runs, the packs, or the other guys. Fabi, continuing to laugh, "All I know is Chris is always gone but makes good money." While they continue to chat on the way into the house, Marisol is talking to Chris.

"You are taking special care to make sure my young friend is safe and treated fairly, right?"

Chris, grabbing his Abuela's shoulder with one hand as his other cradled the basket to his belly, "Yes ma'am! She is in good hands and will make some good money in the process. I promise." Marisol glances at her grandson with a curious face as they get into the house and he places the basket on the kitchen table.

"You two are just in time for supper. Food is ready. You two clean up and come on to the supper table to eat."

Priscilla and Fabi still laughing and talking, both respond to Marisol, "Okay, here we come, as Priscilla goes into Fabi's bathroom to clean up while Fabi sits on the bed looking through some magazines that she was already looking at earlier before going out to the yard with Abuela. After about fifteen minutes, they all join at the kitchen table to enjoy the dinner prepared by Marisol, delicious as usual. Everyone talking and laughing, Chris and Priscilla enjoying the dinner, but both containing anxiety from what was to come next week. Priscilla being the lead on a run for Carlos. Priscilla is filled with anxiety from thinking about not wanting to fuck up next week. Chris with anxiety from wondering if Priscilla was ready for this.

As the week went by fast; with normal routine on the part of Marisol, Fabi, and Chris, Priscilla marked each day anticipating the first run performed by her. She was building up a lot of excitement in her belly and her mind. Hoping it would be as smooth as what she witnessed when Andre did it. Hoping she could just do the runs, make the money, and get out every time. Day by day, she built up more anxiety. Then finally, the day was upon them. A normal morning, breakfast cooked by Abuela. The garden was tended to by Fabi and Abuela. Chris up early, cleaning his van and preparing for the day. Priscilla, sitting on the edge of the couch that she had been sleeping on, folding her blanket and sheet neatly as normal.

After eating, Chris goes into the bathroom, and on the way in, he looks at Priscilla and said, "You'll be ready to go when I come out of the bathroom, right?" Priscilla looked up at him from the kitchen table and nodded her head. Her stomach so full of nervousness by now, that she got up and ran into the bathroom in Fabi's room to use it one more time herself. While they were both in each bathroom, Fabi was out in the yard again with Abuela telling her to tell Chris that she was heading out to meet some friends and walk over to another friend's house, and he didn't need to drop her off.

She kisses Abuela on the forehead. Marisol said, "Be careful out there today sweetheart." Marisol watched Fabi walk out of the front of the yard and onto the sidewalk and down the street. Then Chris appeared outside from his bathroom break and went up to his grandmother to get the news that Fabi had left ahead of them. He went to his van and waited on Priscilla to come out of the house, as Abuela continued to tend to her yard. As Chris sits in the van for about ten minutes, Priscilla bursts out of the door to see that he is in the van waiting.

Marisol, noticing that Priscilla had run out of the house in a hurry, looks up and said, "Be careful out there. Be smart and come back ready to eat young lady."

As Priscilla was climbing up into the passenger side of the van, she looked back at Marisol and said, "Thank you. I will."

Chris put the van into drive, and they headed off. This ride to the factory was much different than the last time. On the last ride, Priscilla was incredibly nervous. Scared even! Because on that day, she honestly didn't know where Chris was taking her. She didn't even know if that would have been her last day on earth. But today, there was a crisp feeling in the air. There was a peculiar smell in the air. Almost as if the smell were sitting on top of the air, ready to be taken in by the nostril of the open-minded reality-seeking individual, who had been seeking revelation. Revelation indeed! Priscilla was seeking today! Needing to experience this run with no hiccups, perfectly executed. To impress Carlos, Chris, and herself! Priscilla just wanted to do this correctly and make her money. Besides, now there was a bit of thirst in her mind for the money. Since in the previous week, while waiting for this day, Chris had taken her out to the garage and broke her off some money; her share for simply accompanying Andre and Dave on the previous run to observe. That take of hers was $30. To Priscilla, thirty dollars was a gold mine! And just for watching! A little bit of running to getaway! What will she get each time for being the person to execute the run to perfection? How much were they making? As Chris drove on to the factory, Priscilla zoned out in her mind, trying to prepare herself for what was to come. She perched herself on the edge of the passenger side window of the van as Chris continued to drive to the destination. As she focused on getting ready, she began to see the birds enveloping each tree along the path of the ride. As it had been every time she's seen the birds, it wasn't just a couple of birds. Again, it was hundreds of birds. A couple hundred. Again, Priscilla found it soothing. It made her aware of who she was. Aware of the situation she was in. Either way, she was prepared for this next adventure. This adventure was becoming her job for the time being.

Chris exits the highway, about an hour and a half away from home. Just as before, Chris pulls into a residential neighborhood, then follows the road up to a street that led to a bunch of huge old buildings that looked like factories. As he parks, Priscilla sees Vic standing there like before. Once again, Vic is standing there smoking a cigarette. They get out of the van and approach the door. Vic gives them a nod to enter. Again, the guys were sitting around a table counting money. The multiple pickup trucks lined up in front of the overhead door, ready to pull out. This time Carlos wasn't there to be seen. David was sitting at the table, looking like he was ready to head out and get the job done. Andre was chilling, counting money, with a look on his face as if he were relieved that he wasn't the runner anymore. The nerve of him feeling good to be handing this job off to a young girl. But the genius of it all for them was Priscilla wouldn't be as noticeable to anyone!

Chris walks over to the table, "Alright everyone. Let's get this party started. Are y'all ready to get it done with the new associate?" Referring to Priscilla. All of the guys chuckle a bit as Priscilla walks up to the table and sits down in a chair next to a stack of money like she was confident and ready. The guys were surprised by this. They just knew she wouldn't be ready. Hell, there was a bet between them that she wouldn't even come back.

Then David replied to Chris, "I'm ready for whatever man. Let's do this." Andre began to throw some money into one of those duffle bags and onto the back of one of the pickup trucks as Priscilla stood there watching.

Andre, as he loaded, looked over at Priscilla and said, "See. Half of the job you don't even need to worry about. I'll continue the loading." With a snicker as he loaded the back of the truck.

George continued counting the money at the table. After loading the truck, David got in and told Priscilla to get on the passenger side this time. Then the overhead door opens as Vic is standing outside of the factory as usual. She looks around as she and David pull away in the truck. David, not being much of a talker, cranks up the radio loud. Probably didn't matter anyway because Priscilla didn't have anything to say. After about 30 minutes, they were approaching a neighborhood with many blocks of row-houses. Kind of looked like duplexes, much like before, but Priscilla could tell this was a different neighborhood, just looked the same. As David parked in a spot that wasn't noticeable, he put the truck in park and turned to Priscilla to check her temperament.

"You ready?"

Priscilla looked at David and gave a nod that she was ready. "I'm ready!"

He looks at her and hands her a small torn-off piece of paper. Must have been something that she missed on the first ride along with him and Andre. The piece of paper had numbers wrote on it, "1322." Priscilla quickly realized what this was, even though she had not remembered the exchange between David and Andre of the piece of paper from the previous run. Priscilla looking at David and confirming that she understood, prepared to get out of the truck and go around to the back to get the bag. Just as she was about to climb out of the truck, David grabs her left arm to stop her.

"Hey! You'll need this. Hope you know how to use it. If you need to." David handing her a small Glock. He also handed her a big folded-up paper bag. She remembered this part, but in her memory of the first run, David grabbed a gun on his own from the glove box. "Put it in your front pocket. Since you don't have a belt on your pants." David told Priscilla. Priscilla, now extremely nervous. She's never even seen a gun up close until she saw David with it last time. Especially didn't know how to use one. But she played it off like she was okay with toting a gun for this run. While playing it cool inside, Priscilla felt her heart pounding and she was about to throw up. But kept her composure in front of David. She hops out of the truck and goes to the bed in the back and uncovers the bed to grab the duffle bag. She starts to walk toward the fourth set of row-houses looking for the number on the paper. She remembers Andre telling her what they were going to do with the bag last time. She eagerly looks for the set of row houses that start with "13" as the beginning numbers of the units. She knew she had to take this bag up to the door of "1322" and go in and give to someone inside, or leave it on the ground at the door, or something. Knowing that she'd get a key to the mailroom like before. She hoped that it would go the same way! After finally seeing the set of row houses with the lead number as 13, her stomach was in knots and she was feeling so sick. She ducked in behind a huge tree, dropped the duffle bags, and made sure she was out of the view of David; then proceeded to bend over next to the tree and vomit every part of the breakfast she'd had this morning, and perhaps some of last night's dinner. What an ordeal! But now she had calmed her nerves by expelling vomit on the bottom of the tree. A bit dizzy, she grabs the duffel bags back up and began to get her clear vision back again.

She headed to the row houses to look for "1322." She approached the door on the fourth set of row-houses. She remembered to stand to the right of the door the whole time like Andre told her before. Remembering from before, she knocks very lightly just two times, then steps back out of the door view to the right. Like the previous time, the doors open slightly ajar, with no visibility into the house as all of the lights are off, Priscilla proceeded to drop the duffle bag onto the ground right in the crevice of the door opening. This time, the bag is gently pulled into the unit by a white arm, no face being revealed. Then the door slams in her face. She stands there looking around the door for the baggie with the key, thinking that maybe she did a step wrong, and she was about to get cheated. Then, from above, a bag floats down behind her head from a window of the unit upstairs. She looks up and tries to get a glance at who threw the bag with the key. No luck. Again, a single key in the baggie. She remembered that Andre had immediately turned and headed to the mailroom of the complex. Though, she was bothered that everything was not the same as before. Still, she proceeded to turn and start to walk swiftly, headed for the mailroom, like before, but she needed to locate it. By now, her heart was about to jump out of her chest. As she walked fast looking for the mailroom, she noticed that she walked by the view of the truck again and saw that David was still sitting there. Some relief! A little! Then she finally saw it in the distance, the building that was the complex mailroom. She approached the door to the mailroom and took the key out of the baggie and put the key in the keyhole on the knob of the door to turn the knob and opened the mailroom door. She entered and began looking up at the mailboxes after she glances at the key. Just like before, what Andre did; she is trying to match the number on the key to one of the boxes as she walks swiftly. Then suddenly, as she is perusing, she sees it! "1322!" Priscilla opened the mailbox, and, in the box, there was a stack of neatly wrapped brown paper rectangles. She grabbed them, about five in all, just like last time. She had a bigger paper bag just like Andre had before. She got it from David before getting out of the truck. She opened the bag and began to swiftly drop each brown box into the big paper bag. She closed the bag by rolling the top down to secure it, just like Andre. Then she slammed the mailbox shut, locked it, then hurried to exit the mailroom. She quickly got her orientation after leaving the mailroom, trying to locate the mailbox as Andre did before. Then, she saw it! The mailbox! She opened the lid and dropped the key into the mailbox. She continued to walk swiftly toward the truck. Got to the truck and hopped in as David began to pull off. "Everything is done. All good?" David confirming the job is done as he pulls off, before fully amping up the speed to leave the complex.

What an experience for a young girl! But now, she was the runner for them! Not knowing the true meaning of what she was doing, or what she would be, as identified by law enforcement, "A Mule!" Priscilla felt like what she just pulled off, could easily be duplicated many times over, without issue. She could make some good money and decide her next move as she grew into this new city. As they ride back to the factory, Priscilla knew this was just the beginning of a new adventure and was ready for whatever it brought. This run felt a little too easy for her. She was of course nervous throughout but felt like she could do this. David pulls up to the factory in no time and Vic gives them the okay to enter as the overhead doors open. Standing there are Chris and the guys. With a look on their faces like they were waiting to hear some bad news. As David parks the truck, Priscilla is looking at the expressions on their faces, knowing they are expecting the worse. After the truck is parked, Priscilla got out of the truck, closed the door behind her, walked over to the money table, and ripped the big brown bag open with force, allowing the paper bricks to fall upon the table, taking the last one to fall out of the bag and slamming it onto the table. "I told y'all I wasn't scared!" Her little heart was pounding! She was doing her best Mob Boss impression to appease the guys. Perhaps to let them know that she was ready for this. Or to convince herself that she was ready. Chris and the guys explode with yells and laughter of happiness. Knowing that Priscilla was indeed the unknown piece they needed to push their money-making ability to greater heights. As they crowd around her celebrating, each grabbing a brick, she zoned out a little, knowing that she would be okay with this, that's if every run was as smooth as this one. She was also thinking about her position in life as the guys celebrated the run. Did she know who she truly was? With that question, Priscilla knew that this was just the beginning of her story after Baltimore. But where it was headed, was yet to be known. After the celebration, and some food, and of course drinks by the guys; Chris and Priscilla were headed home to Fabi and Abuela. On the drive home the two of them talked about each step of the run. Priscilla described each step of hers and explained to Chris how she felt along the way, he was laughing at her.

As she kept saying, "Stop laughing at me."

Chris gained his composure and agreed, "Okay, okay. I'll stop."

As they kept talking on the way home. She opened up a bit more to Chris about the run. "Can I be honest about something?"

Chris replied, "About what?"

Priscilla replied, "You can't tell anyone, the guys. Okay?"

He looked and said, "Alright, alright."

She proceeded to tell, "I got so nervous and sick while looking for the apartment, that I threw up by a tree before I did the exchange." Chris burst out into more laughter as he continued to drive down the road. "See. That's why I didn't want to tell you." Priscilla said as they drove on.

With Chris confirming with Priscilla, "See, the runs are not so bad. I told you."

Sick and Tired

Back in Baltimore, Tricia had proceeded to see the Psychiatrist to seek mental help. That day when Roy saw Tricia and John holding hands while she was headed to the shrink changed everything back home between the two of them. But far more turned out from that day! During the shrink visit, Tricia was taken aback by a few revelations the psychiatrist called out. During the visit, the doctor let Tricia begin the session by telling her why she was there.

Then Dr. Anderson asked Tricia some questions. "You tell me that you've been sick, your daughter is missing, and you have had many fights with your boyfriend Tricia. Everything is centered on your daughter missing. You do know this?" Before Tricia could reply to the Psychiatrist, Dr. Anderson cut her off again, "But, I do need you to know that a lot of this is indeed your fault!" Tricia, with a surprised look on her face, stares at the Dr. feeling like she'd been betrayed already early into this session.

"What... What do you mean, my fault?"

Looking directly at Tricia, the Dr. replies. "It's quite simple, You see! You were trying too hard to juggle your boyfriend, and your daughter, and not making a clear distinction between the worth of both of them. I know she is missing, and presumed kidnapped, but have you had any thought that she may have run away?" As Tricia is more appalled and starting to cry, she began to yell.

"This is why I should have listened to Roy! This is a fucking waste of my time! You are telling me that my baby ran away from me?! Wow! You are unbelievable!"

With a quick reply, the doctor told Tricia, "Did I ever say she ran away from you Tricia? If she did indeed run, what did she run from? That's what we need to figure out! But our time is up today. I'll have to continue this next week." Tricia, sitting in despair, started to think about everything over the last couple of years, her relationship with Roy, her relationship with Priscilla. She was more lost after this initial session. "Of course, we could go on Tricia, but I have a client outside scheduled after you, so next week. But keep in mind, you did jump right to defending Roy as soon as I mentioned Priscilla possibly running away." As the Dr. got up, she handed Tricia a piece of paper. "I also want you to go see my friend, a medical doctor, free of charge. Something else seems to be amiss with your health. It could just be the stress of losing your daughter and the stress of fighting with your boyfriend but let him check you out. On me! Okay?" Tricia, feeling lost, just looks at her, wiped her tears, and left the office. Not knowing what to do next, Tricia decides to head on over to the doctor while she was in mid-town. Might as well, because, at this point, she was lost. Didn't know what to do! She walked slowly to the bus stop and waited on the bench for the next bus that would take her down the road to the doctor's office. Sitting there thinking about her and Priscilla. Priscilla and Roy. She just didn't know how to connect it all, what the shrink was saying about the true reason for her feeling so sick and losing Priscilla. Yet, she sat there until the next bus arrived, then she got in, and went to the doctor's office to be seen. Back at her place, Roy showed up to confront her about what he saw earlier. He parked his car and went up to the door to find it locked and Tricia still not home. He got his key out and went in to confirm she wasn't there; did some snooping around for a few minutes. In Roy's mind, he wanted to see if Tricia had moved on from him. So silly of him to jump the gun and start thinking that way in just one day. But that is how fragile their relationship had gotten during this period of losing and trying to find Priscilla. While looking all through the house for signs, Roy stumbles upon a folder under the china cabinet in the living room. Strange to him, he's never seen this folder. He grabs it and goes over to the dining room table to sit and go through it. Right before going to the table, he went to the front window to peek out of the curtain because he heard chatter outside the house on the front sidewalk. It was a few of Tricia's neighbors. He quickly closed the parted curtain as to not reveal himself in the house, since he knew now that none of the voices were Tricia's and went ahead and sat at the table to look through the folder. What he found blew his mind!

Inside of the folder were the files about Priscilla's Dad. The night of his death, statements from the cops on that night, and documents that could support a cover-up about what happened to him that night. There was also a piece of paper that outlined the possible monetary reward for a lawsuit filed and won against the local police department. All of this was something that Tricia had never mentioned to Roy. He was sure she didn't mention it to anyone. Part of him felt betrayed because he was looking at the money aspect. He also felt that way because this made him know that Tricia wasn't trusting of him. In reality, her not fully trusting him was for good reason, but he now felt that she never did trust him. He put everything back the way he found it and prepared to leave. He then locked up and went back to his car. Just as he was about to pull off, John was pulling up in his car. John rolls his window down to speak to Roy as he is pulling up, and Roy is about to pull off. Roy looks him right in the face, ignores him, and pulls off fast, not speaking at all. John thinking that was extremely weird, because he had done nothing to Roy, convinced himself to pay it no mind and continued to park to go into his house.

As Tricia sat at the doctor's office for about an hour waiting, her name was finally called. She proceeded to the back to see the doctor. "Hello, there ma'am! I understand my good friend Dr. Anderson referred you to come to see me. What is going on?"

Tricia looked up at the doctor as she got her balance on the edge of the bed in the doctor's room. "I've had a lot of stress lately, and I lost my daughter, the police are looking for her."

The doctor asked as he knew about the situation in town. "You're the young lady with the missing girl?"

Tricia said, "Yes. That's me!"

The Doctor replied, "Oh wow! I feel so bad ma'am. I have been doing my part to try and find her as well. I'm Doctor Phillips. And I'm here for you to help figure out why you've been sick."

Tricia looks at him and nods, "Thank you so much."

Then the doctor proceeded with health questions. "What hurts? Other than the stress?"

Tricia replies, "Well, it's my upper back, shoulder, and sometimes my chest. Especially early in the morning."

The doctor sits back in his chair and puts his hand to his chin. "Hmmm... Look, I'm going to send you for x-rays down the hall. If you have the time."

Tricia, looking at him with a sense of relief that someone seemed to care about her well-being for a change, replied, "I have all day Doctor. Thank you."

After leaving the doctor's office, it was quite late, and Tricia was looking for the bus to head home. Still, a bit down from the two doctor visits, she was just all mixed up in her head about Roy, and dearly missing Priscilla. When she gets home and enters the house, something is amiss. She can't quite figure it out, but something just wasn't right. Either way, she made some tea, went into the front room, and sat, watching old love story movies until she fell asleep on the couch for the night. Most of that time spent on the couch was crying into her tea about missing Priscilla and fighting with Roy. At this juncture in her life, everything was seeming to fall apart. Missing who is basically her daughter. On the verge of breaking up with the guy she's liked for so long. Feeling mentally tortured, and also having something wrong with her health that she was praying was nothing, and also massive stress. Just far too much for Tricia, it seemed too much to be able to make it through right now. Each day that passed that week, Tricia was extremely depressed. She barely left that couch. She didn't eat or change clothes. She just lay there, crying and watching T.V. Other than getting up to go to the bathroom, which was not much, since she wasn't eating, Tricia didn't move. Each day, Roy drove past the house as well. In his fit of jealousy, rage, and insecurity, Roy thought that Tricia was still not home. This was because since she was tied to the couch in her fit of depression, she didn't turn on any lights all week, or go outside. Therefore, Roy thought she never came home after the shrink visit. His stupid, jealous mind drifted to thinking that she could be across the street with John since he witnessed the hand-holding incident a few days prior. Roy decided not to enter the house again, especially since he found a way to convince his silly self that Tricia may have something going on with John. In his ignorant mind, how was he to know that the two of them; Tricia and John weren't across the way, watching him go in and out of the house and laughing at him. The mind of a man! A jealous man. Is something else!

As Saturday arrived, Tricia lay on the couch that early afternoon and the light from the sun peaked in between the curtains next to the couch and sat right across her brow to allow her to feel the warmth from the sun on her eyelids. She opened her eyes to the feeling and just stared at the curtains and the ray of light coming in. After about an hour of lying there, she heard a soft tap on the door and then on the window next to the door. It stopped, and she didn't hear anything. A few minutes later, she heard it again. Now, thinking she was dreaming, she sat up on the couch. There it was again. She realized someone was on the porch. So, she mustered up some energy to get off of the couch and pull her wild hair into a ponytail and throw on her robe and go see who was at the door. As she walked to the door, she couldn't help but think to herself, *"About time! It took him all these days to come and check on me! Wow!"* Referring to Roy in her head. Disappointed in him, but still hopeful they could mend the issues. She approached the door to peek through the glass and see John standing there with his hands in his pockets turned halfway toward the street, looking like he was about to give up and leave after his knocks. Knowing she looked like shit! She ran into the kitchen and grabbed a paper towel, wet it, and wiped her face, she also took a swig of water, as she knew she didn't have time to formally freshen up. Not that she wanted to impress or look good for John. She just didn't want a million questions as to why she looked so down. Even though he'd probably be able to tell anyway. She returned to the door and slowly turned the lock to unlock the door. John, just about to leave, heard the lock moving and stopped in mid-step to turn back around. Tricia opens the door, but not the screen, hoping that the screen door would act as a shield for her unkempt appearance.

"Hey Tricia. How, how are you doing? Haven't seen you in a few days." John said through the screen door as he stood there looking at her, with his hand over his eyebrows, blocking the sun that was streaming into the screen further blocking his full sight of Tricia. He continued; "Just coming to check on you and see if you will still be ready to go on the search tonight? Ride with me to the meeting spot? You look like something is wrong?" John standing there trying to figure out why Tricia had been missing for the past couple of days.

She mustered up an explanation, "I, I have just been down a bit with probably a bad cold John. But I'm feeling, feeling a little better today. I, I think, umm yes! I'll be ready tonight! You said six, six o'clock! I'll be ready!" John, standing there looking at her through the screen as if he knew there was more to the story, took her agreement to join him later as an okay to leave and not probe.

"Okay then. I'll see you later. At about six!"

She decides to clean herself up. Besides, this is not who she was! Tricia was normally relentless at fighting for everything. Why should this be any different? She knew it was time to get up, clean up, and continue the search for Priscilla. Also, decide how to mend things with Roy. With that, Tricia went upstairs and headed to the bathroom, and rinsed the tub to start a hot bath. As she sat on the side of the tub with one hand under the running water to make sure it got hot, she began to drift off into thoughts about her and Priscilla together as Priscilla was growing up. Thinking about the day she brought her home from the hospital. Thinking about the first diaper she changed. Thinking about all the times she and Priscilla would stay up late, reading and laughing on the weekends. She so missed Priscilla. As she snapped out of it at the feel of the scorching hot water running on her palm, she stops the tub to allow it to fill and goes to her bedroom to get a change of clothes. On the way to the room, she stops at Priscilla's room and pushes the door open, stands there at the doorway just looking into the empty room, imagining Priscilla, as a little 5-year-old on the floor, playing with toys. She could hear Priscilla laughing with joy as she played. As emotion began to overtake her, she pulled away from the doorway, about to head to her room, when in her peripheral, she sees a spot on the floor. She moves into the room, now intrigued by the spot, and gets closer, down on her knees to examine the spot. It looks like blood. But, why would blood be on the floor, next to the bed? She sat for a few minutes on her knees in front of the spot, trying to think of reasons it would be there, but couldn't think of anything. Did the person who took Priscilla leave this behind? Did Roy see this when he searched? What about the police? How did they miss it? After a few minutes, she got up to proceed with her bath but remained bothered by the spot. After her bath, and relaxing to get her mind right, it was coming up on six o'clock amazingly fast. Tricia gets ready and leaves. As she goes outside, there is John, standing in front of his car door, waiting for her to emerge from the house. With a smile on his face, like he normally has, Tricia notices the smile and couldn't help but feel it was infectious and started smiling as well. "Well good evening my friend!" John said as he opens the passenger door for Tricia, and she smiles even harder as she sits down in the car. Odd, though there had never been anything but a neighborly vibe between the two of them, John was acting very courtly towards Tricia lately. She could tell. But didn't want to figure out why, with so much going on. Maybe it was because he could tell things were falling apart with her and Roy. John closes her door and jogs around to his side, gets in, and starts the car. "Alright! Let's go on over and meet everyone." Just as he put the car into drive and began to pull off from the curb, they heard a loud screeching sound and Roy's car speeds right in front of John's car, causing John to stomp the brakes in a panic to stop his car, barely missing slamming into Roy's car. Tricia and John look at each other, then at Roy's angry face, as the three of them sat in each car. John begins to jump out of his car, as well as Roy and in a second, they are nose-to-nose about to go at it.

While the two are yelling about what Roy just did, and Roy screaming at John asking, "Why is my woman getting in your car?"

Tricia runs over and gets in between the two men. Pulling on Roy's arm to try and stop a swing by either man. "Roy! What the fuck are you doing?" As she pulled him away from John. Other neighbors coming out into the street and getting into the mix by now.

Roy yells at her, "What the fuck are you doing? With him Tricia? Huh!?"

Tricia, continuing to push and pull Roy back toward her porch, yells back at John, who is now being blocked by a couple of neighbors, "I'm so sorry John, I'm so sorry!" Roy getting angrier as he is fussing and being pulled by Tricia kept trying to get out of her grasp. But somehow, she manages to push/pull him up the stairs and into the house.

As she slams the front door shut, they could hear the ruckus of all the neighbors outside and John; not usually an angry man yelling at the top of his voice, "Bring that maniac back outside! Fucking pussy!"

Tricia locks the door and turns to Roy and began screaming at him.

"Why are you acting so crazy?" Tricia yells at Roy.

He yells back. "Why are you creeping around with that fucking weirdo dude?"

Then she returns the screaming, "Creeping? Creeping? You are so fucking ignorant! I am so sick of you and your stupid ass ways!"

Roy responds, "Stupid ass ways?! Fuck you, you crazy bitch! I should have been left you the fuck alone!"

Now in a rage, Tricia yells back at him, "Then leave you asshole! Calling me a bitch! You never liked Priscilla! You never respected my house! You never tried to make this a family! And when needed, you couldn't even be a man and protect my house! Calling me a bitch, you ain't even a fucking man, you punk ass pussy!" As she points her index finger right in front of his nose as she yelled a rebuttal.

He took in her spout and grew angrier, and took her finger and bent it back, breaking her down to one knee, then struck her in the face, knocking her to the ground. "You dirty bitch! Talking about me not stepping up! Look at you now! And I know you kept from me the lawsuit! I saw your folder, you selfish bitch! You are so stupid, you don't even know when you need to help yourself, let alone the little dumb ass girl! I'm out of here bitch!"

As he stepped over her laying on the floor crying, he flings the front door open and charges out of the house. Everyone still outside, but now more neighbors holding John back as Roy gets in his car and screeches off while John is trying to get around everyone to get his hands-on Roy. Roy gets away, and all the neighbors run over to Tricia's house to help her as she lay on the floor in view of the front door. John, still standing in the street looking at Roy drive away down the road, thinking he should jump in his car and follow, but he just stands there and thumps the hood of his car with both fists in rage. The rest of the night, neighbors huddled in Tricia's house, making sure she was okay, and being there for her. Hanging around to make sure that Roy didn't come back. This included John, who was questioning Tricia about how it escalated to the point of Roy putting hands on her. Of course, Tricia didn't answer his questions, and gracefully took the support of her neighbors for a couple of hours until she was able to convince them that she'd be okay alone the rest of the night. As everyone began to leave after a few hours, John is the last to leave, standing in the doorway with Tricia, as other neighbors are leaving and heading back to their homes.

"You do know that I'm not going to go to sleep tonight, right? I'll be right in my front room, looking out to make sure he doesn't come back." John said to Tricia as he stood there in the doorway in front of her.

Ashamed, abused, and embarrassed, she was grateful for John, and everyone on the block. She looks up at John and replies, "I can't thank you enough. I know one day; I'll find a way."

As she displayed a crooked smile, trying to show John that she was still tough enough to get through even tonight! As he turns to walk away down the stairs slowly, Tricia slowly closes the screen door and locks it as John kept taking one step at a time down the stairs, looking back at her in between each foot hitting the next step. She closes the door, locks it, and turns back into the house, and lays back onto the front door, she glances into the living room and notices a blinking light on the answering machine. Her heart starts racing, as she didn't realize that she missed a call, probably ignored the phone ringing earlier in the week, as she lay depressed. She ran over to the couch and hopped over the end to sit next to the table with the phone and answering machine, eager, hoping that it was a call from Priscilla telling where she was. As she pushes the button to hear the recording, it starts, and the voice is that of a man. "Hello Miss Wilson, this is Doctor Phillips! I need you to come down to my office as soon as you can do so! The x-rays and scans revealed something very troubling. We need to rule out any possibility of cancer, do more testing." As she listened to the message, she froze still as tears began to run down her face. This can't be true. This can't be happening to her! Not now! After everything! She yelled out and knocked over the table next to the couch in frustration and just fell to the floor crying and yelling, filled with anguish.

Reality Check

Over time, Priscilla got to become a pro on the runs. The months fly by as she becomes more and more comfortable doing the jobs. The months carried into years, just over two years since her initial arrival in Chicago. Ever since the first one, it's been a breeze and her profit from each run had become one hundred dollars per run. That was a mint for a young girl. She and Chris got closer. Chris even teaches her how to drive sometimes, to show her, just in case a run went bad, and she needed to be the driver to getaway. She and Fabi get closer. More and more time passed, and she grows up wiser and older, while saving her money and doing the runs, getting closer to Marisol as well. Unbelievable that a young black girl in her late teens would be a drug mule in the '80s; in Chicago and getting away with it undetected for the most part! But it was happening! At first glance, anyone would think that these people are taking advantage of this young girl, which they are! The police would probably paint it the same if charges came down. At times, when she was about to go to sleep at night, Priscilla would be thinking about the same thing. But then she would remind herself that she was also using them. To get away from Roy. To allow Tricia to move on with her life with Roy. Not get caught for stealing the bus ticket and crossing state lines as a minor. So, in her mind, it went both ways. By now, she has a regular schedule with the crew, and they are raking in the money. With little to no incident on the runs. Just the times that Priscilla had a couple of encounters with some stray dogs chasing her in some of the apartment complexes. There was the one exception, some months ago when Priscilla realized just how real this could get and was scared beyond her wit on a run.

About a year ago, on a normal setup. With David driving as usual, and Priscilla going through the usual steps of securing the product, she left a mailroom and began to search for the mailbox to drop the key. As she drops the key, she noticed that someone was following her. She didn't bother to look over her shoulder or turn around, she just started to walk faster. Back at the truck on this day, David was blasting some music and not paying his usual attention to see when Priscilla was coming as he'd always done. As Priscilla continued to act like she didn't know the person was behind her; she then noticed another man walking along her right side a few yards away, following her as well. When she noticed this, she picked up more speed and decided to look to the left, there was a third individual some yards away, tracking her steps also. She was boxed in, and they were planning to rob her of the product. The plan for something like this was for David to see it ahead of time and intercept the situation to get Priscilla out of there. The plan even called for David to drive up on the sidewalk, grass, or whatever it took to go get her and get out of the situation. Though he had a gun; the plan was to not use it unless it was necessary. She walked faster and faster, but the three men got closer and closer as she got to the truck. David, still bopping his head to the loud music, didn't notice. As she got within a few feet of the truck, she could hear the music through the closed doors and rolled-up windows. One of the men started to jog toward her. Just then, David flung the passenger door open and the truck started to move. David finally noticed she was being tracked and chased. "Hurry up! Get in!" Priscilla sprinted and jumped into the truck, simultaneously throwing the brown bag with the product into the back seat of the truck and holding onto the door while David began to pull off. At the same time, the man who had begun to run at her grabbed onto the door handle and one of the other men just barely missed grabbing David's door handle. The third man was about to jump onto the back bed of the truck but missed. David sped off as Priscilla held on with all her might to the open door flinging back and forth, now dragging the man holding on. David made a very sharp right turn, the door slammed shut, and the man flew off losing his grip and slid across the street on the pavement. David sped away and quickly entered the highway entrance. They got away!

"What the fuck were you doing? You didn't see those guys? You are supposed to be watching!" Priscilla shook from the incident screamed at David.

David, responding to the accusation, "I did see them, we got away! You're safe, right!"

Still screaming and upset, Priscilla punched David in his shoulder and yelled, "Yeah! But almost too late! What the fuck!"

The two of them didn't talk anymore after the screaming match in the truck on the way back. For some reason, they didn't talk about the incident to the guys either. It was as if both of them didn't want to admit to being caught with their guard down to Chris and Carlos. Which was probably a mistake. After that scary run, David and Priscilla decided to keep it a secret, and the runs that followed were back to normal. They didn't know where those three guys came from, why they were targeted, and the three guys never showed up again. Maybe it was a one-off attempt? They didn't know, and the two of them weren't telling.

Priscilla, a part of the crew. A family member to Marisol, Chris, and Fabi. Outside of the one scare, everything was going well, and she was saving a bunch of money. So much from each run, she hadn't even counted the money yet. She didn't need to count it. She had meals every day from Marisol. She had a buddy in Fabi. A good Boss in Chris. All she needed to do was do this as long as she felt necessary. The time flew by. Run after run, Priscilla and David pulled off with no issues, and she was the perfect decoy to the operation. Though the police had them on the radar, it was hard to pinpoint what they were doing, because no one suspected a girl walking around apartment complexes was a part of an elaborate operation. But she was beginning to age by now. There wasn't any talk of changes in the crew, at least not yet. She and David got close from doing the runs together. As did her and Chris, though more like a brother. On this Saturday, Priscilla woke up to a box sitting on the coffee table next to the couch she slept on. The box was wrapped in a red gift wrap with a bow. Priscilla looked at the box, but didn't think anything of it, since she knew that Fabi was about to graduate in a few weeks from high school, she figured it was a gift wrapped by Marisol for Fabi's graduation and proceeded with her normal routine of folding her sheet and blanket neatly and preparing to go into the kitchen for breakfast, before going on the weekly run with Chris.

Marisol and Fabi, with Chris in tow bust into the living room and startle Priscilla by singing, "Happy Birthday to you!... Happy birthday to you!" The three of them sang, as Priscilla stood there in shock, and humbled, and beginning to cry from the feelings inside of her. She felt like she was a part of their family. It was surreal! She had been with them and in this situation so long, she was on the verge of turning 18 years old. Priscilla forgot that she had shared with Fabi her birthday date. But here they were, her new family singing and celebrating her. It felt weird; being that she had missed a couple of birthday celebrations with her precious Tricia. She didn't even count the last one, because of the events that transpired with her running, hiding, and getting to know Fabi's family and the runs. But a few weeks ago, she and Fabi were talking about Fabi's after graduation plans and she mentioned her birthday. They ate breakfast, then had a piece of the cake as an after-breakfast treat. But this was a run day, so Chris was eager to get out and get the day going.

As they finished the cake, Marisol said, "Christopher, you should let her take the day off. Celebrate."

Priscilla interjected Marisol, "No, it's okay. I don't want to miss my money." Marisol shook her head and waved her hand at them as they all laugh and continue to talk at the kitchen table while Chris was preparing to leave. With a bit more messing around and laughing and talking, Priscilla finally got up and began to get ready to leave with Chris. Giving Marisol a big hug and saying to her, "You're just like a mother to me! I appreciate you so much!" They embraced and Fabi just stood by the table looking at them with this huge smile on her face. Priscilla left and hopped into the van and Fabi couldn't help but think about how a chance meeting on a Greyhound bus ride brought this family an addition that seemed to work out so perfectly. Chris and Priscilla head out to meet up at the factory with the crew. As they drive, Priscilla can't stop grinning. Grinning from the feeling of being appreciated, being included. She hadn't felt this way in a while. Not since she and Tricia first got close when it was just the two of them. Priscilla had always gone between feeling loved and included, to feeling like an orphan, then back. Each change in her life projected the feeling.

Today, they quickly arrived at the factory, as Chris was zooming and bumping the music down the road. As they pull up to the factory, there is Vic, observing everything as usual. They pull into the overhead door and proceed with the routine of prepping for the run. Dave, George, and Andre are all at the table. Carlos was there this time. Priscilla hadn't seen Carlos in a while.

"Young lady. Good to see you. You've made us all so much money. And you are so careful with the runs! Seamless. Yes." Heaping heavy praise on her, Priscilla couldn't do much but smile.

"Thank you, Carlos, Glad to be able to help."

The whole situation was odd. No matter how much money they were making. No matter how "smooth" everything was going. Odd, because these men were using this girl to be a mule in drug trafficking. Morality aside, Priscilla was also getting what she wanted out of it. In usual fashion, the truck is loaded with the bag of cash, and David gets in the driver's seat to get ready to go. Not too far behind is Priscilla to perch into the passenger seat in her normal position. They exit the factory and head out onto the run. The day was quiet. Sun out, and clear skies. Business as usual for a typical run. The two of them focused on the job. David driving, knowing he needs to look out for her, and Priscilla ready to go through the motions of delivering the bags and securing the product, and getting back to David safely. As they pull up to the apartment complex, Priscilla notices that this one is familiar. Matter of fact, this is the one Andre first showed her how it's done. She remembers all the trees on the courtyard on the way to the rows of apartments. In her mind, she can see it; the rusty-looking door slightly opening and the duffle bags getting snatched into the dark apartment. She can still see Andre's face, as he eagerly awaited the key for the mailroom. Going through the memory, she got ready to go to work as David pulled to the curb and parked the pickup truck. This time, she was looking for apartment number "3942" in the 8th set of row houses. She got out of the truck and began to walk over to the rows of the complex. Looking for the one that started with 39. She spots it and headed in that direction. Nothing looked out of the ordinary. Pretty quiet. No one outside. In no time she spotted "3942" and charged toward the door. Following the protocol, Priscilla knocks very lightly just two times, then steps back out of the door view to the left. As she waited for about a full minute, nothing happened.

So, she knocks very lightly just two times again, then steps back again out of the door view to the left. Still nothing. Now she is getting frustrated and anxious. Just as she is about to knock again, the door creeks open. The apartment isn't dark, but no one is in view as she peaks in. She places her hand on the gun in her waist just in case, because now she is on edge. Other than those dogs chasing and those three weird dudes pacing her, something like this had never happened on a run. She knew the rules were to never enter a spot, so she knew how to handle the run in a case like this. But in her mind, she was thinking to herself; *Who the fuck opened the door?* Curious and too confident, Priscilla did the unthinkable! She pushed the door open and slowly walked in as she grabbed one of the straps of the duffle bag. Why? She couldn't help herself. As she entered the apartment, she noticed that the kitchen was straight back, then some rooms after that. To the left was a living room, and to the right was a dining room with a small dining table set. She saw no one in the spot. "Hello!" She said in a soft tone. "Hello!" again. No response. With her hand still touching the gun in her waist, she was debating to just leave or go to the rooms in the back. Way too reckless the situation and what she was doing! She let the bag strap go and proceeded to go into the kitchen and went to the refrigerator to look in. She figured she'd be nosey and see if someone lived here or was this just set up for the exchange. As she opened the refrigerator door, she heard a thump by the front door of the unit and turned slightly from the refrigerator to look to see what the noise was. She heard another thump coming from the back rooms. Now she was startled for real! She let go of the fridge door and began to reach to pull the pistol out of her waistband and then all of a sudden, she felt what felt like a tap on her shoulder.

Priscilla next realized she was sitting on the couch looking up, through a hazy view as her sight came back into focus. She was looking into the barrel of a sawed-off shotgun that was held by a burley-looking man, rusty blonde hair, and a full beard with raggedy clothes. "If you move, your head will be spread all over that fucking wall behind you little lady!" Looking up at this strange man holding a gun in her face, she almost pissed her panties. She also felt a throb on the top of her head. That's when she knew she was in deep shit for not following the protocol. She had been ambushed and hit over the head. She didn't even know how long she'd been out. Scared to death, she remained calm on the couch. "You fucked up little lady! Now I'm going to have to kill you! I think it's about time I made good on all these motherfuckers, get the money and the product, and make myself a pretty wealthy man wherever the fuck I disappear to! And you won't be able to tell anyone! Because I'm going to blow your fucking head off and then chop you up, so they can't find you, you little bitch!" As she sat there, she didn't say a word and she could see her gun in his waistband now. All she was thinking was, why did she go in, and how could she get out now? She was also thinking that David had to realize she was taking too long and be coming soon. So, in her mind, she knew that there was a possibility that she could get out of this. If only David is paying attention this time! Unlike the time she was being tracked by the three dudes. The crazy man, looking at her over the barrel of the shotgun, kicked a chair over to in front of her and pushed it with his foot, careful not to let the aim of the gun leave her; he positioned the chair sideways to be able to point the gun at her and see the front door. "So, before I murder your ass, at least tell me your name." Priscilla remained silent; knowing that at this point, talking or not talking wouldn't change the outcome. But she also kept veering over to the front door. "I see, you ain't gotta talk to me, sweetie! And I see you checking out the door for your buddy. Ha-ha! If he does bring his fucking ass through that door; I'll turn him into a chopped salad, then your head will be the dressing after!" Priscilla, trying not to cry, got more and more nervous. The crazy man continued, "You see, I know he's coming! And I ain't leaving until I take care of both of you! No witnesses baby! Ha-Ha!" She didn't know what to do! She couldn't move or he might shoot her. And she couldn't warn David whenever he comes. It would be useless because this psycho was going to shoot one of them! She needed a play, and she needed it soon! They sat and sat, no David! It seemed like two hours went by. She had no idea how long it had been. And now the crazy guy was getting restless. "Looks like your dumb-ass friend has left you or forgot about you! I need to take care of him too, so I don't have to worry. But I'm ready to go, sweetie! So, I guess your dead body will have to do!"

He is about to get up, when he hears consecutive beeps by the front door, close up on the door. As he reacts by swinging the shotgun to the door, expecting David to burst in. Suddenly he falls back out of the chair that is positioned in between the couch and the door and slams to the floor, with blood running from his head. Priscilla, hearing a single "Pop" before he fell, is terrified. She thought he had shot her! She brings her knees up to her face and cradles her head down. Then her hands are pulled from her face and David is standing there with his brick phone in one hand. "Hurry up! Let's go!" Pulling on her to get out of the unit. As they leave the unit, David carefully pulls the door up to make sure it's closed. She bends down on the way out and grabs the gun out of the crazy man's waist. David left the duffle bag and grabbed the mailbox key. They run. Priscilla headed to the truck, and David started another way.

Priscilla shook and confused now, "Wha... Where are you going?"

David running toward the mailroom yells over his shoulder to her, "Got to finish the job! I'll explain later! Just come on!"

They hauled ass away from the complex. After David collected the product as Priscilla was still shaking throughout, they begin the ride back to the factory. Priscilla, now crying, was in shock. David, upset, but trying to calm down began with the questioning, "Why would you go in!? You know better! You gotta be fucking kidding me! After I finished my 3rd cigarette, and you weren't done, I knew something was up! Damn!" David was so frustrated that Priscilla broke protocol, he went on and on. Trying to muster the courage to justify the stupid decision, Priscilla finally gave a reply to David to cut through the yelling and complaining about her actions.

"I shouldn't have, I know. I just had a feeling someone was trying to get over on us. I don't know what I was thinking." As she continued to wipe the tears rolling down both cheeks. "How did you? What was that noise that tricked him?"

David, rolling his eyes as he steered the truck, "The fuck does it matter? I saved your dumb ass! Damn! Could've gotten both of us killed!" After a few minutes of silence, a break in his ranting, David went on to explain the heroic plot that freed Priscilla. "I crept up and listened to that fucking crackhead go on and on about killing you, and realized, he was tweaking anyway. That's when I decided to try and leave my beeper by the door to get his attention and go around to the kitchen window and page myself with the brick, then take my shot. Lucky first shot, I guess!" Priscilla didn't reply to David's claim of his plan. All she knew is that it worked, they both made it out and they were almost back at the factory. David went on as he entered the gate to the factory and began to pull the truck up to the overhead door, "We finished the job because that's the protocol! That tweaker was either not supposed to be there, turned on his boss, or just plain stupid! The protocol is that their crew is going to clean him up as long as we left the money and got our product. I'm sure their crew found him by now." None of it was making sense to Priscilla, but she just nodded and stayed quiet.

As they get out of the truck, once in the factory, David immediately goes up to Carlos and leads him up to the office, to explain what happened. Carlos was probably going to have to notify the supplier to make sure the tweaker got cleaned up like David told Priscilla. While they went upstairs to the office, Priscilla stood there by the table as George and Andre counted the money. Chris marched right up to her, "What happened out there?" As he put his hand on her shoulder. While breaking down crying, Priscilla explains to Chris step-by-step the events that just transpired on the run. Chris is blown away, and upset that she didn't follow protocol, yet relieved that Priscilla is okay; all in one. "Wow! Don't panic when Carlos comes back. I got you. I'll do the talking. Just answer his questions and stay cool. He might get crazy." After about 20 minutes, Carlos and David emerge from the office and come back down.

"Young lady!!" Carlos goes on, "I can't believe you broke protocol!" As he pounds his fist on the table and some stacks of money fall to the floor. In a low tone, almost like a growl, Carlos said, "You know what I'm going to do to you, young lady?" His voice grows and he is back up to a yelling tone. "You know what I'm going to do to you, young lady!!" Carlos turns his back as everyone is standing frozen. He takes two steps away from them, then turns and walks the two steps back to the table. His voice finally lowers to almost a whisper. "I'm going to let you take some time off. Go home, clear your mind, and come back in three weeks to do the next run. Okay?" All of the guys' eyes were huge, as they couldn't believe it. The last dude that fucked up a run, was, well, missing. Then Carlos looked at Chris and said, "Get her the fuck out of here, and make sure she is ready for next time." Chris was still standing there looking at Carlos nodding in agreement, but not moving because he was still so shocked by the action, which was no action. Carlos raised his voice again and waved his right arm, "I said get the fuck out of here before I change my mind!" Chris and Priscilla leave out of the factory door in a hurry, get in the van, and peel out of the parking lot. They didn't say much on the way back to the house. Both of them were surprised and reeling with adrenaline, from knowing they probably just walked out of a situation in which one or both of them could have been killed today. No music. Just the wind from the windows down. No conversation.

Finality

As Priscilla experienced a life-or-death situation, Tricia was dealing with her mortality. Tricia eventually got up from her living room floor to face the fact that she needed to go to the doctor and do more tests. That day had come and gone. A true diagnosis of Cancer is what those tests revealed. Trying to cope with so much, Tricia went home and just got submerged in the bottles of liquor that filled her liquor cabinet. Depressed because the doctor told her that her cancer was extremely aggressive, and that treatment may help but there was no guarantee. Couple that with her and Roy breaking up. Priscilla is still gone, and her hearing and seeing Roy around town keeping the company of so many women. Tricia was on the brink of destruction. The only good thing that she had in her life now was the fact that her neighbor John had taken a liking to her, and constantly came over to check on her because he wanted to become her man in the absence of Roy. Hell, one day, John even found her passed out, with her front door wide open, drunk from boozing, shortly after her diagnosis. John came in that day, cleaned her up, fed her tea, and stayed with her until she sobered up. So sweet, how John treated Tricia. But she wouldn't take him seriously about a relationship. It was because she knew her time was limited now. Nevertheless, John didn't give up. He kept checking on her to make sure she was okay. She also received a visit from Don in the wake of the news. Frank's old buddy came over to check on her, to see how she was doing in the search for Priscilla. Don himself had been working his connections to try and help locate Priscilla, with no luck. But he kept up the faith that they'd eventually find her. On the day Don visited, Tricia opened up quite a bit, about a lot! Don was taken aback by what Tricia revealed that day he visited. While sitting and talking, Tricia opened up to Don about her and Roy breaking up. As Tricia talked and told him about all the things Roy had done to her, Don could not help but think back to that night when he found out Roy was basically living there, and that he remembered trying to figure out how Tricia could allow that, especially with a young girl in the house. He also was thinking about how he wanted to fuck Roy up that night, that they almost got into a fight. As Tricia talked, he was paying attention, but he was also re-living that incident that night with Roy; when he accused Roy of being the reason Priscilla was acting so weird, as Tricia talked, Don replayed it in his mind:

"Hey man! Is it me? Or does Priscilla seem to act a little different lately? Just saying, I was sitting and talking to her, and every time I brought you up, she seemed to change her disposition, just saying, my man. I'm just saying brother, it seems like it's you! You seem like the reason for Priscilla acting weird!"

As she spoke, Tricia was feeling like Don wasn't listening. "You see what I'm saying, Don?" Don snapped out of his memory of that night, "Yes Tricia, I hear you, you telling me he's done what?" Tricia goes on now that she's confident that Don is paying attention, "Roy has moved on and it's obvious. He's always at the bars, he drives through here with a different bitch in his car all the time! Like he's trying to purposely hurt me or something! I heard that he's on those drugs now. Someone said meth, I've heard crack too." Don, surprised by all of this, replies with that surprise, "Wow!! Are you serious? He is just wild now huh? He hasn't come over here to bother you? Or put his fucking hands on you, has he?" Don asks with authority.

Tricia replies in defense, "No, no, he knows better. I'd fuck him up. I'm ready. Plus, my neighbor John is always looking out for me, and he would come over to help." Then Tricia goes on to reveal a little more about what had happened between her and Roy. "But, before he went on this binge of drugs and prostitutes, something did happen. Don't get mad, because my neighbors all helped, and we took care of it!"

Don sits erect now, "What do you mean, something happened?"

Tricia, now looking sheepish replied, not looking Don in the eyes, "He did come over here and jump on me! He put hands on me, but I fought him off, and my neighbors came to help. I think John followed him to get him." Don, furious as she described the fight in more detail, flashed back to the night when he and Roy were about to throw blows, he sees the night as he zones out on the part when Tricia is describing her and Roy's fight. Thinking about when he and Roy grab each other up, and he threatens to kill Roy, he visualizes Roy's face:

"If I hear anything about Tricia or Priscilla being hurt in any way! I swear, I will come back here and take yo bitch ass out muthafucka!"

Don snaps back again, after thinking about his threat to Roy on that night. Tricia is finishing up the story about the fight between her and Roy, and she began to talk about her illness.

"And with the Cancer, the doctor keeps telling me the treatment might not help, so I haven't committed to it."

Don, now back with full attention, replies, "Look, you need to do what the doctors say, okay? Try to fight this Tricia! All I've ever known you to be is a fighter. You can get through this. Just like one day you will find Priscilla and be back together with her. You can do this sweetie. I know you can." Don pulls Tricia in and embraces her, as she looks at him and breaks down. Don felt it necessary to come clean to Tricia about why he and Roy were about to fight that night. "Do you remember that night I was in town, and it looked like me and Roy had tension?"

Tricia picks her head up and wipes her eyes and replies, "I do. I do. Why do you ask?"

Don looked at her and said, "Well, the only reason I left in a hurry is because it got heated. Because I accused him of being the reason that Priscilla would always be acting so weird. Straight out told him, I think Priscilla only acted weird when he was around. That triggered him, Tricia." Tricia's eyes got big as she pulled back from Don to take in what he was saying. Don goes on, "I'm just saying Tricia, any man that gets all defensive about being accused of making a young girl act weird is guilty. I'm not trying to say I know anything specific, but my heart tells me he's done something to our precious Priscilla. I wouldn't put it past him that he could be the reason she's gone, Tricia."

She got up from the couch. "Don, Don, Don." As she pounded one fist into the other hand. "Don't tell me this mutha…. Don't tell me. No, No." Don gets up also and grabs her shoulders as she is flipping out.

"What Tricia?"

She looked at him and said, "Don. Do you know that the day Priscilla disappeared, I had made a run to the dentist, and left his ass here with her to watch the house? I mean, he was outside doing yard work, but someone supposedly got in and took her or something, according to the police. That fucking pussy says he saw nothing!" She proceeded to pound her fist into her hand. "Damn Don, Damn!" As she fell to the floor on her knees and started crying out again. "God! Please! Don't tell me this man did something to my baby! I did find blood in her room, which the police missed after everything too. God!"

Don picks her up off of the floor and puts her on the couch. "Listen to me, Tricia. Priscilla is alive and well. Somewhere. I know it. He may have chased her away, but his ass ain't stupid enough to do something to her." Tricia looks at him with doubt remaining on her face as she continues to cry. Don went on, "What I would do is go back down to the police station and at least tell them that you suspect Roy had something to do with her disappearance. At least they'll start to look into him. Clear his name or pin it to his worthless ass. Hopefully. It won't hurt anything to do that Tricia and hope they do look into it."

Tricia and Don continued to talk, and she agreed with his sentiment that she should go and talk to the detective again. Just as Don was getting ready to prepare to leave, the doorbell rang. The door was open, with the screen door closed. Tricia got up from the couch and Don followed since he was about to leave anyway. There stood John, with a dish in his hand.

"Hey John." Tricia said as she stood at the door.

John replied, "Oh, hey Tricia. Didn't know you had company. Sorry."

Then Don stepped from behind Tricia to speak to John. "Oh no, I'm like family. I'm just heading out now. Don't let me interrupt your visit. I've heard some good things about you!" Don steps out onto the porch and shakes John's hand. John, appreciative, but also looking at Don with a look as if he wanted to ask, What have you heard? Don goes on as he continues to prepare to walk down the stairs to leave. "It's good to hear that someone has been looking out for my family while that fool Roy is running around town crazy."

Then John got the full picture and replied to Don. "Oh yes, man. We have all been looking out for Tricia ever since that fool went crazy. No chance I let him ever come near Tricia again."

Don looked him up and down. "Glad to hear it. Glad to hear it."

As Don began to go down the stairs, Tricia interjects into their man meeting, "See you later Don. But I hope y'all know that I'm a grown woman. I'm glad y'all are concerned, but I can also fend for myself."

They all laugh as Don leaves and John comes into the house with the dish in hand. "I made you some pasta and sausage Tricia. I hope you like it." Tricia escorts John to the dining room table as she is feeling special that he brought her lunch.

"Aww. Thank you so much, John. I definitely can eat. Haven't been eating much lately anyway, so you're right on time. Have a seat and I'll go get some dishes and utensils."

Tricia heads into the kitchen as John places the dish on the table and sits. She returns to the dining room with the plates and forks in hand and they begin to dig into the pasta John made and talk for hours. About Don and his place in her life as an honorary family member. Roy, and his shenanigans around town. Them still conducting and planning searches for Priscilla. Her illness and her new plans to do what the doctor wanted and try to fight it with treatment. In the middle of their conversation and the meal, John wanted to make sure Tricia truly understood that he was there for her.

"Tricia, can I tell you something? Something heavy I mean."

Tricia stopped in mid-bite of a fork full of pasta to look at John. Wiped her mouth with a napkin and finished chewing. "Yes, yes John. What is it?"

John then proceeded to continue his proclamation to Tricia, "You know that I like you, right? But more than that, I want you to know that I'm going to be here for you every step of the way. I can go to your doctor appointments with you, your treatments. I'll come and spend the night and feed you if I have to Tricia." Tricia was looking at John and was feeling loved by his statement. She knew he liked her but had no idea it was this much. John continued. "What I'm trying to say,

Tricia; is that I feel like I... I love you. I've always loved you. As we've been neighbors and I made sure to always pay attention that you and Priscilla were okay from a distance. We would pass each other by in the stores, or during the neighborhood block parties and small talk. I've always wanted to tell you. But at first, your hands were so full raising Priscilla, then Roy came into the picture. I'm sorry. I probably sound like a creepy stalker or something. I'm..." Tricia got up from her seat and came over to John and pushed his hand with his fork down to the table and gave him the biggest kiss ever. Right on the lips. They kissed passionately for about 40 seconds until they pulled apart and Tricia just stood there looking at him in the eyes.

"John. Thank you. For being here for me. I like you the same. I've always thought you were attractive too. But I never thought you even paid me any attention. It means so much that you would be honest with me. Let's give this a shot. Let's try to figure this out and try to live this life I have left. Together John." She began to cry. It's like Don's visit breathed new life into Tricia. On top of that, she had a great friend and potential lover in John that she could trust.

Meanwhile, speaking of Roy and his shenanigans, he was all around town, doing all the drugs he could find and fucking all the women he could. Even if he had to pay them for it. Roy had fallen so low. Not that he was ever a "Stand-up guy" anyway. But he was at an all-time low in his life. He was feeling the guilt of being the reason that Priscilla was gone. He was feeling the guilt of losing Tricia and it being his fault. Everywhere in the small neighborhood, all he heard were people still talking about Priscilla, and how she was such a sweet girl and how could anyone have done something to her. He was frustrated that it had been a few years, and the neighborhood was still looking for Priscilla. What a terrible man he'd become. Selfish to say the least! He was frustrated because his mother had disowned him due to her being so ashamed of what he'd become. He and his father always had problems; their relationship had gotten worse. Roy also heard through back-channels that Tricia was sick. He was frustrated that she hadn't reached out to him after getting the news that she was sick. He felt like she would come to him if she weren't doing well. He knew that she probably had turned to that damn John! Just like a piece of shit low-life man to blame her for her illness and not coming to him. When a real man would have rushed to make up to her and help her in her time of need. But not Roy. No not Roy! Laying up in a dusty motel. He was laying on the bed, smoking a cigarette, with a sleeping prostitute by his side. He put the cigarette out, grabbed an almost empty bottle of Hennessey, and took the remainder down as he lay, propped up on the headboard. Then he smacked the sleeping woman on her naked ass.

"Get up bitch! It's time for you to hit the road. I got some shit I need to do." The woman, still half-sleep drags herself to sit up on the side of the bed and looks back at Roy.

"Damn man. You don't have to smack my ass so hard! And try to kick me out. What the fuck."

Roy looked at her. "Try to kick you out. Shiiitt. This my spot bitch. You served your purpose. Now get out before I fuck you up." The woman gathered her clothes and began to get dressed and try to leave before he got up and got violent; Roy began to reach for some meth paraphernalia as he talked shit to her. "You just like all the women in my life. That little bitch girl that ran away for nothing and ruined the whole fucking neighborhood. That no-good ex of mine who wants to blame me for everything. And my damn selfish Momma and Daddy, who won't even let me come home to clean up!" As the woman left out of the hotel room, Roy proceeded to tie his arm to prep to get high on the meth needle, then fell slowly back onto the bed to ride his high. A lost soul it seemed.

The Plan

After a few days of sleeping a lot, then sitting out in the yard with Marisol, Priscilla was going stir crazy. She was also still quite shaken from the events of the last run. Chris had been gone for a couple of days. Fabi told Priscilla that he probably went to spend a couple of nights with his girlfriend. Besides still being very scared, thinking about the incident as she sat each day in the yard, or the kitchen for meals, or when chilling with Fabi; Priscilla was having nightmares about it. Not just reliving the crazy guy with the sawed-off shotgun in her face. She was also having nightmares about Carlos, that he may still seek to make her pay for messing up a run. Who knows what he had to pay to make things right with the supplier! Her mind was fucking with her! She was convincing herself that she probably needed to get out of this deal with Carlos and the crew. Besides, what was she doing anyway? She didn't belong! She didn't know what to do. Her mind would not rest, and it was tearing her up. Chris told her not to say a word about any of it to Fabi, so she couldn't vent it out. She was in a predicament for sure. That predicament was making her go crazy! She had to do something but didn't know what. The last thing she wanted to do was run again. So tired of running! She told herself that she wouldn't do any more running. Not to mention the fact that she had gotten so close with Marisol. But her soul was telling her that Carlos wasn't just going to let it be business as usual when she went back. What was she to do!

While Priscilla was mulling her future and safety, Chris was holed up in the apartment where his brother was killed. Trying to gather his mental status. This is because his brother was kidnapped and then killed after filling in on a run for Carlos. Chris, though he wanted to find the killer, blamed himself. He blamed himself because he's the reason his brother got involved in the game in the first place. He was so guilty for pulling him in. Chris knew it was all his fault. So, he just sat there. Sat in that apartment for days. Re-living the days that his brother went missing, never turned up, then his body was found by the police. Tragic! But a lesson. Now he was thinking he almost did the same to Priscilla, not family, but he had also taken a liking to her, and valued her as family. So, he remained in hiding at the apartment, drinking, and thinking about everything. While Priscilla was moping around, wondering what the future held for her, Fabi popped into the living room where Priscilla was laying on the couch. "Hey you! Are you going to just sleep all day every day? Let's get out of the house! You know, like to go to the library; you should come with me!" Priscilla looked at her like she was crazy, talking about going to the library as a way to get out of the house, and rolled her eyes with no reply. Fabi continued with the exercise of persuasion. "So, the reason why I like to hang out at the library is that there are a couple of cute helpers that put the books away. I only go there to hang out and kick it with Will and his buddy Jimmy. They are both cute, you know?" Fabi Grinning from ear to ear and blushing as she described the boys she deemed so cute. Priscilla, staring at Fabi like she was out of her mind, paused a bit longer, and then Boom! That was it!

Priscilla jumped up from her lying position and said, "You know what. I'm down. Let me freshen up, then we can go Fabi. Let's do this." Priscilla got the idea that the library is where she needed to be. With her struggling to decide or build up any type of confidence to tell Chris she wanted out of the game, she all of a sudden got the idea that maybe she could use the library to her advantage regarding getting out of the game. So, she got up and went into the bathroom to get ready to go. After about 15 minutes of getting ready, Priscilla appears from the bathroom to go out to the yard where Fabi and Marisol are sitting in the backyard. "You ready?" Priscilla said to Fabi as she gets out into the yard.

Marisol, looking at the girls, "Oh, you got my young buddy to go to the library, I see. Good to get out of the house." They start to head out of the backyard and onto the sidewalk. Marisol, with a joking tone, yelled as they walked away from her sitting in her yard rocker, "Tell the cute boys I said hello, Hahaha." Marisol laughing as she jokes to them walking away.

Fabi and Priscilla get to the library in no time. A short walk from the house. As they enter the library, Fabi starts to look around for her buddy Will.

"I'm going to go and find the boys, so I can introduce you." Fabi said with energy in her voice.

Priscilla, standing closely behind Fabi said, "Sure! I'll be over here doing a little browsing."

Fabi, not able to contain her excitement to see Will, replies as she walks away. "Okay, I'll be back over here once I find him, and you can meet Jimmy."

Priscilla nodded as she headed over to the computers to activate her plan to try and get out of the game. Priscilla began tapping away on the computer. The goal was to find her uncle in Chicago. Or in Madison, that Tricia always talked about. This was her out! A way to get out of the game! Of course, she didn't want to have to run again. But she needed to do something to get her mind right. Maybe this was it. Maybe reaching out to find her uncle was the way to go. Either way, this was her opportunity. She began to search for a Bill W. Anderson in Madison, Illinois. But, when she entered the info, two things happened. One, Madison, Illinois was way too far from Chicago, basically in Missouri from the map on the search. Also, there weren't any Bill W. Anderson's in Madison, Illinois. There were some Bill W. Anderson's in Madison, Wisconsin, but she knew that Tricia always talked about him living so close to downtown Chicago. She kept scrolling on her search and stumbled upon a Bill W. Anderson, finally. But this one was in a Matteson, Illinois. "Hmmm!" She said with wonder in her voice. Then she looked at the map and saw that Matteson, Illinois was the closest of the three to downtown Chicago. So, she reached for a magazine that was sitting close to the computer and ripped out a piece of the page and grabbed the pencil sitting on the desk, and quickly wrote down the address in Matteson, Illinois. Just as she folded the magazine page up and was about to stuff it in her pocket, Fabi walks up, all alone, after being gone for about ten minutes.

"Hey!"

Priscilla jumps up from the seat and puts both hands in her pocket, concealing that she is stuffing the piece of paper into her pocket. Fabi continued talking as she got closer, "So they didn't come to work today. Both of them. Will didn't even tell me. Wait until I see him. We can go if you want to." Priscilla looked at her, trying to keep an innocent face, as not to reveal that she was up to something.

"Oh, okay. Yeah, I looked at some stuff. The library is still a library, you know?"

Fabi laughed and agreed, "You know what, your right, while picking up the magazine that Priscilla left laying open from tearing out a piece of the back page. Fabi grabbed the end of the torn page with one hand, and looked at Priscilla, then closed the magazine, and threw it back onto the desk. The two of them left out of the library and proceeded to head back to the house.

Sitting on the address for a while, Priscilla was itching to figure out a way to get to Matteson and figure out if this Bill was her uncle. About two days later, Chris shows back up at the house. No one questioned his absence. Pretty much, everyone just operated as normal. Chris picked up where he left off in the home, helping Abuela with the yard and cleaning duties. Then they all gathered for dinner the night he returned. It had been a while, and Marisol insisted to have a family dinner together, so she prepared a hefty meal all day long. They gathered at the table and Marisol felt good. "It's so nice to have you all together. It's been too long! Chris working. Priscilla working. Fabi; always out and about, at the 'Library.'" All of them started laughing as Marisol started to dig into the dish of food and pass the dish to Chris. They took in the meal, laughed, talked, and laughed more. As Chris filled the conversation with lies about where he's been the past couple of days, Fabi talking and holding back on details about her crush on Will, the library helper, and Marisol talking about her garden and the beautiful vegetables she had been harvesting, Priscilla thought of it naturally in the conversation.

"You know, I been wanting to see that Karate movie. You know, with the kid."

Chris interjects, "Oh yeah, I saw that already. It was good."

Fabi and Priscilla, at the same time, say, "Oh you saw it already." They all burst out into laughter.

"We should go see it Fabi." Priscilla said as they laugh.

Fabi, being Fabi, responds immediately, "Let's go tomorrow." Priscilla, knowing she baited Fabi into it, grinned with deceit because she knew Fabi would say that.

"Really! Tomorrow? I… I guess so."

Then Fabi pushes Chris on his shoulder and said, "Take us and drop us off tomorrow. We can take the bus back. Okay?" Chris ignored Fabi at first, having a sidebar with Abuela about how good the food was until Fabi pushes him again and repeats the request to be dropped off at the movie theater.

"Okay, okay, okay! Gosh!" Chris relented as Fabi kept pushing his shoulder and bugging him while they finished the meal.

The next day, as the afternoon approached, Fabi and Priscilla were busy getting ready to go to the movie. Of course, Fabi was getting all dolled up, while Priscilla was focused on the task at hand. Getting dressed regularly, not thinking about trying to impress anyone. "Come on y'all! Let's get out of here!" Chris yells out from the kitchen, ready to head out to his van. Chris was in a hurry for some reason today. As Marisol was out in the yard, as usual, the two girls finally were ready as they both emerged from the two different bathrooms in the house. Chris had already gone outside and was talking to his grandmother while waiting on them. As Fabi and Priscilla came out of the door to the yard, Chris started to walk toward the van, not before kissing his grandmother on her forehead.

"Alright, Abuela. See you later."

Then Fabi, "Bye-bye. Love you!" Fabi said as she swung around the back door heading to the van as she blew a kiss to Marisol. Priscilla in tow waved at Marisol also.

"Be careful kids." Marisol said as she sat rocking in her yard chair.

As they were riding down the road on the way to the theater, Chris wanted to confirm the agenda. "So y'all are going to take the bus back right?" While looking at Fabi in the passenger seat.

Fabi, while checking her make-up again in the mirror replied, "Uh. Yes. I told you yesterday." In a smart tone. They rolled on, and finally arrive at the front of the theater. Priscilla slides the side door of the van open and hops out. While Fabi is still in the van fussing at Chris about knowing which bus to take home after the movie.

Then Fabi closes the door as Chris yells out of the window, "Don't be slamming my door."

Fabi, with the snappy reply, "I didn't slam it." The girls head up to the ticket window to purchase their tickets. As they get to the window; Fabi being Fabi tries to change the program.

"You know what!" While she was looking up at the feature films on the wall. "Let's see the Standby Me movie instead. What do you think?"

Priscilla looks to Fabi like she is crazy, then said, "What? I want to see Karate Kid! That's what we planned. You crazy!" Priscilla thinking in her head; *"Wow, she can't be serious? But this could work out in my favor!"*

Fabi defended her idea, "I'm just saying, the other movie could be better, and we could come back and watch the one you want to see with Will and Jimmy. On a date. Huh, Huh?" Trying to be persuasive as she used her elbow to nudge Priscilla on the arm. Priscilla, now seeing an opportunity to do what she needs to do; but still wanting to play it off replied with a stance of no compromise.

"How about you see that movie, and I see this one? They are only about 20 minutes difference. We could meet up at the bus stop after?" Fabi was disappointed but didn't want to watch the movie Priscilla wanted to see, especially now that she looked at the features on the wall.

"Okay, deal! Meet at the bus stop after and ride home together." The girls went into the theater together after buying tickets and separated into two different auditoriums to go see their respective movies.

A few minutes into the previews, Priscilla gets up and heads back to the entry door of the auditorium. She first peaks out of the door to make sure Fabi hadn't come back out. Then she hurries out of the side door of the theater and makes a b-line for the bus stop. Taking out notes of her research, looking for the bus that would take her to the south suburbs of Chicago. After waiting for only about 5 minutes, just like it was listed on the sign at the bus stop, here comes bus #327 on the 45th minute of the hour. She gets on the bus and pays her fair and quickly finds a seat. The ride was long. What a view for Priscilla this was. Somewhat of a tour of the city. She had no idea where she was going, or if the address she found was even her uncles. All she knew was Tricia talked about this uncle, she'd never met him. So, what if he wasn't her uncle, and thought she was crazy? What if he wasn't alive anymore? All these questions. But she was on the way now. No looking back. As the bus drove on, she kept looking down at the paper with the address; 339 Pleasant Road. Bill Anderson. She couldn't wait to get there to see if it were him. In her mind, Priscilla had convinced herself that she was on a reunion mission. Not that she was on the run again, like she'd promised herself she wouldn't do again. Even though, this is exactly what it was. As the bus gets to an intersection that was in between houses, a shopping center, and a forest preserve, Priscilla felt like this was the stop. She knew she was close, and that the bus wouldn't take her right up to the door. She knew she had to walk a bit, but in which direction? She got off of the bus, and looked around while standing on the corner, then decided that going straight across a huge major road to the neighborhood of houses was the way to go. After she played a little frogger and dodged multiple cars on the road crossing over, Eureka! She saw it! Pleasant Road! She dashed the road and began looking for the house number. She walked house by house. Some people in their yard doing yard work. Some people just sitting on the porch. Some spoke, some just looked at her as she walked on. Then all of a sudden there it was! 339! Her heart started to beat fast as she built up the confidence to go up to the door. Knock, knock, knock; Priscilla gave the door three swift thumps before stepping back from the door and placing her hands behind her back. About a full minute passed; nothing! Knock, knock, knock; again. Another minute passed and nothing. Now she was getting disappointed. Feeling like that long bus ride was a total waste. *"What's the use!"* She thought to herself. As she began to turn around and get ready to leave feeling sad. She walked to the right end of the porch before leaving, bending over the rail, scoping the side of the house to see if she could see to the backyard. She couldn't see that well from this viewpoint and was deciding if she should walk around and trespass the entire yard before leaving. But wasn't sure about doing it since this is a neighborhood where no one knew her. Might look like she was going to break in. As she turned to prepare to walk away and find her way back to the bus stop; a squeaky noise startled her as the screen door of the house creaked open. "Yes! You lost young lady?" A raspy deep voice emerged from inside the house as the door opened further. She was in disbelief as she turned and laid eyes on the source of the voice. There stood a man, about 6'1", very chocolate complexion, gray hair, and a mixed gray and black beard. And this man looked just like Tricia. This was Uncle Bill! Still shocked at his resemblance to her family and his deep voice; she was speechless. "Don't just stand there! You knocked on my door!" Bill added to his surprising introduction. Now, out on the porch, looking her up and down as she stood there looking scared to death, Bill added more. "Look here young lady, we can stand here all day, or you can tell me what you are here for!" Standing there, still uneasy and a bit frozen in time, she got the energy to reply to Bill.

"I… I… I am looking for Bill W. Anderson. Is that you?" Priscilla answered the man.

Starting to smile at her, he replied, "Bill Anderson, I am! Who might you be young lady?"

With a large smile, she replied, "I am Priscilla! Do… Do you have a niece named Tricia?"

Bill, with his face turning from pleasant to shocked, let go of the screen door and let it slam. "Tricia? Tricia? Do you know Tricia? What? How do you know Tricia?" Now they both were surprised, shocked, and intrigued! They both stood there for about 22 seconds which seemed like 5 minutes, with silence, wind, and birds filling the air to provide the sound in the background.

Finally, Priscilla responds, "Tricia is my Momma. Well, Anne was my Momma." With his eyes getting huge and protruding out of his head at her answer, he began to tear up at the mention of Anne's name.

"Tricia never had a daugh…" Pausing in mid-sentence. Then he walks closer to Priscilla and places his hand on her cheek. "Are you. Are you…? You can't be… They told me you were missing." Tying everything together quickly, and filling with emotion, Bill realized he was looking at Anne's daughter. "Priscilla! They said they couldn't find you. Oh My God!" Now, his face was drenched in tears. So was hers as she stood there. Bill turns and grabs the screen door, "Come, come, come on in and have a seat. I can't believe this. I have to." As he went into the house, with Priscilla following him in, he went straight for the phone. That finally made her break her silence since announcing to Bill who she was.

"No, wait! Don't call. We need to talk first. I have to tell you some things that are important before anyone can know I'm here."

The Escape

Bill and Priscilla have a seat at his kitchen table. "Would you like some water? Coffee? Juice?" Priscilla, still not believing that she had found the uncle Bill that Tricia always talked about responded in a low tone while staring at him, blown away with how much he resembled Tricia.

"Umm, no thanks. I'm fine." Bill gets situated in his chair and leans in toward her.

"So, you want to start, or should I?"

Priscilla began to talk with that prompt from Bill. "I had to go. I had to go! I, I just couldn't stay there with that... He was, I couldn't stay there with that man!" Taking a break in her mini-rant, Priscilla tried to clear up what she was saying. "Tricia has this boyfriend. But he is not a good man. He... He..." Priscilla paused, and tears began to well up in her eyes.

Bill, knowing this looked like it was tough for her, reached out across the table and grabbed her hands and said to her, in an attempt to calm her, "Go on, it's okay. I won't tell a soul. I promise."

Priscilla proceeded. "I ran away. I'm not missing. Roy put his hands on me and tried again when Tricia wasn't home. I didn't want to break up what they had, so I didn't say anything. My friends saw it once, at a party

Tricia had. But I stayed quiet." Crying more now, Priscilla put her head down on the table.

Bill, filling with sympathy and some anger about her situation gave his opinion. "You need to tell your aunt about it. We should call at least, even though we will probably have to go… Never mind." Bill stopped short of his last statement, not knowing what Priscilla knew about back home since she had been gone for about two years now.

Priscilla picked her head up and looked at Bill as she was wiping tears away. "You said go? Have to go where? For what?"

Bill then realized that Priscilla had no idea about Tricia being diagnosed with Cancer last year, and not doing well. He knew he had to tell her. "Well, It's your aunt. About a year ago, she was told she has cancer."

As he finished that sentence, Priscilla fell over, out of her chair with a loud shrill. "What. What! What! No no no no no! Not Tricia! No!" On the floor, crying and banging her fists now, Bill got up and picked her up to try and get her off of the floor. By now she was mumbling with the curse words and tears flowing. "It's all my fault. I made her sick. It's all my fault."

Bill proceeded to rub her back as he got her back up onto the chair. "Listen, Priscilla, nothing is your fault. Not her illness. Not you leaving. Not that horrible man that put hands on you. But you have an opportunity to go see her and make it right. I say that, now that we've had this little reunion, we go take a trip to see your aunt. What do you think?"

Priscilla looked at Bill and replied, struck with a sudden fit of rage out of nowhere, "I ain't going to see her. Fuck that. She let that man come between us. She hasn't tried hard enough to find me. Why should I care?" She didn't mean any of that rant.

Bill understood and just continued to rub her back. "It'll be okay. Look, I don't know where you're setup. Uh, staying. But I promise I won't tell Tricia. Until you're ready to talk to her yourself. You should come live with me. I have plenty of room. And I'm your family. Looking so much like my niece Anne. My God you look just like her. Go get your stuff. Whatever you have and stay with me. You can use my car." Priscilla, still angry, and hurt from the news about Tricia, was shocked that he offered to let her stay like this. He didn't know her. But she knew he was going off the emotion of basically seeing his dead niece Anne in her face.

Priscilla agreed to his offering. "Okay, I'll come and stay with you, as long as you promise to give me the time to be ready to reach out or visit Tricia and try to make it right?" Looking up at Bill, over her shoulder for confirmation.

Bill replied, "Yes, whatever you need Priscilla, but you need to decide about making it right sooner rather than later. Time is not as kind as we want it to be sometimes. Bill, knowing that Tricia was doing very badly back in Baltimore, warned Priscilla not to procrastinate. As they continued to talk about back home, this city of Chicago, and Bill growing up with his nieces Anne and Tricia, often having to babysit them, he shared tales of them getting in trouble, and him getting them out of trouble; Priscilla realized that she needed to get back to Fabi before anyone suspected anything. Hoping she would make it back to the city before Fabi got to the bus to go home.

"Uncle Bill. I want to thank you so much for opening up your home to me. And telling me about Tricia's condition. I understand that I need to make it right with my aunt. But I need to go and get my stuff, but I'll be back to stay with you, and we can talk more."

Bill, knowing there was way more to Priscilla's story, decided not to press her. "Okay, Priscilla. Go do what you need to do. As far as anyone knows, you're not here in Chicago. Or they won't hear it from me. Remember what I said about Tricia and time. I'll let you gone on ahead. Takedown my house number, just in case you need me before you make your way back."

Priscilla took out the same paper she used to jot down his address and wrote his house phone number next to the address. She looked at him, and awkwardly stepped in and wrapped her arms around him, catching him off-guard with the hug. He realized and pulled his arms out and around her to give her the most secure embrace. Made her feel welcomed. Made her feel secure. Made her feel loved! Priscilla, back on the bus, headed to the city, thinking heavily about Uncle Bill, Tricia, and everything he told her. He was right! She needed to make things right with Tricia. She knew that she would eventually need to go back home to see Tricia. According to Bill, she didn't need to wait. But for now, she still needed to figure out a way to get out of the game. Get away from doing the runs for Carlos. She knew that it would be next to impossible. Especially now since she had broken protocol. Carlos would need to see that she is still capable to perform the runs with no issue, after the close call with the tweaker.

But how, how could she get out? As the bus wheeled down the road, she began to think deeply about a plan that would work. She hated that she was coming to the reality that she may have to run to get out. How can she become done with running away? One day she would figure it out. In her deep thoughts, she barely realized that the bus was back on the street a block away from the movie theater. When she realized it, she got up from her seat on the bus and quickly pulled the exit request string, just in time before the driver pulled off again. As she got off the bus and ran over to the theater, she saw a bus leaving. That had to be the bus Fabi was on. She is hoping so, then she can get the very next bus, and be not too far behind Fabi, and it'll seem like a just-miss situation coming out of the movies. Right now, with what she was planning to do, she didn't need to bring any extra attention to herself. After waiting, she got the next bus and took it home. Arriving at the stop by the house and charging off of the bus, she could see Fabi a couple of blocks up in front of her. So, she was right! She had just missed Fabi at the theater. Priscilla decided to run and cut Fabi off on the way to the house. She took off, running down an opposite street from where Fabi was walking. Cutting through people's yards, and alleys. Then she got about a block away from the house and slowed down to a walk. Coming up to the same corner that Fabi should be just about now. The spot kitty-corner from their house.

"Heyyyy… What happened? I was looking for you to get on the bus!" Priscilla said it first to Fabi, catching her off guard and cleverly not allowing Fabi to get those words out first. Thus, trying to play with Fabi's mind, because she knew that Fabi was the one waiting and looking for her after the movie.

Priscilla continued with the charade; "How was your movie? Mine was good." Fabi, now thrown off quite a bit, was indeed confused. She knew that she was waiting for Priscilla and something was fishy. But now that Priscilla had ambushed her with the same claim that she had been looking for her; Fabi just rolled with it.

"Girl, I don't know. Maybe I was waiting at the wrong bus stop? That was crazy! But we made it at the same time. My movie was good too. I bet better than the Karate movie. Hahaha." Priscilla took credence to laugh also while trying to be slick and wipe the sweat from her brow and not allowing Fabi to see her doing it. The sweat beads from running that couple blocks to cut Fabi off at the corner. All in all; Fabi didn't suspect anything or didn't care.

Back at home, and back at the kitchen table for dinner, they were doing their usual dinner talking. Chris started to talk to Priscilla about them having to go back to work the day after tomorrow. Priscilla knew it was coming. She had been prepping herself mentally for it since she met Bill, she had drummed up a plan. A plan that could potentially, finally get her out of the orphan, running phase of her life. All of the planning that she had done got her ready, but her stomach was frequently bothering her all day because she knew it was about to be a big deal! What she was going to try to pull off. As they finished the dinner, and the usual conversation ensued, Priscilla zoned out a bit in the mix of the conversation, just going one-by-one looking at all three of them realizing that she was about to burn three good relationships if she made a move. But her gut was telling her that continuing to do the runs could potentially harm her or even get her killed. Looking at Marisol; this woman had become like a mother figure to Priscilla, they've gotten close, Marisol liked Priscilla and vice-versa, she was filling the role that Priscilla lost with running away from Roy and losing Tricia. Fabi, she and Priscilla got as close as sisters. They talked late nights, they joked around all the time, and they've built trust between them. Chris, he's become the older brother she never had, though he had led her down a path that she shouldn't be on, he had looked out for her and put plenty of money in her pocket. Overall, she would miss them if she moved on, but she was scared of the runs after having a shotgun waved in her face being threatened. She was at another crossroads, but one that would probably define the adult years of her life. Priscilla needed to do what had to be done.

The next morning, there they were, Chris and Priscilla, in the van, heading to the factory to begin a day of doing the run. Priscilla was riding quietly on the passenger side, just trying to remain calm and stick to the plan in her head. This was it! She was about to take a stand! No longer would she be used to traffic, no more threat to be killed on the job. Today was the day! As she leaned onto the window to look out, there they were the birds that enveloped every tree that lined the road. Same deal, not just a couple of birds, hundreds of birds. In her mind, she swore she could hear those birds sing and sing and sing. It soothed her as they drove along to go to the factory, curbed her anxiety a little because she was so on edge! She observed the birds all the way to the factory, and then suddenly, the birds were gone, and Vic was standing there as normal. They got out of the van and walked into the factory to see the guys in their normal position, at the table counting money. Carlos was just coming out of the office upstairs to join them. "Hello, my friends. Let's get this beautiful day started." Carlos said in a pretentious voice as he hit the bottom step to get down to the factory floor, where they all were. "So glad to have you back young lady. Hope that you are ready. Refreshed. Re-focused. I know you are young lady. I am not worried." Carlos, with a rant of encouragement, or threats to Priscilla about her getting her mind right to continue doing the runs with no issue. Chris and the guys just look down because they knew this vibe that was coming from Carlos. He meant business but was trying not to come off as enforcing, even though it was his intent. David began to load the duffle bag and get it over to the pickup, like usual.

Carlos, walked right up to Chris and Priscilla and put his hand on her right shoulder, and lowered his voice to a low tone, "You are ready young lady? Is there anything you need to talk about? We can talk if you need to." Acting as if he was giving Priscilla an opportunity for an out.

Priscilla stood there and looked Carlos right in the eyes and said, "I'm ready. Been ready. Nothing has changed." Whether she was able to lie with a straight face, or she had a change of heart on the ride in; Priscilla convinced Carlos, for now, that she was good. She and David proceeded to jump into the pickup truck, Chris joined the guys at the table to count money, and the overhead door rose to allow the truck to exit. They head out.

The truck pulled up to an apartment complex. A new one, Priscilla didn't recognize the location. Here she was! On the brink of making another life change on the journey of her life. She took the paper with the apartment number and made sure she had the gun as normal. Then got out of the truck and went to the back to get the duffle bag of money. David gave her a nod, and she left the truck to go to the apartment. As she entered the complex, she went in between two buildings looking for the apartment number on the paper. There it was! "4298!" As she approached the apartment, she was looking around, side to side and over both shoulders, and up at the windows of the second-floor apartment, windows to see if anyone was paying attention. She got to the door, bag in one hand. She stepped to the doorstop, looked left and right, raises her right hand to do the protocol knocks, then she suddenly turned left and began to walk briskly toward the back of the entire complex. Moving very fast each step until she gets to a large gate encompassing the apartment complex, with a train track right behind it, she got up on the gate, tossed the bag over then proceeded to climb the gate and get over to the other side where the train tracks were. At this point, she grabbed the duffle bag and puts the straps over her head and shoulder to secure it around her back and took off! Running down the center of the train tracks as fast as she can. No one saw her, she just ran! Ran as fast as she could, not looking back, no hesitation! Just running.

After running full speed for about 8 minutes, she had cleared the apartment complex location. Matter of fact, she had entered the back of a different neighborhood. Probably covered just shy of a mile in her sprint. Priscilla was exhausted, afraid, uncertain, and again alone. She finally stopped running and went over to a forest preserve area, near the tracks. A bunch of bushes and trees, she put the duffle bag down on the grass, making sure she was hidden from sight and sat down on top of the bag. Trying to think of her next move. She knew she was going to go to Bill's house, but she didn't know where the hell she was, or how to get to Matteson from her current location. She sat, thinking about Carlos finding out that she is missing. She thought about Chris, getting angry about her fleeing. About Marisol, hurt, to know she was no longer with them. Fabi, missing her friend. David, going crazy once he realizes she is gone and gone with the money. *"Oh shit!"* She thought to herself as she sat there. *"Why didn't I leave the money? Damn! They are going to be looking for me forever with this money!"* At this point, she couldn't turn back now. She had just acted on impulse. She could turn back, but she couldn't, because, what if she goes back, and David sees her returning from the tracks? He'll know what she was about to do. A train was coming very slowly down the tracks, almost at the speed of walking pace. She knew it was going in a south direction. So, she acted on impulse again and got up, grabbed the bag, and went towards the train, and hopped on the first open cart she saw. Will this get her to Bill? She had no idea, but she was taking this ride. This ride away from being exploited. Even if it meant running away again. Something she thought she was done doing.

Sitting in the truck, listening to music, David realized that too much time had passed since Priscilla left. Now he is getting nervous. He turns the truck off, and thinks to himself, *"Don't tell me this stupid ass girl has gone into another apartment? Damn!"* David gets out of the truck, careful to grab his pistol, knowing what he had to do to rescue her the last time they were together. He couldn't believe it. David proceeded to head to the apartment that was the target, "4298!" He weaved through the apartments looking for the number on the door, then he finally sees it. Proceeding with caution as before, David goes up to the door and places his ear on the door. Thinking he'll hear voices as he did before. Nothing! He heard nothing. David proceeded to head to the side of the apartment, to inspect the windows to see if he could determine if Priscilla were inside. After seeing or hearing nothing, David had a decision to make. He knew protocol was to not leave her behind, but how could he figure out if she was in danger? If he just went up and knocked on the door, the protocol was that the person inside knew nothing, or would never speak anything. Besides, if he did just knock, whoever was inside wouldn't just say; "Yes, I kidnapped your run girl!" He had to think of a way to get her out of the apartment again. David proceeded to place his beeper by the door on the ground like before, and call it with his brick phone, just like before, but this time he was going to stay in view of the door, to see if whoever opened the door, looked like they were hiding something or someone, and proceed to act accordingly. He goes across the apartment complex to a walkway with stairs and looks over to the door "4298!" He called the beeper number. It beeped repeatedly, and again. Nothing! No one opened the door. Now he was frustrated. In a fit of rage, unable to believe that she would do this again, David charged over to door "4298" and kicked open the door. Upon him kicking in the door, the person inside opened fire, the protocol for break-ins, and proceeded to fill David's chest with bullets. As the guy saw David, and there was no duffle bag in sight, he ran out of the apartment to make a getaway, leaving David laying on the doorstep to bleed out.

Revelation

Priscilla was back in the south suburbs after figuring out her way with the freight train ride, a bus, and a cab, and walking, was right around the corner from Bill's house. Almost there! By now, the police had found David and had taped the apartment building off to investigate. Carlos and Chris had gotten the news and were sitting in Chris's van in the front of the apartment complex, watching the police go through the investigative motions.

Carlos pissed! "Where is the damn girl!? This should have never happened! Did they take her again?" Chris looking at Carlos, with no answers was both scared and frustrated. Chris's gut told him she ran. Because he knew that's how they met her. Carlos, still ranting, "We need to find her! Now. Let's go! Nothing we can do here. Go back to the factory, so we can strategize." Chris pulled off from the scene and is driving as he is thinking to himself, *"Fabi has to know something!"* They get back to the factory and Carlos immediately got out of the van and hurried into the factory, with Chris right behind him. Carlos starts yelling upon entering, "Everyone stop what you are doing. David is dead! The girl is missing! We have to go and find her. See what she knows. Hope she is alive!" As Carlos is getting the guys' attention, Chris goes over to the other loading dock of the factory to use the phone. Carlos, so busy yelling, and the guys in shock and hurt about the news pay him no attention. Chris got busy dialing, calling home, the phone at Abuela's house.

After two rings, "Hello!" Fabi is the one that answers.

"Hello!" Chris, shaky voice and all, surprised Abuela didn't answer, "Fabi, Fabi! What else do you know about Priscilla?"

Fabi, hearing the tremble in Chris's voice instantly gets scared, "What happened, Chris? What happened?"

Chris, trying to keep his voice steady, and keep Fabi from yelling and getting Abuela's attention, "Fabi, relax! Relax! And listen! What else do you know about Priscilla? She's fine. Just answer the question."

Fabi knew he was lying, but didn't want to anger her cousin, because she could tell something wasn't right. "You better promise me she is okay Chris! All I know is that she kept talking about some uncle, some uncle in Chicago burbs, but she said Madison, so I think she was confused, I think he lives in Wisconsin. She got it all wrong. Now tell me what's wrong! Where is Priscilla?" Fabi gave up some unknown info, then desperately wanted to know about her friend's whereabout and safety.

Chris, with the new information replies, "Fabi, I'll fill you in later. She'll be okay. I promise!"

Fabi adds a last-ditch comment before Chris could hang up, "Chris! She better be!" As Chris hangs up, Carlos walks up behind him, just barely missing the conversation he had on the phone.

"We are about to mobilize. George is going to stay north, Andre out west, you go east, and I'll go south and downtown. We're going to find her! Today! Vic will hang back to see if she shows up here. While we're out, we'll tap our contacts in every part of town to see what they've heard. About David and Priscilla. Got it."

As Carlos finished giving his orders to Chris; Chris began to speak, "Okay, but I got a tip that… Not saying it's the case, but, if she is not taken, she may have family in Madison, Wisconsin."

Carlos, looked at Chris like he just gave up some gold and said, "Really? Now, why would you think she is not taken, Chris?" Carlos moves in closer and grabs Chris by the collar on his shirt. "Why Chris?"

Chris, trying to act cool and not panic, "I'm not saying that. Just saying, we need all options in this situation. Okay!" With his hands up on the side of his face.

Then Carlos let his collar go and said, "Okay man. I trust you. Let's get ready to go search. Since you think you got some inside info, Chris, you switch with George and go north and then Wisconsin and hit up our connects up there."

While the crew began to try and figure out what happened with David and Priscilla, She is back at Bill's house and goes up to the door, just as Bill's about to leave out. "You made it back. Like you said." Bill, grinning while he looked at Priscilla standing on the porch. "I knew you'd come back. Glad you did. I was about to head out to the store. Want to join me?"

Priscilla, drained from running, looking beaten, looked up at Bill and said, "Yes, yes! Can I go and put my bag down and wash up?"

Bill, looked at her huge duffle bag, thinking it was just clothes, moves to the side of the front door, "Sure, sure, go ahead darling. Your room is the one at the back of the house. I'll be out here on the porch waiting for you. Take your time." Bill sits down on a swing on the porch, and Priscilla goes into the house and heads right down the main hall to the back of the house, passing a bedroom on the left, door ajar, must be Bill's, a bathroom on the right, and finally the last room in the back of the house. She opens the door, and it is a cool breeze that hits her. As she enters the room, she sees a twin bed and a nightstand, an armoire, and a closet door. She stands in the middle of the floor of the room and looks around in an entire circle. Then she goes over to the armoire and there is a book sitting on top. She places the duffle bag on the floor and grabs the book. It's a picture book. A lot of people in the pictures, none of which she recognizes. Then, as she gets almost done flipping the picture book pages, she sees two teenage girls standing in front of a porch in a picture posing and smiling. The girl on the left, she immediately knew it was Tricia, the other girl had to be her mom. She saw pictures of Anne before, just not at this age, didn't recognize her at first, but then realized it was indeed her mom. The porch was Tricia's house. She could tell. The house Tricia and Anne grew up in, that she grew up in too. After looking through the picture book, and getting emotional, she put the duffle bag in the closet, which was empty, took out some of the money to buy some clothes, and took the gun out of her waist, and put it up on the shelf of the closet, under some extra pillows that were sitting at the back of the shelf. Went into the bathroom to wash up, and after about ten minutes, went out the front door to join Bill. Incredibly nervous she was, as Bill locked the home, and they went to get into his car to go to the store. Every single truck looked like one of the crew's trucks to her. Every single brown and tan van looked like Chris's van. She had so much anxiety on this trip.

Bill and Priscilla got to the store and went in, she tells Bill, "I'm going to grab a cart and get some things for myself, some girl things."

Bill just looks at her and laughs, "Okay darling. No problem." Bill was simply happy to have someone with him. And they were family. A bonus. They go in different directions as Priscilla made a b-line for the clothes. Needing something to wear, as she left everything back at Fabi's house, not wanting to take clothes and let on that she was about to run away from them. She preferred that it look like she was taken. Priscilla was busy looking through the blouses when she notices a guy staring her down. At first, she gets nervous upon seeing him, about to take off and run. But after noticing that he was someone she never saw before and not one of the guys from the crew, she put her head down to try and not look at him. He was trying to flirt a bit. He liked what he saw. She continued to pretend to not see his advancing glare. As she continued to move along and shop through the women's clothing, she noticed that this guy was still hawking her, trying to get her attention. He kept circling where she stood and looking at her from different angles, throwing smiles and flirty faces. The more she noticed his appearance, she began to feel like he did look familiar. Now she was getting nervous again. The guy was mid-height, black guy, an awkward-looking dresser, and looker. He was wearing a huge earring lined with diamonds in his right ear. As she is trying to connect how she thinks she's seen him before, she still tries to pretend to ignore him. To calm her nerves, she browses the clothing and began to sing to herself, letting a little of the tone out as she shopped. The guy couldn't take it anymore, he decided to approach her. While she is in the middle of a note, singing one of her favorite songs, an old Temptations song that Tricia use to play all the time, the guy walks up.

"Wow! Wow! I've never heard such a beautiful voice. You must be trying to be a professional singer?" The guy said as an impromptu introduction to get to know Priscilla. She finally decided to acknowledge him. Well, with him walking right up on her, how could she not acknowledge him.

"Excuse me?" She said as she continued to sort through the blouses.

The guy replied, "I'm just saying, pretty. Nice body, and a great voice. You are the total package. Can I ask your name?"

Still trying to figure out how she thought she's seen him before, "You tell me your name first. You came up to me."

Stepping back some from her, the guy replies. "I'm Ricky, some call me pretty Ricky." Then he laughs and she laughs also.

"Okay Ricky, What do you want?" Priscilla, not dealing with flirtation before, or ever having a boyfriend, this was a new situation for her. But she tried to play it cool.

Ricky, smiling knowing he had her attention now, "To get to know you. Maybe even help you continue to work on that pretty voice. I've helped some girls before with voice lessons and putting together vocals. The main thing is to continuously practice, and record yourself doing it, play it back, and keep on. You got a recorder? Do you do it?"

Priscilla, though she could sing, never took it seriously at all. Hell, she hadn't even thought about it, being with Tricia, and being just a kid. She only thought about her voice when she was in church and choir.

Priscilla takes in his advances and laughs at his apparent attempt to help her become a singing star, she replies, "Nah, never recorded myself."

Ricky probed more, "So, I know you haven't been around here before, what brings you to this side of town? You from Chicago?"

As she began to answer him, she saw Bill across the aisle. Lying in her reply as to not give up all her info, "Yeah, I'm from around downtown, and I'm visiting my uncle that lives over here." While pointing at Bill walking past.

Ricky turned and looked at Bill, "Oh, I know old Bill. Coolest dude on the block. That's your uncle? Small world." As Ricky identified he knew Bill, it hits Priscilla. The awkward clothes, the name, the earring, out south. This is the dude they blame for Chris's brother's killing. *"Holy shit!"* She thought to herself. She didn't want to give up that she may have known who he is. She just wanted to get out of the situation.

"So, I'm going to go with my uncle and let him know I'm ready. Looks like he is looking for me to leave."

Ricky looking at her trying to leave, "Okay, I see, we should try to get together one day. Can I get your number?"

Priscilla replying as she pushes her cart away, "I don't have a phone."

Ricky gave chase laughing, "Okay. Okay then. I know where good ole Bill lives, maybe we'll cross paths again, and I can give you that recorder for your voice practicing."

As she continued to walk away, she just looked at him over her shoulder, and said, "We'll see. And the name is Priscilla." She catches up with Bill and they check out and leave the store. What an eventful day for Priscilla. She was drained. Just wanted to get to Bill's house and get some food and rest.

For the next couple of days, Priscilla just lay around and rested. Eating here and there and getting much-needed sleep. She needed to re-charge, after living on the edge with Chris and his crew. Bill didn't mind, he knew she had been through something, so he let her rest, and just offered food, and to go out to the store with him if she wanted. Which she declined in the last few days. While she recovered, Chris, Carlos, and the crew were unsuccessful in looking for her. Though they hadn't given up yet. They just could not figure out any leads to what happened that day. No one saw it or heard anything. At this point, Chris and Carlos didn't know if she ran with the money or was kidnapped or dead. Chris spent most of the last few days trying to calm Marisol and Fabi's nerves, telling them that they'll find her. Marisol was torn up. Priscilla took on the role of an additional child for her. She had gotten close to Priscilla. Fabi was in a state of depression about her friend. Because she had the feeling that Priscilla had run away. Just like how she met her on that Greyhound bus. *"Did she go back to Baltimore?"* Fabi kept thinking in her head. Chris had the vibe that she ran to. He even thought about going to Baltimore but wouldn't know which part of Baltimore to go to. So, he didn't try. He managed to hold off Carlos and his anger, by carrying on that she had to have been taken. Even though their supplier denied knowing anything about the incident. Tensions were growing in the business. Chris had to try to find her!

Priscilla finally got out of bed and decided to get up and get some air. She went out onto the porch, where Bill was sitting and drinking some coffee. "There she is. I knew you would eventually need some sunlight." As he giggled with his coffee cup in his hand. "Have a seat sweetheart." Priscilla came over and sat next to Bill on the porch and sat back to just relax. Priscilla sat, taking in the air and the breeze. The two of them sat small talking and catching up more and more. Priscilla, shared stories about her and Tricia as she grew up. Bill, shared stories about back home years ago.

Then Bill asked; "So, what will you do about Roy? Something needs to happen."

Priscilla, thinking before replying, "What could I do? He's a big, grown man. I can't hurt him. I wish I could go and physically do something to his ass." Priscilla, getting angry thinking about it. "Maybe one day, one day, I'll get my revenge on him."

296

Bill, the peaceful type of man, looked at her and said, "You don't have to necessarily hurt him physically. But Tricia needs to know. I think her finding out who he is, will hurt him more than any type of physical damage you could do sweetheart. Plus, you need to talk to Tricia soon. I talked to her the other day; she is not getting any better. And no, she still doesn't know you're here in Chicago." They both sat back and took in what they just discussed, and Priscilla was relieved that she knew she could trust Bill. Finally, a person not trying to exploit her, use her. It was different.

Bill got up after both sat for about half an hour talking and relaxing. He stretched and yawned aloud and started to head back into the house. "You want something to drink Priscilla?"

Almost dosing off, Priscilla replied, "No, no thank you, Uncle Bill."

Priscilla continued to relax and then all of a sudden, "Well, well, well. Look who it is!" There was Ricky, walking up toward the porch, as he was walking by the house. Most likely, not by chance, especially since he already knew Bill before Priscilla showed up. Priscilla couldn't believe it. Smiling at him, trying as hard as she could to not smile, but she couldn't contain it.

"You damn stalker. What are you doing here?"

Ricky laughed, "This is my neighborhood. Last time I checked; I can walk where I want." They both chuckled as Ricky came up to the top step and sat there instead of coming to sit next to her on the bench on the porch. "I would love to get to know you better. You should come and hang out with me." Ricky, giving his best pitch to her. The whole time, Priscilla was trying to resist his charm. They talk and flirt for minutes on in. At a point, Priscilla couldn't hide her attraction to Ricky and began to flirt back with him. As they continue to talk, Ricky convinces her to come to hang out with him, finishing up telling her about his place, "You should come to visit one day. Plus, I can give you that recorder I have, huh, huh? For that singing career of yours. Free of charge." She laughs but is seriously considering coming to hang out with him. What did she have to lose? Though she now knows definitely who he is. The dude that could have potentially killed Chris's brother, but could be innocent. She felt she could trust him. Could it be that she had stumbled upon two trustworthy people in her life in a couple of weeks? Bill, and now Ricky. She throws caution to the wind and gets up from her seat.

"I'll hang out with you." She Caught him off-guard. Ricky was quite surprised. "I'll hang out with you today."

Ricky, even more surprised, stood up, "Huh?"

Priscilla started to go into the house, "Let me grab some things and tell my uncle." As she disappeared into the door. Ricky, standing there with his hand in his pockets, then by his side, in his pocket, didn't know what to do with his hands as he realized he had done it. Got her to come to hang out with him! Priscilla comes back out after a few minutes, with Bill in tow. "Here he is Uncle Bill." Bill comes out onto the porch and looks at Ricky.

"Rick, long time no see. How's your Dad?" Bill already knowing him.

"Oh, he's good. I'll tell him you asked Bill." Maybe it was because she saw that they already knew each other. But she finally didn't feel so uptight.

As they prepared to walk off of the porch, Bill leaned into Priscilla, "Watch out for him. He's okay but watch him." Bill whispered to her as she walked away.

Ricky and Priscilla get to his place, and they enter. His place, modest, a few pieces of furniture, a T.V., not much inside, but clean. They go and sit on the couch and continue their conversation from earlier on the porch. Priscilla, trying to see if she can get Ricky to admit he's a big-time drug dealer and pimp like Fabi told her on the bus, "So, what do you do for a living? Why does everyone know you?"

Ricky, curious as to why she is asking, but not suspecting anything, just laughed, "I'm just popular. That's all. No big thing. I grew up here, know all the families, they know my family. Why do you ask?"

Priscilla didn't want to pry or hint that she already heard about him. "Oh, no reason; just wanted to know. Also, why are you supposed to be this great vocal teacher? Or whatever you brought me here for?"

Ricky, giving a reply, "Ha! I brought you here to hang out. Like I said before. I just think you're cool. Would like to get to know you."

She shook her head, and just laughed, "Okay. I see." Ricky then got up and started to go toward a bedroom.

"Speaking of that, hold on!" He disappeared into the bedroom, and Priscilla started to observe around the room, to see if anything stuck out to reveal his drug dealer label. Seeing nothing before he comes out of the room, he pops out with a small box in his hand.

"Here you go. As I promised, free of charge. Here is a voice recorder, you can use to practice vocals. Do that for a few weeks, and then we can work together."

Priscilla reaching her hand out to take the recorder. "Thank you. You're so nice. But I don't think I'll make it big." Looking at her as he gave her the recorder and held onto it just long enough to allow them to touch hands in the exchange, an element of flirtation continued from earlier.

"Don't underestimate yourself. Sky should be the limit, Priscilla." She takes the recorder and puts it in her pocket. Ricky turned on his T.V. and sat down next to her, and they continued to talk for a few hours and watch T.V. getting to know each other. After a few hours, Priscilla decided it was time to go.

"I guess I'll get ready to leave now! Go check on Uncle Bill." Ricky, not trying to impose will on her on this first get-to-know/date, even though he knew she didn't need to check on Bill.

"Oh, okay. Cool. I'll walk you out. Next time, we should get something to eat or go out to a movie or something."

Priscilla looked at him as they got back outside of the apartment building. "Maybe we can, maybe we can."

Priscilla is walking away from Ricky's building, about to head down the block to go back in the direction of Bill's house. She walks past a liquor store parking lot and hears some chirping in her background,

"Hey sweetie! You must be new meat for Ricky." One voice said, followed by a barrage of laughter by a group of women.

"Yeah, she must be the new bitch on the block." Priscilla stops and turns around after that comment.

"Excuse me!" As she walks over to the crowd of four women. "What the fuck did you just say? You crackhead!" Priscilla, not wanting to be bothered today, approached the woman.

The one-woman took exception to it and walked right up on her. "You heard us! We saw you with Rick. He's a fucking pimp. I don't know what he lied and told you. You are going to have to earn your rank over here little bitch."

Priscilla, thrown by their talk of having rank in a group of prostitutes, got her mad. But now she confirmed the status of Ricky that Fabi claimed on that bus ride. As Priscilla was standing up for herself and defending that she had no interest in becoming "one of them" she was almost jumped by the bunch of prostitutes. They felt she was going to take their money because they saw her with Ricky. She manages to getaway. Slickly, throwing dirt in one of the lady's faces, and runs back to his place. Now she is in the hallway of his apartment and she runs up the stairs and gets to his door. Priscilla is banging on his door, with full force. Ricky finally flings the door open.

"What the fuck! What are you doing? Why are you back? Banging on my door?" Priscilla barged past him and went to stand by the couch and faces the door. He stood there with the door open, the knob in his hand.

She said, "Close the door please." Priscilla still breathing hard from fighting off the women and running up the stairs. "Why the fuck didn't you tell me you were a fucking pimp! So that's why you came to talk to me? You trying to recruit me to be a stinking streetwalker? Huh!?"

Ricky, not knowing how much she knew, denied it. "Hey! I ain't no pimp!"

Priscilla loses it, "Stop fucking lying! Your whores just tried to fucking beat me up by the liquor store. Tell me the truth. They told me you are their pimp."

Ricky, caught off guard, tries to continue to lie, "Okay, okay. They are not mine. I'm just a front man. Okay. I'm not the brains. Okay. They are all a bunch of tweakers, so they lie all the time. They want to get high so bad; they are afraid that you will take money out of their pockets just because you know me. But I'm not the pimp." Priscilla didn't know what to believe. Here she thought she had finally found someone else she could trust. Now this! She began to leave, but Ricky stopped her. "I… I don't think that's a good idea. They can get crazy. And I told you they are not my women. You should stay tonight. Let them go get high, do whatever, and go away before you leave."

Priscilla is appalled! "You expect me to believe that they are not your whores, but you can protect me from them. By hiding me overnight. Get the fuck out of here!" She tries to push him out of the way to go out of the apartment, and he restrains her.

"Listen to me! I could walk you out there, kick their ass and get you home. But if I lay hands on them, my boss will fuck me up. Trust me! Hang out here and leave in the morning. By then, they'll all be somewhere asleep. Look, I'll let you sleep in my room and I'll sleep on the couch." Feeling setup, Priscilla didn't know what to do. But she didn't want to risk having to fight her way away from those women again. Conflicted, she decided to stay, oddly enough.

Priscilla, knowing Bill wasn't going to worry about her, decided to agree to stay. She, of course, didn't sleep.

They both stayed up talking on the couch until about 3 am. They got deep in the weeds with the conversation. At least Ricky did. It seemed that Ricky wanted to get Priscilla to fully trust him. To her surprise, he started to talk about the crew up north, said he knows they blamed him for the murder up there, but he didn't do it. Trying to figure out a way to clear his name. He told Priscilla, "Hell, I even know where it happened. But I didn't do it! I swear it wasn't me!" This was something else to her. She didn't expect him to reveal something like that. It meant a lot. Priscilla was frequently checking out of his window to see that the women were still out there waiting on her. Here and there, one or two of them would leave to get in a John's car and make some money. But they stayed, just like Ricky said. When she finally got sleepy, Priscilla told Ricky to go ahead and sleep in his bed. She remained on the couch and fell asleep there for about a few hours until the sun came up. At about a quarter after six, Priscilla woke up and went over to the window to look, and just like Ricky said, the women were all gone. Priscilla went and looked in Ricky's room to find him knocked out. So, she quietly crept to the front door and snuck out, locking the door handle lock, and leaving, making little to no noise. She exited the apartment building and headed towards Bill's house in a hurry. As Priscilla walked to Bill's, Ricky had gotten up right after she left and went out to the hallway of his apartment building. Ricky went up one flight and to an apartment right above his and took out a key and opened the door. Inside was a living room with beds everywhere. There were the group of women that tried to jump Priscilla last night. Two of them sleep. But the instigator still woke, laying on one of the beds.

"Did it work? Did we scare her enough for you Daddy? Is she going to join us? I bet she felt protected when you told her to wait while she stayed with you. Heard y'all talking all night."

Ricky looked at her, pulled out a wad of money, and threw it at her face. "Shut the fuck up and split the money up between y'all. We'll see how it goes with her." He turns and slams the door and walks back to his apartment. Knowing that Priscilla had no idea that he was indeed trying to recruit her against her will to be one of his street women.

On the way back from Ricky's place, Bill sees Priscilla coming, and runs out to her. "It's Tricia! They moved her to hospice."

As he grabs her to tell her. "What, what, wait Uncle Bill! Calm down!" Priscilla, taken off guard by Bill running out of the house to tell her the news. They walk over to the porch and sit down.

"She's not doing well Priscilla. We have to go; we have to go see her. You gotta make things right before it's too late!" Priscilla, filled with all these different emotions just looks at Bill, then gets up and goes into the house. No more words. Bill follows her into the house and watches as she goes to the back room where she'd been sleeping, and she goes in there and just closes the door without saying anything. She goes to her room and cries all day. Bill just sits and is depressed also. He doesn't want to force Priscilla but is also growing impatient with not going to Baltimore to see Tricia as soon as possible. Yet, he allows it, gives her time to cope with the news. After two days, she got up and told Bill she'll be back, as she went toward the front door and began to exit the house.

Bill looked at her with anxiousness in his eyes, "Priscilla stop! We have to decide when we are going to go see her. You can't keep running from this."

Priscilla stopped and turned to Bill, "I just need a little more time okay. You have to understand Uncle Bill." Bill nodded in agreement but knew they had to get to Baltimore soon. He had already decided in his mind that if she wasn't ready tomorrow, he was going to go without her. Priscilla left and bean to walk down the street. She headed in the direction of Ricky's apartment. She went back to Ricky. As she approached his apartment, some of those girls are hanging outside of the building and are laughing as she walked up. Priscilla saw them but decided to ignore them and walked right on by, bumping one on her entrance into the building.

"Excuse me miss princess! Shit!" One of the women yells as Priscilla pushes her out of the entranceway with the bump.

Priscilla gets up to Ricky's door, and just about to knock when he opens it. "Whoa! Where you come from, and where you been?" Priscilla just collapses into his arms at the door and began to cry. She didn't know what to do. With the news about Tricia, she went to the only place she thought she had gained some trust from someone. Ricky guides her to the couch, and they sit, as she opens up about Tricia, Roy, everything that happened in Baltimore, back home. She didn't mention anything about her time in Chicago. But was quite emotional and remained hugged up on Ricky the whole time she released this information.

"I just, I just, I know I need to go see her, but. But I don't want to or need to see him. I might try to kill him. But she is terribly ill, and I need to see her. Bill needs to see her." Balling her eyes out on his chest, he continues to comfort her. "It's not fair! I have been through so much, and now this. Losing the only person that ever loved me. Why God! Why?" Ricky rubbed her back and shoulders as she continued to vent and cry. Priscilla looked at him as she lay on his chest and he rubbed her back. She continued to stay silent for a few more minutes as she looked up at him. He looked down and then they began to kiss. Their kiss escalated into both of them rubbing and touching each other. Then it escalated to them beginning to strip each other's clothes off. Ricky picked her up and took her into his room. It had begun! Priscilla's first time. She didn't know what to expect. Ricky didn't know she'd never done it. He took his time, and she consented. It happened. Priscilla didn't know how to feel after. Going from pain and hurt to pleasure and passion, she lay there and fell asleep, drained from everything that had happened and the mental drain and toll it had taken on her. Priscilla slept on, for more than two hours. She had just been so drained lately. Ricky had never fallen asleep.

After about an hour, he got up to go and take care of some business. Ricky now knew he had the total trust of Priscilla, and he knew he had to figure out a way to work her into his rotation of ladies. He looked at her as a prize. She was younger, cleaner, and better looking than any of the women in his group. He had big plans for

Priscilla. She woke up to reach over to Ricky in the bed and noticed that he was not laying there. She sat up and grabbed her underwear, she heard him talking, and heard another voice. She crept over to the bedroom door as she put on her underwear. Hearing him in the front room, he was speaking so loudly and had his receiver volume on his phone loud enough that she could also hear the person on the other end of the phone. As she eavesdropped, she could hear him talking about her. She heard him telling someone. "Oh, man. I got a nice clean one for you. She's new. Naïve. And she's open-minded." Priscilla's stomach starts to get sick. Because she knows he is talking about her. She had bought the story that he wasn't the boss and wasn't pimping women. He had lied to her to throw her off the trail, and now he is on the phone and trying to offer her up! She was in disbelief! She wanted to burst out into the living room, tell him off, beat his ass, and march out of there. But she decided to take a different approach. She went over to her clothes and reached in her pocket to pull out the voice recorder that Ricky had given her and goes back to the cracked door and pressed the record button. Ricky, not knowing and still selling the person on the phone, continues to talk about the transaction of offering up Priscilla to him. "Her name is Priscilla. I'm going to bring her to you and tell her you got a job for her! She'll... Yes, She'll buy it! Trust me! Listen, listen to me! Once I leave her with you, you just work your magic and show her the money! She'll get on board!" Sickened, Priscilla almost fainted at the thought that she trusted Ricky. And just gave herself to him. Ricky finally gets off the phone and heads back into the bedroom.

Upon entering, he sees that Priscilla is still in the bed, knocked out. He proceeded to go into the shower and let her continue to sleep. So, he thought. While he showered, she was thinking of things to do. Should she get a knife and kill him? Should she confront him and play the recording. She thought about a better plan and went through his jewelry box. As she dug and dug into the jewelry box, Priscilla was getting frustrated as she couldn't find what she was looking for. Eventually, she dumped the entire contents of the box out on the dresser, sifting through. Just as she saw it, tangled up in some necklaces, the other matching hoop diamond earing to the one Ricky always wore, she heard the shower water turn off! Ricky was exiting the shower! She needed to hurry before he caught her going through his things! As she carefully and quickly put all the jewelry back into the box and closed it to put it back in its place on the dresser, Ricky was turning the knob on the bathroom door, just as she was diving back over to the bed with the earring in her left hand. With Ricky coming out of the bathroom, Priscilla threw the earring on the floor in her pile of clothes and grabbed the covers and threw them to the foot of the bed to look as if she was just getting up from sleeping to get dressed. Close call! Ricky came out of the bathroom to find her sitting on the edge of the bed. Priscilla proceeded to play a role in her new plan. "Hey Daddy! I slept like a damn baby!" As she leaned over to the floor and carefully grabbed her pants, making sure to grab the earring in a manner to hide it with the pants, slipping it into her pants pocket as she began to put the pants on. Ricky, half-dressed, came out of the bathroom and hearing her response gave him supreme confidence that he had flipped her mind, and she was officially one of his women.

"I see you enjoyed yourself. I hope you feel better now. Are you going to be alright? Your aunt and all?" Ricky asked.

Priscilla looked up at him and said, "Yeah, I'll be alright for now." She got up from the foot of the bed and went to him and hugged him and kissed him on his cheek. "I'm glad I got people like you in my corner. I think I'm going to go tell Uncle Bill to get ready to go to Baltimore soon."

Ricky, knowing he had just promised her to an associate, tried to see when she planned to go. "So, when are you planning on telling him to leave for the trip?"

Priscilla, looked at him, knowing what he was up to since she had eavesdropped earlier. "Oh, I'm not sure. We still need to plan it. Flight or drive. So, there's time."

Ricky, responding to her said, "I see. Well, if you ain't busy tomorrow, I want you to meet my friend. An alderman. He says he has connections in the singing industry. He wants to hear you sing."

Priscilla, knowing Ricky is up to some bullshit, plays along. Jumping up on him with apparent excitement,

"Really? Oh wow! Are you serious? Connections? Oh wow! You know you are something else, Ricky! You don't have to do this for me!"

Ricky, blind that she is on to him, looks at her; "I got you! I got you! So, I'll see you tomorrow? About 2?"

Priscilla, put on her shoes to get ready to leave, and said, "Yes! I can't wait, Ricky." Goes back over to him and grabs him and kisses him on the cheek again. Inside, disgusted by him and his audacity.

Flawless Execution

Priscilla now completely outdone by what she had discovered about Ricky, made up in her mind that *"This was it!"* She calmly leaves Ricky's apartment, but on the walk back to Bill's house, she is putting together the ultimate plot. As she approaches the porch of Bill's house, she stops and sits on the porch. She needed to finalize what she was going to do now. No longer would she run! She was about to take control of her life! Take control of everything! She was sick and tired of being used by people and not making them pay. Ricky was about to pay. Somehow. Then it hit her! She had the perfect plan. Priscilla proceeded to go on in the house to talk to Uncle Bill. "Hey Uncle Bill. I have been thinking and you're right. We need to go ahead and make the trip to see Tricia. Maybe we can leave tomorrow? Tomorrow night? Will that work?" Bill, sitting on the couch and watching T.V. was caught off guard by Priscilla's sudden change of heart about going to go see Tricia. But he was pleased about the revelation.

"Huh? Oh, okay. Yes, I have been ready to go. I just was hoping we could go together. Why tomorrow night though?" Priscilla looked at him as she went into the kitchen to grab some water.

Slightly yelling back into the living room to Bill. "I just need to go to the city and take care of a little more business before we go. If that's okay?"

Bill, just glad they would be going to see Tricia now, agreed. "Tomorrow night works for me. But what about flight tickets? You got money?"

Priscilla comes back into the living room and sits on the other end of the couch. "I think it'll be better to just make the drive. Your car can make it? I got money for the gas."

Bill agreed and confirmed that his car would make the trip. "Tomorrow night it is!"

They sit and plan out the trip itinerary. Gas stops on the way. Bathroom stops on the way. By now, Bill had gotten up and went to get his fold-out map of the U.S. and he began to show Priscilla the route he had taken in the past to get to their town in Baltimore.

After all the planning, Priscilla asked Bill, "Can I use your car today? To go to the city to take care of my business I need to tie up?"

Bill didn't hesitate at all, "Yes, yes you can. Besides, this way you can get used to how it drives for the long road we got."

She replied, "Oh, thank you so much, Uncle Bill!" She got up from the couch to head to her room and get prepared for the trip.

As she walked to the back of the house, Bill said, "You might as well fill the tank all the way up on your way back too! So, we can be ready to go!"

Priscilla agreed as she went into her room, "Yes sir! I'll have that tank full when I get back!"

Priscilla, while in the room, gathered some cash out of the duffle bag. She made sure to get the gun from the back of the closet shelf. Then she went over to the nightstand and grabbed a piece of paper out of the drawer and proceeded to write a letter on the paper. She finished the letter and folded it in half and placed it in the duffle bag on top. Then she proceeded to go back to the front of the house to get ready to go.

Bill, still sitting on the couch, laughing at the program he was watching, looked at her, and said, "The keys are over there by the door in my jacket pocket. I guess I'll see you later?"

Priscilla nodded, "Yep! I'll be back and we'll be on our way back home tomorrow!" Priscilla, now in the car, heads out to go back to the city. While driving, she kept reminding herself that she was done! She was about to set everything, and everyone straight and finally get full clarity in her life. Full control in her life! She quickly gets to the city. As she gets back around the neighborhood that Fabi lived in, she pulls up to this apartment building and pulls into the alley behind it. She parks Bill's car in a vacant lot next to the building and proceeded to go into the back of the yard of the building. Upon entering the yard, Priscilla sees that there are two doors, one leading to the basement, and another that looked like it led to the stairway for the apartments. She approached the door and started to try and pick the lock. Down on her knees, trying to pick a lock, which she'd never done before, but saw Tricia do one time they got locked out of the house, and Tricia had done it to get them in the house, but she wasn't having any success.

After about 4 minutes, Priscilla got frustrated and started to look up at windows to see if there was another way she could get in. She was knocked out of the way of the door by it bursting open. Three little boys came running out of the flung open exterior door and knocked her down. The boys so full of energy, looking like they had been released from jail, looked to be excited to be outside and didn't even notice they had knocked her down. As she gathered herself from being knocked back, she stuck her right foot out to block the door from fully closing on her. What luck! As she goes into the door, she looked at the lock and saw that it was a double-enforced industrial-looking lock. Not just a regular residential lock. There was no way she was going to be able to pick that lock. How lucky was she! Priscilla went on to head up to the second-floor apartment and looked at that door and could see that this lock was a basic lock. She proceeded to try her luck a second time. Down on her knees again, she went on to try and pick the door lock. Not even a minute in of trying; "Pop!" The door crept open. She was in. As she entered the kitchen, which was at the back of this apartment, she got an eerie feeling. She explored the rest of the empty apartment, the apartment still furnished and pretty clean. Then she saw a picture on a mantel. It was a boy, a boy that looked like Chris. This was Angel in the picture! To execute part one of her plot, Priscilla had broken into the apartment where Chris's brother had been murdered. She went into the bathroom and kneeled by the toilet and carefully took out the earring she stole from Ricky and placed it in the corner behind the toilet. She sat there a minute. Thinking about Chris and his grief about his brother. Not knowing how he was going to take this. The rest of her plot. But she needed to get up and continue her plan. She got up from the bathroom floor and made sure that she didn't make anything out of place and left the apartment, being sure to lock the back door. She got into Bill's car and pulled off.

Priscilla's next stop was to initiate part two of her plot for control of her life. As she drove down the familiar street, she drove past the library Fabi would always be in just about every day, flirting with Will and his buddy Jimmy. As she drove by the library, Priscilla went about two blocks away and parked the car. She then walked back down to the library and went right up to the entrance door and went to a tree by the entrance and sat down to wait. To not stand out like a sore thumb and look suspicious, Priscilla grabbed a newspaper from the newspaper dispenser by the door and acted like she was reading as people entered and exited the library. For about thirty minutes, she sat and observed the people in and out, just waiting. Then, there she was! Fabi, leaving out of the library alone. Priscilla gets up and walks behind Fabi and places her hand on Fabi's shoulder.

"Stay calm Fabi! Don't make a scene, please!"

Fabi jumps out of her skin and turns around in utter shock! "Priscilla! Oh My God! Priscilla!" Fabi, almost yelling.

Then Priscilla looked at her and put her finger over her mouth to indicate to Fabi to be quiet. "Fabi please, I don't have much time. Can you come with me? Please?"

Fabi, surprised, and upset. "Why should I come with you? Where the fuck have you been Priscilla? Do you know Abuela is sick that you've been missing? Do you know Chris is hurt? Thinking you may be dead. His crew is looking all over for you! And that dude Carlos, I heard he is upset that you disappeared." Then, as Fabi's eyes began to fill with tears, "And I... I..." more tears filling and starting to run down Fabi's face, "I was thinking you had been killed, Priscilla. I thought you were fucking dead!" She pushed Priscilla in the chest, almost knocking her down. Priscilla managed to keep her balance from the push and got up on Fabi to wrap her arms around her and hold her.

"I'm so sorry Fabi! But you've got to let me explain it! Please?" Just come with me and let's talk. Please Fabi!" Fabi, still crying, agrees and they walk down the street and get into Bill's car. Priscilla and Fabi are in the car, and Priscilla looked at Fabi, ready to let it all out. Tell her the whole story about why she's been missing.

"Look Fabi, I ran. But I ran because I was scared."

Fabi interjects, "Scared of what? Not Chris?"

Priscilla continues, "I was scared of what Chris got me into. You don't understand what Chris and the crew do? Do you Fabi? I know you told me that he sells, but he is a pawn!" Fabi stays quiet and looks at Priscilla to indicate to "Go on." Priscilla continues. "Fabi, it's so dangerous. I wasn't just helping them clean up. They had me doing runs to deliver money for drugs.

Fabi chimes in, "Get the fuck out of here. I am not believing for a second that my cousin had you involved in his business. Not a young girl. No fucking way!"

Priscilla comes back to counter, "I'm not saying he's a bad guy Fabi. What I'm saying is he supports the bad guys. He and the crew deliver money and pick up the drugs for Carlos. I believe he is the kingpin, and Chris

315

and the other guys are just the pawns. I hate to say it, but it must be what happened to Angel."

As Priscilla said this, Fabi began to pull on the car door handle, "Let me the fuck out! You're trying to tell me Chris is helping to sell drugs as a peon, and he's the reason Angel is gone. No Way!"

Priscilla won't unlock the door and let Fabi out. "Listen to me Fabi, I just need one favor from you. Please. Chris is not the Boss you think he is. But if I can just talk to him, he'll understand, and a lot of things will be clear, and he can move on. I can move on. I'll make it right with Abuela. Just please help me! If you help me, I promise, you'll be helping Chris too."

Fabi replied. "Why should I believe anything you say? I brought you into my grandmother's home and trusted you. Chris trusted you! And this is what you do! Disappear on us. I shouldn't have been surprised. That's how I met you, Priscilla."

Priscilla, getting mad, stops Fabi in her rant, "Look Fabi. I was almost killed! Doing what Chris had me doing! Did he tell you that? I had a fucking shotgun pointed right in my fucking face. Right on the tip of my nose! By a fucking tweaker. And he was about to kill me. Did Chris tell you all of that? Huh? Did he?" Priscilla yelling in the car now. Fabi got quiet, and sad, and confused at the same time. As long as she could remember, other than when they lost Angel, Chris was perceived to be a Boss. Everyone knew him. How could he be in a situation that he was the one being manipulated and pushed around? It was hard for Fabi to digest. But it all made sense, the more she thought about it. Priscilla continued to talk to her in the car. Now about two hours in, trying to convince Fabi, Priscilla had told her about the first time when Chris took her to the forest preserve. About meeting Carlos. About the stacks and stacks of money in the factory. About the dangers on the runs she did. She eventually convinced Fabi to set up a meeting for her with Chris. She made Fabi promise to set up the meeting later on, in the back of the library, and to tell Chris to come alone. Fabi promised and then got out of the car. As she got out, Priscilla got out too. They walked over to the sidewalk heading back toward the library.

They embrace and Fabi said, "I won't see you anymore after this, will I?"

Priscilla just pulls back a bit and looked at her and said, "I can't call it. But I need to get my life together Fabi. Take control. Stop running from people and things. We may cross paths again, but we'll see. I will always love you and Abuela. For everything. And Fabi. Go and look in my bag of belongings at the house. In there, you'll find all of the money I made working with Chris. This will help you understand how big the operation was that Carlos runs, and you can have the money. As a gift to you for everything, you've done for me." Fabi walks away and Priscilla stands there watching her walk away, hoping she keeps her promise and Chris does come to meet.

While waiting to meet Chris later at the back of the library, hopefully, Priscilla drove over to the block that Marisol's house sat. She parked in the alley about two houses down, in front of a neighbors garage, and walked over to the house. When Priscilla got to the house, she didn't see Chris's van outside. She didn't see Marisol out in the backyard as usual. She walked quietly around the yard and over to the kitchen window. Where she saw Abuela at the stove, looking like she was preparing dinner. Marisol was looking kind of sad as she prepared the food. Priscilla knew that the lady was missing her. After all of their conversations and bonding. She wanted so badly to go in and hug and kiss her and thank her for everything she's done and looking out for her over the time that she stayed with them. Yet, Priscilla didn't want to open those wounds. She stood there, in the window, just watching Marisol. For a while she watched, quietly. Then she took her right hand and kissed it and went on to place that kissed hand on the window glass, as to be passing a final goodbye kiss onto Marisol's forehead through the glass. Priscilla got emotional and bent down out of the view of the window, then crawled out from under the window.

Just as she was about to stand up and head back to the car, there were screeching tire sounds in the front of the house. It was Chris's van. He jumped out and he looked mad! That gave Priscilla confidence that Fabi went along with the plan and told him about the meeting request. Because, the way he pulled up and barged into the house, he was getting ready for something! Priscilla waits for Chris to go into the house and got up and dashed to the car and grabbed the duffle bag. She crept back to the house and snuck down the driveway to the side door of Chris's van and slowly, carefully opened the door and placed the duffle bag on the backbench, then unzipped the bag and unfolded the piece of paper and set it on top of the bag of money. She heard Chris talking. "Okay Abuela, I'll be back later. No, No please no worries! Everything is fine Abuela!" As Chris was trying to convince Marisol that everything was fine, even though he had just burst into the house angry, Priscilla was trying to get away, but she didn't want to let Chris hear the sliding van door, she didn't know what to do. So, she jumped out of the van and kneeled holding the handle of the sliding door and waited for Chris to finish explaining to Marisol that everything was fine.

"No Abuela, no. I told you all is good!"

Marisol replying now, taking his full attention away, "I hope you are being fully truthful to me young man." At the same time, Chris is looking at Marisol as he opens the driver-side door and hops in. He is standing on the doorstep of the driver-side van door as he continues to fuss at her that all is well. Then, as he finally slams the door closed and turns the key in the same motion, Priscilla slides the side door closed, careful not to slam it, and rolls into the bushes that lined the driveway. Chris thinks he hears something in all of the commotion and looks at the sliding door, he sees that it is closed, and pays no extra attention to it. Besides, by now Abuela is in the driveway, still asking questions.

Chris puts the van in reverse and as he pulls back slowly, he is telling Marisol, "Go back in the house, please. Everything is good." Chris pulled off to what would be most likely the meeting with Priscilla.

Priscilla went back to the library to meet Chris. She parked the car in the back of the library and sits and waits. After about an hour, here comes the van. Chris pulled up facing the car she is sitting in. He just sat there, looking at her. Not budging. Neither of them would move first. Then Chris throws his hands up after a 2-minute standoff between them. She hears that he has re-started the van and put it in reverse, and it looks like he is about to pull away. Priscilla got out of the car. Then slowly walked over to the passenger side of Chris's van. Chris is just looking at the passenger door, but the doors are locked. He keeps looking at her through the glass. Then finally, unlocks the door. Priscilla climbs in, she has her gun tucked in her waist, knowing that Chris is strapped too. She didn't know what he might do. He is pissed.

Immediately starts yelling, "Where the fuck is the money bitch? Carlos will kill us both if you got that money! Where have you been? We thought you had been taken or killed like David! Did you see who killed David?"

Priscilla, not knowing about David, her eyes bulged out, "David? What happened to David? What?"

Chris, not believing that she didn't know about David being killed that day, continued to yell at her, "Get the fuck out of here! You probably got him killed! Did you flip sides on us?"

Taking offense, Priscilla yells back to defend herself, "I didn't flip no fucking sides, Chris! Do you understand how scared I was from having a damn sawed-off shotgun pushed into my fucking nose and almost dying? And you and Carlos didn't even take the time to check if I was going to be okay! I'm a fucking girl Chris, I was a fucking teenage girl! Y'all didn't even care! Just wanted to make sure I could keep being your fucking mule! What the fuck! And I had no idea about David!"

Chris, still mad, but starting to see the bigger picture. "Priscilla. You should have talked to me. Why didn't you tell me you were not doing well after that day?"

She snapped back. "Like you and that greedy fuck Carlos would have cared!"

Chris looked at her and shook his head at that comment. "Why did you come back? You know I could just fucking kill you right now, don't you?" As he reached for his gun, Priscilla pulled her gun too. Now they are both sitting in the van, guns drawn on each other. Chris threatens to kill her, and it was likely, especially given that Priscilla had never fired a gun. Chris had used a gun many times over. So, Priscilla was at a disadvantage. "If you don't tell me where the money is, and why you came back right now, I'm going to shoot your ass, Priscilla!"

Priscilla, now shaking as she pointed the gun, and Chris, seeing that she is scared, replied, "Chris wait! I know who killed Angel."

Chris's face turned deep red as he got emotional and his eyes began to fill with the mention of his brother's name. "What bitch! Don't fucking speak my brother's name! Why would you stoop so low to try and meet me to use this as an excuse for you running like a coward?"

Priscilla, replying strongly, "No Chris. It's true! I met the guy who is responsible, while I've been gone! He confessed it to me because he doesn't know who I am, that I know you. I'm not lying."

Chris takes the gun and began to bang it on the steering wheel from frustration. "Why would you do this Priscilla? You know I don't want to kill you. Why would you make this up?"

Priscilla continued, "No, no. I'm not making this up Chris! It's the dude who runs the drug game out south."

Chris flips out even more and starts to punch the window next to him on the driver's door. "Priscilla. Stop the bullshit. I know that guy. The other crew here, up north tried to blame him, but he has no motive. Why would you make this up? Fabi must have told you some stuff, and now you're trying to use it to get out of trouble?"

Priscilla went on to describe the guy. "He's a want-to-be pimp who is an awkward dresser, in the city, out south and he is known to wear a diamond hoop earring. They call him Pretty Ricky. Chris, I know him. I found my uncle, and small world, he lives near my uncle. I got mixed up with him. And one night, while drinking, he told me that he was in the apartment and had a big fight with Angel before he killed him. Matter of fact, he bragged about having such a fight, that he was certain that he may have lost something in the apartment. That even the police couldn't find since they were fighting so hard. Said that most of the fight happened in the bathroom first." Chris was blown away at the specific details that Priscilla had. Even Fabi wouldn't know all of this!

He put his head down and put the gun down. Priscilla put her gun down as well. Chris started to mumble through his emotion and tears. "But why would he? Why?"

Priscilla, knowing she had to act on this emotional state so she could get away, "Chris! Just go back to the apartment. Maybe you missed something. If you figure out that I'm telling the truth, you have to promise me that you'll leave me alone and let me live my life. Tell Carlos to stop looking for me. If you can't prove it was Ricky, here is my uncle's address." Placing a piece of paper on the dashboard. Come get me if you can't prove it. I just ask that you take me out without me knowing it's coming. But investigate and make your decision." Chris looked at the paper on the dash, then at her.

"Priscilla, I appreciate your balls! But you'll just run again, and if I come for you, you'll be long gone!"

Priscilla just looked at him and said as she grabbed the door handle, "Just investigate Chris. But leave me alone if it is Ricky." She steps out of the van, knowing that Chris might grab the gun again and blow her brains out, right there. But somehow kept her calm and said as she closed the door, "Chris! Look in the back of the van." Priscilla walked over to Bill's car and got in and started the car up as Chris got up from his driver seat and climbed to the back of the van. Priscilla pulled off slowly as Chris sat in the back row of the van and saw the duffle bag full of money. He picked up the paper on top of the money to see it was a letter and began to read it as Priscilla drove away:

Chris. I had grown to love you like an older brother. At first, I was just so surprised how you and Fabi took me in, hid me at first. Then Abuela took me in with no hesitation. I felt at home! For the first time in a long time! Chris, I'm only in Chicago because I'm an orphan who was being raised by my aunt. Both my parents died the night I was born. My Dad, in a car accident that is still a mystery. My mom died on the table giving birth to me. My aunt took custody of me, and we were happy. Until she started dating. That man she dated would touch me, and he tried to do some things to me the day I left home. I got away and just ran, ran until I got lucky to get on a bus to Chicago. Where I met Fabi. We became friends and I met

*you and Abuela and finally felt at peace. I appreciated
you looking out to let me make some money. To be honest,
I liked the runs at first. They were exciting. I had no idea
how deep I was getting! But the day that guy tried to kill
me was the straw that made me know I couldn't keep
doing it! I should have come to you. But I didn't want to
have the blame for everything fall on you with Carlos. I
didn't want Carlos to hurt you. So, I left. Here's most of
the money. Please forgive me. Let me move on. Give my
love to Marisol. Just let her know that I'm okay.*

Love you like a brother forever Chris.

Priscilla

Chris finished the letter and put it down in his lap as
he just sat there for a while taking it all in.

Chris finally sobered up from his gloom and reality
check of what happened to Priscilla and his brother. He
climbed back into the driver seat and began to drive over
to the apartment. At the same time, Priscilla is making her
way back to Matteson. Priscilla, on her way to prepare to
play a role. Chris, on his way to prepare to take action, if
necessary. Chris gets to the apartment and just pulls up
and sits out front for a while. He is sitting, thinking to
himself that something doesn't add up! He's been in and
out of that apartment ever since Angel was killed, he
would have seen something left behind. Besides, how
could the police also miss anything? He started to think
he is being played by Priscilla. But he also understands
why she would make up such an extraordinary lie because
she was scared for her life! The reason she ran in the first
place! He knows that his brother would probably still be
alive if he didn't pull him into the game.

Priscilla, now back at Bill's house, pulled up and it was pretty late. She wanted to get some rest and get ready for phase three of her plot to take control of her life. As she went into the house, there was Bill, in his pajamas, pulling a suitcase toward the door. There was also a cooler sitting on the other side of the door. Bill was prepared for their road trip already.

"Hey there! Thought you'd be out all night! You better make sure you get some rest before we pull out tomorrow."

Priscilla looked at the suitcase again, then at the cooler again, then looked at Bill, "I understand Uncle Bill. I'll make sure I'm well-rested by then." She headed to her room and shut the door and laid in bed, getting her mind right for tomorrow.

On the other side of town, in the city, Chris finally built up the nerve to go into the apartment. He went in, as he normally does, and went straight into the living room to look at the picture of Angel and pray. He stood there for a while and thought to himself; *"I hope I don't find anything!"* Chris didn't want to have to take action on Ricky. He was prepared to try and figure out a way to get Carlos his money back and make up a story about how Priscilla got away again. To protect her. He first, goes into the kitchen and looks around on the floor, in the cabinets, under the table. Purposely avoiding the bathroom, that Priscilla mentioned in her story about Ricky bragging. After checking out the kitchen, he convinced himself to go into the bathroom. Not a big room, he knew he wouldn't find anything. How could he? He'd been in there so many times while in the apartment. And where could something be? As he entered the bathroom, he flicked on the lights and got down on the floor to look under the clawfoot tub. There was nothing there and he was relieved. Then he looked next to the cabinet of the sink because there was a small gap between the cabinet and the tub. Nothing. Now he knew Priscilla had made it all up to throw him off the trail while she ran again. He was fine with it. Chris sat back up against the wall on the opposite side of the bathroom and just looked down to the floor. As he raised his head to look up again, something caught in his peripheral. It was behind the toilet, sort of glistening. He got up upon his knees and crawled over to the toilet. Then he saw it, in the corner, against the wall. A hoop earring with diamonds on it. This was Ricky's earring! "That motherfucker!!" Chris screamed out. He knew it was Ricky's because he saw it before, up close one time when they did a deal. In Chris's mind, it was on now. *"I'm about to get that fucker! He'll pay!"* As he got up in a fit of rage, he got to the living room and suddenly collapsed on the floor. The energy from the rage coupled with the relief of knowing who murdered his brother took him down with a blow of emotions. He remained on that floor. Crying all night about his brother, and in his mind, finally solving the mystery drained him.

The next morning arrived and Priscilla had slept until almost the afternoon. With it being close to noon when she focused on the alarm clock on the nightstand, she got up and knew she needed to get cleaned up for the meeting with Ricky's friend at 2 pm. In her mind, she had plotted to play the recording to expose them, and blackmail them, but if needed, take both of them out! She was making sure her gun was ready as she searched for an outfit that was sexy, revealing, but she could also take the gun. She wasn't too much into purses, so she didn't have one. So, she chose some jeans instead of a dress or skirt to layout and get ready to get in the shower. On the way to the bathroom, she noticed the house was quiet. Bill was gone, she confirmed by looking out of the window to see his car was gone. She thought; *"Who knows, he might be checking tire pressure of cleaning the windshield, hell he's old school!"* But it worked out perfect, this way, she could get ready, get out and not have to explain to Bill where she was going. Just handle the next step in the plan, then get the hell out of town.

After getting dolled up and smelling good, Priscilla headed out to go over to Ricky's. When she got there, there was Ricky, sitting in his car and ready to go. She walked up to the car and got in. The whole time, the group of women were standing by his building talking shit while looking at her. She ignored them, got in the car, and kissed Ricky on the cheek.

"Damn girl. You looking and smelling so damn good. My friend is going to like you." Ricky was feeling even better about it now. He felt like Priscilla had fallen in line, just like the other women, and he didn't even have to drug her. Priscilla just smiled as he pulled off from the curb.

"I hope so Ricky. I hope so. Then I'll sing for him and let him know that I'm more than just good looks."

Ricky, forgetting that the singing angle was his original con, was caught off guard a bit, but then remembered as he drove and said, "Yea, yea, yes. Wait until he hears your voice." They pull up to a huge house, near downtown, and Ricky parks the car and then gets out to start walking over to the gate of the house. Didn't even open her door. Priscilla paid it no mind and got out of the car too. They approach the house, and the front door opens to reveal a middle-aged black man with a mix of black and gray hair in both his head and beard.

"Welcome! Welcome!" the man said as they both climbed the stairs to his place.

Ricky chimed in, "Priscilla, this is Alderman Grant. A great, great man in this city."

Priscilla stuck out her hand to shake the alderman's hand, and said, "Very nice to meet you Alderman Grant."

As he looked at Ricky with a sly eye, to confirm that Priscilla was what he was looking for, he said to Priscilla, "Oh honey, just call me Jacob. Ricky tells me you've got quite the vocal ability. Come on in and have a seat." They all go in and sit down in Jacob's huge great room. This place just looked and smelled like money. Priscilla was looking around at the expensive furniture, and artwork on the walls, and thought to herself, *"Damn! So, the alderman's in Chicago getting money like this?"* The alderman got up and offered them drinks. "What would you like to drink? Whiskey is fine?"

Both Priscilla and Ricky said, "Yes. That is good." At the same time.

Just as the alderman was about to get to asking Priscilla some questions, Ricky's beeper starts to go off and continues to. "Oh, excuse me, excuse me Alderman Grant, this is "911" do you mind?"

The alderman turned to Ricky and then to Priscilla and said, "Oh no, it's fine with me. Young lady, are you comfortable showing me your talent if Ricky leaves? I can surely order you a limo to get you back home after."

Priscilla agreed to it, thinking in her mind, *"They planned this! Muthafuckers!"* But she also thought in her mind that they just made her plan even easier. If Ricky leaves, she'll only need to blackmail the alderman. Besides, she just had a gut feeling that it might get sticky and she'd have to learn how to shoot a gun today using it on Ricky. That wasn't a worry anymore.

Ricky got up, looked at Priscilla, and asked, "You sure about this?" Acting like he was so concerned. "I can just bring you back another time with me when I can stay, but this is an emergency beep."

Priscilla played along with their slick game. "No, no, you can go ahead, besides, I get to ride home in style. In a limo. Yay!" She played it off so smooth. Acting like a naïve woman, who wasn't suspicious of any trouble or malice.

Ricky made his way out of the house as he and Jacob talk at the door, while Priscilla remained on the couch, slowly sipping the whiskey. Frowning up as she first tasted it. But still trying it again. After closing and locking the door. Jacob comes back into the great room and has a seat on the couch next to Priscilla.

"So, you have immense talent, I hear. How about we get into exploring those talents right away?" Just as he was about to move in and try to put his hands on Priscilla, she pulls the gun out on the alderman.

"Get the fuck back bitch!" Priscilla yells as she drops the glass on the rug and points the gun in his face. "You thought you were just going to rape me? Take what you wanted from me? That shit is done! Fuck Ricky! He is lucky y'all pulled that shitty ass stunt to get him to leave! Or he would be eating a bullet right fucking now!"

Priscilla, finding a whole new her! An aggressive! Confident, even mean her, had enough! She was about to see her plot through today. As she stands over him, and threatens him, Jacob stays calm.

"Wait, wait! What do you mean rape you? I was going to listen to you sing and then recommend you to my friends in the industry if you're good. I don't know what you mean by taking advantage of you! I was just trying to look out and do a favor for Ricky."

Priscilla rolls her eyes and pulls out the voice recorder. "I'm not stupid, but Ricky is. He didn't know I recorded this." She pushed play on the recorder and let the alderman hear Ricky and his voice discussing selling her to him and giving Ricky money for it. She let it play, as his eyes got huge and surprised. As it played, she said, "I have it all on here. Ricky saying, he was going to sell me to you, and you agreeing to be all for it! Everything!" The alderman still tried to keep his cool and think fast. Because he didn't know her from anyone, didn't know what she was capable of.

"Listen, young lady! We can make this right. Hear me out." He talked her down. "I can get you out of this life. Show you something positive. Forget Ricky. Just give me the recording. Please. Look, I'm sure you know I'm running for Mayor soon. Otherwise, you wouldn't have gone this far."

Priscilla interjects, "You can't get me out of nothing! You can't make my life better; you are just another person trying to use me up for what you can. Wait until the news gets a copy of this recording. You will be ruined. Ricky! He's got something else coming!" Thinking to herself about how she knew that Chris would soon be on Ricky's ass! Her plan was going better than she thought it would. As long as she could complete the blackmail of the alderman.

Jacob starts to speak again, "Well, what do you want then? Money? What? I told you, I could get you out of this type of life. When I become Mayor, I will get you into the alderman's office, a legit job. You can make a difference for the rest of your life."

Priscilla starts to think as she stands there, holding the gun. "I'm sick of being used! I'm sick of being taken for granted and seeing girls get abused!"

Jacob, thinking fast again, replied, "That's just what I'm proposing young lady! If you are doing relevant work in the alderman's office, you can help those women get out and avoid the life." Priscilla stopped to think about what he was saying and was beginning to think it made some sense. Her original plan was to use the recording to get some more money, a couple hundred thousand dollars to live off. But now she wanted to gain some control! She was starting to see a bigger plan! For her life, and other girls and women that would fall prey to men like him and Ricky!

"I want more power than just working in the alderman office." Priscilla standing there looking fierce at the Alderman by now.

Jacob, looking confused a bit at her statement replied, "What do you mean by power?"

Waiving the gun, Priscilla went on. "I want to become an alderman, like you! Get power and be able to shut down the clubs and bars in the city that houses the prostitutes, to help get them out of the life and possibly avoid other girls to get caught up by guys like Ricky!"

Looking at her and taking in her big plans that seemed so unrealistic; Jacob replied the best he could, to try and deter her and have her ask for something else. "Listen! Sure, you can become an alderman, any city resident can, but it takes having an education, which I can tell you haven't been to school lately. No disrespect. Working in the community. Outreach." Priscilla moved the gun in closer to his face as a threat that she was about to pull the trigger, and then he gave in. "Okay, okay, okay. Please, just don't shoot me. If you come back and have got in school, or at least get a G.E.D, I'll get you into the office, and then make sure you get on the ballot to run for my vacated alderman seat and help you win. If you don't blackmail me."

As he sat there, pleading for her to have some mercy, she said, "I'm not going to kill you. But I'm not giving you shit. I'm going to leave and you ain't going to say shit to Ricky or else I'll give the recording to the newspaper. I'm leaving town. But when I get back, you need to hold up your end of the offer. If you win as Mayor, I expect to get your seat. I become the alderman and run things and make changes as I see fit!" He looked at her, impressed with her boldness.

"You know what, as long as you get that gun out of my face, you got a deal. If I win the Mayor's seat, the alderman seat is yours! I'll see to it! Do the things I just mentioned and if you run; you win!"

As Priscilla puts the gun away, she and the alderman talk a little bit more. She tells him that as soon as she sees him win the Mayor's race, she'll be back for what's owed to her. Priscilla gets back to Bill's house later that evening, and she gets Bill to go ahead and get on the road early. She knows that anything can happen now. She's gotten the alderman to agree to the blackmail plot and hoped he keeps his word. But she had the key to him keeping that promise in the recording, and Ricky's time is running out, but she didn't want to take any chances and be in town as all of the shit hit the fan. So, she and Bill were off, on their way home! Back to Baltimore, to allow her to visit Tricia in her last days and make things right! Just like Uncle Bill had begged her to do.

Full Circle

On the road trip, Bill and Priscilla talked and listen to different music along the way. During a long arm of the trip, after a lengthy gas fill-up and snacks, Bill went into telling Priscilla about the night her father died. Priscilla remembers the day a States Attorney came by the house to talk to Tricia. She told Bill about that day, and said, "You know Uncle Bill. That day the man came to talk to Tricia, I listened by the stairs and it sounded like he was trying to tell Tricia she needed to fight, go to court or something." Bill, knowing that there was a conspiracy back home about Frank being killed by a cop, decided to tell Priscilla everything he knew about that night. He started off talking about how her mom, Anne went into labor, and Frank rushed out to get to the hospital. Bill described it as best as he could remember because he had heard it second hand from Tricia and Don.

"Well, I remember it was a tragic night Priscilla. Don told me that he and Frank were huddled in a civil rights office after working the day with others and then they got a call. Don told me he was right there listening as another woman in the office, June took the call. It was Tricia with an anxious yell telling them to tell Frank that Anne was not doing well and there was a risk of losing the baby during labor. That baby was you! But Frank never made it to the hospital. After that night, they found Frank. On the side of the road. Some folk say it looked like murder. The cops in the area said it looked like he was drinking and driving. I think we all know the truth here. But no one ever pursued it to prove the truth. Priscilla, I think the cops killed your Dad!"

Taking in the news the best she could, Priscilla got sad about it all and she mentally added the cops in her hometown to her checklist of revenge. Even though she didn't even know where to start with that. As the road trip moved along, they were just about 3 hours out of town and making great progress. The morning was upon them as they drove along.

Meanwhile, back in Chicago, Chris was planning his hit on Ricky. Ricky, unsuspecting, gave Alderman Grant a call. A call to see how the night turned out for him with Priscilla. Ricky hadn't seen or heard from her since he left her at the alderman's house. So, he wasn't sure about how it went. But he felt like she probably fell in line because she didn't storm over to his place, nor did the alderman call him yelling or complaining. Now he was looking for his money. The phone is ringing and ringing, no answer at the alderman's number. He decides to leave a message. "Hey Alderman Grant, it's Ricky, just calling to see how it went last night. From the way it seems, all good! Just looking for the collect! I'll be by later for it! See you soon." In Ricky's mind, this was no different than their regular program. He often supplied young girls to the alderman. They had an agreement and Ricky got paid. On the other side of the phone, Jacob Grant sat there and listened to every bit of Ricky's voicemail on the machine, after he had let the phone ring and the machine pick it up. Still sitting, thinking about how he fell for the ultimate blackmail by Priscilla. Ricky's call confirmed to him that Priscilla acted alone. He sat, trying to figure out how he could get out of it. He was even thinking to himself, *"How can I get out of paying Ricky now?"* Since Priscilla made him make all those promises.

Ricky hangs up and decides he'll go over there to collect. But first, he planned to visit Priscilla at Bill's house to check on her. Ricky goes out to the parking lot to get in his car, and as he puts the key to the door, all of a sudden, he hears tires screeching to stop right behind him. As he turns around to see that a car looked like it was about to crash into him, he was about to curse them out, but before he could react, Ricky was filled with bullets. A black Lincoln with all tinted windows pulled up and dumped a full clip into Ricky, right where he stood, by his car. Everyone in the vicinity broke out and ran, screaming, even his women. The car made sure to finish him off. Then rolled up the window and took off fleeing the scene. Ricky was lying there, in the street, dead for everyone to see. Priscilla's problem is gone! As some people are scurrying and running for cover, while others are trying to get closer to Ricky's car to see if he was still alive, others calling the police. Here comes Chris walking down the block approaching Ricky's building with a gun in his hand, tucked under his jacket. Just as Chris was about to go into Ricky's building, One of the prostitutes burst out of the building running to the parking lot. "They shot Ricky! They shot Ricky! Oh My God!" Chris sees her and steps to the side quickly, but surprised by what she is saying, he follows her to get a glimpse of

Ricky lying dead. Chris's head is spinning! He was on his way to take Ricky out, but someone beat him to it. He was thinking, *"What The Fuck!"* As he put his gun away in his pocket and got the hell out of there. Now, Chris was paranoid about it. *"Could Priscilla have done this? Did she have some heavy connections? Am I next?"* Chris got to his car and left the scene with so many unanswered questions. One thing was for sure! He was going to make sure that he or no one he knew bothered Priscilla from now on!

As Bill and Priscilla get to Baltimore, they make their way up to the hospital to go where Tricia is in hospice. As they arrive at the hospital and park, Priscilla sees a man that looks like Don. Bill sees him too. They both get out of the car and get his attention. "Don! Don!" They both are yelling out, then Don sees her and runs over there to them.

"Priscilla! Is that you? Priscilla, as Don knows it is her, but also is shocked at how she's become a woman since he'd last seen her." They embrace and Bill comes over to where they are and gives Don a handshake, half hug.

Don's face quickly turned to stone and he delivered the news he just received, "She's doing bad y'all!"

Priscilla starts crying and asking questions, "What's the room number? What else are the doctors saying? She goes on and on." Bill knew this is what they may drive into because he had been trying to warn Priscilla to hurry up and get here. Priscilla was crying and mumbling while Don and Bill tried their best to get her to calm down. She continues to mumble, "No, No! This can't be! I want to make it right! I want to make it right!" They all go into the hospital to talk to the nursing staff. Don took Bill over, as Priscilla decided to wait in the waiting room. She just couldn't do it yet. So, Don took Bill, and they went to see Tricia for Bill's last time. Bill took it quite hard as he stood there over Tricia. As Tricia lay there on all sorts of machines, barely hanging on.

"Hey baby girl. I've missed you. You did a good job with that young lady out there. Do you know she made it to Chicago to find me? If that ain't you Tricia. If that ain't you." Bill put his head down onto her cheek and kissed her one last time. Don put his hand on Bill's shoulder and walked out of the room with him. Just as they were leaving out, Priscilla enters, about to come and pay her last visit to her aunt, her mom that she knew. Bill looked at her and just simply placed his hand on her shoulder as she walked into the room. Priscilla walks in and sees her aunt lying there, almost lifeless. It's all too much for her to bear. But she moves in closer. Then a little closer. Then she walks up to the bed and rubs Tricia's hair, stroking it back.

"I'm so sorry Aunt Trish. I'm so sorry I left. I had to get out and let you live your life." Not wanting to reveal about Roy with Tricia in this condition, Priscilla just talked about them after that statement, about memories of her growing up, Tricia and her doing fun things together. She swore she saw Tricia responding to the memories, thinking that Tricia's eyebrows were slightly moving each time she mentioned good times. "I promise you I'm going to make you proud. I'm getting my life right. I promise. I'm going to do some great things! You just watch me, Aunt Trish. I love you so much. I'm going to think about you every single day." As

338

Priscilla said that, Tricia's face began to look attentive. Her eyes seemed to acknowledge Priscilla in the room with her. Almost as if to let Priscilla know that she is now at peace because she knew Priscilla was okay. In that moment, Tricia's body seemed to relax in a peaceful state, as if finally seeing Priscilla was all she needed to let go. Then she breaks down and just rests her head on Tricia's belly and stays there and cries it all out. She just stayed there with Tricia. It had to be twenty or thirty minutes that she stayed there and cried. Then Priscilla heard Tricia take her last breath as she had her head on Tricia's stomach. Then the nurse came into the room to check and allow them to take the body.

The nurse saw Priscilla lying there on Tricia and gently asked, "Are you going to be okay ma'am?"

Priscilla raised her head and put her right hand on Tricia's face one last time, then turned and looked at the nurse, and said, "I'll be okay." Wiping tears, Priscilla left the room and exited the hospital to find Bill waiting in the car. He looked at her and just nodded as he put the car in drive and pulled away from the hospital. Bill drove over to the neighborhood and the house. They went to Tricia's, as Don had given the house keys to Bill while they were in the parking lot waiting on Priscilla. Don told Bill he had been there in the last days. As well as Tricia's neighbor John. Tricia told them to give the keys to Bill and allow him to stay there and help plan the service. Don said that everything for the service was already taken care of by Tricia and that if Priscilla happened to turn up, everything was hers. If not, everything was Bill's. They pull up to the house and Priscilla is just looking at the house.

"Are we supposed to stay here?" She asks Bill.

Bill responds. "Yes, unless you can't do it?" Priscilla sat still for a little bit, then responded, "I can do it." They both go into the house.

At the house, Priscilla is looking at all of the papers that Tricia had stacked so neatly on the table in preparation. She finds the case labeled important papers and sees a folder. The folder contained documents that spelled out what happened to Frank. Priscilla is taken aback by this. It all matched up! What she heard the day the States Attorney visited Tricia, what she heard over the years, and what Bill just told her on the road trip. Her Dad was most likely killed by the cops. She planned to keep this folder. Look into this one day and get vengeance or justice for her father. As she continued to look through everything, Bill came into the living room, after being in the bathroom freshening up from the road trip. He joined her, and they sat up all night looking at pictures together, going back down memory lane. With Bill filling in the details about the older pictures of people she didn't quite remember or recognize.

The next morning, Bill had gotten up early and prepared breakfast, and a lot of it! Priscilla woke up to the aroma of bacon and eggs and biscuits and coffee. She also heard the sound of many voices. As she made her way downstairs, she saw that the front room had a few people, and the dining room table was just about full. The morning breakfast was a spread, and most of the neighbors were there, in the house. There was John from across the street naturally. May, Tricia's friend from church was there, Pastor Shaw. Other church members, some of Priscilla's friends like Jackie, Susie and Carla, and Charity. A lot of people were there! It was like a block party reunion in the house. As she got to the bottom step, everyone got silent. They couldn't believe it was her. They knew she was back. But couldn't believe it. Everyone was in shock at seeing the grown version of Priscilla. Besides, the last time they saw her, she was a teenager. They all came up to her, one-by-one to hug and talk to her and console her. While the reunion was going on and on, suddenly there was a big bang at the door, the screen door flung open, there stood Roy, reeking of alcohol and everything else, with a scantily clad woman by his side.

"So ain't nobody bother to tell me the bitch died!"

Pastor Shaw jumped up from his chair immediately with Don and John and Bill jumping up as well. "Whoa, whoa!" Pastor Shaw said as he ran to the door to grab Roy and try to keep him outside.

Everyone else watching as the altercation escalated. With John now at the door entrance as well.

Roy yelling, "You fucking heard me! Get your fucking hands off me man! I wanna know why no one told me she died! When is the damn funeral? No one told me that either!"

Now John is rolling up his sleeves, getting ready to go out there and do some damage to Roy! While Don is trying to hold him back. Roy is halfway in the house, and halfway on the porch, trying to get in, ranting and drunken raving at everyone, while all the men are at the door trying to not let a fight breakout. The women are inside, some scared, and some talking shit to Roy too, like they are ready to go whoop his ass too! Then, just as Roy is losing it and people trying to restrain him, Roy notices that he sees a woman that looks like Priscilla.

"Wait! Wait a damn minute! Is that Priscilla? Wait a minute! Hold on!" Don, still holding John back, and Pastor trying to walk Roy down the porch steps to get him to leave. By now, someone had called the police. Roy kept fighting trying to get past the Pastor, "So you decided to come back after she died huh? You little scary bitch! But I must say, you looking real fucking hot, now that you are a grown woman! I could do some work on you now!" With that comment, Priscilla charged the door to attack Roy, but in her charge, she knocked Don down and John got free and tackled Roy off of the top step of the porch and onto the concrete. You could hear Roy's back snap.

Nevertheless, John began whaling on Roy's face; punch after punch after punch until his fists were bloody. By the time the police began to pull up, Roy was knocked out with a bloody face, and Don and Bill somehow managed to get John off the top of Roy and they left him there, bloody on the ground. The scantily clad woman was right there next to him on the ground as the police walked up, drawing guns. Pastor Shaw walked up and said, "Excuse me, officers, the person just ran away who beat him up. We tried to stop him." The cops started to look down the block to see if they saw someone running away. The pastor knew the back story and made an executive decision to not allow John to go to jail for defending Tricia's house and defending Priscilla. They kept him hid in the house in the bathroom until the cops left the house. The scantily clad woman that was with Roy was no good to describe what she saw to the police either. She was so high; she didn't even know where she was. Eventually, the cops got an ambulance to the scene to take Roy to the hospital and they left, and everyone at the house just hung out, talking about what had just happened, remembering Tricia, and catching up with Priscilla. On a sidebar, Pastor cornered Bill and Don and began telling them a story about Roy, when Roy was younger. This pieced together a lot about Roy for Bill, as Priscilla had told him about what Roy did, but he was having a hard time believing it, pastor explained:

It was a regular church Sunday, and I had just finished my sermon and headed into the basement to check on the women of the church who were preparing meals for the congregation. We would always sell after-service dinners to the congregation. To add to the church funds, and avoid families having to go home and cook or go to a restaurant. Anyhow, as I get into the basement, I hear a woman screaming and thumps behind it. As I come around the corner, it's sister Jackson, pulling Roy out of the girls' bathroom and beating him on the top of his head and screaming at him, just behind them was a young girl church member, Uh... Judy. Judy was just walking out of that bathroom like a zombie, face full of tears, and her blouse open and pants unzipped! And sister Jackson was yelling at Roy, saying "Why were you doing that to that girl?"

"I, of course, intervened, separated everyone, talked to each of them separately. Talked to Roy, and I'm telling you, even at such a young age, he didn't get it! He couldn't explain why he was in that bathroom molesting that girl Judy. Scared Judy from then on. I decided to keep an eye on Roy as much as I could, didn't tell his Dad, because his Dad may have killed him! Knowing what I know now, I wish I would have told on Roy then. I was afraid it would ruin his life to tell on him. But he turned out for the worse anyway."

"My God!" Bill, very surprised by this story, was shocked and appalled! He consoled the pastor and told him, "You did your best pastor! We can't go back now!" They continued to talk more, and Bill was contemplating telling Priscilla about this. Wishing he could have told Tricia about it! As the day went on, and some people left, some people stayed and Priscilla was sitting, having some drinks, and reminiscing with some of her old friends. She kept zoning out and thinking that she was going to make Roy pay! Then she realizes that she has a hunger for revenge on everyone who ever did her wrong. In between her losing Tricia to cancer, being used by all these different people, and overcoming so much, she made a conscious decision that she was going to get Roy's ass, one way or another.

While Bill and Priscilla took care of the remaining business to get ready for the funeral, the day had come up fast. The services were that morning. Bill was up, in his suit and drinking coffee. Priscilla was coming down the stairs in her black dress, coming to finish her makeup in the mirror in the downstairs bathroom. The limo to pick them up was already sitting outside the house. They got done getting ready and went ahead and left the house to go over to the church for the services. Today was a somber day. A day of reflection. For the entire neighborhood. For, these same people, many years ago, were in this same mood, doing this same march to go and lay Frank and Anne to rest. All too familiar was the feeling. As they approached the church in the limo. There was no worry about Roy showing up to mess this up, for he was severely injured during that fall when John tackled him. He had just been released from the hospital and was at his rinky-dink apartment, laid up in pain and on pain killers, back swollen from the injury. Luckily for him, one of his female friends stayed with him today to help him recover for a few hours. Of course, she was looking for some drugs to do it. The services for Tricia were peaceful, orderly, nice and a true tribute to the woman that gave her life to raise her niece that was left as an Orphan. One-by-one, each person got up to pay respects and say something meaningful and nice about Tricia. Ending with Priscilla, who gave the most eloquent and precious Eulogy for her aunt:

"There are not many words in the English language that has enough meaning or carry enough weight to describe what you mean to me! What you did to raise me and show me how to be a good person! A selfless person. A person that put God first! I know that we didn't always see things the same. But I always adored your charm and intelligence. I wanted to be you. You were my Mom! Even though I knew about my real Mom, you did a good job at making me feel like I always had a Mom. I wish I didn't have to leave you when I did. Never said goodbye. But when you left, I thought you didn't say goodbye. But now I know that you had been with me the whole time, in spirit. Guiding me to get back home and navigate life. I know you will be with me every day for the rest of my life. I love you, Tricia. Forever!"

After the service, everyone got together for a repast to share food, memories, and turn the sadness into some type of happiness. They all gathered and talked, ate, and congregated for hours into the evening. Everything was finalized and Priscilla was getting things in order, to sell the old house. Bill and Priscilla decided it would be best to go ahead and sell the house. Sad, that it had been in the family for so long. But at this point, Priscilla had decided that she would start her new life in Chicago instead of Baltimore. Bill wasn't leaving his home in Matteson. But what Bill didn't know, was that Priscilla had an agreement with the alderman, soon to be Mayor of the city back in Chicago. Priscilla still didn't know about Ricky because she didn't have any main contacts back in Chicago. Talking to realtors and buyers, her head was spinning. She decided to take a break from that and take care of some other business. Besides, she had heard in the neighborhood that Roy was back up on his feet, quicker than the doctors expected. He was back on the streets and in the bars and clubs talking about how he was going to get John and make him pay. Make Priscilla pay as well! Priscilla knew that she had to do something about Roy. Especially since she had plans to do some big things in Chicago. As evening approached, Priscilla got dressed and went out to the club scene. She told Bill that she needed to go and have a drink or two with some girls before they head back to Chicago. Bill had no issue with it, as they had planned to leave the day after tomorrow anyway. Plenty of time for her to get rest. Priscilla went barhopping alone. Bar by bar, looking for Roy. After about two bars, a nightclub, and a strip club, she was about to give up, when she was driving down the boulevard and Eureka! There he was! Going into a dirty strip club at the end of the block. Priscilla jumped into action. Parked the car a few blocks away and proceeded to go into the same strip club.

She entered the strip club and made sure to keep a low profile, getting a table in the back corner of the club. At first, she doesn't see him. Now she's wondering if she had been seen by him at some point while parking the car. Then boom! There he was, coming from out of a personal dance room with a stripper. Priscilla is thinking to herself *"Damn! Who gets a dance as soon as they walk up in the damn strip club? Fucking desperate!"* She stays at her table in the corner of the bar, well-hidden from sight, and just watches him. For about three hours, she sees his routine. Have some drinks, go outside for a smoke, then come back in and take a dancer for a private session. But something was off. He was never in the backroom long enough for a real lap dance? What was going on? Priscilla had to figure it out. So, she decided to find out. She took out some dollars and sat them on the table and sure enough, a dancer comes over to her.

"Hey sweetie! I see you must want some attention, huh?" The dancer said to Priscilla.

Priscilla, not knowing how to act in a strip club, said, "Umm yeah, yes! I want some attention." The dancer grabs her by the wrist and pulls Priscilla up from her table. Priscilla grabs her drink and her dollars and follows the dancer to a private room. The whole time, she is watching Roy at the bar, also making sure he doesn't see her. They get to the private room, and the dancer told her to sit down on the couch. The dancer proceeded to take her top off and started to dance around to the music being played. Just as the dancer was walking over to try and straddle Priscilla; Priscilla said, "Wait! I just want to talk!"

The dancer, confused, said, "You ain't no cop, are you? Shit! Don't tell me they about to bust this place again!"

Priscilla, not sure what the girl meant said, "No, no, I'm not a cop! But I want to ask you something."

The dancer looks at her and said, "Okay. What do you want to know?"

Priscilla goes on, "That guy out there, in the red shirt. He's had a lot of dances tonight, but short. Why?"

The dancer pulls the curtain back to look out onto the floor and spots Roy, then turns around to Priscilla, "You talking about Roy!" Then she starts laughing. Priscilla is thrown by this because she doesn't know what is so funny.

"What! What about Roy!"

The dancer looks at her and said, "He's a dopehead. All he does is take women in the back to see who is down to go back to his place and get high with him. If you ain't doing drugs, he doesn't want a dance, all the girls know it. But his dumbass gets so high and drunk that he can't even remember who the addict girls in the club are. Me. I don't do that shit. So, that's why you saw me leave out fast too." Priscilla couldn't believe it. This guy was only looking for women to get high with. To use them and their earnings for the night to keep his habit going.

Priscilla thought and then began to ask the stripper, "Okay. Can you do me a favor?"

The dancer looked at her and said, "You look like a nice girl. What can I do for you?"

Priscilla sat up straight on the couch and told her, "Send me an addict girl in here." The dancer, looking crazy at Priscilla agrees to do it. After about a few minutes in the private room with one of the addict girls, Priscilla walks out and then walks out of the club and gets in her car and sits. Waiting for Roy to leave the club. The addict girl comes out of the private room with a wad of money and stuffs it into her bra, then headed over to Roy to get him to go into the private room.

After about an hour or so, Roy comes out of the club with the girl and they get into his car and drive off. Priscilla follows him slowly and not too close. Roy and the girl go into his place and another hour goes by. Shortly after the hour passes, the girl emerges from Roy's place and sticks her head out of the door. She looks around for Priscilla's car, and gives her a nod, and proceeded to leave his front door ajar, and walked off into the night. Priscilla got out of her car and headed over to Roy's place. There he was, laid out on the bed, drunk and high and not knowing where the hell he is. Riding his high to the fullest, with a band and a needle still hanging from his vein. That's when Priscilla walked over to the bed and looked at him, while he was half out of it and half there. He thinks he recognizes her but can't make her out fully at first because of his high. "Prisci... Prisci..." Drooling at the moth as he thinks he knows who is standing over him. Priscilla leans in over the bed and takes out a syringe and sticks it into his arm, replacing the one that's hanging out of his arm. Giving him a lethal dose of Meth, and he was already high. She walks out of his apartment, gently closing and locking the door. Leaving him to die of an overdose. Priscilla felt a thrill!

A thrill of vengeance! For her! For Tricia! For everything, this man had put them both through. She weirdly felt happy after surely killing a man. As morbid as it was, she felt an immense relief, and pleasure from getting vengeance.

Priscilla took care of her business, secret business, and public business. She and Bill were headed back to Chicago. Bill felt a sense of peace. Knowing that Tricia had received a respectable and loving homegoing. Priscilla felt a sense of empowerment! Knowing that she got rid of Roy and she was going back to Chicago where she held the big card to play to get what she wanted. Here she was on the precipice of full control of her own life. She couldn't be in a better mood on the road trip back. They arrive back in Matteson, Illinois in the late evening and they are worn out. Bill gets into the house and immediately is looking to lay down.

"Alright, Priscilla. I'm tired. I'm going to lay down for the night."

Priscilla looked at Bill and said, "I understand Uncle Bill. It was a long draining trip. I'm going to sit here and eat a quick sandwich before I lay down."

Bill goes into his room and closes the door, and Priscilla proceeded to make a sandwich and goes over to the T.V. to turn it on and watch something. As she is about to turn the station, she notices that the evening news is on. She backs up to look and listen and then sits on the couch with her sandwich to watch the news. While watching the evening news, the lead story is about Alderman Grant leading in the Mayoral race polls. Priscilla sits up and can't believe it! This guy is about to win, and she holds the ticket that could drown his entire career. She is ecstatic! Thinking to herself; *"I hate that it had to come this way, but so many people used me anyway!"* As she gets some energy from the news of the Mayor's race, she began to chomp on her sandwich and then the next news story almost made her choke on her sandwich!

> *Here on channel six news, we are following up on the deadly drive-up shooting last week of the known Matteson resident Rick Marshall. Rick was believed to be known in the neighborhood as Pretty Ricky. The police currently have no leads on his murder but have the below hotline for any information. Some residents say Rick was a good guy, while some others paint him as a drug dealer and pimp of Matteson. No one knows the true story. The police want answers. That's the news at ten. Goodnight.*

Priscilla is blown away by the news. She can't believe it. Chris did it. He took Ricky out. She is overjoyed. All the obstacles in her life appear to be getting terminated. She had been through so much, she just couldn't believe that she had no one else to worry about, as long as the soon-to-be new Mayor Jacob Grant kept his word. Which he was almost certain to do, given the evidence she has on that recording. She finishes her sandwich, turns the T.V. off, and goes to bed. Priscilla slept well that night. Probably the best she'd slept in a while.

Becoming

The next year or so, Priscilla began to dedicate her time to get her education. She enrolled into a G.E.D program at a south suburban junior college to get what she remembered alderman Grant claimed she needed to get the power she wanted in her blackmail scheme. While working to get her G.E.D. Priscilla took trips into the city and spent time in the worst neighborhoods. Always carrying her gun, she just would sit and watch the streetwalkers. Observing them and their pimps. Trying to see how they became victim to the game and the life. She mentally documented everything, to start formulating a plan to help these types of women get away from this grip of abuse. As she flirted with the danger of the streets, by day, she finished the G.E.D program and then registered for college to get an associate degree, by night; she visited strip clubs, bars and even went into crack houses to truly understand the games men would play on these young girls minds. She worked tirelessly, studying while helping Uncle Bill around the house and to investigate how so many girls got caught up in street life. After it was all said and done, it all paid off! Priscilla wasted no time going back to Alderman Grant when he was on the verge of winning the mayoral race to stick the recording back into his face and force him to pay up! She got on the ticket for his vacated alderman seat, and Jacob pulled all of his strings to ensure her victory. Often campaigning for her. He even evoked his mayoral campaign team to work for her bid for the alderman seat. It all went according to plan, her plan at least.

***

"Well now, it's so great to see you, Governor Johnson. It's been a while since we last spoke." Priscilla said, now attending a political gala, rubbing shoulders with city politicians as part of her new life.

A big heavyset white man turned to reply; "Yes, yes. A while indeed. I am hoping that all the programs you've been implementing are going well. I hear exceptionally good things about the program for abused women. It seems to have taken off and made an incredibly positive impression on the Mayor. Speaking of the Mayor."

The Governor turns to see the Mayor being escorted into the huge ballroom event. Then people start to crowd around as the Mayor of the city enters the room. A city gala event, full of politicians drinking and laughing, and talking. Several celebrities also filled the room. There stood Priscilla, in a casual dress, taking in the conversation and the drinks, then someone taps her on the shoulder.

"Hi there, Alderman Tibbs. Looks like you've made good on our arrangement."

Priscilla looked at Mayor Grant and agreed, "Yes! I guess I did make good on it."

The Mayor went on, "You know, I never thought you meant well and was going to do so much outreach and help these girls in the inner-city. I have to tip my cap to you. Give you the respect and praise that's due."

Priscilla stood there, knowing that she wouldn't or couldn't be in this position without having blackmailed this guy. But at the same time, she thought to herself, and often reminded herself. *"This motherfucker tried to buy me like a prostitute!"* Yet, she smiled and agreed and kept it professional and political. Besides, she was making such a great name for herself, who knew what the future held for her in this city.

The Mayor turned to walk away, "Keep up the great work. We'll talk soon." As he went up to the podium to address the Gala. Priscilla thinking to herself; *"We will talk soon! Sooner than you think!"*

Here she was, making a name for herself, with the Mayor, the governor, celebrities in the city. Making a difference for underprivileged girls and women in the city. She was so successful; she had begun plans to pilot similar programs for women back in Baltimore with local aldermen in that city. Priscilla had taken control of her life. This was her life's work now. A politician. Who would have thought it? With all the success, everything wasn't all that rosy. About three years had passed. Uncle Bill had a massive heart attack and died last year. She had lost touch with her friends in Baltimore again. Yet, she had built such a positive reputation in the city that she was gaining power. Her work in the community was unmatched. She eventually reconnected with Fabi, though they hadn't hung out in over a year, from Priscilla being so busy. She had just spent so much time in the community working. Because of her, the Chicago community had overcome the rape and abuse of girls and weans addicts off of drugs. Truly accomplished. Who would have thought that she would be able to help girls and women try to avoid what she experienced! This was her life's work! But, was she happy? "What else was missing?" Something she always asked herself. As she continues to work and make more progress in her seat, she continually gains more and more popularity. She even saw a political show one morning in which they were pointing to her as the next Mayor of the city within the next decade as an up-and-comer.

One morning, while approaching her alderman office, Priscilla was approached by a strange woman. "Excuse me, excuse me!" The woman said as she got Priscilla's attention. "I know you don't remember me, but I just want to apologize and tell you that I am grateful and proud of you." Priscilla, caught so off-guard by this strange woman, looked her up-and-down and remained silent because she had no idea what the woman was talking about, nor who the hell she was. "I... I used to be one of Ricky's women. I am ashamed to say that I was there the day we tried to jump you and kept laughing at you. We should have... I should have tried to tell you what Ricky was going to do to you. But I was afraid. I'm so, so sorry." Priscilla, now starting to piece together an image of this woman a few years back when she was mixed up with Ricky, is now starting to see it and responds to the lady.

"I think I do remember you now. You were the one standing in the back looking like you didn't want any part of what the other three women were doing like you didn't want to hurt me."

The woman replies, "I just wanted to get an opportunity to apologize and tell you that your programs for women in the city are working. I'm proof of it! You saved my life! And not just because Ricky was killed. I would have got into your program even if he were alive and would be better off still."

Priscilla, humbled, and appreciative replies again, "Thank you so much for coming to me and telling me. And here, take my card. Don't hesitate to reach out to me if you need anything. I promise! Matter of fact. I'll sign the back, and if you ever need shelter or anything and you go to one of the centers, show them my signature, and they'll take care of you! By the way, what is your name?"

The woman looks sheepishly at Priscilla as she takes the card and replies, "I'm Debra."

Smiling at Debra now as she reaches for the office door handle, Priscilla looked at her one last time and said, "Debra. You've made my day, my week, my year! I'm so happy we reconnected." Debra agrees as she puts the card in her pocket and began to walk away as Priscilla goes into her office building.

***

The years kept rolling by as Priscilla continued to do good things. By now, Mayor Grant was rolling along as a successful mayor and on the verge of an election run to remain seated, which was almost a formality, with his popularity! She couldn't help but think that he owed it to her, because she never exposed him to the public. But she kept it to herself and lived in the success that was her own. One day she took a trip. "Hold on, hold on please." Mayor Grant was saying as he went to open the front door to stop the doorbell ringing while holding a phone up to his head. As he opens the door, there stood Priscilla.

Surprised, he said, "Priscilla, what brings you here unexpectedly?"

Priscilla replies, "Well, as you said the last time we chatted, we have a lot of catching up to do."

He replied, "Well, come on in, make yourself at home." The mayor replied but couldn't help but feel that she was here to get something. He had a gut feeling. Something wasn't right. Why would she show up out of the blue? "Can I get you a drink?" The mayor said.

Priscilla replied, "Sure, let me get a glass of your finest whiskey if you have some."

He looked over his shoulder at Priscilla, "Indeed I do." As he made the drinks, he couldn't help but get the conversation started. "So, what is up Priscilla? Have I told you just how proud of you I am?" Priscilla sat there, fiddling with her hands as he came back into the room with the drinks.

"I need some advice. I know your planning on running again, but I want to find out how I can start to think about preparing for a similar career way down the line in the future if that's what I wanted?"

The mayor sat back and thought about her question. "Oh wow! Oh wow! So, are you saying, to become the mayor in the future? Come on Priscilla, I ain't leaving no time soon!"

They both laugh, and she replies, "No, Oh no, That's not what I meant! I just want to get the best advice on how to navigate this city and the political landscape for when I do get the stripes and get older, and you decide you're done, then I can run. I'm not thinking about this anytime soon. Not at all."

Feeling a little relief, Jacob sat back and took a sip of his Whiskey, "Well Priscilla, I have to tell you, the way we met, how things turned out, I would never think I would be sitting here talking to you on the eve of me announcing my re-election run bid and would have never thought that you would be alderman and asking me for career advice. I owe you! You could have exposed me. Let's keep drinking, then we'll talk about the best moves you can make to get ready, as I did." They sat and drank and talked for hours until she left to go home that night. Often laughing and thinking about years passed. They hit it off. Seemed like they had begun to create a bond. Student/apprentice type of bond. Priscilla was there for it all! All of the advice she could soak up! She was taking notes in her mental notebook. Hanging on every piece of advice he gave as the night grew later. Eventually, they both start to get sleepy, and Priscilla leaves his place at about 3 am. As she stumbled to her car, half-drunk, she had a huge grin on her face and happiness in her heart. She felt like she had just got the keys to the palace. Here she was, in her early twenties, an alderman, and strong advice on how to build a successful political career to run for mayor one day. What a ride she had been on.

The next morning, Priscilla is up early, hadn't slept at all. At her place, she grabs her keys and hops in her car, and drives down to the river walk. Priscilla, now standing at the river walk, is holding the morning paper as she stares off into the sky. As she stands there, taking in the breeze, she suddenly sees a huge flock of birds, a couple hundred, all flying in unison. Then she looked back down at the trees across the river walk in the park and saw the birds that enveloped the trees in the park. This wasn't just a couple of birds. It was hundreds of birds. Those birds were singing and singing. Priscilla found it so very soothing. In her mind, she was perched back on the window stoop at Tricia's house for a few minutes. It was her mental freedom. Her guide on her path to let her know she was traveling correctly! Then she raised the daily paper to eye level and on the front page, there was the news:

"City Mayor found dead this morning. Believed to have died in his sleep. He was the strongest candidate as he was about to begin his defense to remain mayor. Who can step into his shoes?"

She tossed the paper into the river and gets in her car and drives down to her alderman office. As she is driving, she is thinking about Tricia, the old neighborhood. Chris, Fabi and Marisol, Ricky, Uncle Bill, Roy, everyone, her whole life, replaying in her head as she drives. She arrives at her office, she parks and sits for a while, finishing reflecting on her life. Then she turns off the car, walks into the office and grabs a stack of papers, and stares at them for minutes, just thinking about her life again. Finally, she gets up and grabs her keys and the papers she was staring at. The papers were the city clerk's office filing papers to enter the election to run for mayor of the city. Priscilla gets back in her car and leaves her office, driving down the lakefront, with the wind bustling through the car. Maybe this is it! Maybe this is the time in her life that Priscilla won't have to be bothered by someone who wants to take advantage of her. Maybe this is the point in her life where she doesn't have to worry about running from anyone or anything. Maybe she had reached a point of full control; and finally, able to avoid dealing with the choice of picking to eliminate people and negative factors from her life. Priscilla can't help but think to herself, if she is a victim of circumstance, or if her just being her, brings the negative people and situations into her life. What if her father and mother never died that night? Did she solve that and get closure? Would her parents in her life have made a difference? What if she would have stayed with Tricia and been there for her? So many questions, thoughts, and possibilities. But here she was, on the precipice of a new chapter in life....